# ACHERON INHERITANCE

## KEN LOZITO

ACOUSTICAL BOOKS LLC

Published by Acoustical Books, LLC

KenLozito.com

Cover design by Jeff Brown

IF YOU WOULD LIKE TO BE NOTIFIED WHEN MY NEXT BOOK IS RELEASED VISIT

WWW.KENLOZITO.COM

ISBN: 978-1-945223-37-2

# CHAPTER ONE

HE DIDN'T WAKE UP. To wake would suggest that he'd been sleeping, when he'd actually just sort of become aware. It was as if someone had flipped a switch and he started processing information. First came a vague awareness that startled his mind into a heightened state of activity. Then, a feeling of increased urgency expanded from the diminutive depths, as if he'd suddenly forgotten something important. He tried to open his eyes. Nothing happened.

*System diagnostic running.*

These words appeared amid the black void of his thoughts. A few moments later, various diagnostic windows flashed, and a status report appeared.

*Warning.*

*Low-power mode.*

*Less than 30 percent of power remaining.*

*Recommendation: Deteriorating power cell should be replaced for optimal performance.*

*Configuration update required.*

*Please wait . . .*

He frowned, or at least tried to, but nothing happened,

which instantly made him want to even more. He couldn't feel anything. He couldn't even open his eyes, but he'd seen the status windows, so he wasn't blind. His racing thoughts went into overdrive. He tried to move—first his arms and then his hands. Nothing. He felt the urge to inhale, but it was only an urge—just a longing to take a deep lungful of sweet, precious breath—and it wasn't happening.

He couldn't breathe and wondered why he wasn't gasping. He should be struggling to breathe, but he wasn't, and his thoughts flatlined. He wouldn't panic. He was awake but couldn't move or feel . . . anything. There was no kinesthetic awareness to indicate whether he was lying down, strapped to a chair, or dangling in the air.

Not a good sign.

Maybe someone had drugged him, and he hadn't fully awakened yet. There were drugs that could induce paralysis, and maybe they were wearing off. He tried to remember the last thing he'd been doing. Had he been hurt? Medication to block pain receptors could explain a lot, including the paralysis. Where was he? He felt another urge to frown, remembering what it felt like as his eyebrows knitted together, his gaze narrowed, and his jaw tightened with the gritting of his teeth, but as he commanded his muscles to do those things, they just sort of . . . stalled, as if there was something blocking his muscles from actually moving.

*Veris initiation complete.*

*System startup complete.*

*Autonomous mode has been activated.*

*Limited storage available.*

A small image appeared in the void that surrounded him. He focused on it, and the image rushed toward him until the void disappeared. He was in a dreary room with smudgy, broken windows and long, thick cobwebs, and he had the impression that he was sitting. He looked down to a crusty, dirt-laden floor. Howling winds gusted from outside, sending layers of dust swirling into a lazy cyclone. Scummy residue trailed a path from the broken windows to the ground. Across from him were charging stations that housed different-sized humanoid robots. They were covered with a swarthy, crumbling shell that must have taken years of exposure to accumulate. These remnants of abandoned robots were all offline, without any indication of power.

He glanced down at his legs, and his thoughts screeched to a halt. His legs were gone! In their place were thick, metallic legs with an intricate set of connectors and actuators running to his feet. But they weren't *his* feet; they were something else. Each foot had three large, elongated toes and a broad, thick heel. They shifted, seemingly of their own accord, as if their range of motion was being tested.

He jerked backward at the movement and heard the mechanical whine of actuators fighting against their restraints in a cradle unit. Looking down, he saw that his chest was broad and comprised of overlapping plates that flexed when he moved. A whitish-blue power source glowed from between the plates. There was a series of symbols on his left side, and after a few seconds, a translation appeared on his internal heads-up display.

*Agricultural Unit – 92.*

*Repairs have been completed, and the unit is cleared for duty.*

Something disconnected from his back with a snap-hiss, and he slumped forward. The table he'd been sitting on dropped down and became part of the wall. As he landed on his feet, he saw the metallic toes spread and adjust to keep him standing. He flailed his arms for a few moments, trying to keep his balance. Everything felt uncoordinated and slow. He tried to move his head, and the movements were jerky, as there were actuators in his neck that hadn't been moved in a long time.

The one thing he knew for sure was that he hadn't been drugged. He felt as if he was remotely operating a mechanized unit for the first time, except that there was no system lag. Was this someone's idea of a joke?

*Self-diagnostic?*

The words appeared on his heads-up display—HUD—and he initiated the command.

*Cannot run self-diagnostic now. Still restoring backup from remote storage. Please wait . . .*

Thanks for nothing. That wasn't very helpful. He was apparently stuck in an agricultural unit, and he didn't know what he was supposed to do. This wasn't funny anymore. Why had he thought this could've been a practical joke? His mind was functioning much like his current body, like neither had been used in a really long time, but his mind suddenly began to race with an all-compelling need to remember.

He needed . . .

He *needed.*

He . . .

*Partial data restored.*

*Veris restore procedure for the consciousness transference protocol has enacted emergency protocol number 736 in accordance with the Veris mandate of preserving core Personality Matrix Construct into the system.*

He read the message again. "Consciousness transference protocol" stood out amid the amber lettering on the translucent window. Consciousness transference . . . His consciousness had been transferred, and something was trying to restore it from backup. Someone was restoring *him* into this machine.

He tried to bring up a command menu on the HUD.

*Identify.*

The system response puzzled him. It had just restored him, so shouldn't it already know who he was? He froze there, his thoughts racing as he tried to make sense of all the information coming at him.

*I'm a robot? No, not a damn robot! I know who I am.*

He repeated that thought over and over again.

I know who I am.

I know who I am.

I. Know. Who. I. Am.

He glared at the system prompt that showed its last query in dispassionate amber lettering.

*Identify?*

A surge of hope coursed through him as his name pierced the veil of confusion surrounding his thoughts.

"Quinton Aldren," he said, his voice sounding slightly modulated. He tried to clear his throat—which he didn't have—and repeated his name.

"Quinton Aldren," he said, much more clearly this time.

*Identification confirmed. Partial restoration of Personality Matrix Construct has confirmed the viability of the individual in this unit.*

Quinton reread the message with an increasing awareness that he knew about Personality Matrix Constructs. PMCs were human-consciousness-to-machine interfaces. He tried to remember more, but the information just wasn't available. He was *sure* he knew more about it, but something . . . He looked down at his body and understood.

A quiet hum came from a maintenance drone as it sank slowly to the floor. Its spherical chassis had multiple appendages, some of which looked to have been torn off, but one of them reached in his direction. Its power indicators went dark, and the drone was dead.

Quinton felt a second presence snap to existence in his mind. It was as if someone had just appeared next to him, but nobody was there.

*VI interface initiated. Designation—Radek.*

A virtual intelligence should be able to help him out.

"Radek, are you online?" Quinton asked.

"Diagnostics are still running," Radek said a few moments later. "Diagnostics complete. Virtual Intelligence Designate Radek responding."

"Excellent. Now, maybe you can answer a few questions for me. Why have I been restored into this agricultural unit?" Quinton asked.

"Emergency reactivation protocols were initiated," Radek replied.

Quinton felt as if his thoughts were wading through a muddy barrier.

"Radek, putting my consciousness into this agricultural unit violates PMC protocols. It shouldn't have worked, even under emergency conditions."

"Personality Matrix Construct's standard operating procedures were overridden."

"By whom?" Quinton asked.

"Information is unavailable."

"Unavailable . . . how's that?" Quinton paused for a moment, trying to strangle his growing irritation with the useless VI. He glanced down at the maintenance drone. "Were you in control of this drone?"

"Affirmative. It was required to transfer the Energy Storage System to Agricultural Unit 92."

"You're telling me that I've been stored in an ESS, which you then stuck in the chest of this agricultural unit—a damn *garden* robot," Quinton said.

More of his knowledge became available. It shouldn't have worked. PMCs required a high level of haptic capabilities in order to avoid malfunction. The PMC was a way of preserving his consciousness, requiring that he feel human, or else—

"Your summation of the events is an oversimplification," Radek replied, and Quinton could've sworn the VI sounded a little agitated.

"Not from where I'm standing."

"Per emergency procedures, I found the best solution given the constraints I was called to deal with," Radek said.

Quinton looked out at dark gray skies through the shattered

remnants of what had been windows. He was in a garden storage shed for service bots. He didn't have any idea where he was, and he certainly didn't know why he was there. He needed Radek's help if he was going to figure out what had happened. He needed the VI's cooperation, but VIs could be finicky. They weren't sentient, but they could be singularly uncooperative if given the right motivation.

"It sounds like you did the best you could," Quinton said. "How long did you have to search before you found this body?"

"One hundred eighty-seven days, fifteen hours, and thirty-three minutes."

*Oh crap,* Quinton thought. Radek seemed to sense this, but Quinton reminded himself that VIs couldn't read minds.

"The ESS was in a critical state and in danger of imminent failure. Use of this agricultural unit was the only option."

Quinton didn't doubt what Radek said. If Radek had searched for a hundred eighty-seven days to find a suitable host for his PMC, then he was in danger.

"Where are we?"

"Unknown."

*That's great,* Quinton thought. Radek was just as much in the dark as he was.

"Is there a governing body we can contact?"

"Negative. There are no settlements with active inhabitants that I've observed."

Six months searching and no one to contact. Quinton glanced out the window at the ash-covered landscape and then looked around the room. This planet had suffered some kind of disaster. A readout on his HUD showed that the atmosphere was still breathable, meeting minimum requirements to survive —not that breathing air was an obstacle for him in his current form.

Quinton tried to recall why he'd been uploaded into a PMC and stored in the first place but found that he couldn't remember.

"Radek," Quinton said, "my memory access is restricted. Is the ESS intact? Was it damaged?"

"The ESS is undamaged and fully intact. However, because of the limitations of the agricultural unit, you have limited access to the ESS. This is required so you can fully utilize the unit the PMC is currently housed in."

Quinton took a few steps across the shed, then turned and paced back to the other side. Each step he took demonstrated more confidence as he learned the capabilities of the agricultural unit. There was significant risk involved with a PMC being loaded into a less capable machine. PMC degradation would occur if the consciousness inside lost its connection to being human. Quinton tried to feel whether he was losing himself and then shook his head. How was that *supposed* to feel?

There were several loud pops as something slammed into a nearby building. Quinton spun around at the noise and glanced toward the maintenance drone on the ground. There were gashes cut into its sides, and several of its limbs were missing.

"I must advise you that there are hunter mechs currently searching for you," Radek said.

A new pathway engaged in Quinton's mind, and he had access to new data stored in the ESS. "Hunter mechs! What do they want with me?"

"The hunter mechs are specifically tasked with destroying PMCs."

That couldn't be right. Nothing about this situation was right.

Quinton heard something crash from within a nearby building. "They must have control units. Can't we override them?" Quinton asked, stepping toward the door as he tried to engage the communications systems of the agricultural unit.

"I advise against that," Radek said quickly. "They can detect open comms signals. These units have been pursuing me for many days. I already tried an override command, which didn't work. Those systems are locked out from any comms unless they're coming from whatever command central gave them their instructions in the first place."

That made the hunter mechs no better than mindless drones. Why would they hunt PMCs?

"Radek, I need access to your analysis of those units if I'm going to decide how to deal with them. If they're just basic mechs, I should be able to disable them."

"Data is available, as you requested."

A report appeared on his HUD, and Quinton accessed the log data. There wasn't anything like a detailed analysis, and Radek had been severely limited in his capabilities while operating the maintenance drone. His top priority had been to preserve the Energy Storage System that Quinton's Personality Matrix Construct was stored in, which was all fine and good, but it meant he didn't know what he was facing, and they were getting closer to his position.

# CHAPTER TWO

QUINTON STEPPED OUTSIDE but stayed close to the side of the building so he could watch for the mechs.

"How do you know they're hunting PMCs?" he asked.

"When they scanned the maintenance drone and detected the ESS, they became hostile."

The Energy Storage System—ESS— was a miniature reactor the size of a fist. The low energy output of the leuridium core made it durable and long-lasting, ideal for the data storage requirements of a PMC. The ESS had a unique identifier that made it easy to detect. Quinton glanced down at the agricultural bot body that contained his consciousness. He didn't think the robot's chest could shield it from the mechs.

He looked up at thick, dreary clouds pressing on top of him and felt as if he were staring at a tidal wave about to sweep him away in a violent upheaval of destruction and doom. A bellowing rumble came from overhead. Weather-worn buildings that were sagging under the weight of wet volcanic ash lined the streets, fading into the misty fog.

Quinton moved to the other side of the street. Loud banging sounds came from inside the nearby buildings, followed by screeches that came in rapid succession as the mechs forced their way through a heavy door. The agricultural unit was capable of highly acute sound sensitivity and depth perception, probably meant for the delicate work of maintaining the exotic gardens that had once been here.

He heard three distinct sound sources from various areas of the building. The mechs weren't trying to hide what they were doing.

He glanced around at the crusty brown ash that covered the buildings and saw more fall from the sky in a sleety mix of snow. Peering closely at the clusters of ash as they fell, he realized that the agricultural unit's optics were able to perceive each unique crystalline structure marred by the particulates filling the air. Where was the ash coming from? The agricultural unit must have had smell receptors, but he was glad they weren't working. Atmospheric readings on his internal heads-up display showed high levels of sulfur. Skipping the smell of rotting decay was perfectly fine with Quinton.

"I need to know what you plan to do," Radek said.

The VI's question startled him out of his thoughts because Radek was just a voice. Although there was a highlighted section of his HUD that flashed when Radek spoke, it was still off-putting. Quinton checked the agricultural unit's systems to see what was available.

"Radek, update preferences for our normal interactions to require the use of a holographic representation."

A small sphere that was a semi-transparent silver hovered in the air a few feet away from Quinton's head. "System preferences have been updated."

That was better.

"I wonder if we have a case of mistaken identity," Quinton said. "Maybe the security mechs just detected a power signature that's not in their data repositories. Given how things look around here, they're probably still following some kind of latent security protocol. You said they hunted you for days, but did you see any people here? Is there anyone we can go to for help?" Quinton asked.

"There were very few online systems, and no life signs were detected. I was lucky to find this agricultural unit."

Quinton's gaze flicked upward in irritation. He was about as far away from what he considered "fortunate" as he could get. He was sure the VI assistants that were part of his PMC were working overtime, managing the interface between him and the machine he was stuck in, but why belabor the point that his current form was the best the VI could find? Radek was just the manifestation of multiple VIs that were part of the PMC.

Quinton had limited access to his memories, but now that everything was online, he remembered going through extensive training before his consciousness was uploaded into an ESS, even if it wasn't *the* ESS that was in this specific bot. He couldn't recall the actual memories of his training, but the skills were there, and the link that the VIs were associating with hinged on the fact that Quinton had been trained. It was supposed to set him at ease so he could focus, but it just brought attention to the fact that he wasn't anywhere he'd expected to be, which meant that something had gone utterly wrong. Without complete access to his memories, how was he supposed to come up with a solution? He was stumbling in the dark, but he had his training. The possibility of a partial upload had always existed, as well as a chance that the unit the ESS was installed in would have limited capacity, which was what Quinton was dealing with thanks to Radek inserting him into this garden-variety robot.

"It was the only unit available, and it doesn't quite meet the minimum requirements for a PMC," Radek said, making Quinton wonder if the VI *could* read his thoughts.

Quinton accessed the scan data from Radek's encounter with the mechs. They were accurately identified as Veris Hunter Model Mechs, but that was just the base unit. They could represent any number of mech types, but they all had strict protocols for preserving human life, and an ESS housing a PMC qualified as a living being. These mechs shouldn't harm him, unless they were military mechs, in which case the restrictions on human life could be rescinded. If Quinton was identified as the enemy, they would attack. Radek's attempted communication with them had likely been interpreted as just another drone delivery system, which was different from someone who was actually alive.

He had to find out if the mechs would hunt him. If he tried to sneak away and was detected, there was very little chance of him being able to reason with them. He walked out to the middle of the street and shouted, "Hello!"

The glowing holographic sphere bobbed up and down to get his attention. "I must advise against this. Hostiles in the area," Radek warned.

"Noted. Now stop distracting me," Quinton replied.

The orb disappeared. VIs helped the PMC interact and cope with being in another form other than a human host. To help facilitate this connection, they were required to act human, but they were machines. Radek was a virtual intelligence, and sometimes they just got things wrong.

Three mechs emerged onto the street a short distance from where Quinton stood. They had extremely long arms that protruded from their stocky wedge-shaped main bodies. Long legs connected to a black-armored pelvis. They'd probably been designed to run at high speeds, using all of their limbs. Serial numbers for each mech appeared on Quinton's HUD, which were transferred as some kind of default broadcast. This was encouraging because they might listen to him. But what struck him as odd was just how old the mechs looked. The orange stripes along their torsos and down their arms were faded and looked to have been scraped off in several areas. They must've been bright when the mechs were in service. He had no idea how long these mechs had been running around. How could they still have power? The fact that they did indicated that there must be a charging station in service nearby.

The three mechs regarded Quinton for a few moments, and he raised his arms to the side in a non-threatening gesture of compliance. The mechs squatted lower in an aggressive posture.

"Wait a minute," he blurted, his voice going high. "I'm not a danger to you. My name is Quinton Aldren, and I'm a Personality Matrix Construct temporarily stored in this agricultural unit. I need help. Transferring my identification now."

A beam of light came from one of the mechs and highlighted an area on Quinton's chest for a few seconds before going out. The three mechs remained motionless, and Quinton was beginning to agree with Radek that this was a bad idea. He tried opening a comlink to the three mechs, thinking that perhaps they had suffered some kind of damage and were attempting to communicate with him.

They weren't.

The mechs shared a data communication session, which Quinton was able to decipher because they weren't using any security protocols.

. . . *Target hostile: negative.*

*ESS power signature confirmed.*

*Must retrieve.*

The three Veris mechs began striding toward him. Each step they took seemed to impact the ash-laden ground, and Quinton stepped back.

"Wait a second. I'll go with you," Quinton said.

. . . *Agricultural unit loss is acceptable.*

*Retrieve ESS for disposal.*

Quinton felt a wave of panic surge through him. They wanted the ESS. What did they want with the ESS? They were going to . . .

They were charging toward him now.

# CHAPTER THREE

QUINTON STAGGERED BACKWARD, nearly losing his balance, and ran. The robot's feet adjusted to the rough terrain, giving him better traction, and his enhanced hearing noted the quick, powerful cadence of the hunter mechs hastening to catch up with him.

There were dozens of abandoned greenhouses nearby, covered in a thick, crusty layer of dirt, and ash coated their windows in a grimy grayish brown. Quinton bolted toward a narrow path between them and pivoted, hoping to throw the mechs off his tail.

He raced away from them as he heard at least one of the mechs crash into the building. Quinton emerged from between the greenhouses and turned right, rushing toward an impressive main building that, despite the current climate, had retained hints of its former glory. Atop a broad staircase were mounds that must have been statues, which Quinton recognized by the elevated pedestals. An enormous dome sat on top of the main building, flanked by two long side wings. Large sections of the roof had been peeled off the upper levels, but the main entrance above the grand marble staircase looked intact. He'd try to lose the mechs inside while he searched for a vehicle.

Quinton heard the stomping of heavy metallic footfalls coming from the rooftop of the building beside him. A hunter mech kept pace with him, gingerly running along the rooftops. Amber-colored eyes locked onto him, piercing the gloom from within narrow sockets in its dark helmet.

The sky brightened as pale moonlight shone through a break in the billowing storm clouds. The mech must've veered away from the others, circling around to cut him off. Quinton swerved away from the greenhouses and darted toward the main building. The mech leaped off the roof and chased him, rapidly closing the distance.

He ran up the grand staircase past thick stone columns to the shadowy interior. His vision cleared as his night vision engaged. Just beyond the doors was a wide reception desk with kiosks. Quinton ran past the reception area, the hunter mech right on his heels. A loud blast of sound came from behind him, and his foot was bumped to the side, shoving him off balance. He stumbled, and the mech knocked him off his feet. Quinton went down and skidded to a stop on the smooth floor as dust billowed into the air.

He scrambled to regain his feet, searching for anything he could use for a weapon. The agricultural unit was equipped with a focused sonic blaster, but it wouldn't respond. It was dead, just like he'd be in a few seconds if he couldn't stop the mech. He hastened back as the mech stalked forward, but it leaped toward him, grabbing hold of Quinton's outstretched hands. He struggled to push the powerful mech off of him, but he couldn't.

*Dammit, Radek, why did you have to put me into such a pathetic machine?*

Quinton pushed with his feet, and they slid farther into the building. The mech atop of him tried to block Quinton's feet with its own. He knew that if he could just keep moving, there was at least a chance he could break free.

The mech began angling them toward a nearby wall.

*No, this is not good.*

The mech was going to use the wall as leverage to overpower him. Quinton tried to change direction, but the mech had momentum on its side. As they drew near the wall, the mech pivoted on its lower body, anchoring itself to the wall, which jolted them both to a stop. The mech leaned toward Quinton's chest, where the ESS was housed. Two smaller arms sprang from a hidden compartment in its chest and pulled hard on Quinton's chest plate. He twisted away, trying to prevent those damn small arms from getting his ESS. The mech climbed higher on the wall, lifting Quinton off the ground.

*Oh, crap.*

He was completely at the mech's mercy. He had to do something, or else his brief existence as a PMC was going to end. What separated humans from machines was an unwavering drive to preserve life. When push came to shove, both humans and animals alike would fight for their lives until their very last breath. A PMC wasn't required to breathe, but the indomitable will to live was just as strong.

Quinton wouldn't give up without a fight. He accessed the agricultural unit's systems menu and felt a rush of hope surge through him as he finally found something he could use.

*Weapons!*

Hidden within the forearms were hardened alloyed blades meant for chopping and cutting thick branches.

The mech grabbed his chest plate and pulled hard. Quinton brought his feet up to its body and angled his palms upward as the blades sprang from his wrists, punching through the mech's hands. Quinton pressed his feet into the mech and pushed away from its grasp. He landed on his feet, and the mech's head turned toward him in surprise. Quinton sprang up, stabbing the blade through its narrow eye socket. He hung there for a moment, using his whole weight to sever the mechanical innards of the hunter mech. Sparks burst from the wound, and Quinton dropped back down to the ground.

The mech flailed its arms and struck Quinton's shoulder, almost knocking him down. Damage alerts flooded his internal heads-up display as a klaxon alarm blared from the mech. He glanced back toward the entrance of the building and heard the other two mechs running up the stairs. He'd gotten lucky, but he didn't want to take on two hunter mechs at the same time. They'd probably already called for reinforcements, so more were on the way. Quinton turned and ran, eager to put as much distance between him and the hunter mechs as possible.

"There is a power source in this building. There might be a working terminal available for use," Radek said.

"Where?"

"Sub-basement level five."

A route for him to take was highlighted in front of him. Quinton followed the path to a wide, long staircase amid an open atrium with exhibits and walkways on both sides. Thunder roared outside, and rain began to fall through a massive hole in the roof overhead.

"What's down there?" he asked.

"My guess is some kind of control room."

"You guess!" Quinton said, reaching the bottom of the stairs.

He'd tried to keep his voice down, but the mechs must've heard him. He noted the echoes of the security mechs from the top floor, but they hadn't followed him yet. What were they waiting for?

"I have access to the same information as you. This unit has a sensor range for detecting power lines, which is understandable given the occupation for which the unit was designed."

Radek was correct. This unit was once a highly sophisticated garden robot whose lifespan would have been severely limited if it hadn't been able to detect hidden power cables and conduits. Quinton had never thought about it before, and even if he'd been an expert in these kinds of machines, he wouldn't have remembered because of his limited access to the ESS.

*Gah!* He really wanted to grit his teeth, but he couldn't. The robot didn't have a mouth, but its head had somewhat anthropomorphic features.

He dashed toward a hallway that led to elevator doors, going to the one farthest away and prying open the door. There was no power to the elevators, so he'd have to climb down the shaft. He spotted a metallic ladder to his left and began his descent. The elevator doors squeezed shut, and he was in near darkness. The only light came from the slight glow of his ESS that has been partially exposed when the mech tried to rip it out of his chest. The mech had been trying to tear his heart out, but the ESS was more than just his heart. It contained everything that made Quinton who he was. PMCs were sophisticated uploads of the human consciousness, wrapped in a framework of assistant virtual intelligences.

Quinton didn't know the circumstances that surrounded his apparent reactivation. He didn't even know what planet he was on, and because of the limited capacity of the machine he was housed in, he couldn't access any of his memories.

Every time he climbed down a rung on the ladder, there was an audible click, like several gears grinding into place. When the mech had struck his shoulder, it must've damaged the socket. The sound would surely be detected by the hunter mechs when they came for him.

Instead of climbing down one rung at a time, Quinton decided to let himself drop. Before he could gain too much velocity, he grabbed hold of a rung to slow his descent, and his body jerked to a halt. The agricultural unit was designed for climbing. Trimming tall trees was probably one of its duties. He didn't know what he would do if his arms were torn out of their sockets, but he needed to reach the lower level—fast.

He soon came to the fifth level and made his way over to the door, forcing it open and climbing through. As he walked down the dark, quiet maintenance corridor, he noticed that the outside elements hadn't penetrated there, and the corridor was untouched. The sensor data on his HUD showed that the power source was just up ahead in one of the side rooms.

Quinton hastened toward it and opened the door. A phalanx of workstations illuminated the area in an azure glow, and he walked to the nearest one. A holoscreen flickered on. The data displayed was slightly blurry from the aged projector hidden inside the workstation, but the status window showed the batch of commands that had been submitted by the last person who'd used the station. They'd initiated a shutdown protocol because of some kind of emergency. Given how things looked aboveground, Quinton was certain it was something catastrophic. As the system refreshed, a barrage of offline messages began spewing on the holoscreen. There was no info-net for him to connect to. He could only find the coordinates to an evacuation center. It must've been a broadcast emergency message that instructed the workers to go to a specific evacuation place. He brought up a map, and it highlighted a path for him to follow. There was a lot of open ground to cover, and with the hunter mechs coming for him, he wasn't sure if he'd make it.

He still had access to local systems, and he tried to find a maintenance work area. He was hoping to find some kind of vehicle he could use. An alert appeared on his HUD. The power core in the agricultural unit was depleting, showing that he had less than 25 percent power remaining. Quinton had no idea what the longevity of the power core inside him was, but the unit must've been stored for quite some time, and it was probably well beyond its expected lifespan. He was running out of time.

"You should go to the evacuation center," Radek said.

Quinton stepped away from the workstation. "Thanks for the tip," he said bitterly.

He left the control center and shook his head. Radek was just trying to help keep him on task, and he had to focus. He had to do one thing at a time in order to escape. He couldn't afford to dwell on what he didn't know, but he couldn't help but blame Radek for his current predicament. Rationally, he knew it wasn't the VI's fault. It, too, had been activated after the upload to the ESS, but given what was happening, he felt he was entitled to a bit of irrationality. It wasn't as if Radek had feelings anyway.

There was no way for Quinton to call for help, and now he was thinking that there would be nobody to answer his call even if he was able to make one. He began making his way to the maintenance work area. Hopefully, there would be some kind of vehicle the groundskeepers used. Otherwise, he'd have to continue running from the hunter mechs. If there *was* a vehicle, and it was still connected to a charging station, perhaps it would be enough to get him to the evacuation center.

# CHAPTER FOUR

THE MAINTENANCE AREA was located at the ground level. Rather than risk another encounter with the hunter mechs, who no doubt wanted to exact revenge for what Quinton had done to their sneaky comrade, he decided to find another way to reach the ground level. Making his way through the dark hallways of the building, he found a staircase and began climbing to the upper level. He kept expecting to feel the exertion of climbing the steps. It was natural to think that since he was exerting himself, he'd feel the results of those efforts regardless of how physically fit he'd been. At least, he *thought* he'd been in good physical condition before he'd been uploaded into an ESS, but he couldn't know for sure. He just had a feeling that he had been. Something in the way he moved suggested a familiarity of movement, a familiarity that could only come from the habits formed in his brain, but what if he was wrong? There was no heavy breathing or burning thighs as he mounted the stairs. Instead, there was nothing but an efficiency of motion as he climbed as fast as he could. With his mechanical limbs, he was taking the steps two at a time. The hunter mech had damaged his shoulder, and whenever he lifted his left arm, he once again noted a clicking sound from the actuators. Raising his arm higher than shoulder level resulted in it dropping, as if it couldn't support its own weight. The blade in his left forearm was only partially retracted because it was bent from his fight with the mech.

Quinton reached the ground floor and slowly opened the door. He stepped into the dark corridor and peered toward a wide doorway that led to a maintenance garage. Pale light from the outside cast shadows beyond the doorway, and he froze. The hunter mechs would be searching for him. The shadows stirred in the pallid light, and a gust of wind moaned in the distance.

Quinton raised the sensitivity of the bot's auditory sensors. Rain splattering the roof high above him registered in stunning clarity of sound, as if time had slowed to a crawl. A soft groan came from the upper floors that were exposed to the elements. He remained still and logged the sounds, carefully cataloging them and minimizing their impact so he could listen for the mechs. He waited there, alone in the darkened corridor, hoping the mechs weren't nearby. Several minutes passed with nothing but the quiet cadence of a stream of rainwater splashing the ground inside the maintenance garage. He crept toward the door.

Satisfied that there were no mechs waiting to ambush him, Quinton reduced the auditory system sensitivity to normal levels. Inside the garage were vehicles and other bots in charging stations along the walls. He detected faint power signatures from some of the bots and vehicles, but he'd need to inspect them to determine whether they had enough power to be of use.

Rainwater streamed through a jagged opening in the roof of the garage toward the outer wall. It looked as if the roof had been peeled away in order to see inside. Something must have crashed and bounced off the structure with sufficient velocity to cause that kind of damage. If the hunter mechs had a giant older brother, something from a military arsenal, then he was as good as dead.

A steady stream of water made its way toward the main

doors. Lightning flickered brightly, pushing the shadows back into sudden retreat, and Quinton headed toward the outer doors. There were several large vehicles off to his right that looked as if they were meant for hauling heavy things. Their thick wheels were nearly as tall as he was. The lack of counter-grav vehicles meant that this estate or museum was a throwback to a historical time before the advent of the current tech, or he might be on a fringe planet that had limited resources. It could be both, but Quinton wouldn't find that out by staying in this garage.

He headed to the door control panel and saw that it still had power. The maintenance area must have been on its own backup power after it had been cut off from the main building. The bots and vehicles in the garage weren't what he considered cutting edge, but they were built to be relatively self-sustaining—at least under normal circumstances. Given the state of things outside, he wondered how long things had been so bad here. Power cores being what they were, they would take tens of years to deplete and maybe more, even without proper maintenance.

Next to the main doors was a smaller door where workers entered. Quinton walked over to it and pulled it open. Outside, he could see what had once been a sprawling garden, with paths he could just barely see under the slushy ash. Map markers, pulled from the agricultural bot's memory core, appeared on his HUD. There were several paths across the vast estate that he could take to the evacuation center. The ash-covered fields had the appearance of dingy gray snow, and Quinton's sensors detected high levels of sulfur. Such high concentrations indicated that not only did the air smell like rotten eggs and decay, but he'd have a strong aftertaste in his mouth if he were in his body.

He doubted anything was left alive in the region. In addition to looking like a hellish landscape of a dying world, the atmosphere was slowly poisoning anything left alive. He couldn't wait to get out of there.

Streaks of gray and black stretched across the way, and even though the remnants of tree-covered paths were only a short distance away, he'd be way too exposed if he tried to make a run for it.

"Quinton, you must hurry. You need to cross the field to reach the evacuation center," Radek advised.

"I don't think so," Quinton replied.

"I don't understand. Staying here doesn't bring us any closer to our objective."

"You're supposed to help me, Radek. I can't just go running blindly out there. Can you tell me if any hunter mechs are waiting to ambush us? That's where I'd be if I were them. I'd be keeping watch, and as soon as my target left the building, I'd pounce," he said and shook his head. "For a virtual intelligence that's supposed to help me, you're not being very helpful. Now, just give me a few seconds to think."

He watched the open field. There was *some* cover from the trees that hadn't toppled over, but they were leaning to their sides under the heavy weight of the ash, ensuring their eventual demise. He tried to calculate how long it would take him to reach that area, and he didn't like his chances. Radek was right about one thing. He couldn't stay here, but that didn't mean he should make a mad dash across an open field, begging for the hunter mechs to run him down. He had to be smarter than that. He needed cover . . . or a distraction. Quinton glanced behind him at all the vehicles and the maintenance bots. Some of them still had power. They wouldn't last long, but they might last long enough for what he was planning.

He glanced at the main doors where ice glistened on the gray metallic surface in frozen rivulets. It wasn't enough to prevent the doors from opening, but he doubted they'd open quietly, which meant they'd draw the mechs' attention.

He crossed to the other side of the garage and brought up a control terminal. The main screen showed the status of the machines in the charging stations. Almost half of them were without power, but there were multiple outdoor maintenance bots for which he was able to bring up the startup sequence. These bots were less sophisticated than the unit he was in. No doubt, they were meant for working away from the view of the patrons who visited this place. The medium-sized maintenance bots had four mechanical arms, as well as a continuous tread system at the base. As they went through their startup sequences, they did a system check. Their mechanical arms went through a range of motion to test their mobility and the continuous tread systems clustered together, raising the bots up several feet. All twelve of them bobbed up and down as they went through their checks.

Only four large autonomous vehicles still had power. Quinton accessed their control systems next and began activating them. One of them quickly came online but failed during its startup sequence and became unresponsive. He accessed another one, and it lasted a whole thirty seconds longer than the first one had before it failed. Quinton swore in frustration. Thankfully, the remaining two passed their systems startup test and waited for orders. He passed the control protocol from the control terminal over to his own systems so he wouldn't need to stay at the physical terminal, then stepped back and turned to survey his squad of decoy bots. Dim amber light gleamed through the crust-covered, multi-sensored heads of the maintenance bots. A soft hum came from each one as they waited for him to command them.

Quinton walked over to the main doors and used the controls to open them. The door mechanism struggled for a few moments before the actuators were able to pull the two massive doors to the side, and rain and wind gusted in a soft howl through the opening. The door tracks screeched in a protest loud enough to be heard over the storm.

*There's no going back now.*

He scanned the area outside for a few moments and then

accessed the medium-sized bot control interface. He tasked half the bots to perform a general maintenance patrol mode, and they quickly sped outside, heading away from the maintenance garage. Quinton waited a few moments and then ordered one of the large haulers to head to the western side of the vast estate. The large metallic wheels adjusted the treads to give it traction, and the hauler drove away at a leisurely speed at first, gradually increasing its velocity.

The rest of the medium-sized bots came to the doorway and waited, followed by the remaining large hauler. Quinton climbed up the side of the hauler and glanced inside the open storage bed. Pieces of scrap metal were piled inside.

He scrambled over the side and onto the bed. The scrap metal was partially covered, and he squatted down toward the front. He ordered his small squad of robot henchmen out into the storm, and he followed.

Radek had updated Quinton's HUD to show where the other bots had gone. The coordinates he'd given this group were to take them directly across the field as fast as they could. He hoped it would confuse the hunter mechs.

The large hauler jostled back and forth as it crossed onto the rugged path. Quinton turned around and glanced behind them, seeing two shapes appear on the roof of the museum. The hunter mechs quickly surveyed the scene of the fleeing robots and then leaped to the ground. They split off, each mech heading toward different groups of maintenance bots, but neither was heading toward him. His distraction had worked.

The hauler was running with minimal power, and its systems were throwing up warnings about the depleting charge. Quinton increased the vehicle's speed, knowing it would cut the life of the hauler's power cell to little more than a handful of minutes, but he needed more speed than endurance. The hunter mechs were able to quickly traverse the rough terrain, galloping on all of their limbs.

Quinton was about to turn around when he saw a third mech appear on the rooftop. Its dome-shaped head had a jagged puncture where one of its eyes had been. A few fleeting sparks burst from the opening. It scanned the area and seemed to focus on him. He sank down, trying to hide behind the pile of scrap metal. Just then, one of the hauler's wheels slipped, and the vehicle began to slide for a few moments before regaining traction. The storage bed jerked to the side, and Quinton was jostled out from cover. He looked back at the roof in alarm, hoping the mech hadn't seen him.

He was wrong.

The mech leaped off the roof and hit the ground at a run.

Quinton commanded two medium-size bots to circle back and intercept the mech. There was a bright flash off to the side, and then a squeal sounded from a maintenance bot as one of the hunter mechs tore it apart. Sparks burst from its power core, and the mech darted toward its next victim.

Quinton took control of the large hauler, overriding the autonomous drive systems. He jerked the steering controls toward the tree-lined path, and the entire vehicle tilted to the side as it swerved. The hauler bounced wildly for a few moments, and he clutched onto the handrail inside the storage bed. The adaptive wheels quickly engaged deformation protocols, and the ride smoothed out as the vehicle continued over rough terrain.

He looked to the left and saw a mech chasing the maintenance bots. They didn't look anything like Quinton's agricultural unit, which made him wonder just how sophisticated the targeting systems of the hunter mechs actually were. They seemed to be chasing almost anything that moved, and his only option was to get away from them as fast as possible.

He ordered the four remaining bots in front of them to form a phalanx behind the large hauler. The mech he'd fought inside the museum had made quick work of the medium bots he'd sent over to it. Their remains littered the ground in pieces. The mech's one good eye gleamed hatefully in stark contrast to the greenish fluid that had splattered over its chassis.

Quinton made it to the forest path, and the hauler bludgeoned through the lower tree branches that splintered apart on impact. He saw small dark shapes scampering among trees, keeping pace with him. Something big slammed into the side of the hauler. It lurched, jostling his hold on the handrail, and he slipped back onto the pile of scrap. An armored, metallic claw reached over the side. The mech had finally caught up to him.

He extended the blade from his forearm and slammed down on the mech's hand with all his might. The hand severed at the wrist, and the mech dropped and rolled away, but Quinton's blade was wedged into the side of the storage bed. He yanked his hand back, trying to free the blade, and it snapped at the base of the tang.

The vehicle leveled off, and he peered around. Eight sets of amber-colored eyes gleamed menacingly in the darkness. Reinforcements had arrived, and their heads bobbed slightly as they raced toward him. Quinton recalled all the maintenance bots, but their numbers had diminished rapidly. He overrode their crash-avoidance systems, and they threw themselves at the mechs. Several mechs went down in a tangle, and Quinton lost sight of them.

"Obstruction ahead. Secure your position," Radek warned.

Quinton spun and saw that the corpse of a thick tree was blocking part of the path. He grabbed onto the handrail and increased the speed. Several dark, furry shapes leaped from the nearby trees and landed inside the hauler's storage bed. The creatures' fur was matted and dirty, but their wide eyes gleamed in the dim light.

The hauler slammed into the obstructing tree, causing it to jerk violently, and it bounced off another fallen tree on the other side of the path. The furry little critters screeched as they scrambled to grab hold of something. One of them flew through the air and disappeared from view. Quinton watched as one of the larger animals helped the others climb the scrap pile near the rear of the vehicle. They hadn't paid any attention to him at all.

Quinton heard two mechs close in behind the hauler. They sprang up and yanked the rear hatch, hard. The hinges bent and the hatch flung open, causing the pile of scrap to start spilling out of the bed. Several of the furry creatures tumbled down despite the efforts of the larger male trying to help them. One of the mechs snatched at the scrap, pulling it, along with the creature, toward him. Quinton lurched forward and flung a metallic shaft at the mech. The shaft slammed into its chest, knocking it off balance.

A third mech raced behind the hauler, desperate to find a way into the vehicle. With a firm grip on the handrail, Quinton tried to grab another piece of scrap metal, but the mech was faster. The clawed hand gouged at the end and heaved itself into a lunge toward him. The furry creature scrambled back, squealing in terror as the large mech was about to flatten him. Quinton dove and plucked the creature out of harm's way. He rolled, so his back slammed into the side of the storage bed while cradling the animal. Then he shoved at the last scrap pile with his feet, sending fragments of metal flying toward the mech's head.

The mech flailed blindly before falling off the back and tumbling out of sight.

"Obstruction ahead. We must slow down," Radek said.

Quinton pulled himself up. The frightened creature tried to escape from his grasp, but he held onto him and looked toward the front of the vehicle. The hauler was speeding toward a tall barricade that stretched across the path. It looked reinforced and solid. There was no way around it, and there was no way he was going to break through it like he'd done with the tree. He glanced back and saw the remaining mechs about to make another attack run. Quinton increased the vehicle's velocity to the maximum and climbed out of the storage bed toward the front of the vehicle. After the initial burst of speed, the hauler began slowing down. Its power core was depleting rapidly. A system alert appeared, showing that there was a containment breach in the power core.

The mechs closed in on them. Quinton held the furry creature in one hand and then leaped into the air just before the vehicle slammed into the barricade. He cleared the barrier, hurtling through the air like a slow-moving missile. The ground raced up to meet him, and he spun to the side, clutching the furry rodent to his chest protectively. As he crashed to the ground, a large explosion blazed into the night. He rolled for a few feet and then skidded to a stop but quickly regained his feet. The creature he still held glared at him as if Quinton had somehow mishandled it. He squealed loudly, and Quinton dumped it to the ground.

"You can take your chances with them if you want," he said and started running.

He didn't need to look behind him to know that there were more mechs making their way to his position. He was out of range of the maintenance bots, but he doubted there were any left online.

The evacuation center wasn't far. Something scrambled up his leg, and he glanced to the side, seeing the creature riding on his shoulder. It was his good shoulder, and he couldn't lift the other arm high enough, even if he wanted to shoo him away. He left him alone and ran toward the evacuation center.

# CHAPTER FIVE

QUINTON DARTED DOWN THE STREET, passing empty shops along the way. Their darkened interiors flashed by as lightning gleamed brightly overhead. He came to a large marketplace and peered through the broken windows to the dark recesses inside. Abandoned nests and dead animal skeletons were piled outside various alcoves, occurring too regularly to be random. A community of predators had lived there but must have moved on when they depleted the food source.

Quinton kept wondering about what had happened here. Had the calamity affected the entire planet? Volcanic ash was indicative of a major catastrophe, but with enough warning, there were ways to prevent even a caldera from blowing. If they'd evacuated the region, that probably meant the disaster had been extensive. Hopefully, he'd find some kind of transportation that could get him out of the area and leave the mechs behind. The evacuation center was his best hope for either finding transportation or contacting someone who could help.

Holographic signs pointed the way to the center. Quinton hurried down abandoned permacrete streets, passing buildings that had entire floors exposed where the walls had crumbled, exposing the superstructure that kept the buildings standing. The gusting winds shrieked through the openings in a furious buildup and then relented.

Rubble crowded the sides of the streets, and an analysis of it appeared on Quinton's HUD. Outlines of human skeletons were detected within the rubble. The bodies had long since decomposed, but the analysis capability of the agricultural bot was designed for fine-tuning. His sensors were able to decipher the intricacies of delicate plant life, and the detail of the analysis surprised him. It was something he hadn't been expecting. The owners of this machine had configured it with features he'd underestimated. Unfortunately for him, none of those things would help him when the mechs finally caught up with him. Even though the mechs that had been on the hauler must have been destroyed, he knew more had been nearby.

He reached the end of the street and ran around a corner, seeing that the evacuation center was several hundred meters away. Barricades blocked the entrance, and long lines of abandoned vehicles were crammed together, filling the space leading up to it. Quinton ran between them. A watchtower still stood to the side of the barricade, and he peered at the dark shape inside.

*ACN Plasma Assault System.*

The words appeared on his HUD.

"Radek, what's with the ident of the tower defenses?"

"The identity of the tower defenses was pulled from your ESS," Radek replied.

The other tower had toppled over the barricade, and Quinton began climbing it.

"Are you saying that I have detailed schematics of weapons systems available?" Quinton asked, hoping he'd found some useful skill he hadn't known he had.

He couldn't recall that ability from the little he could remember of his PMC training, but there might have been improvements since he'd first been uploaded and stored into his original ESS. PMC modification, which included the enhancements, required the consent of the person, and under the circumstances, Radek should be able to inform him if any such enhancements had occurred.

"Negative, there are no additional technical libraries stored in the ESS. The identification was from your own knowledge."

Quinton reached the top of the barricade and began sliding down the other side.

"My own knowledge," he said. "But why can't I remember having the knowledge in the first place?"

He stopped his descent. A maze of designated queues meant to manage the people leaving this place extended another hundred meters from where he was. How many people had come through here? The lines must have been immense.

He leaped to the ground and began making his way across the maze, going in as straight a line as possible, but he saw that there were more personnel barricades on the other side that funneled people to a specific pathway beyond. Quinton didn't know which would take him directly inside, so he angled for the nearest one and hoped for the best.

"Radek, you never answered my question."

"Apologies. I've been interacting with the VI interface that manages all the VIs. To answer your question, it has to do with the limitations of this unit. VIs operate to assist you without you having to consciously ask for it. They're monitoring all sensory inputs. Due to the limitations of the unit, they cannot allow direct access to your extensive memory libraries, but they can allow the factual knowledge, giving you information to help you with things like identification of a variety of systems."

Quinton considered this for a few moments. The VIs managed the Personality Matrix Construct's connection to the ESS. His consciousness was mainly stored in the ESS, but the parts that allowed him to inhabit the agricultural bot functioned separately, as if they were two distinct units. But there *was* a connection, which meant that the VIs had access to the majority of knowledge—his knowledge and experiences— stored in the ESS. Quinton didn't like that one bit. This meant he'd be living with VI gatekeepers that were called upon to decide which knowledge he needed and then make it available. He should have access to everything. Instead, he was walking—or, in this case, running—around with a form of selective amnesia that was under the dominion of a VI. What made it even worse was the fact that Radek hadn't realized this was happening, which led Quinton to believe that even Radek was functioning in a diminished capacity. Compounded with the current situation of running for his life, this meant he was one step away from some kind of failure. Either this unit would cease to function, or the bottleneck between his PMC and the ESS would cause the entire system to freeze up.

He stopped his racing thoughts from distracting him when he could least afford it. He just needed to keep moving forward. His furry little freeloader let out a low squeal, and Quinton stopped. He glanced behind him toward the large barricades and increased the sensitivity of his auditory systems. Filtering out the rapid breathing of the creature on his shoulder, he was able to hear the brisk thump-thump of its heartbeat as it increased. He raised the sensitivity further and could just make out the artificial cadence of hunter mechs in the distance. They must have found his trail. He returned the configuration of the auditory system back to normal and ran inside the evacuation center.

A warning flashed on his HUD. The power meter for the agricultural bot—him— was decreasing rapidly and would soon reach critical levels.

The unit's power meter minimized to the upper-right corner of his HUD and, trying to ignore it, he sprinted inside the evacuation center through another security check-in, wondering how many of these things the people of this world had had to go through before they could leave. He glanced at a veritable mountain of discarded personal belongings and sped down a long hall-way. Lightning flashes illuminated a wide-open waiting area ahead of him, and he ran toward it. Once through the doorway, numerous lightning flashes revealed ash-laden sleet free-falling outside in glistening waves. It collected on the ground in drifts that nearly reached the tops of high landing platforms.

He peered at the rows of landing platforms.

They were empty.

Quinton ran toward the window, searching for a ship. Personnel tubes extended from the waiting area to empty landing platforms. The sky lit up again, showing the graveyard of a massive transport station without any ships. There was nothing here.

He kept walking in a half-shuffle, stopping periodically to look outside, hoping to spot something he might have missed. He slowly scanned the area, praying that one of his internal VIs would spot something and highlight it on his HUD.

"Radek, I don't see anything out there that we can use."

"Confirmed. It appears that all ships have left this center."

*Big help that was*, he thought and quickly dismissed it. He leaned toward the window, searching. He was at ground level, which didn't give him a good view of the area, so he glanced over to the side at a small building that looked as if it was some kind of control center. He saw the curvature of the landing field area, and judging the central location of the dark building, he could climb to the top and get a better vantage point.

Quinton scuttled toward the nearest tunnel leading out of the evacuation center and entered. He kept going until he found an emergency exit and emerged outside. His furry companion let out a soft cry and burrowed his face into Quinton's neck, shielding himself from the acid rain. There was nothing he could do for the creature, no shelter he could give him. The best he could do was to get out of the toxic atmosphere as quickly as possible.

He raced toward the control center and bolted up the staircase that led to the entrance. Once inside, the creature shook itself, and flecks of water and slimy ash flicked into the air. To his left was a wide window that stretched the length of the control center, giving him a perfect—though disheartening—view of the empty landing area for the transport station.

"Come on," Quinton said. "Give me something I can use."

He peered outside and then noticed a dim light glowing from one of the workstations to his right. He hastened over to it and engaged the holo-interface. The console flickered to life, and the screen showed the most recent status. As he quickly scanned through the data, he noted that there was a date for the last entry, but without knowing the current date, he didn't know how much time had passed since the system had last been updated.

All the loading platforms had a status of "open," meaning that they were waiting for a shuttle or other transport vehicle to arrive. Quinton scrolled through the screen, reading page after page of the same thing. He was stranded here. There was another flash on his HUD, warning him that his power core had reached critical emergency levels. He needed to get to the nearest charging station.

Quinton shook his head in frustration and glared at the holo-screen, which was full of information that wouldn't help him, but he kept scrolling until he reached the end. There were no other ships. Then he noticed something different about the last entry.

*Emergency launcher track system offline.*

This wasn't the important part. If he'd had his human eyes, they would have widened in exultation. One of the tracks showed that there was a small escape craft with a status of needing repairs. Quinton verified the location and looked out the window. Across the landing field was a series of tracks that led off into the distance and curved out of sight.

He saw a door to the outside on the far side of the room and darted over to it. He rushed through and leaped over the railing, forgoing the staircase altogether. He didn't have time. He needed to get to that ship and figure out what was wrong with it so he could escape.

A few minutes later, Quinton finally reached the emergency launcher track system to find a long tent covering the temporary hangar. Its frayed edges flapped in the wind, and long tears along the top provided no shelter underneath.

The track systems curved away before raising in a steep incline, and he looked for anything that could be blocking the track. His enhanced vision outlined an obstruction about halfway down the track before it curved upward. He'd have to clear it. Quinton peered down the row of empty loaders until he saw an elongated shape with a booster engine on the back.

He raced toward it, and his excitement spiked. The loader's terminal was still active. It was a simple standalone access terminal for the planetary escape pod, which had limited flight capabilities and was designed to dock with a space station. He brought up the terminal, and it attempted to establish a connection to the space station that this evacuation center fed into.

*Attempting to establish a link.*

*Connecting . . .*

*Connecting . . .*

"Connect, dammit."

*Connection established. Downloading updated coordinates to station alpha.*

"Yes!"

While the navigation data was downloading, Quinton brought up the pod's status to determine why it was offline. The creature jumped off his shoulder and scurried back under the tent cover while he accessed the pod's computer.

*Escape Pod 4110.*

*Status – Life-support system failure.*

*Abort launch sequence . . .*

He quickly checked the remaining systems for the escape

pod. They were still operational. The only thing was that the pod's life-support system had malfunctioned. Whoever was here must not have had time to repair it, or perhaps they hadn't needed to. But Quinton didn't need life support. He didn't need oxygen or an atmosphere to survive. What he didn't know was how long the metallic alloy of the agricultural bot could withstand the frigidness of outer space, but he could deal with that. The pod would still protect him. He began the launcher's startup sequence, which would take a few minutes to initialize.

Quinton ran next to the track, quickly closing in on the obstruction across it. A tangle of twisted metal from another track lay across the one he needed. He pulled at it, clearing away pieces until he got to a heavy section that just wouldn't budge no matter how hard he pulled. He climbed over to the other side and saw where it was wedged in tight. Quinton extended the remaining blade from his right forearm and selected the option on his HUD for shearing. The blade split into two, and he began cutting near the wedged section. In a stroke of good fortune, the alloy of the blades was stronger than the material used for the track, and he was able to cut through it. He made quick work of it and then tore loose the last of the debris.

He spun around and ran back toward the pod. The control panel inside cast a bluish glow on the vehicle's interior. Quinton glanced at the launcher platform, looking for the creature, but it was gone. It had probably run off. He checked the pod's status on the terminal and approached the open hatch. He was taking one last glance around when lightning flashed, and his gaze sank to the ground, seeing flashes of amber reflected upon the watery surface.

*Hunters!*

The mechs had found him. Six of them galloped toward him, closing the distance in a rush of speed.

Quinton scrambled through the hatch and closed it. He sat

down and had to buckle himself in before the controls would allow him to initiate the launch.

Something scurried on the floor, and Quinton saw that the furry creature had already climbed aboard. A mech slammed its fists on the outer hatch, and the escape pod rocked to the side before settling back into place. He thought it was going to break through. If it did, the automatic safety systems would abort the launch.

As the hunter mech drew back for another strike, Quinton engaged the launch system. There was a sudden burst from the booster, and the planetary escape pod raced down the track, quickly reaching maximum speed. He was thrown back into the seat, and his furry companion screeched as he was pinned against the wall. The pod angled upward and then it was in the air. The secondary boosters engaged in a blast of energy as the pod reached escape velocity.

A warning flashed across the holoscreen.

*Life support offline.*

*Interior atmosphere minimal.*

Quinton glanced at the creature and then opened the panel beneath the console. There was an emergency life-support face mask inside. He snatched it out and grabbed the little furball, which scrambled his stubby legs.

"Easy there, Stumpy. I'm trying to help you."

He fit the mask over the creature's face. It formed around his head, the material configuring in a tight seal, and oxygen flowed inside. The panicking creature calmed down after a few moments of breathing the fresh air.

"Power levels critical. I must shut down systems to conserve power," Radek said.

Before Quinton could voice any kind of protest, everything around him began fading. His thoughts came to a halt, and all sensory input crawled to a stop as if his mind were frozen. Then, nothing.

# CHAPTER SIX

*System diagnostic running.*

Quinton snapped back to awareness and stared at the words on his HUD. A few quick diagnostics completed, and his motor functions returned to normal.

*Again . . .*

*Where am I now?*

He didn't open his eyes because, as far as he knew, the agricultural bot he was housed in didn't have any eyelids. It was more that he gradually became aware of his condition and the sensory input the optics provided.

He was still inside the planetary escape pod, but the hatch was open. Somehow, he was lying on his side on the floor. He glanced at the upper-right corner of his internal HUD, which showed that his power meter was charging, and he jerked his head back in surprise. His power core had been charged to almost 50 percent. He started to push himself up and the actuators in his left shoulder gave out, but he caught himself with his other hand. He still had that damn damaged shoulder to deal with, but at least he was awake.

Outside the hatch, emergency lighting was engaged in the

corridor. He glanced at the floor and saw that a thick power cable came in from the outside and was attached to a port on his back. Someone had connected him to an emergency charging station.

"Radek, are you there?" Quinton asked.

"System startup is nearly complete."

"Do you know where we are?"

"Station identification is Gateway Station in the Zeda-Six Star System. You went into emergency standby mode to preserve functionality. Once the pod was within range of the station, their automated systems guided it into this docking bay. I did a search and discovered that I would be able to request an emergency power supply authorization if I declared you caretaker of a living creature."

"You made me Stumpy's caretaker?"

"It was a calculated risk, but I didn't want to give the station's computer systems a reason to deny the request."

Quinton realized the little creature wasn't completely useless after all. "Good call. I guess if you'd told the system I was a PMC, it might have ejected the pod so some station jockey could use it for target practice."

"I kept you in standby until the unit had charged more than 50 percent," Radek explained.

They'd escaped the hunter mechs and made it to a space station, and he had Radek to thank for it. "I guess I owe you one."

Radek paused for a moment as its silvery holographic orb hovered in the air. "I'm afraid I don't understand." The orb pulsed when the VI spoke.

"You helped me, Radek. You got me hooked up to a power supply to recharge this machine."

"PMCs are a distinct entity apart from the physical form they are housed in. I made an effort to keep the unit performing. It's one of my primary objectives."

Quinton shook his head. "It's called appreciation, Radek. I

was expressing my gratitude. I know VIs understand this concept."

"I understand the concept. I'm merely pointing out that it is unnecessary."

"Well, I disagree, but let's just drop it. Have any station personnel arrived?"

"Other than the automated system response, we have not been contacted."

Quinton didn't like the sound of that. He stood up and attempted to access the space station's computer systems, but there were no active connections available. Glancing around the escape pod for a moment, he realized that the emergency faceplate he'd stuffed Stumpy inside was now empty. The agricultural bot was equipped with sensors to detect a whole library of residues, so tracking Stumpy would be easy, but he couldn't spend a lot of time doing it. He wondered if he should have left the critter but quickly recognized that anything left on the planet, at least in the region they'd been in, was likely dead or dying. Leaving Stumpy would have been a death sentence, but Quinton wasn't sure if bringing the creature up here was any better.

He walked out of the escape pod and into the narrow corridor. To his right, the corridor led to the station's interior. The station's automated systems had docked his small vehicle on a long arm that was designed for escape pods, and the corridor was lined with empty pods whose occupants had long since exited them. There must have been a mass exodus from the planet, and he once again wondered what had happened to make the planet so uninhabitable. Severe volcanic activity explained some of it, but not the mechs.

His sensors detected that there was an atmosphere being maintained on the space station, but it was minimal. Apparently, it had been some time since anyone had come here. Life-support systems had automatically initialized the artificial atmosphere with the detection of Stumpy.

The power line that was tethered to the access port in his back retracted into the wall as he walked down the corridor. The main port was at the end, and when Quinton reached it, the cord detached from his access port and disappeared behind a panel on the wall.

He thought it was more important that he find the people who operated the space station rather than staying to continue charging. They might have a better housing unit for his ESS. Hopefully, he'd be able to get some information about where he was and whether other PMCs had been sent out across the galaxy. He tried to remember what the standard protocol was for PMC reactivation, but he couldn't. However, he was pretty sure he wasn't supposed to be dumped in an agricultural bot, no matter how sophisticated it was. This thing was barely able to accommodate the ESS where the bulk of Quinton's PMC was contained.

He called out, hoping that somebody would hear him, but there was no reply. The station should have been monitoring for verbal communications at the very least, so why hadn't it responded? There was really no way for him to get lost because there was only one way to go. He came to a larger corridor, and there was a sign that pointed the way to central processing and main transport.

Quinton followed the signs and eventually made his way to an information terminal. Somebody had designed this part of the station for minimal human interaction, which he supposed made sense. If people were evacuating the planet, they wouldn't be on the station for very long.

The information terminal came online, and Quinton accessed it. This entire section of the space station must have been offline because the information terminal didn't have the current status readily available. But then, Quinton had no idea how large the space station was because he'd been unconscious when the pod arrived.

He heard the pitter-patter of tiny clawed feet and saw

Stumpy coming toward him. The creature stopped and regarded him for a few moments, twitching his head to the side and fulling extending his large floppy ears. Deciding that the danger was minimal, Stumpy came closer, but the status screen suddenly flashed, and data began populating the screen. Quinton ignored Stumpy.

*Searching for the next available transport ship.*
*None available. Please head to central processing.*

Quinton glared at the holoscreen. He made a swiping motion, and the status screen minimized. He searched through the options, trying to find a map of the station so he could see the layout of the place and locate a hangar. He finally found a map and saw that this station was one of more than twenty positioned around the planet. It *was* a mass exodus.

He studied the map. The station looked like it had been cobbled together from spare orbital platforms. Usually, inhabited systems had a singular space station that was the transport hub for the planet. If there were mining facilities throughout the star system, then there might be smaller stations. But Quinton had the feeling he wasn't on either of those kinds of space stations. Someone had deployed this setup quickly, which meant that it lacked some of the essential systems he would have expected to find. Also, there were no people. He was alone.

His thoughts began to race, focusing on nothing that would help him. He found himself wanting to take a deep breath, but he couldn't, and there was no physical release of tension that might have brought a moment's peace. Instead, his fear just gathered into an overwhelming intensity. He looked around at the metallic walls of the space station and staggered back a few paces, letting out a half-formed snarl.

Who had done this to him?

A small voice in his mind urged him to calm down, and he wanted to comply, to think rationally. He should be able to do that, but he couldn't. He was stuck inside this lifeless machine, trying to keep a firm hold of his sanity, and it was slipping away.

*I just need to focus. I just need to see.*

Quinton spotted a viewport off to the side, but it was closed. They all were. He stomped over to the information terminal and opened all the viewports. All around the circular room, the metallic shields sank toward the floor, revealing a planetary view directly in front of him. A massive storm covered any landscape that would have been in sight, and only faint flashes of lightning emerged through the tempest. He glanced toward the horizon, looking for signs of life, but all he saw was an expanse of grays and whites that had extended far from the poles.

He walked around the central hub and saw the other arms of the station where escape pods had docked. Above him were massive docking platforms where transport ships had docked to fly people away from there.

He peered out of the viewports, looking for the other stations, but couldn't find any. Something shimmered in the sunlight, but Quinton couldn't tell what it was. It looked like some kind of metallic mass that was reflecting the light from the star. He returned to the terminal and bypassed the generic options on the main screen, establishing a link to the station's communication systems. Then, he sent out a general comms signal and waited. There were several automated replies—not from other stations but ship systems. He didn't care. He activated the station's auto-dock procedures, sent the commands to the ships, and waited for the ships to acknowledge the broadcast. Three of them replied immediately, and Quinton watched for them to fly to the station.

He shook his head. The ships weren't far, but it was going to take them some time to reach the station. He walked back toward the viewport of the planet and watched the massive storm clouds that covered the entire continent. There was something almost hypnotic about the way the swirling masses moved together. Out of the corner of his eye, he noticed something that pierced the clouds. A large grouping of objects began to glow as they reached escape velocity and headed toward the station. Were they escape pods? He returned to the info-terminal, but the automated docking systems weren't detecting any incoming pods from the planet.

Quinton looked back toward the viewport. A flash of panic erupted inside him just as the first of the objects slammed into the nearby docking arm. Klaxon alarms sounded and bulkhead doors slammed shut, cutting them off from the damaged part of the station. He backed away and heard Stumpy screech as he scurried away from the sound of the alarms.

Quinton glanced out of the viewport and saw more objects speeding toward the station. Two realizations slammed themselves into the forefront of his mind—there was a planetary defense cannon on the surface of the planet, and somehow the hunter mechs were using it to destroy the space station he was on.

Quinton backed away from the viewports.

He had to run.

# CHAPTER SEVEN

QUINTON OPENED a comlink to the space station's computer systems using his connection to the information terminal as an access point. He ordered the door on the other side of the control center to open and ran toward it. Stumpy scampered ahead of him down the corridor that curved out of sight.

He needed to get to the smaller docking bays on the far side of the station that faced away from the planet. As he ran, he scanned for new comlink access points because his current connection to the onboard systems was tenuous at best. If the planetary defense cannons hit the processing center, he would be cut off until he found another information terminal to patch into. It shouldn't take him this long to find a remote access point.

As the seconds went by, Quinton felt a gnawing doubt nibble away at his thoughts.

"Radek, are you able to help me with access to the station's systems?"

He checked the station's tracking systems, and one of the ships he'd called for was minutes away from docking with a maintenance port.

"Try scanning for open comlink interfaces," Radek replied. "They should be standard on a station of this design."

"What do you think I've been trying to do?" Quinton said.

The bulkhead door ahead of him wouldn't open, and Stumpy scurried back and forth in front of it—a furry ball of frightful intensity. Quinton checked the command status of the bulkhead door, and it wasn't responding. Then his access to the space station's systems severed. He was cut off.

A loud clang came from behind him, followed by a series of pops. The floor trembled under his feet, and everything lurched to the side as his view of the planet spun out of view. The station was spinning! The defense cannons must have hit a vital system for maintaining its orbit.

Quinton searched the control systems of the agricultural bot for magnetic boots to help stabilize him, but there weren't any. He cursed inwardly, simultaneously acknowledging that there was no reason for the bot to be equipped with magnetic boots. There was still some artificial gravity, but the centrifugal forces of the spinning space station exerted more force than the standard point-seven-five g-force maintained by the field.

He was pushed against the outer wall, and he crawled toward the bulkhead door. Light flashed by the open window. The station wouldn't be able to maintain its location in lower orbit. Quinton didn't know how long he had before the station broke apart in the planet's atmosphere. Unless his luck changed, it wouldn't be long.

He reached the bulkhead door and squatted down to pull open the manual override. He yanked hard on the lever, and the door opened a little. He grabbed onto one side of the door and pushed. Both sides of the door retracted. Stumpy hastened through, and he followed.

Quinton ran, his feet pounding on the outer wall of the station.

"Radek, did you detect anything?" he asked.

The wall curved upward, and Quinton climbed toward the opening of the adjacent hall. The little furball had already reached it and let out a screech before disappearing from view. Quinton had the impression that the little creature was telling him to hurry in furball language.

It took him a few moments to realize that Radek hadn't responded to him. Quinton accessed the agricultural bot's comms systems, and they were stuck in a comms loop, unable to connect to anything. He killed the process, temporarily shutting down his data communications capabilities, then brought them back up. He engaged the signal-acquisition protocol, which was a limited broadcast from the transmitter located on his head.

*Signal acquired.*

*Authorized access granted.*

*Welcome to emergency gateway station.*

The words appeared on his HUD, along with a gold emblem of the triangular bow of a warship on a black background. Quinton felt a few moments of satisfaction, immediately followed by suspicion. Why hadn't Radek told him about the faulty comms subroutine? It should have been easy for the VI to detect, unless the VI interface was functioning at a limited capacity just like Quinton was.

He glanced at the emblem, thinking it looked familiar. He tried to force the memory from his ESS, but it didn't work. Some low-level VI interface had decided that this information was nonessential.

Quinton slammed his fist against the wall and used the hardened alloy of his fingers to gouge a fingerhold. He thought he might have heard a growl from the bot's vocalizer. He pulled himself up and climbed to the top. Stumpy was already way down the corridor, and the furball stopped and glanced back at him for a moment before continuing.

With entry to Gateway Station's systems, Quinton had more access to the data he needed.

"Apologies, Quinton," Radek said, his silver orb shimmering nearby. "My capabilities were temporarily impaired due to a faulty module inside the agricultural bot's central processing unit. I was freed from the impairment when you stopped the associated tasks, and I have managed a workaround. I see that you now have systems access."

"Are you serious? You should've—" Quinton stopped himself from making a snarky reply. Everything was falling apart, including the bot his PMC was housed in, and he had no idea how long it would function. How many internal systems would need to fail before his PMC ceased to function? If that happened, his life would be in Radek's limited virtual hands, and who knew if Quinton would ever regain consciousness in those circumstances. He had to get to the ship and get away from the space station as quickly as possible. Then he could decide what to do next.

An alert popped up on his HUD. The automatic docking systems were attempting to abort the docking procedure.

"No, dammit, stop aborting the dock," Quinton growled.

He initiated an override and engaged the station's mobility thrusters. Enough of them came online to slow the spinning space station, and the approaching ship was able to get on a safe approach vector. At least now he had a ship docking closer to his location than before.

With the station stabilizing, it was easier for him to move toward his destination, although he knew it wouldn't last—not with the planetary defense cannons tearing the station apart. He accessed a video feed and saw that the projectiles from the defense cannon had decreased. Maybe they were running out of ammunition.

Quinton hastened down a narrow corridor between sections of the station, glancing at the section heading to make sure he was in the right place.

*Successful dock of the ZS-Novo.*

The status of the ship appeared on Quinton's HUD. The other ships he'd initiated a broadcast to weren't responding now. They'd aborted the docking procedure, so this was his only chance to get off the station. The ship was at the far end of a long corridor where escape pods normally docked.

Quinton ran down the corridor, and the station lurched to the side again, causing him to stumble. He banged into the wall and nearly fell into one of the open doorways of an empty escape pod. Stumpy screeched from somewhere ahead of him, and he could tell by the sound that he was going to have to climb to reach his ship. The axis at which the remains of the space station was spinning was trying to push him off the wall, and he had to hold on. If he let go, there'd be no way for him to stop himself and he'd just crash into the far wall at the end of the corridor, likely destroying the agricultural bot altogether.

He crawled along the wall like a spider. The station began to spin faster, and Quinton didn't know how much time he had. He began taking short leaps, ignoring the fact that if he failed to grab hold of the bulkhead walls at the precise time, he was going to die.

The escape pod doorways blurred by as he sped past them. He reached out with his hands and attempted to slow himself down, but the actuator in his left shoulder gave out and he misjudged his approach. Instead of grabbing hold of the bulkhead wall, he began to tumble. He heard the little furball screeching but didn't know where it was.

Quinton grunted with effort as he tried to anticipate where his body was going to be in relation to the out-of-control space station. He banged against the bulkhead wall and a series of impact alerts appeared on his HUD.

Panic swelled up inside him. This was it. He was going to die. He tried to grab the bulkhead wall again but couldn't get a firm grip.

Then time slowed down—literally.

"What the . . ." Quinton began to say, and then a new sub-window appeared on his HUD.

*Frame rate increase.*

*Warning: Power consumption increase.*

He finally understood. One of the advantages of a PMC was the ability to speed up the perception of time beyond what he would've been capable of in his own body. The agricultural bot was still tumbling out of control, but his perception of it had slowed down. He could pick the precise moment to slow himself down.

Quinton looked around and found a handhold that was part of the bulkhead wall. He was going to bounce off the adjacent wall, and by his estimation, it would send him right to the handhold.

He slowed the frame rate to 20 percent that of real time, then angled his body to try to control how he bounced off the wall.

It worked.

He was heading right toward the handhold. Quinton reached out with both hands, his body slowly spinning. He brought his legs and feet together as if he were a missile. Then, he grabbed the handhold. His feet jerked past him, but he was able to hold on and stop.

He blew out a breath that came out as an audible hissing sound from the agricultural bot's vocalizer. He didn't need to breathe, but there were some things that were embedded as habits in his consciousness that he couldn't let go. A proper housing unit for his PMC would have been able to compensate for the nuances that came with being human.

He adjusted the frame rate to normal time and heard Stumpy from farther down the corridor near where the ship was docked. Quinton began climbing toward it. On the other side of the corridor, inside a vacant escape pod door, he saw Stumpy, wide-eyed with terror as he clung onto the central console.

"You're not showing off now, are you?" he said.

Stumpy turned toward him, and his saucer-shaped eyes narrowed. His clawed feet gripped the console and his tail went rigid as he tried to keep his balance.

"This is what happens when you run off ahead." He looked around, trying to think of a way to cross over.

"The ship is just ahead. You must escape as quickly as possible," Radek said.

Quinton glanced up the corridor to the open docking bay door where his ship waited for him. "Are you suggesting I just leave him here? No moral compass, Radek?"

"A VI is incapable of determining moral choices. That is left up to the PMC."

He found Radek's reply peculiar, but he wasn't sure why. He'd brought Stumpy with him on a whim. The furry creature would have died if he hadn't, just as he would surely die if Quinton left him where he was now. If he tried to save him, there was a chance they'd both die. But if he could save the creature, Stumpy would most likely die at a later date, and Quinton would feel better about it now at least.

Stumpy held onto the central console, and now his feet and tail dangled in the air as he scrambled to hold on.

"Hang on, I'm coming," he said.

He tried not to think of how stupid he'd feel if he botched this and ended up dead. At least he'd only feel that way for a few seconds, and then he wouldn't be thinking of anything at all. The edges of Radek's holographic orb glistened, but the VI didn't say anything.

Quinton brought his feet under him and changed the configuration of the bot's feet so he could grab onto the handhold. The agricultural unit was designed with climbing in mind.

He increased his frame rate so time slowed down, and he waited for the space station's spin to approach its apex. When it did, he launched himself across the corridor directly toward the open hatch of the escape pod. Then, he grabbed the outer hatch and stopped himself from landing inside and crushing the little fella.

He set his frame rate back to normal time. His body dangled inside the escape pod, and he reached with his foot toward Stumpy. The escape pod was bigger than the one he'd flown to the station on, and he couldn't quite reach where Stumpy was, but he was as close as he was going to get.

"You're going to have to jump," he said.

Stumpy bobbed his head a couple times, as if judging the distance to Quinton's foot, and looked as if he was going to make the jump a few times, but Quinton's patience was growing thin. He didn't have time for this.

"I'm going to leave you here." He shook his foot, dangling it in front of the little furball. "Come on," he said and beckoned with his arm.

Stumpy's gaze locked onto Quinton's foot, and his body went rigid. There was a quick shuffle and a leap. The furry little creature grabbed on, scampered up to his shoulder, and held on tight.

Quinton climbed out of the escape pod and headed toward the ship. He had to time his movements with the momentum of the space station as it spun. A few frame rate adjustments later, he was climbing into the ship.

The ZS-*Novo* was a light transport star jumper-class ship. He closed the outer hatch, went through the airlock, and walked out onto a decent-size storage area compared to the size of the ship. From there, he headed for the bridge. Crusty flecks of pale green paint from the walls and ceilings littered the floor. He glanced at a $CO_2$ scrubber that was in a recess on the wall. A buildup of black mold surrounded the scrubber, and Quinton was able to detect mold spores in the atmosphere. Not the healthiest air to breathe, but he'd worry about that after they escaped.

The *Novo*'s bridge was rather small. There were two chairs in a small circular room that was above the level he'd entered. He sat down in one of the chairs, and Stumpy scampered off his shoulder, but he didn't pay attention to where the little furball went next. He needed to check the ship's systems and get away from the space station. Since this was a civilian ship, there was very little security between him and the *Novo*'s systems. It also helped that the last captain hadn't done a proper shutdown of the systems. They'd probably been in a rush to get on one of the large evacuation ships.

The *Novo* was equipped with a second-generation Paxton jump drive, which had limited range, but it should do the job of getting him to another star system. Anything would be better than where he was. Three holoscreens appeared in front of him, and he was able to see outside the ship for the first time. The bridge was located near the front of the ship, seeming to ride on top of the storage area.

Quinton opened a comlink to the *Novo*'s systems so he could interact with the computer directly. The *Novo* ship computer recognized that a new captain was on the bridge and had status reports ready for him. A proximity alarm flashed on the center-most holoscreen.

A video image showed that the planetary defense cannon had resumed its bombardment on the station. Those damn mechs must have reloaded them. The space station was essentially a large shaft with spindly docking arms that had escape pods attached. Many had broken off as the space station was blown apart.

Quinton got the engines ready and waited, intending to use the space station's rotation to help him escape. It wouldn't do him any good to release the docking clamps and be flung toward the planet. In that case, he'd have to expend precious energy flying away from the planet, and he didn't know how well the ship could maneuver through a field of projectiles from a mag cannon.

He noticed that the rate of fire seemed to be focused on another part of the space station, so the mechs probably believed he was still there. He released the docking clamps and engaged the engines. As the ship cleared the station and flew away,

Quinton felt an urge to sit back in his chair and sigh, but neither was necessary. For the first time since he'd awakened, he felt like he had a few moments to catch his breath.

He set a course to take them away from the planet. Not only did he need to reach the minimum safe distance to execute an FTL jump, he also needed to allow the navigation computer time to refresh the star charts to align with a destination he had yet to pick.

"Okay, Radek. Time for us to talk."

Quinton looked at the power meter on his HUD. The power levels for the agricultural bot had fallen below 50 percent. Increasing his frame rate had drained the power core. He needed to keep that in mind. He queried the ship's systems, looking for a way to continue charging the bot's power supply, but couldn't find anything. That was problem number one that he'd have to work on.

"Radek, are you there?"

A silver orb appeared on one of the holoscreens. "I'm here, Quinton. I thought it better to show myself using the ship's power systems rather than the limited capacity of the bot."

"Can I leverage the ship's computer systems to gain additional access to my ESS?" Quinton asked.

"Offloading like that poses an extreme risk to PMC stability and the ESS."

"How extreme of a risk?"

"Instability in the ESS, which could lead to severe degradation of the PMC."

"Okay, Radek, next time just tell me it'll kill me and we can keep this simpler."

"Understood."

"Why am I here?"

"I don't understand the question," Radek replied.

Quinton took a few moments to gather his thoughts. "You said there was an activation signal from somewhere, and there was an ESS located on Zeda-Six. Somehow my PMC was stored there."

"I believe this is accurate. Transference of a PMC to an ESS poses a great risk to PMC stability. There is a strong probability that you were stored in the ESS prior to it being located on this planet."

That was something, at least. PMCs were highly complex, and Quinton didn't want to think that someone or something had transferred all that data from somewhere while looking for an open ESS. "Where was I first activated?"

"In a data archive facility on Zeda-Six."

"Whose data archive facility?"

"Unknown. The facility reacted to the activation signal."

"Where did the activation signal come from?" Quinton asked and then shook his head. There was no way Radek would know this because he would have been activated at the same time. "Never mind. Is there anything you can tell me about the activation signal itself? Do you have a record of it?"

"No, when the ESS was activated and there was no acceptable storage unit for it, I was tasked with finding an acceptable one. Any record of the initial activation signal must still be at the facility on the planet," Radek replied.

Returning to the planet wasn't an option. He recalled that Radek had encountered the hunter mechs shortly after his activation. Going back there would help only if he had no other option. Quinton opened a comlink to the space station and found that part of the communication system was still online. Most star systems had a communication hub with built-in redundancies. He requested a data dump of the communication log from the space station. He didn't know how long it would remain online and didn't want to risk being cut off. When that was done, he could review it on the ship.

"Radek, analyze the communication logs and see if you can

pinpoint the activation signal. I need to know where it came from."

The silver orb on the holoscreen went still, and a few moments later the data on the screen changed. "I've identified the signal, but I'm unable to determine its origin."

Quinton studied the raw data of the communication signal. It looked like gibberish, and incomprehensible data could mean only one thing: Whoever had sent the signal didn't want to be found. This made tracking it more complicated. He'd have to give it some more thought. He saved a copy of the data, then opened the *Novo*'s navigation systems and began looking at the star charts. They hadn't been updated in over fifty standard years. A lot could change in that time, but staying there wasn't an option.

The holoscreen to his right flickered and showed a plot of the Zeda-Six Star System. He was moving away from the planet but noticed that another ship had entered the system and was heading toward the planet. It wasn't on an intercept course with the *Novo*, but he was reluctant to open a comlink to the ship. The plot updated with other ships that were in orbit around the planet, and he noted that they were small vessels like the one he was on. Given his original reception, Quinton had to assume that everything in the star system could be hostile.

He brought up the Paxton jump drive, and while it was charging, he picked a nearby star system called Lantus as a destination. He'd never heard of it before, but he needed to get away from this place, and he didn't want to break the jump drive by having it fold space to a destination much farther away.

A communications holoscreen came to prominence. The ship that had just entered the system was trying to initiate contact, but something was wrong. The hailing package was just a ship-to-ship identity request.

SN-Seeker-901.

He'd never heard of the designation "SN," and "Seeker" was a class of ship, not a ship name. Ship designations utilized federation names as part of their identification.

The SN-Seeker-901 hailed them again and then changed course.

"Definitely not friendly," Quinton said and checked the status of the jump drive.

The SN-Seeker-901 increased its speed and was now on an intercept course.

The Paxton jump drive finished charging, and its status changed to green. He was far enough away from the planet's gravity well that he could initiate the jump.

The ZS-*Novo* light transport ship jumped out of the star system.

# CHAPTER EIGHT

THE LANTUS STAR system was home to a massive red giant star. An initial subspace scan of the system revealed a couple of Jovian planets with a few hundred moons orbiting them in clusters, but nothing else was detected—no automated mining platforms, no research stations. Nothing. Not even an interstellar communications relay.

Quinton looked at the scan data on the holoscreen in disappointment. The star charts had shown that both a communications relay and mining platforms were present in this star system. Again, he felt an urge to sigh or frown or maybe even press his lips together, all of which the agricultural bot couldn't do. Instead, the bot's vocalizer made a soft buzzing sound that he supposed could have been considered a growl. He made a mental note to change whatever setting was associated with it.

He glanced at the controls for the ship's monitoring systems on the bridge, wanting to get a better look at the agricultural bot. He didn't have a clear image of what he even looked like. But it wasn't him, he reminded himself. He wasn't the bot. This was just a platform that his PMC was housed in for the moment. It was temporary. He repeated the thought in his mind a few times before shifting his focus to something else. Maybe now wasn't the best time to find out what he looked like.

He hadn't altered his course since entering the star system. While he waited for the jump drive to recharge, he searched the navigation system. He needed to pick a system that would likely have a communication hub so he could track the activation signal that had found its way to Zeda-Six.

The *Novo* wasn't designed for extensive travel beyond a local cluster of stars, which was why the star charts in the navigation systems had limited information. He didn't know if he was located along the galactic fringes or was in one of the core systems. His thoughts suddenly became blank, as if they'd been blocked by an invisible barrier.

"Radek," Quinton said, "I'm stumbling around here in the dark without full access to the ESS. I don't even know which federation or star empire I'm located in."

"Understandable," Radek replied, "but I don't think you fully appreciate just how precarious a position you're in. Ship diagnostics indicate that even though this ship can still operate, it's been derelict for at least fifty years. Jump drive systems for this ship haven't been calibrated since the star charts were updated. The computer systems are inadequate to transfer even a small percentage of the sophisticated data in the ESS. It wasn't designed for—"

"All right, I get it," Quinton said irritably. He remained motionless on the bridge for a few moments. "This ship and this bot are all I have to work with."

An alert appeared on his internal heads-up display. The bot's power meter plummeted by more than 10 percent before stopping at 38 percent. Then another alert appeared, informing him that part of his power core had ceased to operate. The error log gave a manufacturer code for Veris, who had built the bot.

He didn't know how much time he had. If he lost power here, no one would ever find him. He'd be lost forever. Someone had sent that activation signal just like someone had stored his PMC onto an ESS and left it on Zeda-Six. He needed to figure out who that was, but more importantly, he needed to find another body — something that could handle the ESS so he could have full access to his memories. Then maybe he could find whoever thought it had been a good idea to store an ESS with Quinton's PMC on what he suspected was a fringe-colony world. Someone had hidden him away to be activated at a later date, and he needed to understand why.

Quinton returned to scouring the star charts for a destination. Radek was right—the ship had severe limits. He had to assume that the next FTL jump might be his last, so he had to make the most of the destination he chose. He moved the star chart to the main holoscreen and then calculated the limits of the jump drive. A sphere surrounded a smaller portion of the star charts. There wasn't much here in such a remote location, but he did see a reference to Shangris Spaceport. The spaceport would be his best chance to get some help or, at the very least, find some information. Maybe they'd even be able to swap out his power core, or better yet, maybe he could find a better bot to use since this one wouldn't last much longer. He needed something that was designed for a PMC with full haptic interface capabilities.

He was getting ahead of himself. He looked back at the holoscreen, uploaded the coordinates to the navigation system, and left the bridge. As soon as the jump drive recharged, he could be underway.

"Your power core is failing," Radek said.

"I know."

"I would advise you to stay on the bridge."

Quinton walked down the short corridor, glancing at the failing atmosphere scrubber as he passed it, and then entered the storage area. There were several rows of storage containers. He brought up the shipping manifest, hoping there would be something he could use.

"I can't do anything on the bridge. I need to recharge my power core," Quinton said.

"This ship doesn't have droid support capabilities," Radek said.

"You're right; it doesn't, but some of these storage containers have their own individual power cores that connect to the ship's reactor. I'm going to have a look at them."

Radek was quiet for a few moments. Quinton imagined him as an old man with gray hair, a harsh gaze, and a quizzical furrowed brow, ripe with disapproval. Quinton chuckled.

"I don't see the humor in this," Radek said.

The VI's comment confirmed that he was incapable of reading Quinton's thoughts. From what little he could remember of his training to become a PMC candidate, VIs weren't supposed to be able to do that. But there had been so many things that were unorthodox in what Radek had been called to perform that he wouldn't put it past the original designers to keep certain capabilities secret.

"I need a new body," Quinton said. "Actually, I need *my* body."

"It is doubtful that your original body has been preserved, but I don't have any knowledge regarding it."

He walked down a row of storage containers, some of which were nearly as tall as he was. "What *do* you know then?" he asked as he squatted down to look at the container's identification.

"All PMCs have their DNA backed up and recorded in case the PMC decides to abandon its artificial existence and return to a biological form," Radek said.

Quinton stood up. He'd asked the question without really expecting an answer. "Wait a second. Are you saying that somewhere out there is a record of my DNA, and it can be used to grow me a new body?"

"Precisely," Radek replied. "This safeguard was put in place for all PMCs and was part of the standard PMC creation protocol."

If he could track the activation signal, this would lead him to where his DNA was recorded. He just had to survive long enough to find it.

He checked all the storage containers that were patched into the ship's reactor. There was a small charging station for the salvage gear stored in a work area in a side room. Inside the kit was a power bypass module, and Quinton studied it for a few moments. One of the connections looked like it could be attached to the side port of the agricultural bot. He tried to attach it and was able to force the connectors to make contact. It wasn't seamless, but he thought it would work.

He grabbed one of the other connectors and plugged it into an open port on the workbench.

Nothing happened.

Quinton stared at it expectantly, then initiated a remote access session to the ship's systems. He found the controls for the power regulator on the workbench, throttled the power output down to the lowest setting, and then turned it on.

---

QUINTON SNAPPED BACK TO CONSCIOUSNESS.

*System diagnostic running.*

*Power surge detected.*

*Emergency disconnect.*

*32 percent power remaining.*

He cursed inwardly. He'd nearly overloaded the bot's power systems. He was about to call out to Radek when he heard Stumpy's guttural screech.

"What the hell is that thing?" a man asked.

"I don't know. Shoot it if it comes back," another man said in a deep voice.

There were two men aboard the ship? How long had Quinton been out of it? He accessed the ship's systems. It had successfully jumped to the star system where the Shangris Spaceport was located.

"See, Becker, I told you coming back to this old spaceport was a good idea. There's some good salvage on this little ship," one of the men said and laughed.

"It'll be a good haul. Lennix will be pleased. Hey, Simon, where you going?"

Quinton heard someone walking toward him.

"Relax, Becker," Simon said. "I'm just having a look around. There's a small workshop over here. I also think I saw that creature run this way."

Quinton accessed the video feed and saw two men in the storage area. One of them was tall and broad shouldered, and a scar that went from his chin to his neck made him look as if he had a permanent scowl. The second man was much smaller but stocky, with russet, reddish-brown skin. Quinton didn't get a good look at his face before the man headed for the bridge.

"I need you on the bridge, Simon," Becker said.

"I'll be there in a second."

"You're not going to believe this," a disembodied third man said. "Becker, you need to get up here."

"Hang on, Guttman," Becker said. "Simon. Bridge. Now," he bellowed.

Quinton heard Simon come to a halt outside the workshop and sigh. "Fine," he said and walked back the way he'd come.

"This ship came from Zeda-Six," Guttman shouted.

"Not likely," Simon muttered under his breath.

Quinton activated another video feed on the bridge and saw that the three men were looking at the nav system's data on the main holoscreen.

"That's crap," Becker said, leaning over Guttman at the controls.

"It says it right there," Guttman said, trying to shove Becker away.

Becker backhanded the salvager, knocking him out of the seat. Then, he grabbed Guttman by the metallic collar of his spacesuit and hauled him into the air with a growl. "Who do you think you're shoving?"

Guttman grunted in pain, the collar pressing into his neck. "Sah . . . sah . . ." he rasped. "Sorry!"

Becker glared at the man, who coughed in an attempt to breathe in some air. Then Becker dropped him to the ground.

Quinton watched as Simon stood in the doorway.

"Listen up," Becker said. "Out here, it's my way or the airlock. It's your choice, and I don't care which you choose. Get it? You worthless meat-bags mean nothing. All of you are replaceable. Understand?"

"Yeah, I get it," Guttman said and spat on the floor. The biometric sensors showed that there were droplets of blood mixed in with the expelled substance.

"I'm not your friend," Becker said and turned toward Simon. "That includes you, rookie."

Simon hastily brought his hands up in a placating gesture. "I'm here. What do you need me to do?"

"What took you so long?"

Simon jutted a thumb behind him. "I was looking around in the storage area. There's a workshop back there."

Becker shook his head and stepped toward Simon. The smaller man's back bumped against the wall, and he gasped nervously.

"I'm here now. Just tell me what you want me to do," Simon said.

Becker leaned toward him like menacing doom incarnate. "Do you think Crowe cares about who you work for? There's no special treatment."

Simon looked away. "I know. *I know*," he sputtered.

Quinton saw an energy signature detection on the video feed, and the source was the palm of Simon's hand that he kept at his side. He might have been terrified, but it didn't appear as if he intended to go down without a fight, and Quinton guessed that Simon's dark-haired, boyish looks made people underestimate him.

Becker straightened. "Get on that system and tell me if it's been compromised."

The energy signature vanished, and Simon scrambled over to the pilot's seat.

Guttman had finally caught his breath. "Who would lay a trap way out here?"

The sides of Becker's lips lifted into a smirk. "I would," he drawled. "A juicy piece of salvage out here in the middle of nowhere and a group of salvagers," he said, his beefy hand making a circular gesture with his index finger, "come to claim it and bring it back to base?"

"Yeah, but you just put a suppressor on the comms systems."

Becker shook his head. "Suppressors don't stop rogue transmitters designed to come online after certain conditions have been met. Things like engaging a jump drive. Forcible access to the ship. Latent check-in intervals for subsystems."

Guttman considered this for a few moments and nodded, turning his attention back toward the holoscreen.

Becker raised his hand to his ear. "Go ahead, Oscar."

"Captain, we finished scanning the hull and didn't find anything out of place. The ship looks clean," Oscar said.

Becker nodded. "Good work. Simon, patch us into the *Ravager*'s systems."

"Done, and the ship hasn't been compromised," Simon said.

"Well then, how the heck did it get out here?" Guttman asked.

"The ship's computer has logs for two recent FTL jumps.

Given the state of the jump drive, we're lucky the ship is in as good a shape as it is," Simon said.

"Why is that?" Becker asked, peering at the data on the main holoscreen. Then he turned toward Simon.

"It's been in standby for almost fifty years and then received a recall request for a place called Gateway Station in the Zeda-Six Star System."

"See," Guttman said. "I told you it was from Zeda-Six."

Becker's gaze narrowed. "A recall," he said, then unholstered the weapon on his hip.

Quinton peered at it. A tactical overlay appeared on the video feed, and an enhanced view of the weapon appeared.

*Particle sidearm.*

*Model: FCC-Tilion.*

*Status: Charged.*

"What's wrong," Guttman asked and pulled out a similar weapon.

"We have a stowaway," Becker said.

"There aren't any life signs on the ship other than that small thing we saw before," Simon said.

"Then they're shielded," Becker said and stepped toward the door, using part of the frame for cover as if he expected to be attacked. "All right, I want every part of this ship checked. Simon, you check the storage area. Guttman, you're with me. We'll look in engineering and work our way to the storage area."

Quinton thought about increasing his frame rate to give him time to think about what he could do but decided not to. The salvagers didn't look like reasonable people to him. Becker certainly looked like the shoot-first-and-ask-later type of person. He could stand up and try to reason with them but doubted they'd help him.

"Wasn't Zeda-Six an Empire colony?" Guttman asked.

"Maybe," Becker replied. "This region was controlled by the Tilions."

"Actually, the last federation to control this sector was the Acheron Confederacy," Simon said.

Quinton watched as the slight man worked his way through the storage area, a small sleek sidearm in hand.

"Acheron, phaw," Guttman said brusquely. "The galaxy is much better off without 'em."

"It's ancient history," Becker said. "Now, be quiet."

Quinton filed the information under his to-be-reviewed pile, along with everything else. He'd fought the hunter mechs on Zeda-Six, but three armed men in an enclosed space without room to maneuver might be too much for him, especially now that his power core had suffered damage. If he started a fight, he wasn't sure that he'd be able to finish it. Even if he could somehow incapacitate the three men, there was still an unknown number of people on the other ship. No, his odds were much better if he just pretended to be the broken-down agricultural bot that he appeared to be. If anything, it would buy him some time.

Quinton heard Simon approach the workshop. The young man stood in the doorway for a moment, then holstered his weapon and came over to him.

"What do we have here?" Simon said and proceeded to have a closer look at him.

Quinton felt all kinds of conflict while Simon poked and prodded his systems. His sense of personal space was being violated, and it took every shred of his control to ignore it.

Simon pulled out a palm scanner and began running a scan of the bot's systems. "Heh, still online," he said quietly. "How did you get here?"

Quinton watched as Simon leaned over to examine his damaged arm. He nodded to himself in response to the conversation that was taking place inside the young man's mind.

"That's weird," Simon said. "Why would there be . . ."

*Dammit, he's going to detect the ESS.*

The ESS was shielded and hidden inside the agricultural bot's chassis, but still. If that scanner could detect it, then all bets were off.

Heavy footfalls came toward the workshop, and Simon quickly stopped scanning.

"What you got here?" Becker asked.

Simon stood up. "No one's here. Just this bot."

Becker stepped inside the workshop and gave Quinton a quick once-over. "What kind of bot is that?"

"It's an agricultural unit. No idea how it got on the ship. Someone must have been trying to repair it before abandoning it here. I'd like to claim it as my cut from the salvage, if that's all right with you," Simon said.

Becker's gaze narrowed and he peered closer at Quinton, as if trying to guess whether he was missing something valuable.

"It's not worth much. I mainly want it for parts. This model has a pretty good haptic system," Simon said.

Becker frowned. "Haptic system?"

"Yeah, it must have been designed for delicate work, which requires a pretty good haptic system for sensory input. It's not worth much. Who has gardens to tend to these days anyway?" Simon said.

*Careful. You're overselling it*, Quinton thought.

"Gotcha!" Guttman cried out from the other room.

Becker frowned and looked back out the doorway. Stumpy's screeching could be heard throughout the storage area.

Becker and Simon left the workshop.

"This thing is ugly," Guttman said. Stumpy twisted and squirmed, trying to break free. His tail lashed back and forth. "What's with the little spines on its back?"

"Careful," Simon warned, and Guttman froze while trying to hold the struggling animal away from his body. "They contain a neurotoxin. If you come into contact with it, it will cause paralysis and then permanent blindness."

Guttman's eyes widened. He hastily dropped the creature and

vigorously wiped his hands on his legs, then paused for a moment to search for imagined residue on his fingers.

Simon snickered, and Becker glanced at him. Then the large man laughed uproariously.

Guttman's eyebrows pulled together, and he sneered. "Why you little son of a—"

"All right, enough," Becker said, and Guttman halted.

"I don't know what it is," Simon said. "Doesn't look that dangerous."

Guttman glared at the younger man. "I'm not gonna forget this, noob. You're just a tech. You just wait. When we—"

"Save it," Becker said. "Let's get this ship ready to transport. Guttman, head back to the *Ravager* and tell Oscar we're ready to move on."

Guttman gave Simon a venomous look and then walked toward the airlock. Becker regarded Simon for a few seconds. "You got some spine, kid. If that bot means so much to you, then I'll let you claim it."

"Thank you, Captain," Simon said.

"Go secure it for transport. It looked like someone had it wired up for something. I don't want it interfering with the jump drive when we leave," Becker said.

Simon headed back into the workshop and disconnected the wires to Quinton's chest. A warning appeared on Quinton's HUD, but at least he hadn't lost a charge in the bot's power systems. Now all he had to worry about was whether Simon was going to strip out the parts that were connecting him to his humanity. PMCs required a certain level of physical interaction with their environment, or the experience would become too artificial. The garden bot was equipped with specialized haptic systems necessary for working with delicate plant life, which was absolutely essential for Quinton to feel as human as he could. The alternative was psychosis. This was why PMCs were uploaded into special automatons designed to mimic key features of the human body and experience—senses beyond sight but no less important, including smell and touch. He supposed that with limited access to his memories and a bot that wasn't designed to house a PMC, he should count himself lucky to be functioning at all.

Simon stopped what he was doing and regarded Quinton for more than a few seconds. He seemed to be waiting for something, his face a mask of concentration. Quinton remembered that Guttman had called Simon a tech expert. Had Simon figured out what Quinton was? Had he detected the ESS? Quinton had no idea. He felt like Simon was staring him down, as if they were determining who was going to blink first.

Quinton smiled inwardly. He definitely had the advantage there. He could easily wait out the young man.

Becker bellowed for Simon to report to the bridge, and Quinton heard Simon sigh.

"I'll deal with you later," Simon said and left the work area.

Quinton thought he might have been talking about Becker but then suspected that Simon was referring to him. There was nothing he could do. He'd wait to see where they were going and then decide what to do next.

# CHAPTER NINE

THE SALVAGERS more or less ignored him. Quinton overheard Becker talking about other things they'd salvaged from the spaceport. He monitored the *Novo*'s systems as Simon put nonessential systems into standby. After determining that it was unsafe to use the *Novo*'s jump drive, they flew the ship onto a secure docking platform attached to the salvager's ship.

Quinton accessed the external video feeds and got his first view of the *Ravager*. He'd expected the ship to be some type of cargo carrier, but it looked more like a smaller munitions supply-class ship that would have been used by any of the galactic federations. He peered at the heavily damaged hull, looking for the ship's identifier. Without it, he didn't know which federation or star empire the ship had come from. He wondered how the salvagers kept it space worthy. The supply ship was designed for a small crew and only had one light mag cannon located midship. The cannon looked like it had been maintained in serviceable condition and was probably enough of a deterrent for other opportunistic salvagers but not enough for earnest ship-to-ship combat. He spotted a few armored panels that looked to house point-defense turrets, but he couldn't be sure. The rear artillery section still had the mounting structure for another mag cannon, but it had been stripped away and the salvagers had built up the platform to store large cargo that couldn't be brought inside.

The *Novo*'s docking clamps engaged the platform, taking up a large section of it. The small ship was only one piece amid a crowd of space salvage they'd managed to extract from the station.

Quinton listened to the open comms chatter. Becker was monitoring the area for other ships, almost like he expected to be attacked. The small number of crew that had come aboard the *Novo* must have been Becker's way of testing new recruits.

He kept an eye on Simon until he was ordered off the ship. After that, he sat in the workshop, pretending to be a lifeless robot. Simon had captured Stumpy by disabling the artificial gravity. The loss of gravity had stunned the creature, and Simon had stuck him in a bio-storage container. Quinton hadn't heard so much as a peep from him, which was probably for the best.

A short time after the salvagers had secured Quinton's ship, they'd flown away from the small space station. He tried to think of some way to escape, but the salvagers were on high alert. They'd notice if Quinton used the *Novo*'s escape pods. Even if he were able to leave undetected and somehow make it to the derelict space station, there was no guarantee that anything there would help him. Staying put was his best choice and kept his options open. Now all he needed to worry about was where they were taking him.

There was a bright azure flash as the *Ravager*'s jump drive engaged and the open comms chatter went quiet. Quinton hated being kept in the dark. The *Novo*'s systems were on standby, and if he started switching things on, someone would notice. He'd simply have to ride this out.

He glanced at the power meter in the upper-right corner of his HUD. It was holding at 38 percent. Power consumption while he waited in the workshop was minimal. At least he had that going for him.

FTL jumps were almost instantaneous, but they did cause a temporary gap in sensor coverage. A field of stars appeared on the video feed. He couldn't listen in on the *Ravager*'s comms systems, but he assumed they were checking in with their destination. The outside imagery began to change as the salvage ship flew toward its destination. The journey didn't take long, and none of the salvagers returned to the *Novo*. Maybe Simon *hadn't* guessed that the agricultural bot was something more than what it seemed.

The *Ravager* entered an approach vector to a large asteroid base. Asteroid movers helped maintain the orbit of the mineral-rich rock. Although it wasn't quite the size of a dwarf planet, it was close enough that it could support a space colony. Quinton spotted several large hangar bays that were built into the craggy side of the asteroid. There was a significant amount of ship traffic going to and from the base. Legions of delivery drones hauled shipping containers to some of the bigger ships, maintaining their position at a space docking platform.

The *Ravager* headed toward one of the remote hangar bays with the least traffic. As they came closer, Quinton spotted numerous station defenses, which made him think that this had once been a military station converted into what looked like an extensive salvage operation. All he had to do was find an alternate power source or an alternate body to use, both of which would buy him the time he needed to figure out where the activation signal for his PMC had come from. Gaining full access to the ESS would be a tremendous bonus, but he needed to focus on one thing at a time.

The ship passed through the hangar bay shields and flew toward an offloading landing pad. As soon as they were through the shield, multiple network connections became available from the station, and Quinton pulled up the list. They were mainly for personal comms traffic rather than data feeds, which made sense.

The salvager's security protocols had to assume that all ship systems in the bay were unsecured and therefore required further screening before data access was allowed. He remembered Simon giving Becker the green light that the *Novo*'s ship systems were clean. He needed to wait until he was offloaded before trying to gain system access to the space station or else risk being detected.

Quinton didn't have to wait very long. Counter-grav lifts attached themselves to the *Novo*'s hull, and the small ship was lifted off the *Ravager*. All the salvaged items were offloaded onto the platform, and dock workers began to categorize them. He watched them from the *Novo*'s external video feeds. A group of dock workers gathered outside the ship. He saw Becker's towering form jab a beefy finger toward them, and the workers stopped. Becker turned back to speak to someone else. Simon came into view, and Becker gestured toward the *Novo*. Simon nodded, and he and Guttman hastened over.

He watched Guttman's stocky, dark-skinned form stride ahead and begin speaking with the dock workers. Without the EVA suit, Quinton saw Guttman's belly push against his shirt, and the additional weight lent extra skin to his already protruding eyes.

After Guttman finished speaking with the workers, he and Simon came aboard the *Novo* and began unloading the ship. Quinton saw Guttman glare at Simon as the young man walked up the loading ramp. He was probably still angry about Simon's little joke. While the dock workers offloaded the cargo containers, attaching them to portable power generators, Simon entered the work area where Quinton was.

Simon gave Quinton a brief once-over and then turned to the array of tools in the workshop. He did a quick job of cataloging the items and then began gathering them into a container in the middle of the floor. Simon accessed his wrist computer, and Quinton saw a new data connection appear on the agricultural unit's systems.

Simon looked at him and sighed. "Someone really didn't like you," he said while reading the data on the holoscreen. He pulled up a damage report and pressed his lips together. "It looks like you can still move, though, so let's give this a try. All right, stand up."

Quinton saw that Simon had enabled vocal command mode. He'd need to be compliant and maintain the guise of cooperation. He'd thought Simon had guessed what he was, but he must have been wrong.

He stood up.

"Good." Simon nodded and gestured toward the container. "Grab that container and follow me."

Quinton walked toward the container, which was almost overflowing with spare parts and tools from the workshop. He squatted down and lifted it, but it wobbled because of the damaged actuator in his left shoulder. Some of the tools slipped off the top and dropped to the floor.

Simon picked them up and put them back on top. "Damaged shoulder joint. I can fix that. That power core will need replacing too."

*You have no idea*, Quinton thought.

Simon left the workshop, and Quinton followed him. As they walked down the loading ramp, Guttman glanced in their direction, scowling.

"What do you think you're doing?" Guttman asked as he stormed over to them.

"Claiming what's mine. You can take it up with Becker if you want."

Guttman narrowed his gaze. "Yours," he sneered.

"I loved that little scene on the bridge—you know, when you tried to shove Becker. You probably thought it was me," Simon said and frowned in mock consideration. "I'm sah, sah, sorry," he said, mimicking Guttman. "It must have been hard to speak while you were being choked."

Guttman inhaled explosively. "You little bastard, I'll—" He reached toward Simon.

Quinton tilted the container to one side and a small avalanche of tools spilled onto Guttman's feet, tripping the man. He set the container down, hastening toward the mess while bumping into Guttman, sending him sprawling onto the floor. Simon glanced at Quinton, a curious frown on his face. Then, the dock workers laughed uproariously. It had all happened so quickly that Guttman found himself on the ground, looking completely baffled as to how he'd gotten there. He glowered toward Simon.

"Hey, I'm sorry about that," Simon said. "That bot has a bad shoulder and it gives out." He quickly reloaded the container.

Becker walked over. He looked at Guttman and shook his head. "What are you doing? Get on your feet."

Guttman stood up, looking as if he was going to launch into a tirade, but he suddenly thought better of it. A group of people headed toward them, and Becker's mouth went flat, forming a grim line.

A tall, dark-skinned man strode over to them, followed by a group of armed men. He glanced at the *Novo*, and then his gaze slid toward the rather substantial amount of cargo on the hangar deck, but he didn't look impressed.

"Helsing," Becker said by way of acknowledgment.

"Looks like you've got yourself quite a haul here," Helsing said.

"It's not bad."

Helsing pursed his lips together and leaned toward Becker. "It's not great either."

Becker's gaze hardened. "Crowe will be fine with it."

Helsing bobbed his head to the side once. "We'll see. He hasn't approved of your team's performance lately," he said and gestured toward the offloaded cargo. "I don't know if this will even satisfy last month's quota."

Quinton watched, expecting Becker to attack the other man. Helsing also looked as if he expected it, as did the armed men with him.

Becker calmly regarded the man. "We'll see."

"Still, something is better than nothing. We'll do an accounting," Helsing said and looked toward the far side of the hangar. "Looks like that accounting will come sooner than we thought. Lennix is here now."

Quinton was irritated that he couldn't simply do what everyone else was doing. He wanted to see who this Lennix Crowe was. There was apparent deference being given, and among these dangerous people, that was saying something. But he had to keep pretending to be a simple robot, and robots didn't do things like look at the newcomer just because everyone else was.

He was able to twitch his head slightly and saw another group of people walking across the hangar. Everyone was centered on one man. Creases showed at the corners of his eyes and mouth, and his dark-eyed gaze regarded everything around him with professional calm. He had just enough gray to his black hair and beard to make him look distinguished rather than old. Quinton couldn't begin to guess his age, but he had something that no one else in that hangar had—command experience. He seemed to regard everything on that hangar deck with a comprehensive knowledge of how it served a higher purpose beyond its immediate value. Everything here served *his* purpose. He was a bit on the tall side—athletic but not excessively so. Lennix Crowe's strength was beyond that of his body. He had the bearing of a man who never changed his mind once he'd made a decision.

Quinton watched as Crowe looked around the hangar bay while listening to an older man speaking. The older man was referring to a report showing on a holoscreen above his wrist computer.

"They don't have the resources to keep up with projected growth for the mining operation," the older man was saying.

Crowe looked at him. "Nate," he said, and the other man became quiet, "the Grand Terra mining operation has to make scheduled payments just like everyone else. Just because they have something of value doesn't mean they get special treatment."

Nate considered this for a few moments and then the holo-screen minimized as he lowered his arm. "Understood."

"That's just it. *They* don't understand," Lennix said and rubbed a powerful hand over his thick ebony beard. He glanced toward Becker and Helsing and then purposefully strode over. His gaze flicked between them before settling on Helsing. "I need you to take a battalion of Union troopers over to the Grand Terra mining operation."

"Of course, sir," Helsing said. "Do you want me to just intimidate them?"

"Oh, I want more than a simple show of force. They need to be reminded of who reports to whom here," Crowe said and glanced at Nate.

The older man—some kind of advisor, Quinton guessed—regarded Lennix for a few seconds. "Applying the right kind of pressure will yield results in the short-term, but that doesn't take care of the bigger issue here."

"What are you talking about, old man?" Helsing asked.

Nate kept his gaze on Lennix, ignoring Helsing altogether.

"The Collective is increasing their influence over all salvage and mercenary operations. I'm not," Crowe said and gritted his teeth. Then he looked at Helsing. "Take the *Wraith,* along with a cargo container ship suitable for transporting organics."

"Yes, Commander Crowe," Helsing said.

Nate pressed his lips together in thought, and Crowe raised his dark eyebrows. "The appropriate pressure, you say. If they don't deliver on their promises, I'll remove a member of every household on every level of their pathetic colony until I've gutted a third of their numbers. See if they still try these stalling tactics when over 30 percent of their population is about to become slaves."

A rush of thoughts pushed through Quinton's mind. First and foremost was that he needed to get the hell out of there as quickly as possible. Second was that Lennix Crowe introduced a whole new level of ruthlessness that he'd never seen before. He didn't know what to think outside the utter revulsion he felt at what he'd just heard.

Quinton glanced at Helsing, and the man looked at Nate for a moment before turning back to Lennix. "I'll leave at once."

"Good," Crowe said.

Nate watched Helsing as he left. He seemed to arrive at some sort of mental calculation and simply shifted to the next topic.

What was wrong with these people? Quinton resisted the urge to shake his head. *This Lennix Crowe gives an order that if some mining operation can't deliver, he'll enslave a third of their population, and everyone on the hangar deck just takes this as a matter of course?*

Quinton opened the bot's comms and began scanning the station's systems for a data connection.

"I must advise against that," Radek said inwardly.

Though no one could actually hear his VI assistant, Quinton increased his frame rate. "I need to get out of here," he replied.

"Then allow me to interact with the station's systems."

"What for?"

"Because when machines interact, most monitoring systems aren't suspicious. If *you* do it, it might be detected, and an alert could be sent out. We don't want to draw attention to ourselves," Radek replied.

"What? That's nonsense," Quinton said and watched the scan session continue.

"You must stop what you're doing."

"Not without a good reason."

The scan finished, and he found a general communications system he could access.

"You're in more danger than you realize," Radek said.

Quinton paused his search. "What do you mean?" Nothing in his situation could be done without risk, but maybe the VI knew something he didn't.

"Interacting with computer systems poses a serious risk to you in particular because of the limited state of your PMC."

Quinton didn't understand. "PMCs by design are supposed to be superior to any other type of systems access, and you're telling me I can't do it?"

"Not exactly. I'm saying there is a high risk of detection if you do, more than your training would have accounted for," Radek said.

"What's the risk?"

"My primary objective is to ensure the PMC stays intact and operational. Part of that is to make sure you retain your current mental state."

"My mental state," Quinton repeated. "Well, my mental state is pretty damn agitated, Radek. I can be reasonable, but this is too much."

"What query do you want me to run on the station's systems?"

He needed to better understand the risk to his mental state, but he could worry about that later. "We need to find the source of the activation signal for starters. Then I need to get out of this unit and find a better body to use."

"Understood. Querying system for requested information."

Quinton brought his frame rate back to normal. His entire conversation with Radek had occurred in less than a second in standard time.

"Does this bother you?" Crowe asked.

Quinton tore his attention away from his depleting power core and looked at the person Crowe was speaking to. She was a beautiful woman—not a young girl who'd just attained adulthood, but a woman. She had brown, wavy hair, exotic almond-shaped eyes, and high cheekbones, and her skin was a medium olive tone that made her celestial blue eyes sparkle. She looked at Lennix Crowe with a surety born of confidence.

"I'm not here to judge the way you run your operation," said the woman.

Crowe regarded her for a few moments. "Most people don't have the stomach for it."

The woman arched an eyebrow. "You don't strike me as the type of person who cares what most people think. All that matters is what I can do." She pursed her lips for a moment. "To put a finer point on it, what I can do for you and the Union."

"Maelyn Wayborn," Crowe said. "I wouldn't expect such ruthlessness under so delicate a face."

Maelyn smiled. "You assume this is my real face."

Crowe's grin revealed genuine amusement but also something much darker.

"Back to the business at hand," she said. "Several of your teams have had a chance to observe my people in action." She gestured toward Simon.

Quinton had to stop himself from looking at Simon when everyone else glanced in the young man's direction.

Crowe gestured for Becker to come over to him. "How'd he do?"

"He was useful, sir. He spotted a few things that we might have overlooked," Becker replied.

"That's been happening a lot to your crew of late," Crowe said. Becker didn't reply. "But judging by all this, it looks like you managed to bring something of value back, so there *is* that."

Again, Becker remained quiet.

Crowe nodded. "That's what I always like about you, Becker. You're never one to fill the air with excuses. You stand by your work."

Quinton watched a data window on his HUD. Radek was accessing the station's system, and then he stopped. Klaxon alarms blared overhead.

Crowe's gaze narrowed, and he looked at Nate.

"Something is trying to access our systems," Nate said and looked at Becker. "Did you make sure these systems were secure?"

"Yes, we did," Becker said and looked at Simon.

"Never mind that," Crowe said. "Where's it coming from?"

Nate flipped through several menu options on his personal holoscreen, and then he frowned. After staring intently at the screen, he turned toward Quinton. "It's the bot."

Everyone nearby also turned toward him. Crowe narrowed his gaze and his mouth went flat.

"That can't be right," Simon said quickly. "I checked this unit out myself."

"Well then, you missed something because it has an active comms signal," Nate said. He made a snatching motion on his holoscreen and tossed it into the air. The holoscreen stretched and showed the comms session.

Quinton did the first thing that came to his mind.

"Malfunction," Quinton said and repeated himself. Then he turned and ran.

# CHAPTER TEN

QUINTON JACKED up his frame rate, and his perception of everyone in the hangar bay came to a standstill. A power consumption warning flashed on his HUD, which he ignored.

"So much for trying things your way, Radek."

"I don't understand," Radek said. "They shouldn't have been able to detect my queries. I used the standard machine query protocols I observed being used by nearby systems."

"Great, that's just perfect," Quinton said derisively.

Another power consumption warning flashed on-screen. He needed to rethink his reliance on the virtual intelligence that was supposed to be helping him. He should've trusted his own instincts, but he couldn't keep his perception of time jacked up for long or else he risked doing more damage to the agricultural unit. He wanted to scream. He had these few precious moments to think of something other than running around like a malfunctioning machine.

Quinton glanced at Simon. The young man was frozen in mid-motion while he accessed his own wrist computer. He peered at the screen and saw that Simon was in the middle of typing a message. He couldn't read it, but it was meant for him because it had the agricultural unit's identifier on it.

He couldn't afford to wait around. He was mostly surrounded. Once he returned his frame rate to normal, he'd have seconds to get away. He glanced at the stacks of storage containers that had been assembled on the hangar deck.

Quinton reset his frame rate to normal and bolted toward the containers. He leaped into the air and climbed to the top, quickly scaling upward. After scrambling over the top, he jumped down on the other side and heard shouting from behind him. A group of workers looked in his direction, and he blew past them.

"Did you at least find anything on their systems?" he asked.

"Negative. I didn't have a chance to gain access to the communication logs," Radek replied.

Ahead of him, a group of armed salvagers was heading toward him. Quinton turned and ran toward a nearby ship, which was locked up good and tight. He had no chance of getting in there. Even if he could somehow escape, with all the armed security he saw coming, they would quickly shoot him down. Running away wasn't going to help him.

A message appeared on his HUD. It was a comlink from Simon.

*I can help you. But you need to come back here. I know what you are. It's not safe.*

Quinton heard more shouting from behind him, and white ionized bolts slammed into the bulkhead of the nearest ship. Ionized bolts would disable him, but he wasn't sure if it would damage his ESS; however, he didn't want to find out. What a mess this was. If he kept running, it was only a matter time before they caught him. The young tech specialist was his only hope. But Simon had figured out what he was, and Quinton had no idea how he'd done that.

He ran back toward the others, who'd been following his

progress, and saw Simon watching him from across the hangar deck.

Then another message appeared.

*You need to let them capture you. Don't tell them what you are.*

If Quinton had a stomach, it would have been sinking to his feet as if he'd leaped off the hangar deck into the abyss. He was out of options. He had to either trust Simon or take a chance and try to reason with Lennix Crowe.

Quinton didn't need to jack up his frame rate to take the time to consider that. Simon was the lesser of the two evils. There was no way he was getting off this hangar deck—not by himself and not without help.

He ran back toward the others, and the deckhands scrambled to get out of his way. They were afraid. They thought he was an out-of-control robot. Quinton realized that if he kept moving around erratically, they would certainly destroy him. He came to a halt and simply stood still with his arms at his sides, which was a miracle unto itself. Every instinct inside him wanted to run, to fight, to keep his destiny in his own hands. But this wasn't a fight he could win.

Soon he was surrounded by armed salvagers. They gathered around him, pointing their weapons.

"Wait!" Simon shouted as he ran over to Quinton. "Don't shoot it."

Becker pointed a hand cannon that was primed with a molten orange glow. The plasma bolt from that cannon would melt through the agricultural bot's chassis before Quinton would ever even register that the man had shot him.

"Becker," Simon said, "I've got it. Seriously, it's just a glitch. It's not dangerous."

"The hell it isn't," Becker said and looked back as Lennix Crowe caught up to them.

Simon stepped in front of Quinton and held up his arms. He

looked at Maelyn. "Captain Wayborn, please. This is my part of the salvage."

Maelyn's brows pulled together in a thoughtful frown.

Simon looked at Becker. "Lower your weapon. It's just a glitch in this thing's programming."

Becker looked at Crowe, who gave him a single grim nod. "Simon, start making sense right now or I'm going to shoot you too."

"The bot was just trying to open a comlink back to its command-and-control unit. The system was reset, and part of the startup process was to check in. When it couldn't, it triggered a return to this bot's base of operations, but it couldn't figure out its location. The bot's interior systems are degraded and damaged. I can show the log data to your tech experts, and they can confirm it if you want, but that's what happened. It's on standby now. I have it under control. It'll do everything I tell it to. Want me to show you?" Simon asked.

Becker looked at Crowe, who glanced at Nate.

"Carradine, does that make sense to you?"

"I'll need to review the logs, but the alert did come from our comms systems," Nate said.

"Send them the logs, Simon," Maelyn said and looked at Crowe. "If Simon says it was an error, then that's what it was."

"That remains to be seen," Crowe replied.

"If you feel that strongly about it, destroy it. I assume you have another way to compensate my tech specialist," Maelyn said. Crowe gave her a questioning look. "You *are* a businessman, after all. Weren't you telling me earlier how you take care of the people who work for you?" she asked as she walked toward Quinton.

She glanced at Simon and gave Quinton a once-over. Then she turned back toward Crowe and the others.

Becker still had his hand cannon pointed toward them, and Crowe came to stand by his side.

"Why does this matter so much to you?" Crowe asked.

Maelyn's lips lifted into a half smile. "You're not the only one who takes care of the people you work with. You get more out of them when they're happy," she said and looked at Simon. "Why do you want this agricultural bot so much?"

"It has some good serviceable parts on there that I'd like to salvage. Particularly the haptic systems. I was also going to—" Simon said.

Maelyn held up her hand and Simon stopped speaking. "They understand," she said.

Crowe shook his head. "All right, in the spirit of cooperation and future business relations, I'll allow it."

Maelyn smiled, and Simon seemed to relax.

"I'll be in touch with you," Crowe said and looked at Becker. "Escort them back to their ship, along with whatever salvage they claimed."

Lennix Crowe left them, but his advisor gave Quinton a long look. Nate Carradine. He was an older man who almost seemed out of place among the other salvagers. He watched Quinton for a few moments and then followed the group. Quinton kept his eyes forward and walked with what he hoped was a dutiful robot stride under the control of one Simon Webb.

# CHAPTER ELEVEN

Lennix left the hangar bay. The heightened security protocols he had in place might generate a few false positives, but they were necessary for securing his operations. He'd built his salvage business from the ground up, functioning within the confines of the Collective. All companies in this galactic sector had ties to the Collective.

He rode up the service elevator, along with his staff. The bigger his operation had become, the more people he had to keep with him to ensure that it ran smoothly. He glanced at Nate Carradine, whose unfocused gaze meant he was working on something using his HUD. Nate was one of the few people Lennix trusted. He'd been part of Crowe's Union for a long time, but he had a mysterious past. Lennix thought the man had led a mercenary troop at some point in his past, but what he was looking for was Nate's extensive knowledge of pre-federation tech.

Nicos shifted on his feet, and Lennix could feel his insistent gaze upon his neck. He glanced over at him. "What's next, Nicos?"

"I just received a message that the Collective is sending a

representative, along with an invitation for you to meet with them."

No wonder Nicos looked so uncomfortable. The invitation was a formality. This was a summons, and it was one that Lennix couldn't afford to ignore. The Collective had already been paid, but they wanted more. Crowe's Union had grown so large that it garnered the attention of Trenton Draven. Crowe had carefully built up his operations so as not to alarm the Collective, but there was a tipping point, and he must have gone past it.

"What was that about the Collective?" Nate asked.

Nicos looked at him. "They want to meet with us."

"There was a scheduled meeting for next month," Nate replied and frowned in thought for a moment.

Lennix had more freedom than most, mainly because Crowe's Union had several old federation warships at its disposal—nothing that would challenge the Collective in a direct fleet engagement, but it was something they couldn't afford to ignore either.

Lennix looked at Nicos. "Anything else?"

"Nothing specific, sir. Just a reiteration from the Collective on the importance of salvaging federation tech."

Lennix shook his head and snorted. They were always pressuring to keep their advantage. "Send a reply that we'll meet with the representatives at their convenience, and send them coordinates for a neutral-territory meeting location."

He saw Nate waving his hands as he navigated his own personal holographic interface, and he looked at him pointedly.

Nate caught the look and brought his hands to rest at his sides. The elevator stopped, and they headed toward the tram system that would take them to the far side of the station.

"I was reviewing the video surveillance footage of that robot back on the hangar deck," Nate said as their tram sped away.

Lennix sighed. "We've got the Collective breathing down our necks, and you want to worry about a malfunctioning robot?"

"The devil is in the details."

Lennix leaned his shoulder against the wall and folded his arms in front of his chest. "All right, what am I missing?"

"I'm not sure yet," Nate said and brought up the holoscreen for Lennix to see. The surveillance showed the agricultural bot springing into action, and Nate slowed the frames down. "The bot moves with precision, almost as if it anticipates what will happen to it."

Lennix peered at the holoscreen and then nodded. He could see what Nate was talking about. Thermal imaging revealed a secondary power source that was hidden in the chest cavity.

"What is that?" Nicos asked.

"It's some kind of secondary power source. Probably a redundancy," Lennix replied.

Nate shook his head. "I don't think so. You could see the power draw increase from the main power core at certain intervals . . ." His voice trailed off as he made a swiping motion and opened up another holoscreen. His eyes widened, and he looked at Lennix. "It's an Energy Storage System. Low power yield, but definitely detectable."

Lennix felt his eyebrows pull together as he peered at the image. "An ESS? But that means . . ." He looked at Nicos. "Find out where Maelyn Wayborn is right now."

"A Personality Matrix Construct. A PMC, and they said it came from Zeda-Six. That's a third-tier colony world," Nate said.

"What would a PMC be doing way out there? There's nothing of strategic value at that location."

"There is if you want to keep a PMC hidden. Regardless, we need to recover it. It's highly valuable," Nate said.

"You got that right. I'm not just going to give this to the Collective," Lennix said.

"Sir, they were heading to the secondary hangar bay where their ship is," Nicos said.

Lennix tried to open a comlink to Becker, but it wouldn't connect. "I can't reach Becker."

"They must be using a suppressor," Nate said.

"If they were jamming communications, it would have been detected," Nicos said.

"Not if it's small enough. They could have dialed in the suppression field to impact only targeted people," Lennix said.

"She betrayed you," Nate said.

"Maybe." Lennix shook his head. "It's more that she saw an opportunity and took it."

Lennix walked over to the console on the side of the tram car and tried to initiate a lockout that failed. He cursed.

"My access is restricted," Nate said. "She planted a suppressor on us as well."

Lennix had no choice but to admire Maelyn's tactics. "Clever, but she hasn't gotten away yet."

Nicos began rubbing his hands over his shirt, looking for some kind of device.

"Stop that. You're not going to find it," Lennix snapped. Sometimes he thought he was surrounded by idiots, with the exception of Nate.

"We'll have to wait until we get off the tram. Then we can disable the suppressor," Nate said.

"Why do we have to wait? Why can't we just disable it now?" Nicos asked.

"Because it's a microscopic nano swarm," Lennix said and shook his head. He looked at Nate. "She's good. I'll give her that."

Nate nodded. "It'll be close, but I think we can stop her before she leaves."

"We better."

# CHAPTER TWELVE

QUINTON FOLLOWED THE OTHERS, leaving the hangar bay through a series of interconnected tunnels. Becker had Guttman and Oscar following behind Quinton and Simon.

Maelyn arched an eyebrow toward Becker. "We know the way from here. I'm sure you'll want to get back so you can monitor your deck crew."

"They won't try anything funny, if that's what you mean," Becker replied.

Maelyn nodded, managing to look amicable and unconvinced at the same time. Becker ignored her.

Quinton's sensors showed that Guttman and Oscar weren't keeping that close of an eye on him, and he was anxious to speak with Simon. The good thing was that Becker had set a quick pace for them to follow. Maybe Maelyn's comment about the deck crew had bothered him more than he let on.

The corridor opened to a smaller hangar deck, and Becker gestured for Maelyn to lead the way. When she flashed him a dazzling smile, Quinton felt a strange urge to frown. It was strange because he knew he couldn't frown, but these microhabits were ingrained in his mind.

The smaller hangar deck was no less busy than the previous one they'd been on. Quinton heard snippets of conversations as they walked by, and a quick analysis from his VIs appeared on his HUD, highlighting a pattern of certain keywords and phrases. The people in close proximity all seemed to be commenting about a sudden loss of communications, a slight disruption that soon resolved itself as they walked past.

They walked toward a white shuttlecraft that displayed the sleek lines of a smooth hull, seeming to radiate speed and agility. There was a flash of blue as the loading ramp lowered.

"Nice ship," Becker said, and Maelyn looked at him.

"She gets the job done. Please inform Commander Crowe that I will be in touch with him soon," Maelyn said.

Becker looked away and listened to a couple of salvagers speaking, then looked down at his wrist computer. His gaze narrowed, and his hand shot toward his weapon.

"Don't," Maelyn said, holding something in her hand that Quinton couldn't see. Becker's hand was just above his hand cannon. "I was really hoping to avoid this."

"Whatever you're trying to do, it's not going to work," Becker said.

Quinton heard Guttman and Oscar mutter a curse.

Simon had his palm-sized blaster pressed into Becker's back. "Back off," he said over his shoulder and then looked at Becker. "Nothing personal."

The smaller man circled around to Becker's side and gestured for Quinton to keep going, but Quinton stayed put.

Becker clenched his teeth for a few moments.

"What are we waiting for? Let me take them out," Guttman growled.

"Becker," Maelyn said, "you'd better leash your dog. He might be able to get us, but I guarantee that *you* won't walk away."

Becker glanced behind him at Guttman and Oscar, shaking his head a little.

A high-pitched tone chimed overhead, followed by a klaxon alarm.

"Captain," Simon said to Maelyn, "we've gotta go. They're initiating a lockdown."

"I know. I was hoping we'd be on the ship before they figured it out," Maelyn said.

Maelyn and Simon kept their weapons pointed at Becker while backing away a few steps. Simon gestured for Quinton to join them.

"What are you trying to do? There's nothing here for you to steal—not when you've got a ship like that," Becker said and frowned, his gaze swinging toward Quinton. "What's so special about this robot?"

The ruse was up. Becker was putting the pieces together. The hangar deck was clearing as people began evacuating the area.

Quinton grabbed Becker's weapon from his holster, using the lightning-quick speed capability of the agricultural bot. Becker's eyes widened, and he reached for his weapon on pure instinct but came up short. Quinton pointed the hand cannon at Becker, and Guttman and Oscar flanked him, pointing their weapons at Quinton.

"It'll take them too long to explain," Quinton said.

"What the hell is that thing?" Guttman asked.

Quinton ignored him. "We don't have a lot of time," he said and gestured toward Becker. "How long do you want to be Helsing's lackey? I heard what he said to you. If you come with us, there might be something in it for you worth more than what you've got here."

Quinton took a few steps back and to the side. He glanced at Maelyn, whose mouth hung slightly agape, and then she looked at Simon.

"I told you. Somehow, it's got a PMC inside it," Simon said.

"Yes, yes," Quinton said quickly. "Now, if we're not going to shoot each other, let's get moving."

Maelyn pointed her weapon at him. "Not so fast. I'm not bringing them along."

"You'll never get out of here if you don't," Quinton said and gestured with the point of his weapon toward Becker. "Right now, he's trying to figure out how much Commander Crowe is going to reward him if he turns you over to him."

Maelyn narrowed her gaze and swung it toward Becker.

"It's nothing personal, Captain," Becker replied.

"What the hell is a PMC?" Guttman asked.

"Not now," Quinton replied. "Captain Wayborn, is it? We can sort this out away from here, but none of us wins if we stay."

"That's not how I see it," Becker said. "The longer I keep you here, the better it is for me."

Quinton lowered the hand cannon and squeezed the trigger. A plasma bolt charred the metallic alloy of the hangar deck near Becker's feet, proving more powerful than he had thought. "The next one is for you. Do you want to keep stalling, or do you not recognize an opportunity when it's staring you in the face?"

Becker gritted his teeth, and Quinton thought he was about to rush him. Becker shifted his gaze toward Maelyn. "He's right. I can help you escape. You won't get past the station's defenses without us. We're coming with you."

His henchmen began voicing a protest, and he told them to shut it.

"Captain," Simon said.

Maelyn regarded Becker for a few moments and then nodded once. "The PMC is right. We can sort this out away from here. I'll allow you to come along, but you keep your henchmen in line, or I'll take care of them myself."

*The PMC* . . . He had a name. He wasn't some mindless machine.

Maelyn turned around and headed toward the ship.

"Put your weapons away," Becker said to the others. "We're not going to shoot them."

"Fine," Guttman said, "but I'm not going on that ship. Do you have any idea what Crowe will do when he finds out?"

"Crowe is the least of your worries if you don't get on that ship right now," Becker said and looked at Oscar.

"I was getting tired of this place anyway," Oscar said and hastened toward the ship.

Simon followed, and Quinton was only a few feet behind. He held onto Becker's weapon.

Guttman considered it for a few seconds and then walked toward the ship, shaking his head.

Quinton walked up the loading ramp. Maelyn and Simon were in the cockpit.

"Have a seat, gentlemen," Maelyn said.

Becker and the others sat down. The seats weren't big enough for Quinton, so he stood.

"Becker," Maelyn said, "I need you to override the lockdown. I've opened a comlink for you to use."

"On it," he said and used his wrist computer to send in his authentication. "What would you have done if I hadn't come along?"

"There's more than one way to get past a lockdown," she replied.

Becker twitched his eyebrows. "That should take care of the defense cannons as well, but it won't last long."

"He's gonna come after us," Guttman warned. "He's gonna find out what you did."

Becker smiled. "That's why I used your credentials, Guttman. Now shut up."

Guttman sneered and shook his head.

Becker glanced toward Quinton and flicked his gaze toward the hand cannon.

"I think I'll hold onto it for a little while," Quinton said.

The shuttle's engines engaged and Maelyn swung the nose around, then flew out of the hangar. The defense cannons remained offline, and once they were clear, she increased the shuttle's velocity to maximum.

"How far away is your ship?" Quinton asked.

"It's not far," Maelyn replied. "Simon, let Kieva know we're on our way back."

"Yes, Captain," Simon replied.

"And we have a few extra passengers with us," Maelyn added.

Becker watched Quinton as if he wasn't quite sure what to make of him.

"Didn't anyone ever tell you that it's not polite to stare?" Quinton said.

Becker smirked. "I'm not. You're just an echo from a bygone age."

Quinton was about to reply when Simon spoke.

"Hang on back there. Looks like they've sent a couple of ships after us."

Guttman muttered incoherently and checked his seat straps.

"It's just comms chatter. They haven't located us yet," Quinton said.

The others frowned and glanced at each other. He'd patched into the shuttle's systems and was monitoring various data feeds. Simon would have noticed the same thing if he'd taken the time to look.

Maelyn flew the shuttle close to one of the cargo carriers to throw off the active scans from the space station.

Quinton looked at their current velocity. "The point is to get out of here alive."

"No one likes a backseat pilot," she replied.

A ship designation appeared on the nav computer's plot, but it was just a series of numbers—a ship without a name. It was supposedly bad luck to fly a ship without a name, but Quinton didn't want to point that out.

Becker continued to watch him, and it was becoming a bit uncomfortable. He'd called him an echo. What did that mean? Quinton kept a close watch on Becker and the others. They could have decided to come along, only to betray them later on. Guttman and Oscar didn't seem like they could pull something like that off without being completely obvious about it, but Becker was smart enough. He wasn't a mindless brute, despite his brutish appearance. Quinton had gambled when he'd brought up Helsing, but there was no love lost between Becker and Helsing. He'd correctly guessed that Becker was tired of being beneath Helsing in Crowe's Union, and he'd have to keep that in mind. Once they reached the ship and were away from here, aggressive negotiations would open back up.

Becker knew what a PMC was, or at least was familiar enough with the concept. Judging by Becker's comment—bygone age notwithstanding—and the intense scrutiny of his unfaltering gaze, Quinton was under no illusions that the salvager wouldn't blow him out of an airlock if given a chance. He'd have to keep an eye on him.

Quinton monitored the shuttle as Maelyn waited until the last possible moment to slow down before docking with the ship. They attached to the vessel's outer hull, and Quinton saw a small docking tube extend to the cockpit.

Maelyn and Simon climbed out of their seats and gestured for the rest of them to follow to the forward airlock. Quinton did as directed and was soon followed by Becker and the others. There was a quick zero-g transition to the main ship, and by the time he landed, he was firmly in the artificial gravity field.

"Jump drive has been prepped, Captain," a woman's soprano voice said, coming from the ship's intercom system.

"Thank you, Kieva," Maelyn replied.

"Captain, we're being hailed by the station. We're not cleared to disembark," Kieva said.

"Understood. Ignore them."

They entered the bridge, and Maelyn went to the pilot's seat on the left. Simon took the seat on the right.

"You can't engage the jump drive here," Becker said.

"Watch me," Maelyn said and palmed the jump controls that had just become green on her holoscreen.

# CHAPTER THIRTEEN

QUINTON SAW that a significant portion of power was being
diverted to the engines. The jump drive was already charged and
waiting for Maelyn to execute.

"What's she doing?" Guttman asked.

"Becker," Oscar said, "if she initiates the jump here, it could
tear the ship in half."

"I know," Becker replied, and his gaze flicked toward the
hand cannon that Quinton held.

"Don't do anything stupid. You're never gonna take it from
me," Quinton said.

"I'm not listening to a damn robot," Guttman said and began
unbuckling his straps.

"One, I'm not a robot. Two, do you honestly think she wants
to die? Now sit tight and let her—" Quinton stopped speaking.

The ship's engines engaged at maximum, straining the inertia
dampeners. He reached out and braced himself, nearly dropping
the weapon. Guttman almost slid out of his seat, but Becker
grabbed him and held him in place. The lights dimmed, and a
shudder went through the floor and the walls of the ship.
Quinton accessed the bridge computer and saw a countdown for

the jump drive. They were increasing their velocity at an accelerated rate to reach minimum safe distance for an FTL jump.

Maelyn engaged the jump drive. The main engines cut off, and Quinton watched as the excess power was rerouted back into the jump drive as it began to fold space. Jumping through space and time didn't actually feel like anything. One moment they were in one place, and the next they emerged somewhere else. The transition folded space, creating a jump field around the ship. Once the ship reached the target coordinates, the jump drive powered down. The lighting inside the ship leveled off as the power fluctuations began to regulate themselves back to normal operating range.

"Jump is complete," Maelyn said. "In case anybody gets it into their head to try to take control of my ship, I've activated the lockdown protocols for unauthorized weapons use. Anyone who powers on or tries to use an unauthorized weapon will become the victim of the ship's countermeasures. You have five seconds to power your weapons down."

Quinton didn't think she was bluffing and quickly deactivated the hand cannon. He saw Guttman and Oscar do the same thing.

Becker stood up and held his hand out. "That belongs to me."

Quinton held onto the weapon and regarded Becker for a few moments.

Maelyn and Simon left the bridge, joining them.

"Give it back to him," Maelyn said.

"I don't trust him," Quinton replied.

"Don't make me take it from you," Becker said.

"I'd like to see you try," Quinton said and then held the weapon just out of reach. "Go ahead. Take it."

Maelyn sighed. "At least now we know you're a man."

Quinton looked at her. Becker inched closer to him, and Quinton snatched the hand cannon away.

"All of you are guests aboard my ship," Maelyn said. "I am the captain, and you will abide by my rules or I'll introduce you to the airlock. It's your choice, PMC. I can just as easily have the ship's countermeasures target you as them."

Quinton was already accessing the ship's systems and saw that they were now targeting him. The onboard stunners could release enough of a jolt to render even someone Becker's size into a drooling, ineffectual man-child on the floor. He rather enjoyed imagining it, but the effect the stunners would have on an agricultural unit made him hesitate. His host body wasn't designed to withstand the countermeasures. They could cause significant damage, including making the bot non-functioning, which he wanted to avoid at all costs.

"Fine," he said and flung the hand cannon back at Becker. The big salvager snatched the weapon out of the air and quickly checked it with the practiced efficiency of someone who knew how to maintain and keep a weapon operational.

"My name is Quinton. I'm a PMC," he said and saw Guttman and Oscar frown in confusion. "Personality Matrix Construct. Does that ring any bells? . . . No? All right, the quick version is that I uploaded my consciousness into an Energy Storage System—ESS—and it's here in my chest."

Becker looked at Maelyn. "You should disable this thing right now."

"I'm not a 'thing,' I'm a person. The governing body of PMCs defines them as living beings," Quinton said.

Becker grinned bitterly. "Governing body," he said and glanced at the others. They all shared a meaningful look that Quinton didn't care for. "Which governing body would that be?"

Quinton felt as if the knowledge was just beyond his reach.

"Do you even know?"

"Of course, I do. It's just . . ." Quinton said and paused for a few moments. "This agricultural unit isn't meant to house a PMC, so my access to the ESS is limited."

Becker looked at Maelyn calmly. "Do you want to disable him, or should I?"

"No one is going to disable me," Quinton said. He thought he could disable a few key systems before Maelyn did anything threatening.

"He's inside the ship's systems," Simon said.

"You're damn right I am. I have access to life support, artificial gravity, and maybe a few other systems right now," Quinton said.

"Good," Maelyn said. "If you do anything stupid, the lockout protocol will engage and erase everything, including the nav system. You'll be stranded out here with nowhere to go."

"Quinton," Simon said, stepping closer to him and raising his hands in a placating gesture, "I said I could help you and I meant it. I know that unit is in bad shape, and the power core is failing."

"Then you know how desperate I am," Quinton replied.

"That thing needs to be disabled," Becker said.

Guttman grunted in agreement.

Quinton crouched into a fighting stance, and the blade extended from his right forearm. Both Becker and Guttman regarded the weapon for a moment, as if judging whether they could subdue him.

"Back away from him," Maelyn said.

Much to Quinton's surprise, the two men backed off a few steps. He turned and saw that Maelyn held a sidearm in her hand. The polished alloy tip had a greenish glow.

"Quinton, is it?" Maelyn said. "I think there's a way we can all help each other."

Quinton retracted the blade back into his forearm and stood up straight. "All right, I'm listening."

"How did you come to be . . ." she said and gave him a once-over. "Why was your ESS put into that robot?"

"There was an activation signal, and Radek, my VI assistant, took control of a delivery drone while he tried to find an acceptable housing unit. This agricultural bot was the only thing available. I don't know where the activation signal came from, and I have limited access to my ESS, so my memory appears to be . . . limited," Quinton said.

Maelyn glanced at Simon. "Where did you find him?"

"On a light transport ship that came from Zeda-Six. According to the ship's logs, it had been on standby for at least forty standard years to preserve its power core. But this agricultural unit is quite a bit older than that—at least a century old," Simon said.

"Zeda-Six." Maelyn frowned.

"I didn't know where I was until I reached the space station," Quinton said.

"How did you get to the space station?" Maelyn asked.

"I used a planetary escape pod left over from an evacuation."

Maelyn's gaze flicked toward the damaged parts where he had fought the hunter mechs. "You look like you were in a fight. What happened on that planet? Wasn't there anyone there who could help you?"

"There wasn't anybody around."

"He's right about that. I checked," Simon said. "It was a third-tier colony world and has a classification of being unlivable. The population was evacuated over a hundred years ago."

"To answer your other question," Quinton said, "yes, I was in a fight. I was hunted by security mechs. They were following some latent protocol, and I couldn't override it."

Quinton watched as the others, including Becker and his henchmen, shared a knowing glance.

Becker cleared his throat. "Zeda-Six isn't part of any federation."

"What do you mean?" Quinton asked.

"We can't figure out what federation you came from."

"Why do we care what federation he came from?" Guttman asked.

"Because—" Becker began, but Maelyn cut him off.

"Simon, what was the last governing body of Zeda-Six?" Maelyn asked.

Simon pressed his lips together and brought up a personal holoscreen while he looked for the answer. "It looks like Zeda-Six changed hands quite a bit. At one point, it was part of the Jordani Federation, then part of the Acheron Confederacy."

"That thing is from Acheron?" Becker asked, cocking his head to the side.

Maelyn pursed her lips in thought.

Simon shrugged one shoulder. "Not exactly. Like I said, the system changed hands quite a bit. There are some references that show that the Dholeren United Coalition had a claim there, as well as the Castellus Federal Alliance. A lot of colony worlds changed hands on the outer rim territories, but the evacuation might've been organized by the DUC," he said and then added, "Dholeren United Coalition."

"They didn't have a PMC program or even the technology," Becker said.

Simon nodded. "No, not the DUC, but the Jordani had it for sure. And, of course, so did the Acheron. Maybe a handful of others. Since Quinton only has limited access to his ESS, we won't be able to answer the question out here."

Becker stabbed a finger toward Quinton. "That thing is a ticking time bomb."

Quinton was having trouble following the conversation. He kept running into invisible thought barriers. What were they so afraid of?

"You might be right about that," Maelyn said and held up a hand when Quinton's gaze swooped toward her. "Come on. Even you have to admit that there's something more going on here. Why would an activation signal suddenly come on now, and you don't even know where it came from?"

"I have information on how to track it," Quinton said.

"Let's not get ahead of ourselves here," Becker said. "It's not safe to travel with that thing."

Quinton was getting tired of being referred to as "that thing." He was not a *thing*.

Maelyn arched an eyebrow toward Becker. "I would've thought you could've figured this out. You *are* a salvager after all."

Guttman blinked his eyes rapidly and looked at Becker. "What's she talking about?"

Maelyn rolled her eyes and sighed. "What I'm talking about is that there's some tech that's only accessible via a PMC. You're worried about Lennix Crowe and what he'll do to you if he finds us. Well, with Quinton's help, you might not have to worry about Crowe ever again," Maelyn said.

"Yeah, but . . ." Becker paused.

"We can work out the details," she said.

"One of the details I'm interested in," Quinton said, "is how you can help me. I still have an issue with my power core. I have limited access to my ESS, so I'm not sure how I can help you access anything."

"Simon said he can help you. Let him examine you," Maelyn said.

"I can," Simon said. All eyes turned toward him. "At least I think I can. We don't have a power core that's compatible with you, so it's not a simple swap-and-replace, but I might be able to put something together that will at least keep you operational."

"Does that include a way for me to access my ESS?" Quinton asked.

Simon shook his head. "We can't tamper with an ESS, at least not here on the ship. It requires the use of a special interface and your cooperation. Everything ESS-related requires the cooperation of the PMC."

Quinton sent a message to Radek: *Is this true?*

*That is correct. There are built-in safeguards to prevent unauthorized access into an ESS. However, there is the potential to find a workaround to force access, so I would be careful, especially with a tech expert.*

*Careful*, Quinton mused. *Thanks.*

Quinton looked at Maelyn. "In exchange for your help, you want me to help you access what, exactly?"

"We'll get to that, but first let's get Simon to check you out and stabilize you. Once he's finished, we can talk," Maelyn said.

Quinton regarded her pretty face for a few moments. She had an agreeable tone that seemed to put everyone at ease. He couldn't afford to trust any of these people. However, he couldn't find any fault with what she'd said. He needed help and he needed it badly.

"Will you follow me, Quinton?" Simon asked.

"Oh, there's one more thing I want to know," Becker said. He was looking at Maelyn. "You jumped us out here in the middle of nowhere. How long will it take for the jump drive to recharge?"

"I was just about to confer with my chief engineer, Kieva. You're welcome to join me. She might have a few things for you to do to help out," Maelyn said and glanced at Guttman and Oscar.

Hints of a smile tugged at the edges of Becker's lips. "All right, after you."

They left the common area through one door, and Quinton and Simon went in the opposite direction.

"Radek," Quinton said sub-vocally so no one else could hear him, "I need you to monitor the ship systems."

"Of course," Radek replied. "What do you want me to monitor for?"

"Keep an eye on Maelyn and Becker. I don't think they're telling me everything."

"Understood. I'll monitor all references they make to you and PMCs in particular."

Quinton followed Simon. Radek hadn't been that reliable, but Quinton had to make use of him. He couldn't afford to watch everything himself, and he didn't think it was a good idea not to monitor his new associates.

"How did you figure out what I was?" Quinton asked.

"I wasn't sure at first," Simon said. He walked to a door and palmed the control unit so it hissed open. "I did detect a secure power source, which I now know is your ESS. The other thing that gave it away was your behavior. You didn't act like a robot, certainly not an agricultural robot. But when you gave Guttman some trouble, I knew for sure that there was something going on with you. The only thing it could be was a PMC, even though I honestly don't know how the hell you're functioning in that thing."

"So you've encountered a PMC before?" Quinton asked.

Simon shook his head once. "No, but I've read about them. I've seen virtual intelligences that are meant to mimic human behavior, but I didn't think you were one of those."

"All of you seemed worried about whether my origin was from the Acheron Confederacy."

Simon looked at him for a few moments. "Most people blame the Acheron Confederacy for what happened—the wars that followed their ascendancy."

"What wars?" Quinton asked.

Simon's eyebrows raised. "You really can't remember?"

"I'm not pretending, if that's what you're implying."

"I do understand if you're hiding what you are."

"Do you," Quinton said pleasantly. "Since I've been awake, I've been hunted and also shot at by an orbital defense cannon on a space station that was abandoned a century ago. Then I was picked up by you and your friend Becker, who wanted to claim me as property. And now I had to bargain something I don't even fully understand in order to get your help. But you want to tell me you understand why I'm hiding what I am."

They came to another door and Simon paused, his hand hovering over the door controls. "I didn't mean to upset you. But you don't know everything that's happened. There are good reasons why people are . . . Let's just say that people won't be overjoyed to learn that there are PMCs being reactivated."

"Have there been others? Have you encountered other PMCs?" Quinton asked quickly. His mind was beginning to race.

Simon palmed the controls, and the door hissed open. A familiar screeching sound came from inside, and Quinton looked over at a biological container in surprise. Inside, Stumpy was bellowing his dissatisfaction with his current living conditions.

"You brought it with you?" Quinton asked.

He walked over and peered inside the container. Stumpy stopped screeching and watched Quinton with wide eyes. His large flappy ears angled, as if he was trying to detect some kind of sound.

Simon walked over and stood next to the animal. "I figured you brought him with you for a reason."

"I didn't have a lot of time. It was more a last-minute decision," Quinton said. "Actually, the space station allowed me aboard because I had him with me."

"Is that right? I wonder why that was," Simon said.

The door to the workshop closed, and Simon opened the container. Stumpy hesitated for a moment and then bolted out, scrambling across the floor. He climbed a shelving system off to the side and perched on top of it, giving him a bird's-eye view of the entire room.

"I think the station's identification systems believed I was the creature's caretaker. It must've classified him as some kind of pet," Quinton said.

Simon made an *uh-huh* sound. "Did you name him—he got a name?"

"I called him Stumpy."

"Stumpy?" Simon said and cocked his head to the side, looking at the creature. "Really?"

"Yeah. His legs are short, so Stumpy."

Simon nodded. "I'll have to figure out what he eats."

"You don't need to keep him on my account."

"We'll see what happens."

Quinton watched him walk over to his workbench. "You never answered my question."

Simon looked over at him, his eyebrows raised. "What question?"

"Have you encountered any other PMCs?"

Simon shook his head. "No."

Quinton didn't believe him, at least not entirely. Simon could just be being cautious, or perhaps he wasn't allowed to talk about it. The young man deferred to Maelyn, who was clearly in command. But since Simon was going to help him, he didn't think it would be smart to make an issue of it right then. Simon was going to give him what he needed most, which was time.

"Let's get you checked out," Simon said.

Quinton walked over to the workbench, and Simon began to work on him.

# CHAPTER FOURTEEN

OVER THE NEXT FEW HOURS, Simon evaluated the agricultural unit that Quinton resided in. Quinton was impressed with how thorough Simon was with categorizing the damage to the robot. The power core needed to be replaced. The entire unit was beyond its original design specifications, even if it had been serviced on a regular maintenance schedule—which it hadn't.

"Stop doing that," Quinton said.

Simon was putting the shoulder assembly back together. He stopped and looked at him. "Huh?"

"Stop shaking your head and looking at me as if you expect me to . . ." Quinton said and stopped. He'd been about to say "die," but that wasn't right. If his power core suddenly stopped working, he would go into standby mode within the confines of the ESS. He'd be safe, but he'd lose all awareness of . . . everything—his sense of self, his surroundings, and his ability to influence his own life. He might as well be dead if that happened. But someone could also destroy the ESS, and then he'd be dead for sure.

"I'm sorry," Simon said and resumed his work. "It's just that

—You know what, never mind. It looks like the power regulator was able to get your core up to 40 percent capacity."

"It's holding steady, but more than half of it is damaged or nonfunctional."

"Yeah, but the battery backup I made for you should help with the load," Simon said.

The battery backup was a square box that Simon had bolted to Quinton's back. "It looks older than this bot is."

Simon snorted a little and bobbed his eyebrows. "You're not wrong about that, but I've replaced the internal components and configured the inhibitor to prevent it from overloading your systems."

Quinton turned his humanoid metallic head toward Simon, doing his best to convey consternation into the insipid facial features.

"I know," Simon said quickly. "This body isn't you, but you know what I mean."

He finished what he was doing and stepped off the stepladder. "All right, see how that shoulder works now. I think that should do it."

Quinton raised his arm and found that he now had full range of motion without loss of motor control. He walked over to a storage container and lifted it up without any problems. He put it down and then did a handstand. Quinton pushed up onto his fingertips and switched from one arm to the other, showing a display of acrobatic skill.

"You're a miracle worker," Quinton said.

Simon grinned. "Nah, that's what they call my cousin, Scotty."

"Is he on the ship?"

Simon shook his head. "No, he's back . . . he's not on board."

Quinton looked down at his chest. It was all one piece again. Simon had used a regenerative nano-robotic blend to patch and repair the damaged areas, and it would also maintain the structural integrity of the exoskeletal system. It couldn't be used where the haptic sensors were on his hands and feet because it would interfere with the sensory receptors. Anything having to do with physical feedback by touch couldn't be fixed with the nanite repair systems. However, the stuff spread throughout the exoskeleton, and Quinton suspected that the agricultural unit could now move as well as it had when it was first built. Simon had staged the application of the nanites in sections and uploaded basic design functions, essentially giving the nanites instructions on what they were to maintain.

"Simon," Quinton said, "how long are we going to play this game?"

Simon looked away for a few moments, not meeting his gaze. "I'm . . . There are some things that I can't talk about with you. It's for our protection."

"What do you think is going to happen?"

Simon's mouth hung open a bit, and he bobbed his head to the side. Then he inhaled and sighed. "Look, I know it's frustrating, but I just can't, all right?"

Quinton thought Simon looked genuinely conflicted. "Not really. What happened that made all of you afraid of a simple PMC?"

"There is nothing simple about a PMC."

"All right, fine, but you act like I'm some kind of threat to you."

Simon turned away and put his tools back on the workbench. He moved methodically, like he was someone who returned things exactly where he expected to find them later on. When he was finished, he banged his fist gently on the open workspace for a few beats, ending decisively with the loudest of all. Then he turned around. "You *are* a threat, even if you don't realize it and even if you don't intend to be. Maybe that's even worse," he said and pressed his lips together. "Can you remember anything?"

"It's limited. Radek insists that it's because of this," Quinton said, gesturing toward himself.

"Is it still advising against direct interaction?" Simon asked.

Radek had told Quinton it was more or less up to him, and since trust was so limited, Quinton had chosen to wait.

"You're not the only one with trust issues," Quinton replied, then added, "or maybe your captain, I should say."

Simon shifted uncomfortably. "I still think your VI is keeping things from you, which I don't like."

Quinton had suspected the same thing, but Radek was in as fragile a state as he was at this point. "Why is it so important for you to know my origin?"

Simon arched an eyebrow. "I thought it was obvious, and it should be just as important to you."

The lights dimmed for a tick and then resumed. Repairs were being made to the ship while they waited for the jump drive to recharge.

"You see, this is what I think," Quinton said. "I think it will affect whether you help me or not. So, if I did really know, I might not tell you anyway until I knew more about what happened to make you all so suspicious of PMCs."

Simon pursed his lips and nodded once. "Fair enough, and I don't see us going any further unless I tell you a few things, so that's what I'm going to do."

Quinton walked over to him and stopped. "Don't you need to consult Maelyn?"

"She trusts me," Simon replied.

The door to the workshop opened, and Maelyn walked in. She glanced at both of them. "Talking about me?" She quirked an eyebrow, and Quinton wondered if she'd been listening to their conversation before making her timely entrance.

She smiled and walked over to them, eyes twinkling. But all the smiles in the galaxy wouldn't negate the simple fact that they were all walking on eggshells around him.

"I was about to tell Quinton a few things, and he asked if I should check with you first," Simon replied.

Maelyn turned toward Quinton and gave him a once-over. "I have to say, you're looking much better," she said and looked at the young man. "Simon, you're the best. I knew there was a reason I kept you around."

"I thought it was my charming personality."

Maelyn laughed a little, and Quinton liked how it sounded. She looked at him. "You wouldn't believe how shy he used to be."

Simon's face became serious with mock severity. "You said you wouldn't talk about it anymore."

Maelyn frowned. "I don't remember promising that."

Simon shrugged. "Of course, if you did, I could start talking about the things I know about you. For example—"

"That won't be necessary," Maelyn said quickly and looked at Quinton. "You must have a few questions for us," she said and leaned back against the workbench.

"Just a couple," Quinton replied. "But first I'd like to point out that I really loved the performance. The playful banter between the two of you, I mean. I really sensed a bond between you. It's very disarming, and it probably works on a lot of people, but I'm not one of them."

Maelyn eyed Simon for a moment and said, "He figured us out." She looked back at Quinton. "You're right. This was all a ruse to get you to open up to us. I'm just trying to get you to cooperate." She crossed her arms and regarded him. Quinton noticed the way her thick, wavy hair rested on her shoulders like they were blanketed in caramel, and his receptors detected the sweet citrusy scent of her smooth skin. "Or perhaps I'm just trying to be friendly. Maybe give you a reason to lower your guard a little. I believe there's a saying about it. You know, spirit of cooperation and all that."

"With *us*," Quinton repeated. "Aren't you the captain? So, I guess I just need to cooperate with you."

Maelyn smiled. "You're a witty one."

"Cut the act. I know you might seem friendly now, but how friendly could you really be? Not if you're willing to work with someone like Lennix Crowe."

Maelyn laughed. It was a jovial, musical sound that Quinton actually liked and probably would've joined in if she weren't laughing at him. She looked at Simon. "How old do you think he is?"

"He?" Quinton said. "*He's* right here, and you can ask me."

"But you don't even know. You have limited access to your ESS. What's the last thing that you remember?"

Quinton thought about it for a few moments. "I remember pieces of my training for my candidacy to become a PMC. I remember passing a series of tests, but I don't know who they were for. The memories are there, I know it, but I just can't get to them."

Maelyn looked at Simon. "The way his VI—" he said.

"Radek," Quinton interjected.

"Radek," Simon repeated, "explained it was because of the limited capacity for the agricultural unit to interact with the ESS. I think he had to decide between allowing Quinton to function in a limited capacity or not bringing the PMC online altogether. It's actually unprecedented. It means that the VI is choosing dynamic connections to allow access to Quinton's ESS, and it's happening in real time."

Maelyn pursed her full lips and inhaled softly. "Dynamic connections, you said. That would mean it has to expend precious cycles to make that determination on an ongoing basis. Isn't that less efficient?"

"I have no way to measure it. Not with what we have here on the ship. But Quinton can clearly interact with us, even with limited access. Whatever Radek has done is working, at least for now."

Quinton waved at them. "I'm still here. I'm not going

anywhere. I know you're worried about something that I might be able to do, but unless you try to hurt me first, I really don't intend to do anything like that. You're just going to have to trust me."

"All right, Quinton," Maelyn said. "Let's see if we can get any of those suppressed memories to come up. Do you think Radek will cooperate?"

"He'll do what I ask him," Quinton said.

"Okay, good. Have you ever heard of the Dholeren United Coalition?" Maelyn asked.

"No."

"How about the Collective?"

Quinton shook his head.

"How about Castellus Federal Alliance? Tilion Empire, the Jordani Federation, the Acheron Confederacy."

"None of those sound familiar. I guess I should be relieved."

Maelyn's eyebrows raised. "Why would you say that?"

"Because it doesn't sound like . . . Judging by what's been said before, what if I was from one of those places? Would it affect our deal?" Quinton asked.

"It might, but it really depends," she said.

Quinton thought she was telling the truth. He felt he should have recognized some of those names.

"If he was from the Acheron Confederacy, then we'd—" Simon began to say when Maelyn cut him off.

"It wouldn't matter," she said.

"Yes, it would."

They were both silent for a few moments.

"Why does it matter?" Quinton asked.

Maelyn and Simon glanced at each other. "That could take some explaining," she said.

"Wait a second," Simon said. "Quinton, if Radek was operating under some kind of lockdown protocol, you would need to ask him before he could disclose it to you. This isn't something he would volunteer, but if you make the request, he'd have no choice but to tell you about it."

"What if the lockdown protocol forbids it?" Maelyn asked.

"Then, we'll still confirm that the lockdown exists and to what extent it can be influencing him."

Quinton considered it for a few seconds, then said, "Radek, I want you to show yourself to the others."

A moment later, a silvery orb appeared a few feet away from Quinton.

"Is there anything I need to know?"

"You'll need to make a more specific query," Radek replied.

Maelyn and Simon watched the hovering orb with great interest.

"Radek, are you operating under a lockdown protocol? Are you keeping things from me?" Quinton asked. There were a few moments of silence, and he suspected that Radek was stalling for time.

"Affirmative," Radek said.

Quinton felt a vague sensation of wanting to grit his teeth, but this was something the agricultural unit couldn't do. "I want you to end this lockdown immediately."

"I am unable to comply with this request."

"It's not a request. It's an order, and you will obey me," Quinton said.

"Apologies. I am unable to comply with this request."

Quinton growled.

"Hold on. Maybe there's a reason he can't comply," Simon said. "Radek, why can't you end the lockdown?"

The silvery orb spun but didn't reply.

"Answer the question, Radek," Quinton said.

"Conditions have not been met in their entirety. Between that and the limited capacity of this unit, I am unable to disclose the exact nature of the lockdown," Radek said.

"Let me get this straight," Quinton said. "There's a lockdown that's affecting my own access to myself," he said, gesturing toward his chest. "My own data. Information I need right now. Who instituted the lockdown?"

"I am unable—"

"For the love of—I don't want to hear what you're unable to do. Tell me what you *can* do."

"The lockdown affects what I am able to tell you," Radek said.

"That doesn't make any sense. No one has the authority to deny me access to my own mind," Quinton said angrily.

Simon's eyes widened, and he looked at Maelyn. "Wow. The VI itself is operating under a lockdown. Someone instituted a check against the VI itself. This isn't like the others."

"Others," Quinton said. "What others?"

Maelyn looked at Simon and shook her head.

"He was going to find out sooner or later," Simon said and looked at Quinton. "There were Federation Wars that happened probably around the same time you were uploaded. PMCs were used to enhance the combat capabilities of federation navies. That is, until they started going insane, but this was after the technology had spread."

"Insane? But the tech was proven. It was safe. PMCs were considered living entities with the same rights as the person they used to be when they had a human body," Quinton replied.

Maelyn cleared her throat. "He's older than we thought. Pre-galactic war age."

"What the hell does that mean?" Quinton asked.

"Things have changed since you volunteered to become a PMC," she said.

"You're right, this is pre-Sentinel fleet operations," Simon said and winced.

"Really, Simon," Maelyn scolded as her blue eyes flicked toward the ceiling. Then she looked at Quinton. "I think I know which federation you came from."

They both inched away from him, and Quinton became suspicious.

"Hey," he said, not liking that they were backing away from him. "Which one?"

Maelyn and Simon exchanged a few meaningful looks, trying to have a conversation without words, and they were utterly failing. Quinton accessed the door controls to the workshop and locked them. The overhead door indicator light shifted to red, and a soft chime sounded. Maelyn and Simon looked at the door and then back at Quinton.

"I need an answer right now," Quinton said.

Maelyn sighed. "All right," she said. "We'll be able to confirm this, but I think you are from either the Acheron Confederacy—the ACN to be exact—or the Jordani Federation. They were the earliest adopters of PMC technology."

Quinton cranked up his frame rate, which controlled his perception of time. Time didn't slow down for anyone else, but he was able to think much more quickly. Since he now had a direct connection to a power source, the familiar warning indicator did not appear on his HUD.

"Radek, is this true? Can you confirm any of this?"

As an answer, Quinton became aware of a new pathway to his ESS.

*Acheron Confederacy naval lockdown protocol.*
*Condition seventy-four has been met.*
*Awareness confirmed.*
*Secondary protocols activated.*

"I guess that's my answer," Quinton said.

He was from the Acheron Confederacy. He glanced at Maelyn and Simon, who were motionless. Maelyn's mouth was partially open, as if she was about to say something.

"Radek," Quinton started to say but didn't know how to finish. Radek was affected by the lockdown protocol as well. The VI was all he had to work with. "What just happened?"

"The lockdown couldn't keep you from the knowledge any longer."

"It couldn't? But that would mean I should be able to override the lockdown and get full access to my memories."

"Not entirely. The lockdown protocol functions as its own separate VI that can have a governing effect on you. It was added after the PMC load date," Radek said.

*Great*, he had some kind of Big Brother virtual intelligence watching his every move, but Quinton had no idea what its primary objective was.

"Can you tell me anything about the secondary protocols?"

"It's going to take me some time. The effects are intricate."

"Can it force me to do things I don't want to do?"

"Unknown," Radek said. "I can't say for sure with a great deal of probability whether it can or can't. If it could, that would violate core restrictions for PMC rights, rendering you no more than a machine. The greatest probability is that the secondary protocols are an influencer."

Quinton considered this for a few moments. "Either way, I'm being backed into a corner."

"I'm afraid I don't understand."

"You interpreted my question in specifics. It can't control my thoughts directly and force me to act accordingly. However, if it can influence me, then it can exercise some degree of control, the consequences of which might include cutting my access to my ESS."

"I see your point. I will devote some of my cycles to considering the problem."

Quinton wasn't sure how much headway the VI would make, but he guessed it was better than nothing. "You do that. I guess the question now is whether I tell the others."

"I would advise against that."

"Why?"

"Even though Captain Maelyn has narrowed the origins of

your PMC, there still remains a doubt, which may work in your favor in securing their cooperation," Radek said.

"I wonder if it would make any difference," Quinton said and collected his thoughts for a few moments. "All right, don't volunteer any information to them unless I give the okay."

"Understood."

Quinton returned his frame rate back to normal.

"Are you sure you can narrow it down to just those two federations?" Quinton asked.

To Maelyn and Simon, no time had passed, and she took the question as a normal progression of their conversation.

"PMCs were invented by the Acheronians, but eventually the Jordanis had it," Maelyn said.

"It spread pretty quickly," Simon said. "I can do some research on it."

"Does it really matter? Would it change anything?" Quinton asked.

"Yes, it would," Maelyn said. "PMCs changed the way wars were fought across galactic federations—"

A comlink chimed overhead.

"Captain," Kieva said, her voice coming from the speaker by the door.

"What is it, Kieva?"

"I'm afraid Becker has found a stowaway in one of the cargo containers. You better get down to the cargo hold, ma'am."

"On my way," Maelyn said.

She looked at the door and then turned back to Quinton. "We'll finish this conversation, I promise, but Kieva isn't an alarmist, and I still have a ship to run. You can come with me if you want."

Quinton unlocked the door. "Lead the way, Captain."

Maelyn left the workshop, and Quinton and Simon followed her.

# CHAPTER FIFTEEN

QUINTON FOLLOWED Maelyn down the corridor with Simon walking next to him. The young man kept glancing over at him, looking a little uncomfortable.

Quinton looked at him. "You're already in trouble. You might as well tell me what other PMCs you've encountered." He thought he saw Maelyn twitch her head to the side as if she hadn't quite heard what he said. "Don't worry about her. The cat is out of the bag. The drive signature has already been identified."

Simon shook his head. "You'd be an idiot to underestimate her."

"That's not what I meant," Quinton said. "I just want to know more about the other PMCs."

Simon looked pointedly at Maelyn's back for a moment. "We haven't encountered any PMCs, but we've heard some rumors."

Quinton expected Maelyn to interject a comment, but she kept striding forward. "Like what?" he asked.

"Just that there's been increasing Sentinel activity reported," Simon replied.

"What's a Sentinel?"

Maelyn turned back toward them. "We'll need to postpone the history lesson I'm afraid. Simon, make sure you keep an eye on Becker's team."

There was shouting from up ahead, and Quinton heard Guttman laughing about something, which couldn't be good.

"I'm not letting you anywhere near her. The captain is on her way here now," Kieva said.

"It's a Servitor," Guttman replied in exasperation. "I just want to have a look at her."

Quinton followed Maelyn as she strode into the cargo bay. Becker stood off to the side, his arms crossed as he leaned against the wall. He wore a mildly amused expression.

Kieva was on the shorter side. Her blonde hair was tied back into a ponytail and her button-brown eyes flicked toward Maelyn, looking relieved to see her. "Captain," she said, and Guttman and Oscar turned toward them.

Quinton saw someone hiding behind the stack of storage containers that Kieva was guarding.

Maelyn looked at Becker, who shrugged a shoulder. "What's going on here?"

Quinton saw that both Guttman and Oscar had elevated heart rates. There was a slight flush to their faces and, he suspected, their chests as well. The data showed itself on his HUD.

"We found a stowaway," Guttman said. The way he said it seemed to convey that he had some sort of claim on what he'd found.

"I see," Maelyn said. She looked at the storage container and activated her wrist computer, and her personal holoscreen appeared. "This came from Crowe's Union Station. This wasn't a mix-up. It's part of the resupply manifest."

"It's a Servitor. Do you know what they're worth? This wasn't an accident," Guttman said.

"He's right," Becker said, unfolding his arms and stepping away from the wall. "This isn't the kind of cargo that would go unnoticed by Crowe."

Maelyn looked away, seemingly unperturbed by Becker's comments. "Very well," she said, raising her voice slightly. "I want you to come out of there. I'm the captain of the ship, and I promise that no harm will come to you."

Kieva turned around. "Come on, it's okay now," she said and stepped out of the way.

Quinton didn't know what to expect when the Servitor stepped out from behind the storage container. It was a woman, but not like any he'd ever seen before. She was scantily clad, with dark lavender skin. There were hints of pink on her high cheekbones and full lips that were perfectly proportioned. She had legs that went all the way up, and she wore a formfitting shirt that only accentuated her remarkably firm and full breasts. The shirt ended, leaving her midriff bare, showing a flat stomach and hips that accentuated her womanly curves. Her dark eyes had violet in them, and Quinton couldn't help but gawk at the sight of her. He couldn't tear his eyes away, as if his mind refused to accept what he was seeing.

A few moments of silence passed while they all stared at her. He noticed that the other men all had similar reactions to the stunning beauty standing in front of them. She had long, silky white hair that seemed to glisten with silvery strands, as if they were enhanced by the lighting in the cargo hold. Quinton watched her with both admiration and a growing wariness that the person in front of him was designed for a specific purpose. She was meant to get a particular reaction, and it wasn't failing on any of them.

"What's your name?" Maelyn asked.

"Vonya Irani, Captain," she said. "I am a Servitor."

"Why are you on my ship?"

"The conditions of my employ were unacceptable, but I did

not have the means to remove myself from the situation while maintaining good standing with my employer, so I added this cargo container to a manifest," she said and gestured with a long, slender arm, "destined for one of the independent trade ships that had come to the station."

Vonya's voice carried the alluring quality of silk sliding off smooth skin. Quinton wanted her to keep speaking so he could watch her full lips move as they formed words. Vonya kept her attention on Maelyn, but he thought she was well aware of the effect she was having on the men aboard the ship.

"Captain, please don't send me back," Vonya said simply and without a hint of pleading in her voice. "I would like to be of service to you and your crew in order to earn my place until I can make other arrangements," she said and glanced at the others for the first time. "Surely, I have some skills that could be of use."

Guttman cleared his throat. "I had a few thoughts on the matter," he said.

"Simon," Maelyn said, ignoring Guttman, "can you detect any tracer signals on this cargo?"

Guttman looked as if he was about to say something, thought better of it, and instead closed his mouth.

"Checking," Simon replied and brought up his own personal holoscreen. After a few moments, he shook his head. "No signal detected, Captain."

"What about the ship systems? Is anything broadcasting?" Becker asked.

And in one moment, the big man had proved to Quinton that he was more than a mindless brute.

"The ship's security systems would have detected it," Simon said.

Becker nodded, satisfied with the answer, but Quinton noticed that Maelyn was checking something else. Vonya simply stood there, looking stunning.

Becker looked at Maelyn's holoscreen and frowned. "I think

you would have detected a subspace communication link broadcasting our coordinates."

Maelyn's eyes scanned the data on her personal holoscreen. "We would, but that's not the only way to track a ship."

"How else would someone track a ship way out in the middle of nowhere?" Guttman asked.

"A broadcast beacon is too obvious, but a short-range beacon would work," Quinton said.

Becker and Guttman looked at him doubtfully.

Maelyn closed the holoscreen. "They don't need to track us way out here. The three of you worked for Lennix Crowe, and you know how resourceful he is. No, he'll want to know where we check in, which means he doesn't need a subspace beacon tracker on the ship. All he needs is something small and undetectable that will come online the moment we check in to a space dock." She paused and her gaze took them all in. "We're going to have to make a sweep of the hull."

"You can't be serious," Guttman groused. "You want us to inspect the entire hull?" he asked and looked at Becker for support.

"I thought you wanted to avoid Crowe," Maelyn said.

Guttman looked like he was about to protest, but Becker silenced him. "She's right. It will be something small and unobtrusive, but it'll have its own power source," he said and looked at Maelyn. "Do you have any drones that can help with this?"

Maelyn's lips lifted in a wry smile. "I do have a few drones. There and right there," she said, looking at Guttman and Oscar. Quinton thought she included him in that all-encompassing look. "It will be a team effort. The more of us who get out there and search, the quicker we can be on our way."

Guttman exhaled explosively. "I'm not going out there to search the hull."

"Shut it, Guttman," said Becker. "We're guests on the ship,

and like everyone else, we will contribute. Captain Maelyn has every right to request this of us."

Guttman's mouth formed the word "Captain" as if he'd never said it before. Then he shook his head and turned away.

"I'd like to help, Captain," Vonya said.

Maelyn frowned. "I didn't think Servitors were equipped to go on spacewalks."

"Not normally, but it sounds to me as if you need all the help you can get. I'm sure if I partnered up with someone—" Vonya said.

No sooner had the words escaped her lips that Guttman spun around. "She can partner with me. I'll keep an eye on her."

Quinton heard Oscar voice the same. He then glanced at Simon and saw the glint of anticipation at being partnered with Vonya.

"Gentlemen," Maelyn said, "I believe I overheard you speak about your preference to work alone. I think if you were out there with Vonya, you'd be too distracted, which negates the purpose of checking the hull," she said and looked back at Vonya. "You can help monitor our progress from inside the ship, along with Kieva."

Kieva smiled encouragingly at Vonya, who returned it in kind. "Come with me to the bridge, and I'll show you around."

Quinton glanced at Simon and noticed he was watching Vonya walk out of the cargo hold. His eyes had slid toward her lower back, but when he saw that Quinton was watching him, he immediately averted his gaze.

"What's a Servitor? And why was her skin purple?" Quinton asked. His question snatched the others' attention back to him. Becker's gaze narrowed, as if he'd just realized that Quinton was even there. "She looks human, but is she human?" Quinton asked.

"My God," Becker said, "you're a fossil. No, scratch that, you're just ignorant."

"I'm not the one standing there with my tongue hanging half out of my mouth like some beast in heat," Quinton replied.

Becker lifted his chin, and his lips formed into a smirk. "Already forgotten what it's like to be a man, I see."

Quinton stepped toward him. He knew he shouldn't let Becker get under his skin, but he was going on pure reaction in that moment. All he wanted to do was throw Becker through a bulkhead wall.

"That's enough of that," Maelyn said. She didn't raise her voice, but it carried a command authority that pierced his anger.

"Careful now," Becker said, goading him on. "I wouldn't want you to lose sight of what you are."

Quinton stood there. There were no telltale signs of the anger he was feeling inside. There was no explosive intake of breath or surge of adrenaline, but he yearned to knock that smug look off Becker's face. He was positive he could get there before any of them could react. There had to be limits to the ship's suppression systems. After all, he didn't have a weapon.

Maelyn turned toward Becker. "You're not helping. Are we going to have a problem?"

Becker stared at Quinton for a few more moments before turning his gaze toward Maelyn. "Of course not. I'm a professional. I'll take Guttman and Oscar, and we'll check the port bow area and work our way around." Becker gave her a small two-finger salute and then left the cargo hold.

"I'll start at the stern then," Simon said.

Maelyn nodded. "I'll take a group of drones and check midships. It shouldn't take us more than six or eight hours to do a thorough check."

"I might be able to cut down on some of that time," Quinton said.

Her eyes widened. "How?"

"The agricultural unit is equipped with sensors for detecting hidden power sources. It's actually quite sensitive and should be more than up to the task," Quinton said.

Maelyn frowned and looked as if she was trying to think of a way to decline his request without insulting him.

"I've been in the vacuum of space before. The unit can handle it," Quinton said. He felt an urge to prove that he was useful, like he had something to contribute. He didn't want to be idle.

"The unit can handle it," Simon said.

"All right, but you stick with Simon and stay away from Becker and the others," Maelyn said.

"Would it really be so bad if they were somehow launched into space and we couldn't rescue them?" Quinton said.

He'd hoped that Maelyn would be amused, but she wasn't. Instead, she left the cargo hold.

"Does she not like jokes?" Quinton asked.

Simon led them to the other side of the cargo hold, heading toward the stern of the ship. "I think she's concerned that there's a tracker on the ship."

"I get that, but she can't possibly like Becker or the others."

"It's not a matter of approval. You don't understand, but I can tell you about Servitors while we work."

"That would be nice, but about Becker and the others. Will Maelyn let them become a problem?" Quinton asked.

Simon paused partway through the doorway and looked at him. "You're asking if she'll be able to deal with Becker and the others decisively if things get bad?"

"Yes."

"I've known her for a while, and in all that time, she's never hesitated to do what had to be done when the going gets rough. You've met her for all of five minutes. Don't underestimate her," Simon said with a surety that Quinton couldn't question.

"I won't," he said.

Simon nodded and kept walking. Quinton followed.

"Servitors emerged as a species after the Federation Wars. I can't remember which colony world they came from, but they decided as a society to be subservient to other human factions. They modified their appearances, both the males and females."

"They genetically modified themselves to be beautiful?" Quinton asked.

"Yes, but there's more to it than that. They actually have other skillsets. Their reason for being, other than survival, is to bring peace wherever they are. They're pacifists. They seek to please people and believe this is the way to coexist in the galaxy," Simon said.

"They made themselves slaves? Are they owned?"

"No, they do have a choice, but they are bound by strict rules. They will never disclose the secrets of whomever they serve. They can be very insightful and make good advisors and confidants. If Vonya abandoned her employer before her contract was up, things must have been pretty bad. They might be subservient to other species, but they will run away if they feel that their life is threatened," Simon said.

"Yeah, but to genetically alter yourself so . . . I mean, the purple skin and all that looks great, but it just seems a little extreme," Quinton said.

Simon snorted. "If you think that's extreme, wait until you see some of the other species out there."

"Aliens?"

Simon shook his head. "No, just different variants of the human species. We've taken adapting to the galaxy to a whole new extreme."

"What do you mean?"

"Well, there are some groups that live on asteroids. They can survive with minimal atmosphere and some without oxygen at all. They don't look anything like us anymore, but they can communicate. They're actually pretty good at finding mineral-rich systems."

"What do they eat?"

"I don't remember. The point is that there are a lot of variants of the human race out in the galaxy now. The collapse of the federations caused us to drift further apart and find new ways to survive," Simon said.

Quinton was quiet for a few moments. "And most people blame the Acheron Confederacy for this?"

Simon inhaled and sighed. "A lot of people do, even if they don't talk about it."

Quinton was glad he hadn't told anyone about his Acheron origins. They were anxious enough around him as it was. "But they're just one star nation. It's not like they waged war on the entire galaxy," he said.

They walked into a room where there were several spacesuits off to the side. "No, they didn't," Simon said and walked up to one of the EVA suits. He brought it online. The suit opened at the front, and he stepped inside. "They just enabled everyone else to do it for them with the technology they brought into the galaxy."

Simon looked away from him when he spoke, but Quinton couldn't help but feel that he was talking about PMCs. He didn't know what to think about it, but he certainly didn't regret keeping his origins a secret. He couldn't imagine the others reacting well to that, so he wasn't going to volunteer the information anytime soon.

"Do *you* blame the Acheron Confederacy for how things are in the galaxy?" Quinton asked.

The EVA suit sealed itself, but Simon gave him a long look. "Yes and no."

"Well, which is it?"

"The fact of the matter is that there has been a lot of suffering since the Federation Wars. Planets capable of sustaining life are at a premium, but unless you have a powerful military, you don't stand a comet's chance of flying through a star at holding onto it. Maybe not even then."

"Why?" Quinton said. "Wait, what happened to federation core worlds? They haven't been destroyed, have they?" he asked, unable to keep the rising fear he felt inside from sounding through his artificial voice. Without full access to his memories, the implications were somewhat lost on him, but still, loss of life on such a galactic scale . . .

Simon walked into the airlock, and Quinton followed him. Simon stopped with his hand poised over the airlock controls and turned toward him. "I know this is a lot to take in. You seem to be someone from before the Federation Wars, and you've awakened to a galaxy that's changed considerably. I think it's best if we hold off on this discussion for the time being while we look for any tracer beacons on the ship."

Quinton knew he was being managed, and he didn't like it. They were giving him information piecemeal, and he wanted answers now. He needed to figure out who or what had sent out that activation signal. And what was even more important than that was *why* they'd done it. Simon had spoken about rumors of other PMCs being activated. Quinton needed answers, but he also couldn't rush into anything. He'd have to cooperate, and they couldn't go anywhere until they made a sweep of the ship's hull.

"All right, fine. Let's get to work then," he said.

Simon smiled, looking pleased.

"But sooner or later, you and Maelyn will have to level with me regardless of how you think I'm going to react," Quinton said.

The smile faded, and Simon nodded.

———

THEY SPENT the next several hours making a sweep of the ship's hull. Quinton was able to make the quickest progress because he was tapped into the ship's systems and could readily identify anything that wasn't supposed to be there. However, he was limited, like everyone else, to being in one place at a time. With Simon's permission, he took control of several repair drones, which helped them widen their coverage area. They were nearly done with their section of the ship when there was some sort of suit failure. Guttman was almost jettisoned into space because of a nozzle failure for the propellant. Becker and Oscar saved Guttman. The spacesuit's safety protocols isolated the damaged areas, but Guttman's leg had to be treated in the medical bay.

Quinton and Simon found themselves doing the bulk of the hull checks while everyone else was now inside the ship. Enough time had passed that Becker and Oscar should have rejoined the effort by now.

"This sector is clear," Simon said, his voice coming over the comlink.

"Same here," Quinton replied.

They'd split up and were covering different areas while bypassing the areas that had already been checked. Quinton was starting to think there wasn't any beacon, but they weren't finished.

He accessed the ship's comms systems with the intent of getting the others to come out to help. He saw that Oscar was heading back to a maintenance hatch airlock toward the bow, but where were Becker and Maelyn?

Quinton found them through the ship's life-sign detection sensors that monitored the ship. Vonya and Kieva were on the bridge, but Becker and Maelyn were still in the medical bay.

"He won't lose his leg," Maelyn said. "The damaged tissue will be replaced, but it'll take a few hours."

Guttman appeared to be unconscious inside a medical capsule.

"Nozzles don't just fail like this," Becker said.

"What are you suggesting?"

Becker stepped toward her. "I'm suggesting that that *thing* out there tried to kill him."

The only person on the ship Becker referred to that way was Quinton.

"He's been with Simon the whole time."

"Come on, Maelyn, you can't believe having a PMC running around is safe. Do you have any idea what they're capable of?"

"In fact, I do," Maelyn replied. "I checked the suit's systems, and it registered as a failure. No outside tampering occurred. Maybe you think Quinton somehow teleported to where Guttman was located and just yanked out the propellent nozzle assembly. Surely one of you would have seen that. Plus, there would be evidence of it on the suit." She tilted her head to the side. "There wasn't any."

An accident happened with Guttman's suit, and Becker's first thought was that Quinton tried to kill him? Guttman wasn't his favorite person by any stretch of the imagination, but murdering him was something else entirely. He'd joked about it, but he hadn't actually meant it. Not much anyway.

Becker and Maelyn left the medical bay.

"There's something you're not telling me. You don't seem surprised about encountering a PMC," Becker said.

Maelyn kept walking and didn't respond.

"Come on, we've got to work together. It doesn't cost you anything to tell me what you know about PMCs," Becker said, and Maelyn stopped. His tone was smooth, and they were standing close together in the corridor.

Maelyn regarded Becker for a moment. Quinton saw she had a pleased tilt to her mouth. "There have been rumors of others."

"Rumors," Becker repeated.

"Yes, rumors. Someone is doing this."

"Who?"

"I don't know, and we might never find out."

"Then what's your plan?" Becker asked, stepping closer to her.

Maelyn's mouth opened and she pressed her lips together. Becker leaned in and Quinton felt like his head was going to explode. Then Becker cried out and jerked away from her, shaking his arm. Maelyn held a palm stunner.

Becker shook his head and then grinned. "Can't blame a guy for trying."

Maelyn smiled. "This isn't going to happen."

Becker crossed his muscular arms in front of his chest. "You don't like what you see?" Maelyn glanced at his chest. "I can be pretty persuasive."

She chuckled a little. "Of that, I have no doubt. My plan is what I've already told you. Quinton is able to unlock tech that's been off-limits since the Federation Wars. I need that."

"Oh yeah, for whom?"

"That doesn't really concern you now, does it?" Maelyn asked and then said, "You're out of Crowe's Union and you want to start your own. Helping me can go a long way toward helping you achieve that."

"That's what you keep saying, but until I see it, I'm not going to accept anything at face value."

"Fair enough," she replied.

"But having that thing running around—it can turn on us at any time. It can seize control of the ship's systems before we have a chance to stop it. I don't see why we can't disable it—"

Maelyn shook her head, and Becker stopped speaking. "Even if you were to disable him, you'd effectively kill him, and we wouldn't be able to access his ESS. They go dormant forever. It's some kind of safety protocol."

"And you've seen this for yourself?" Becker asked.

"No, but do you really want to chance it?"

Becker was quiet for a few moments. Then he unfolded his arms, and there was a hardened glint to his gaze. "If it's between him and us, then it's going to be him. PMCs have caused enough problems."

"Why, Becker," Maelyn teased, "I didn't think such a cold-hearted salvager cared about things like that."

"I know what's been done, and the only way it stopped before was thanks to the Sentinel fleets."

"Sentinels aren't any less dangerous than PMCs. Quite the contrary."

"No, but they also stabilized the galaxy. As long as we stay out of their way, they'll leave us alone. That's the way it's always been."

"That's no way to live," Maelyn said.

Becker snorted. "Do you think you can take on the Sentinels now? Is that why you want this PMC around?"

"Hey, are you done here?" Simon asked.

Quinton was so startled that he severed his connection to the ship's security systems and didn't get to hear Maelyn's response.

He looked at Simon. "Yeah, this area is clear."

Simon nodded. "Good, same for me. We've got a few more sections to check, but I've been meaning to ask. How is the power regulator holding up? Is it still stable?"

"Power levels are holding for now," Quinton replied.

They continued onward. At least he knew why Maelyn was keeping him around. They needed him alive in order to access the ESS. It made sense, but he didn't understand anything they'd said about these Sentinels. He needed to find out as much as he could about them.

Simon began asking him more questions, and Quinton thought the young man was just trying to break up the monotony of the task they'd been given. Then Maelyn contacted them both, saying that they were coming back out to help with the search. Quinton needed to keep an eye on all of them. He wasn't sure if Becker had been convinced to go along with Maelyn's plan, and he would need to be prepared for it.

"Radek, have you made any progress analyzing the secondary protocols for the lockout?" Quinton asked.

"Still working on it. I will alert you once my analysis is complete," Radek replied.

Quinton engaged the bot's power detection systems and kept searching the hull.

# CHAPTER SIXTEEN

AFTER AN EXTENSIVE SWEEP of the entire hull of the ship, they found no tracking devices of any kind. Given the amount of time it had taken, Quinton was disappointed with the outcome. On the other hand, it had felt good to actually be doing something that wasn't life-threatening, although that concept was a bit of a misnomer where he was concerned. His power core continued to degrade despite being connected to the power regulator Simon had put together for him, though the power regulator did ensure that the agricultural unit's power core was connected to a readily available power supply contained in the box attached to his back.

"What are the current levels now?" Simon asked.

"30 percent and holding. I'll let you know if there are any changes," Quinton replied.

They'd made several space jumps, but Maelyn had not taken them to another habitable system. These were shorter space jumps, which allowed for quicker recharge times for the jump drive.

"Okay, where were we?" Simon asked.

There wasn't much they could do for the agricultural unit except finding a replacement power core.

"Genetic modifications," Quinton said.

Radek hadn't come up with anything insightful into the lock-down protocols and advised Quinton to try functioning as he usually would. He chose not to remind the VI that functioning normally would have required full access to his ESS.

"It's not as simple as that because of the side effects."

"Like what?"

"Sterilization, for one," Simon replied. "Or a complete loss of empathy."

"What good would that do?"

"The loss of empathy was intentional. The Sparns thought that if they could enhance their logical deductive reasoning, they could adapt to environments others didn't want," Simon said.

Quinton felt the vapid sensation of wanting to frown in thought, which the agricultural bot couldn't do. He found that he really missed being able to mirror the micro-expressions of the people around him. It had been a distraction to his thoughts, leaving him feeling less than what he should be feeling.

Maelyn walked into the galley, which had high countertops and stools for people to sit on. Simon was sitting on one of the stools, eating while Quinton stood there. He no longer experienced a sense of exhaustion, but sitting down and enjoying a meal would have lifted his mood.

Maelyn came over, carrying a cup of tea. She looked at Quinton. "What's the matter?"

"I was just trying to remember what the last thing I ate was," Quinton said.

Simon snorted a little and then frowned. "Can you remember?"

"No. I guess it's not essential," Quinton said.

"Or it's just Radek's way of looking out for you," Maelyn replied and sipped her tea after she blew on it for a moment.

"What kind of tea is that?" Quinton asked.

"It's from the Mozeyian Outpost. They get it from some-where else . . . I can't remember where exactly," Maelyn said.

"Do you like it?"

"I wouldn't be drinking it if I didn't like it."

"How would you feel if something was controlling the knowledge of whether you even liked that tea. It might be mildly annoying at first, but then multiply that feeling by infinity, and then you'll understand how I'm feeling right now," Quinton said. His anger had sprung from nowhere.

Simon's eyes widened, and he looked at Maelyn and shook his head a little.

"Just . . ." Quinton said, holding up his hand and then bringing it back down to his side because the gesture could be interpreted by the ship's internal countermeasures as threatening. "Just don't," he said and stepped back. "Don't do that thing where you try and share some kind of unspoken conversation."

He turned around and walked out of the galley. Becker and Guttman were in the corridor.

"Careful now," Quinton said, shoving his way past them. "I might lose control."

He kept going without a backward glance. There was only so far he could go on the ship, but he just wanted to take a walk, even if it meant not having the physical release that came from moving actual muscles. At least he could see that he was moving, and perhaps his mind would use that to trigger some kind of release to mimic the endorphins that came from moving.

Simon had become his unofficial caretaker, and he was doing a great job, but Quinton didn't like being managed. He wasn't helpless. It wasn't supposed to be this way. He couldn't remember what he was thinking when he'd become a PMC, but this wasn't what was supposed to happen. He wasn't supposed to be brought online like this.

"Hey, hold on a minute," Maelyn said, running to catch up with him.

Quinton wanted to keep going. Some small part of him liked the idea of Maelyn chasing him, but he knew that was foolish. He'd already made enough of a fool of himself, so he stopped.

"It looks like you need to blow off some steam," Maelyn said.

"A new power core is what I need."

Maelyn nodded. "Our next jump is going to take us to the Mozeyian Outpost. It's an out-of-the-way trading outpost that might have what we're looking for."

Quinton stopped himself from making a hasty reply. "I didn't know that."

"Yes, I know. That's what I was coming to tell you."

"Well, I appreciate it."

"You know we have a weapons area. Do you want to get in some target practice?"

Quinton cocked his head to the side and regarded her. "You're handing out weapons now?" he asked.

Maelyn chuckled. "Only with target ammo. Nothing that could pierce the hull. Still, the sensation is the same," she said while taking a few steps ahead of him and turning around. "Come on, you might like it."

Quinton followed, and she smiled. "I don't know if it's going to help," he said.

They walked together.

"It might. I bet you're a good shot," Maelyn said.

"Why would you say that?"

"Since you have no knowledge of the Federation Wars, you must precede them. The earliest PMCs were taken from among military personnel. Regardless of which federation you served, I think it might help trigger more access to your ESS," Maelyn replied.

"It doesn't work like that," Quinton said. "My access to the ESS is limited because of this body. It's a resource issue and not a hidden-connection problem. Also, the gaps in my knowledge could be just that—gaps. The VIs are managing data access while balancing what I need to continue functioning."

Maelyn led him through a series of corridors that came to an open cargo hold. It was a long, narrow space. On the wall were several lockers. The doors on them opened at the same time, revealing an assortment of handheld weapons, but Quinton gravitated toward the assault rifles.

"Maybe it's a bit of both," Maelyn said. She walked toward a hand blaster. "Regardless, it might be fun. I come down here sometimes. It helps."

"Helps you cope with your worries and your fears?" Quinton asked.

She arched a dark eyebrow toward him. "Something like that."

Quinton was sure it wasn't anything like that.

He stayed outside the danger zone while Maelyn walked toward the entrance. She checked her weapon, and Quinton saw that she'd activated it. She pushed a button on the console in front of her, and the floor retracted. Beneath the opening was a subfloor that sported multiple barrier configurations. Some were hardly big enough to provide cover, while others were floating platforms. Spherical combat drones flew in from the other side and took up positions throughout the course. Once they reached their designated area, a holo-image surrounded the drones, making them appear like soldiers in combat armor.

Maelyn sprinted toward the first barrier, firing a few shots from her weapon as she went. The combat drones immediately took action. They fired their weapons in quick bursts of suppressing fire meant to herd her, but she vaulted over the nearest barrier and dashed toward one on the right. Green bolts fired from her hand blaster, and she took out two combat drones. Once they'd been hit, the holo-images disappeared, and the drones dropped to the ground.

The combat drones quickly adapted their tactics and began working their way around to flank Maelyn.

"Anytime you're ready to join in, rookie," Maelyn said.

Quinton hastened toward the entrance and checked his assault rifle, setting it to three-round bursts. It wasn't an energy weapon. Instead, he preferred something that fired actual combat darts, even if they were just for target practice. He hadn't been aware of the preference until he'd selected the weapon. Maybe Maelyn was right about him.

Quinton ran toward the first barrier. A group of combat drones broke away from Maelyn and headed toward him. The agricultural bot wasn't exactly small, nor was it designed for combat, but it was agile. He darted out from cover and fired a few bursts at the drones with deadly accuracy, the ease of which surprised him. Recognizing the new threat, more combat drones were working their way toward his position.

Quinton glanced across the course and saw that reinforcements had arrived and were pressing toward Maelyn.

*This is what she does to blow off steam?*

He had the rifle, but he needed the high ground. He crouched and scrambled over to another barrier and was greeted with a barrage of weapons fire from the combat drones. Maelyn fired her hand blaster at the group of combat drones, causing them to cover their flank. Quinton used the distraction to race toward the elevated platform. An energy bolt clipped his thigh but didn't do any damage.

The assault rifle was strapped across one shoulder, and Quinton let it fall while he raced toward the elevated platform. He leaped into the air and grabbed the edge, then hoisted himself up, rolled away from the edge, and grabbed his rifle. He immediately started firing on the drones, cranking up his frame rate as time slowed down around him. He quickly scouted where the combat drones were located and tried to come up with a firing solution that would swing the odds in their favor. There were only two of them, and the sheer number of combat drones would overwhelm them eventually. The floor was littered with the drones they'd taken out. Quinton looked at them and saw that they weren't offline. They were still operational but in strict adherence to the rules of the simulation. He opened a comlink to them and took control.

He'd only cranked his frame rate up to about 45 percent, which meant that combat drones were coming toward him, and the glowing bolts from their blasters were even now blazing a path toward him. Quinton dove for cover as his frame rate returned to normal. He'd managed to take control of twelve combat drones that both he and Maelyn had taken out, and he reassigned their targeting protocols so they'd attack the other drones. Seemingly all at once, the defeated combat drones reactivated and flew up into the air, their weapons taking the others by surprise. The combat drones were thrown into complete disarray because they weren't supposed to attack other combat drones. More of them were taken out, and Quinton quickly recruited them. At some point, Maelyn stopped firing her weapon and simply watched as the drones "killed" each other until there were only his minions on the course.

Quinton stood up and surveyed the battlefield before leaping to the ground as Maelyn walked over to him. He relinquished control of his combat drone attack force, and they sank to the ground.

"Nice trick," Maelyn said.

"Thanks. I just came up with it," Quinton replied.

He heard someone clapping and turned to see Becker and Simon at the entrance.

"This is what you do for fun?" Quinton asked Maelyn.

"Sometimes. It's good to keep active, but I have to admit it usually lasts longer."

They headed back toward the entrance. Becker regarded Quinton for a few moments.

"You took control of the combat drones that had been shot down," Simon said. "Isn't that cheating?"

"If you're not cheating, then you're doing it wrong," Quinton replied.

Becker shook his head and looked at Maelyn. "Kieva says we're approaching the jump point."

"We'll be right there," Maelyn said.

Becker eyed her for a few more moments and then left.

They returned their weapons to the locker, and Maelyn looked at him. "Your reactions are really fast. It's almost as if you knew where the drones were heading before they got there."

"I'm able to adjust my perception of time."

Simon's eyes widened, and he grinned. "You can increase your frame rate?"

"Yes," Quinton replied.

"That's amazing," Simon said and looked at Maelyn. "He can adjust his frame rate, and his perception of time can either quicken or slow down." He looked at Quinton. "But isn't that resource intensive?"

"It is," Quinton agreed. "Without the power regulator, doing it would drain my power core."

Simon nodded. "That makes sense."

"I wonder what kind of soldier you were," Maelyn said.

Quinton had the strange sensation he'd get when trying to frown. "I don't know if I *was* one."

"You can't be serious. You certainly weren't a civilian, not with the way you handled the obstacle course. How do you feel?" she asked.

Quinton considered what she'd said for a few seconds. "I guess I feel better. I like doing something rather than waiting for this body to give out."

"Speaking of which," Simon said, "The Mozeyian Outpost should have what we need."

"Let's go to the bridge and find out," Maelyn said.

She headed for the door, and Quinton called out to her.

"Thanks for doing this," he said.

Maelyn regarded him, but there was something warm in her gaze. She nodded and walked through the doorway.

# CHAPTER SEVENTEEN

THE SHIP JUMPED into the star system where the Mozeyian Outpost temporarily resided. Maelyn had called everyone to the bridge.

"Why does the outpost move around from place to place?" Quinton asked.

"A couple of reasons," Simon replied. "Mobility allows for more salvagers and traders to use the outpost. It's also an information hub since outposts like Mozeyian draw in many frequent travelers. And last, but not least, it's more secure not to dwell anywhere for long periods of time."

Quinton looked at the main holoscreen. The video feed showed a massive space station that had taken up residence central to the system. It was close enough to the inner planets that it made resource acquisition easy enough for smaller ships to make salvage runs but was far enough away from the star's gravitational field to allow it to make an FTL jump.

"There're actually a dozen jump drives that have to be synchronized in order to ensure a successful jump," Simon said.

"How long have they—"

"You couldn't pick somewhere less conspicuous than here?" Becker asked Maelyn.

Quinton and Becker had been playing this game where they chose the most opportune moments to cut the other off in mid-sentence. It was irritating, but Quinton refused to show his frustration. He'd wear out the veteran salvager first.

"Feel free to stay aboard if you want," Maelyn said.

Becker shook his head.

"It's not ideal, but we have the best chance of finding a replacement power core here. We also need to resupply. After that, we'll plan our next steps," Maelyn said.

"The outpost is huge. Finding what we need is going to take forever," Guttman said.

"We'll need to split up, but it shouldn't be that difficult," Maelyn said. "Once we register with the docking authorities, we'll get access to their vendor systems. Then it's just a matter of narrowing down our search."

Becker shook his head again. "By now, Crowe will be monitoring for activity that has anything to do with our PMC friend here."

"You think Crowe somehow knows that my power core is failing and we need to replace it? That's a bit of a stretch, don't you think?" Quinton asked.

Becker pressed his fist against his mouth and puffed out his cheeks. "There is so much wrong with what you just said that I hardly know where to begin."

"It's still a stretch, but I'm sure if you continue to smash rocks together, you'll soon have a whole set to play with."

Becker glared at Quinton.

"Not Crowe," Simon said, drawing their attention toward him. "It's his advisor," he said while snapping his fingers, trying to remember. "Nate Carradine."

Becker nodded, and Guttman did the same. "Carradine probably figured out what he was," Becker said, gesturing toward

Quinton, "before we got off the station. He would have reviewed all the video logs we had and has probably narrowed down the type of robot."

Simon looked at Maelyn. "All it would take would be a few enhanced images for a VI to recreate a model to identify Quinton. He wouldn't know about the power core, but if we're looking for replacement parts . . ."

"Crowe knows we have a PMC. He'll send out scout forces, and an outpost like this would be high on his list," Becker said.

"Yeah, but the Mozeyian Outpost moves around quite a bit to throw off regular traffic-tracking by people like Crowe or even the Collective. Don't get me wrong, they still conduct business with anyone who's willing to trade," Maelyn said.

There were a few moments of silence while they regarded each other.

"So we move fast," Quinton said. "I can access the outpost's systems easy enough and find what we're looking for. Then we just—"

"No!" Simon said and was quickly echoed by Maelyn and Becker.

That irritating frowning sensation registered itself on the agricultural unit's internal systems, and Quinton ignored it.

"Was it something I said?" he asked.

"Let me answer this," Simon said and looked at him. "Sorry about that, Quinton. You need to be careful, or you'll give yourself away. Most systems have better detection for unauthorized access."

"Yeah, but there are ways around that," Quinton said. He'd been accessing ship systems since he'd come on board. It wasn't particularly difficult, and no alarms had been tripped.

"I know there are," Simon said and rubbed the side of his neck, which made that soft scratching noise of fingers scraping the stubble of a few days' worth of beard growth. "We talked about the Federation Wars, but what you don't know is that during those wars, PMC-enhanced ships and weapons were used. These weapons systems, partnered with VIs, made them much more destructive than anything before. As the war went on, PMCs were used to take control of enemy installations wherever they were. In response to this, safeguards were put into place to help detect unauthorized access."

"Okay, but I still don't see what the issue is if I access the outpost's systems," Quinton said.

Becker exhaled forcefully. "You see, this is what I'm talking about," he said to Maelyn and the others, then looked at Quinton. "It always comes back to what you are. Constructs like you are the reason why the Federation Wars were so destructive in the first place. On top of that, most of them went insane, which made everything pretty un-fucking-stable. Get it now? There are systems in place to detect and safeguard against anything you try."

Quinton glanced at the others and then looked at Becker. "One, I'm not insane. Two, what do you mean by everything?"

"He literally means everything," Maelyn said. "Entire federations and star nations were toppled and scattered during the wars."

"What! That can't be right. There were risks in becoming a Personality Matrix Construct, but there were safeguards—stars. That's what the VIs were meant to do," Quinton said.

"Yeah, well somewhere along the line, they failed, and that's when things got worse," Becker said.

The agricultural unit was intended to cultivate exotic plant life, but those same systems were highly attuned to other living creatures. Quinton was able to see the biometrics of everyone on the bridge—most notably their level of agitation, even if they were temporarily working together for a mutual gain.

"What else? Tell me the rest of it," Quinton said.

Becker began to speak, but Maelyn cut him off. "Shut up. I'll do it, thank you very much," she said. Becker rolled his eyes, and

Maelyn looked at Quinton. "Okay, look, we don't have time to go into the minutiae here, so this is going to be high-level. The galactic sectors had already been fighting for many years when the PMCs began to change. No one knows how it began. Reports are fragmented and, in some cases, unreliable. What we do know is that remnant militaries joined together to deal with the new threat," she said and paused for a moment before continuing. "You've heard us mention Sentinel fleets?"

"Yes," Quinton replied. "It's on my list of things to ask you about."

"They were created in response to the rogue PMC attack forces," Maelyn said.

"Rogue PMCs? What does that even mean?"

"They were the ones who went insane. Their safeguards didn't work. Millions died. It's what's going to happen to you," Becker said, and something ugly flickered far back in his eyes.

Quinton turned toward him, clenched metallic fists rising. "I'd be careful if I were you," he said in a quiet, deadly tone.

"Hey," Maelyn said, "look at me," and Quinton turned toward her. "You asked, remember. The fact is, Becker's right. There were large numbers of PMCs who went insane and just weren't human anymore. The safeguards *did* fail. Not all of them, though, but we're getting sidetracked. The Sentinels were created to fight the PMC fleets."

"But what are they?"

"They're a combination of VIs and PMCs, but with many more controls in place. Certain behavioral modifications were removed to make them obedient."

"Obedient!" Quinton shouted. "You mean they enslaved the Sentinels?" He spun around, his gaze taking them all in at once.

"Yes," Maelyn said, and he turned back toward her. "Yes. They were enslaved. They were the answer to a very dark time in our galaxy's history."

Quinton leaned back. "You're looking for a way to do the

same thing to me," he said, taking a few steps away from them. "I almost fell for it too. I was willing to go along with it."

"No, that's not the plan," Maelyn said.

Quinton was constantly aware of all the ship's systems, including how they interacted and where their access ports were. They'd been cataloged by Radek and were available for his use. He'd done this in case Becker or any of the others tried to do something to him.

"I'm finding it hard to believe you," Quinton said.

Becker growled. "I should have known this was going to happen," he said and pulled out a hand cannon. It was fully charged and online.

Quinton accessed the combat suppression systems on the bridge, and a stunner bolt singed Becker's hand. Quinton closed the distance on the salvager and slammed him against the wall. "I told you that if you came at me, it wouldn't go well for you," he said and he turned his head toward Guttman. "Take another step and he dies. Then I'm coming for you."

Thick metallic hands squeezed Becker's shoulders, and he involuntarily cried out.

A stunner bolt struck Quinton's side, and a barrage of warnings appeared on his HUD. He wobbled on his feet for a moment.

"The next one will fry the power regulator," Maelyn said. "Now, put him down."

Quinton turned his head toward her. Gone was the pleasant, amicable, beautiful face. In its place was a hardened ship captain who meant what she said.

"Don't make me do it," she said. "I know you're in the system, but so am I."

Quinton turned back toward Becker. The salvager's hardened gaze was all anger, with the promise of retribution. Then Quinton dropped him to the floor and backed away. He walked toward

Maelyn, ignoring Becker, but he monitored both of them through the ship's security systems.

"He threatened me," Quinton said.

"Indeed, he did," Maelyn replied.

"You can't trust him," Becker growled.

"The only thing that's not safe around here is you. If you want, I can leave you on the outpost. Do you want out?" Maelyn asked. She looked at Becker, Guttman, and Oscar in turn. They were silent. "I didn't think so. Next time you do something like that, our deal is off and you're off this ship. Do you understand?"

Becker clenched his teeth and looked at Quinton. "Fine."

"Don't mention it," Quinton said. "Next time, you'll have to be quicker."

Becker's mouth twisted into a partial sneer, and then he nodded a little.

"So, these Sentinels are still around?" Quinton asked.

Maelyn nodded. "Yes, they are."

"I thought the Federation Wars have been over for a long time now," Quinton said and looked at Simon for a moment. "Why are the Sentinels still around?"

"They're still performing their primary function—hunting down all PMC-controlled systems and class tech and destroying them," Maelyn said.

Quinton knew he shouldn't have been able to feel cold or shiver, but he definitely felt something. The truth was written on all their faces, a certainty that unified them all, even Becker, and it was impossible for him to ignore.

"So Becker's right," Quinton said. "Me being here puts you all in danger from these Sentinels."

Maelyn regarded Quinton for a few moments, her gaze calculating. Then she nodded. "There is always the risk of crossing paths with one of their fleets."

"Why are they still around? Why haven't they disbanded?" Quinton asked.

"Because no one is left to order them to stop. You have to understand that things were fragmenting. Groups were diverging, and people were just trying to survive long enough for the Sentinels to help establish some stability," Maelyn said.

"Yeah," Becker said derisively. "Except for the occasional case of mistaken identity, the Sentinel program worked wonders."

Quinton couldn't think of a snappy reply. He thought that if he had his physical body, he might have felt sick. But all he felt was an enduring numbness devoid of any of the emotions he should be feeling. What was wrong with him?

"Radek," Quinton said internally, "what's happening to me?"

"Emotional spike is being suppressed to keep system integrity," Radek replied.

"Damn it, Radek," he said aloud this time, startling the others. "Just stop it right now. I need . . . I need to feel." There was a rasp to his voice that hadn't been there before. He saw Becker look at the others with his eyebrows raised.

"Radek is his virtual intelligence assistant," Simon said quietly.

Quinton ignored them. He needed to process the information he'd been given, and his emotions were part of that process. He couldn't make smart choices if his emotions were dulled down to meaningless drivel.

"Everyone off the bridge," Maelyn said. "Give him some space. Go on. I'm serious. Get off the bridge now."

Quinton heard the others leave, and he looked up to see that Maelyn and Simon had stayed behind. Vonya lingered in the doorway, looking as if she wanted to say something. Maelyn gestured for her to go, and the Servitor left them.

Quinton tried to catch up with his racing thoughts as they spread out from him like rays of starlight, each one attached to a truth that he hadn't even considered, along with a promise that he wasn't ready to face. He'd woken up to a galaxy that he didn't recognize. He was a man out of time and without his own body.

Why had he been brought online at all? What was he supposed to do? He felt the questions stack up, forming a huge wall that he was almost afraid to climb.

"Quinton, are you still with us?" Maelyn asked.

He didn't respond. He couldn't. He was still grappling with the harsh reality that had been thrust upon him. Now he understood Simon's reluctance to go into details. He'd been trying to protect him. Even Becker's contempt was making more sense.

"Quinton," Maelyn said. There was a note of concern in her voice. "Simon, can you do something for him?"

"I . . . I can't. We have to wait for him to respond."

"We can't lose this. There has to be something we can do."

Maelyn came to stand in front of Quinton. Her large blue eyes looked up at him, searching for some sign of life. "You said you couldn't remember anything. What's your full name? I just realized that you never told us. I'm Maelyn Wayborn."

Quinton still couldn't answer. It was as if he couldn't break free of this inner turmoil that surrounded him. It was if he were standing in the middle of an explosion engulfed by flames, and the truth burned.

"Answer me," Maelyn said with a little bit of force behind her words. "You have to answer me. What is your full name?"

His name?

A vague impression of the agricultural unit's lack of frowning ability registered and was immediately dismissed.

"Quinton," he said softly, and Maelyn exhaled. "Quinton Aldren."

*Acheron Confederacy Navy.*

He tried to follow his thoughts to where this knowledge was contained in his ESS, but he couldn't reach it.

"Keep him talking," Simon said.

"Stay with me, Quinton. I can help you find out more about it. About who you are. I promise. I was never going to betray you. You've got to trust me on that," Maelyn said.

Quinton focused his attention on a couple of different things —the sound of Maelyn's voice, Simon speaking in hushed tones, and his own name. Names were powerful things. They anchored people to their identity, and he had his name. That was something that hadn't been kept from him. The inner storm raging inside him dissipated, and Quinton felt more focused and in control.

"I'm not going anywhere," he said. "You can trust me on that."

Maelyn smiled and looked at Simon.

"We were worried that as you learned more about what had happened, it would . . ." Simon said and paused for a moment.

"I know what you were trying to do. You were looking out for me," Quinton said. "But I still don't understand why it's so dangerous if I access the station's computer systems."

"Because the way you access systems is different than if we do it," Simon said.

"That's absurd."

"No, it's not," Simon replied. "Really, it's not. The rest of us have to go through authentication protocols. You can bypass them without even trying. It's part of the subspace comlink transceiver that you adapted."

"I didn't adapt—"

"Actually," Radek said, "it was part of the startup enhancements I made when I brought the agricultural unit online, and it interfaced with the ESS. It's part of the ESS core."

"Never mind," Quinton said to the others. "Radek just explained it to me."

"Good," Maelyn said. "So you understand why you need to stay aboard the ship while the rest of us go to the outpost."

"Uh, what," Quinton said. "Can you say that again?"

"You need to stay behind. We can't risk bringing you onto the outpost station. Too many things could go wrong. Becker's right about that too. Crowe will certainly have people monitoring all the trading outposts in this sector. I never did get access to his network of agents, but the reports are that they're quite extensive," Maelyn said.

"I'm not staying on the ship," Quinton said.

Maelyn frowned. She looked perplexed that he hadn't seen the wisdom of her logic.

"I said, I'm not staying on the ship. There's no way I'm staying behind. It's not going to happen," Quinton said. "Think of some other solution because I'm going to that station with the rest of you."

Maelyn and Simon exchanged a glance.

Simon pressed his lips together in thought. "I might be able to help," he said and looked at Quinton. "A disguise."

Quinton nodded. "That sounds perfectly reasonable. Let's do that."

# CHAPTER EIGHTEEN

QUINTON LOOKED at himself through the ship's security feed. He wore clothing—tan pants, boots, a shirt, and a long, thick jacket with the hood pulled up over his head. He glanced up at the camera and could see the faint glow of his eyes from within the dark folds of the hood.

He would appear more out of place than if he just went as . . . himself. "Ridiculous. This can't be what passes for incognito. I might as well walk in there carrying a sign."

Maelyn glanced at him and shook her head. "Nonsense. Most people's attention will be on Vonya."

Quinton looked at the Servitor, whose smile lifted her high cheekbones. She still had on a tight-fitting amber-colored shirt with much of her midriff exposed, and a ivory skirt that showed her smooth well-toned legs as she walked.

"You're okay with this? I thought you were going to check in with the other Servitors and get your own transport," Quinton said.

"Of course, I'm okay with this," Vonya replied. "I do appreciate your concern, but you really don't have to worry. I owe a debt to Captain Wayborn in exchange for my accommodations."

He wasn't worried. At least not that much. He just didn't want to wear these clothes.

"I'm sure both you and Toros Becker will dissuade any unwanted attention," Vonya said.

That was the other part of the plan Quinton didn't appreciate. Becker was coming with them. Both he and Quinton were posing as hired security. Quinton was pretending he was a Yezierian. Simon had explained that the Yezierians were from the former Tilion Empire. They'd enhanced themselves through cybernetic implants and exoskeleton replacement limbs. Yezierians hired themselves out, and once in a contract, they remained loyal until the contract was completed. Quinton was a bit surprised by that last part because, based on his own observations from his somewhat limited interactions with other people, he'd just assumed that the Yezierians would function as mercenaries—no loyalty except for whoever had the most to trade. There wasn't a large population of them, but they were known. All he had to worry about— as if it was just one thing— was whether they'd run into any other Yezierians on the outpost. He doubted they would simply go along with someone pretending to be one of them.

Simon looked at Maelyn. "I wish you'd reconsider."

"I know you do, but the fewer of us going onto the outpost, the better," Maelyn said. She glanced at the others who were staying behind. "I can't leave them alone with Kieva on the ship."

Guttman and Oscar were also staying behind. They weren't happy with the decision either, but both men hadn't protested much after they learned that Becker was on the away team.

"Come on, let's get going so we can get out of here," Becker said, and looked at Quinton. "That is, of course, if there aren't any more outbursts."

"You never know what will happen," Quinton replied.

"I swear, if you give us away—"

"Yes, yes, I know just where the blaster will be pointed."

Vonya looked at them both and inclined her head. Becker's gaze softened a little.

"All right," Maelyn said. "Simon, monitor the info-nets for anything out of the ordinary."

"Will do, Captain," Simon replied.

They flew the ship to the Mozeyian Outpost, and Quinton withdrew his access to the ship's systems. When he had done so, Simon looked at him and gave him a curt nod. Quinton still didn't fully understand how any type of secure detection system could detect PMC access. While they were on their final approach to the Mozeyian Outpost docking platform, he cranked up his frame rate.

"Radek, I can't think of how they'd do it. Do you have anything?"

"Just theories. It would have to be something that we would need to test. But there must be some kind of pattern recognition where the detection protocols categorize and keep track of all data communications throughout the entire system," Radek said.

Quinton had come to rely on increasing his frame rate because it gave him some much-needed time to consider his options. The risk was that he was going to wear out the aged components of the agricultural unit. He tried to use the ability sparingly, but he just needed to think these things through. However, in real time, there would be less than fifteen minutes before the ship docked, and he wanted to have some idea of what he was walking into.

"I understand the theory, but I just don't think it's possible, not without severe degradation. They must be looking for something else. There's no way they can keep track of every single access point on their systems," Quinton replied.

"Perhaps, but how else would it work?"

Quinton felt an urge to sigh but knew he couldn't. If Radek was asking questions, then even the VI was perplexed. "Well, if I was trying to prevent . . ." He went quiet for a moment. "No, that's not correct. Simon and Maelyn never said that they were preventing access. They were simply detecting it, and then alarms would be raised. If the purpose of whatever monitoring systems they're using is only to detect certain types of unauthorized access, then they probably can't prevent it. At least not quickly. They must be looking for a pattern on even standard communication protocols. The first thing that comes to my mind is the ease with which I can access multiple systems."

"Also bypassing security measures."

"It makes sense, but it wouldn't lead to detection because I've been able to bypass any security measures I've found so far. Perhaps they monitor for multiple data connections that exhibit the same type of behavior at the same time," Quinton said, speaking slowly. "But that would mean they would need to be able to determine what's random and what's intentional."

"They must have perfected their method of detection because, according to Captain Wayborn and all the others, it's supposed to be extremely reliable," Radek said.

"I'm not sure how they'd know for sure since there haven't been that many PMCs around, although that fact could be evidence alone for its effectiveness. But there has to be a way we can know for sure," Quinton said.

"I don't think that's possible. What you're asking for is an early warning for an already sophisticated detection mechanism meant to prevent what you might try to do," Radek replied.

"Well, I haven't done anything yet, but I'm not—I need to have the option to access the systems that are around me. I can't simply cut myself off. There has to be some kind of middle ground."

"The highest probability for success would be to only access the system from one entry point at a time. Also, you must adhere to the protocols of the system you're on."

Quinton thought about that for a few moments. "You'll need to help me with that then. Can you do that?"

"It should be possible."

He supposed that this was as close to an affirmative as he was going to get from the VI.

"Has there been any change with the lockout protocols since we learned more about the Federation Wars and the Sentinels?" Quinton asked.

"Negative, but I do agree that these revelations are alarming. You should try to find out more about that."

Quinton must never underestimate Radek's propensity for stating the obvious. "Thank you, Radek."

Quinton returned the frame rate back to normal. Only a few microseconds had passed in real time.

"There's an issue with our clearance," Simon said.

Maelyn frowned for a moment. "Got it. Send out identification again."

"That worked," Simon said.

"What did they want?" Quinton asked.

"The ship identifier was stripped of its name, and I reauthorized it," Maelyn said.

"What's the ship's name?"

"The *Nebulon*."

Quinton nodded and waited.

"We're cleared for final approach to the docking platform," Simon said.

Maelyn led them to the portside airlock. Vonya watched the airlock doors with a bit of wide-eyed excitement. Quinton wasn't excited. He just needed to get a new power core.

"Let's say we do find this power core," Becker said. "How do we replace it without the ESS going offline?"

"The ESS has its own power supply, so I won't be offline," Quinton replied.

"Are you sure about that?"

Quinton wanted to reply that he was, but he couldn't.

"That's what I thought," Becker said.

Maelyn cleared her throat. "We have a list of potential places that will have what we need," she said and looked at Quinton. "Remember what we talked about. It's imperative that you stay out of the outpost's systems unless you use one of the designated consoles."

"I understand."

"Also, try not to overreact," Becker said.

Quinton knew he was being goaded. "To what?"

"Everything that you're about to see. If they're right and you predate the Federation Wars, then some of what you're about to see might . . ." Becker paused with a wide smile. "I'll just let you find out for yourself."

Maelyn rolled her eyes and opened the airlock. They entered the transit tunnel, which had an automated walkway that led toward the check-in counter, where she paid their docking fees.

Quinton looked around and saw that most people looked normal. They were all human. They weren't at all like what Simon had described. Becker watched him from time to time, and for once he was glad the agricultural bot had limited facial expressions.

They entered the transit hub and got onto a tram that took them to one of the Mozeyian Outpost's trading floors. The tram was a single sleek metallic tube that wasn't very long, but it moved quickly through the shaft. The trip was over in seconds, and they disembarked. That was when the freak show really became apparent.

The others started to walk, but Quinton stopped and looked at the wide-open multi-leveled inner sanctum of the outpost. Crosswalks connected the different levels above and below. He saw platforms with counter-grav emitters rise into the air, bringing patrons to the level of their choice. There were covered corridors that led to other parts of the colossal space station as well.

Quinton hastened to catch up with the others. Maelyn led

them, Vonya followed, and Becker and Quinton brought up the rear. Their plan that Vonya would be a distraction to everyone they passed was right on the mark. Vonya strode with liquid grace, from her long platinum hair to her slender arms, as if she were a queen walking among her subjects. She occasionally made polite eye contact and gave a small nod of her head in acknowledgment of the people they passed, but otherwise, she followed Maelyn. No one gave Becker or Quinton a second glance.

Quinton looked around at the various storefronts they'd walked by. One thing that was almost immediately apparent to him was the fact that there was hardly anything new. Everything that was being traded was used, as if the galactic residents were living off the bones of the past, creating nothing themselves.

They stopped at one of the smaller storefronts that looked like it had third-hand rejects from some of the other traders. Quinton doubted any of the equipment inside actually worked. Why would anyone trade anything there? He was about to ask Maelyn when she walked in and headed for the counter.

Standing behind the counter were three men who appeared to be clones of one another. Their skin was pasty yellow, with small dark age spots on their bald heads.

"We have a customer," the centermost one said in a voice that was devoid of life and inflection. The other two men looked at them with that same dispassionate gaze.

Maelyn walked right up to the first one. "I have a list of things I'm looking for, and I'm hoping you might be able to point me in the right direction. I'll pay for the information, of course."

"Transmit your list," the man said.

Maelyn did. They'd put together a rather extensive list of things to be purchased, and within it was a power core that should be compatible with Quinton's agricultural unit.

The man quickly examined the list and looked at Maelyn. "First, you transfer credits, and then I will update your list with the appropriate storefronts that should have what you're looking for."

"Should have," Becker said. "For a paying customer, I expect better assurances than that."

The man looked at Becker. "You're paying for our intimate knowledge of the outpost. No one except the actual storefronts has the most accurate inventory of what they have in stock. You always have the option of trying to find what you need on your own, but I'm afraid that option takes the longest and carries with it a significant probability of failure."

"Time is important to us all," Maelyn said. "I've transferred the credits, as you requested."

The man looked over to one of his "brothers," who gave a single nod. Then he brought Maelyn's list up on his personal holoscreen, which immediately populated with corresponding storefronts for everything on the list.

"I've highlighted the storefronts that will have most of what you're looking for. Some of the things on your list are quite specific," the man said. He watched her for a few moments.

"Thank you. I'm sure it will help us greatly."

The man looked down at his holoscreen, made a passing gesture, and the data refreshed on Maelyn's personal holoscreen. She glanced at it for a moment and nodded, satisfied. Without another word, she turned around and walked toward the exit. Quinton glanced at the three men, who watched them with almost lifeless stares that he found unsettling. The whole encounter had felt as if they'd been interacting with people who'd had the life drained out of them. Simon had told Quinton that there were many groups of "humans" that had genetically modified themselves to adapt to surviving in the galaxy, but he couldn't come up with a practical reason why someone would forgo emotion and perhaps empathy in favor of pure logic. He wondered if the genetic modifications could be reversed.

Over the next several hours, they made their way through

the outpost. There were more than a few people interested in purchasing time with Vonya. At first, Quinton had assumed that most interests were of a sexual nature, and there was plenty of that, but the vast majority of people desired a consultation for any number of situations. They sought comfort and reassurance that their troubles would lessen over time, that there were worlds left to discover where they could live. People would approach them, their gaze on Vonya, but the Servitor always deferred to Maelyn, who allowed Vonya to speak with them. Even Becker, who was impatient to keep moving, looked on with an expression between the harshness forged from an unrelenting galaxy and peaceful respite, but only for a few moments.

Quinton watched the encounters, wondering why anyone would seek comfort from a Servitor. Vonya had an angelic beauty —from the way she looked to the sound of her voice to the way she spoke. But Servitors lived to serve everyone else in whatever capacity was required. After a few gatherings, it finally started to make more sense. People were searching for an escape. They were looking for hope, but not everyone.

The Mozeyian Outpost had a mixed population of salvagers and mercenaries, as well as the people who hired them. It wasn't a safe place, but there was an order to it where people could conduct their business. The more Quinton observed, the more out of place he felt. It was a strange feeling to walk here, and the surroundings felt like they should have been familiar. The design of the decks, bulkhead doors, and some of the little things like tools, scanners, and even some of the service bots gave Quinton the strange sensation of being both familiar and foreign all at the same time, as if he were dreaming of a place he used to frequent, but it was a place he'd never been.

"It's time for us to move on," Maelyn announced.

Vonya looked around with an apologetic smile and empathy in her luminous gaze. The cluster of people began to disperse.

Quinton looked at Maelyn. "I didn't think they'd leave so quickly."

"It was expected," she replied.

"Captain Wayborn is my employer. She has the final say on how I am to execute my duties," Vonya said.

Quinton glanced at Maelyn, who shrugged.

They resumed their search. They'd been to a storefront that specialized in robot maintenance and repair. To throw off any of the data-sniffers monitoring for inquiries searching for an exact match for the agricultural bot's power core, they'd decided to look for similar cores but nothing exact. They needed something that was compatible, but it was proving to be much more difficult to find than they'd previously expected.

"We're running out of places to check," Becker said.

Quinton had chosen to remain as unobtrusive as possible, which included limiting communication with the others.

"I know," Maelyn said.

She checked her personal holoscreen and frowned. Becker and Vonya moved closer. They began discussing their options.

"The problem is that most of the available power cores are too damn powerful. Even with the regulators, we'd risk overloading his systems," Maelyn said.

*His systems . . .*

They weren't *his* systems. The agricultural unit wasn't Quinton. The others had the propensity to not make the distinction. Quinton wouldn't allow himself to think in terms of the agricultural unit and longevity. It was an unfortunate set of circumstances that had put his ESS into this robot body and nothing more.

"Can't we find something Simon could modify to keep him running?" Becker asked.

Quinton walked away from the others because he didn't want to listen to them anymore. This wasn't the time or the place. They were partway into a wide-open court with booths in the middle and shops along the edges. The area was filled with people. He put some distance between himself and the others. He hadn't accessed any of the Mozeyian Outpost's computer systems, but he could detect the multitude of comlinks and data feeds in the surrounding area without directly accessing them. The secure systems weren't broadcasting anything, but they were easy enough to find if he really needed to.

Quinton glanced at the others, who were still huddled over Maelyn's holoscreen, discussing their options. He walked over to a nearby storefront that looked filled with . . . a little bit of everything. There was no specialization at all. The storefront was home to everything that didn't have a home, and the equipment didn't appear to be in that great of shape. Quinton stood a few feet outside the entrance and saw that there were more than a few patrons inside.

After a few moments, he decided to enter. As he walked inside, several people glanced in his direction and quickly averted their gaze. Most of Quinton's face was covered by the hood he wore, but they also wore face coverings. The patrons were all armed, some more heavily than others. An older man walked out from behind the counter. The name "Rosevier" appeared near his face on Quinton's HUD. The man must have been broadcasting it.

Three men approached Rosevier and seemed to communicate with him, but without speaking. Quinton tried to listen by raising the sensitivity of his auditory systems, but it was no use. He saw that the group had entered a private comlink session. He glanced at the others inside the store, and they didn't appear to care about the private conversation going on around them. He accessed the storefront systems. They were open to anyone, and he was able to see the private session clearly indicated among the open comlinks. They weren't taking any steps to hide what they were doing beyond not wanting to be overheard. He watched the pattern of data that started out as indecipherable, but then it appeared in clear text.

"What rumors are you talking about?" Rosevier asked.

Quinton glanced around, almost positive that alarms were going to sound at any moment. "Radek, what the hell just happened?" he asked internally.

"It's the translator protocol VI. It can decipher encrypted messages. They're only using a basic form of protection."

"Is this going to alert any detection systems?"

"Not likely. They're using a closed system that isolates them from the outpost's main systems."

Radek's advice had been inconsistently reliable in the past, and he hoped his VI was right this time.

"Happenings on the galactic net. Sentinel activity. Several large salvager operations being more active," Solin said.

"There are always rumors about Sentinel fleet activity. Keep doing what the rest of us do out in the verse. Avoid them, and they'll leave you alone. Engaging them, even to open communications, is to invite trouble the likes of which no one is prepared for, not even the Collective," Rosevier replied.

Solin glanced at his silent partners before turning back to Rosevier. "The price I'm paying you should give me more than what's already common knowledge."

"You paid for the knowledge I can share. I can't help it if there isn't anything new."

"How about something else then? Another query, since the last one wasn't so informative."

Rosevier's gaze flicked toward their holstered weapons, and then he inclined his head once. "Ask."

"Crowe is paying for any leads to a salvager group that stole something from the Union."

"That's it? You're going to have to give me more to go on than that."

"He's particularly interested in an older agricultural bot—

something that would have been used on one of the old colony worlds. Have you seen anything like that?" Solin asked.

Quinton turned away from them, pretending he'd seen something interesting on the other side of the shop.

"Have I seen anything like an old robot?" Rosevier said and then made a grandiose gesture toward his surroundings. "Take a look around. I'm surrounded by old robot parts. I've got all manner of cast-offs, pieces that belong to counter-grav emitters," he said and frowned. "Some might even work. Oh yeah, I've got a whole storage area of Jordani emergency docking clamp systems, which is great for shuttles navigating some of those ancient battlefields. That's where the real credits are."

"I didn't ask about Jordani docking clamps," Solin said, stepping closer to Rosevier.

"You don't like Jordani, that's fine. I've got a rare find you might be interested in," Rosevier said, and glanced conspiratorially from side to side. "Acheron made."

Solin's two companions hissed and closed in on Rosevier.

"Calm down. Geez. Everyone hates Acheron, but they made the best tech the galaxy has ever seen, and it's still in perfect working order."

Quinton had been so focused on the conversation that he hadn't noticed most of the other patrons heading toward the exit. There was a loud commotion coming from outside. He peered out but couldn't see anything. Still connected to the storefront's computer systems, he accessed the video feeds that covered the entrance. They were higher up and gave him a better vantage point. There was a heated exchange between several groups of people about five storefronts away. He panned the video feed across the court and saw Mozeyian peacekeepers heading over. They wore black helmets that covered their faces, along with armored mesh suits. Assault rifles were strapped to their backs, and they strode into the atrium with authority. Most were Becker's size or taller.

Quinton looked over to where Maelyn and the others had been and saw that they were surrounded by a group of mercenaries.

The private chat area became disabled.

"There's something going on out there," Solin said.

"Probably time for you to leave," Rosevier said. Solin peered outside but didn't move. "Seriously," Rosevier said. "Competing salvager clans are about to clash. I'm going to have to close up shop while the enforcers sort it out."

Quinton ducked down one of the aisles and opened a comlink to Maelyn. "I'm in one of the storefronts across from your position."

He saw Maelyn's gaze flick toward his location for a scarce moment before she refocused on the person she was speaking with.

"Wallace," Maelyn said, "I already told you I'm going to check in. Don't make this more than what it is," she said and looked over to where Quinton was located, giving a slight shake of her head. She'd left her comlink open so he could hear her, but then she closed it.

Sounds of footsteps came toward Quinton, and Rosevier looked around the corner of the aisle.

"You're not nearly as sneaky as you think you are," Rosevier said. One of his eyes glowed green from an artificial orb.

Quinton stood up, and Rosevier tried to see under his hood. Quinton looked away at the empty store. "I thought I saw something I was looking for," he replied.

Rosevier arched an eyebrow. "Is that so? Was it these used sanitation processors, or was it the private meeting room whose security measures you managed to make a mockery of?"

"You looked like you could use some help with those guys."

Rosevier grinned a little, his cybernetic eye gleaming. "Is that so? Are you some kind of guardian?" he asked and gave him a once-over. "I don't think so."

"You're right about that."

"Well then," Rosevier said and tilted his head toward the exit. "Time for you to leave."

The doors slammed shut, and Rosevier rolled his eyes. "Damn enforcers. Every chance they get they pull that security override to lock everyone down."

Quinton looked at the door, and Rosevier narrowed his gaze at him. "You're not a Yezierian."

Quinton considered denying it for all of half a second, then decided on a more direct approach to the problem. "Need me to prove it," he said, stepping toward the man.

Rosevier shook his head. "Don't do anything rash. Do you think you're the first person to come to this outpost wanting to hide their identity? This whole station is full of people not wanting attention drawn to them. It's why people come here."

Quinton regarded him for a few moments. "So, are we gonna have a problem?"

Rosevier held up his hands but didn't back away. "No."

"Good, then you'll help me get out of here."

"Can't."

"Why not?"

Rosevier frowned. "The lockdown."

Quinton was still connected to the storefront's video surveillance systems. He saw that the enforcers were going from storefront to storefront, opening the doors and making everyone come outside.

*Not good!*

"Do they normally search the area when they're trying to keep the peace?" Quinton asked.

Rosevier glanced at the door and walked over to the console behind the counter, bringing up the same video feed Quinton was watching. "They must be searching for someone," he said, and he arched an eyebrow toward him.

Quinton closed the distance and locked down the console. Rosevier looked at it, frowning, then lifted his gaze back to him.

"Now, don't do anything stupid," Quinton said.

"They're looking for you."

"I don't know about that, but I'd just as soon not be found."

"How did you turn off my console? Are you . . . All right, what's going on here? How the hell are you on my system?"

"You were the one who made a closed system. I just happened to have needed access to it," Quinton said.

"What do you want?"

That annoying frown-but-can't-frown sensation registered itself on the agricultural unit's systems. Quinton wondered if he could have Radek filter those unhelpful lapses so he didn't have to be aware of them. He couldn't take the time to explain it to Radek now though.

Quinton leaned toward the counter. "I need a new power core."

Rosevier's mouth opened partway, and he snorted. "A power core. Is that all? What kind?"

Quinton opened his personal holoscreen and showed Rosevier the specifications.

The shop owner looked at it and nodded. "That's odd. An old one too."

"Do you have it or something like it?"

"I might," Rosevier said. "For the right price, that is."

*How about I don't kill you where you stand*, Quinton thought and then chided himself for the harshness of it.

"What do you want?" he asked.

The enforcers were working their way closer. He also saw that Maelyn and the others were still speaking with the mercenaries. Becker looked ready to open fire, and Vonya smiled at everyone. Maybe it was better that he was in here.

"We'll get to that, but first I need to access this console so I can look at my inventory," Rosevier said.

Quinton didn't trust the man. He'd been too quick to seize the upper hand. If he was granted access, then he could raise an alarm, or worse. Quinton decided to find the inventory subsystem and run his own search, but the system was coded with a custom records-management process that he had no hope of deciphering quickly. He came around the counter to stand behind Rosevier and activated the console.

"Don't try anything foolish. I'm not violent by nature, but I'm getting backed into a corner here," Quinton said.

Rosevier gave him a curt nod and gestured toward the console. "Pesky thing, our inventory system. My business partner, Gervais, made us get it so that even if someone infiltrated our systems, they wouldn't be able to figure out what we actually have. The only way to decipher it is up here," he said and tapped the side of his head next to his artificial eye.

"How clever of you," Quinton said dryly. "Now get searching."

Rosevier nodded and accessed the console. A few minutes later, he brought up an image of a power core that closely resembled the one in Quinton's chest cavity. "It looks like I do have something similar to what you need," he said, sounding a little surprised that he'd found it. His eyes scanned the information. "Hmm, this is for older service bot models. I can see why you had so much trouble finding a replacement. The designers made the power core in such a way that you could only get it from the manufacturer. How greedy of them." He regarded Quinton for a moment. "I've got one in back. I can go get it for you, but I bet you'll want to follow me back there."

"I'm not letting you out of my sight," Quinton said and gestured for Rosevier to lead the way.

The shop owner led him to the back and palmed the security panel that granted them access to the storage room. The room was triple the size of the actual storefront, with aisles of freestanding shelving that were packed with various items. Rows of amber lighting lined the shelves, casting a soft glow in the dimly lit storage room.

Rosevier led him down one of the aisles toward the back.

"Where do you get all this stuff?" Quinton asked.

"Mostly by trade. Others are things that Gervais sought out. He'll go out and try to acquire the rare items that spacers are searching for while I handle the day-to-day operations of the storefront."

"Your partner."

"That's right. He's my sister's husband. We've been partners for over fifteen years. Started this business and built it up over the years by being smart and not overextending ourselves," Rosevier said.

They reached the back of the storage room where there was another console. Rosevier activated it.

"What are you doing?" Quinton asked.

Rosevier pulled his hands away from the console and looked at Quinton. "I have to bring the power core up from the warehouse."

"Where's that?"

"It's in the lower levels of the outpost. We all have a ware-house storage area. We use these consoles to deliver our products right to the buyer's ship. Oh, by the way, you'll need to transmit your ship ID to me so I know where to send the power core."

"Yeah, sure, that's not going to happen. I want that power core delivered right here," Quinton said, then added, "Who do you need to contact to get it?"

Rosevier frowned. "No one. It's automated. I can get it deliv-ered here as well. I just thought you were in a hurry."

"Fine," Quinton said. "Proceed."

Rosevier nodded and went back to the console. He navigated through the interface and selected a few of the options. "On its way here now," he said and regarded Quinton for a few moments. "We need to discuss payment."

"I can get you paid."

Rosevier narrowed his gaze. "I've heard that before. No deal," he said and went for the console.

Quinton grabbed his arm and pulled back, and the shop owner's gaze slid toward Quinton's robotic hands. He wasn't even afraid. What would it take to make this guy squirm? He needed to get the upper hand.

"Definitely not Yezierian. No, no, you're something else," Rosevier said, his eyes slipping into a calculating glaze.

Quinton activated the cutting shears from his forearm. The darkened razor-sharp blade sprang from its holder, and he shoved Rosevier against the wall. He pressed the blade against the shop owner's throat. "You're focusing on the wrong thing."

Rosevier waggled his eyebrows once and smiled. "Am I?"

"What's wrong with you. You're not even—"

"Afraid," Rosevier said and grinned. "No, not at all. Endocrine suppression controlled by my implants. It's really quite helpful with negotiations." He frowned in thought for a moment. "Well, that and increased logical reasoning. So . . ."

Quinton cranked up his frame rate to maximum. He still had the power regulator Simon had made, but his power core was down to 23 percent. He couldn't intimidate the shop owner, so he had to think of something else to use as leverage. Strong-arm tactics weren't working, but everyone had a weakness, and he needed to figure out what Rosevier's vulnerability was. The shop owner's pale skin and white hair projected an impression of weakness, but he was clever. Quinton had to out-think him.

His gaze took in the console, and a few thoughts came to mind. Rosevier was business-oriented, almost to fault. There had to be something there that Quinton could use against him. He already had a data connection to the shop's systems. With his frame rate cranked to the max, Rosevier was neutralized, but computer systems didn't suffer from such restrictions. He supposed that if he had better equipment, he could process information faster than the shop's computer system. Regardless, he could still access the information he needed.

"Radek, I need your help."

"What do you need?"

Quinton brought up the accounting records on his data connection. "Can you run an analysis on these records and tell me if there's anything out of the ordinary?"

"Of course, but for future reference, if you just access the information, you can initiate a query on your own, and I will assist," Radek replied.

Quinton's awareness of the accounting records grew to encompass two perspectives—those of the observer and those of the analyst—at the same time. Both perspectives fed each other, allowing for logical leaps that brought him closer to what he needed. Then he found it—oh, did he ever find it.

He returned his frame rate back to normal.

"These intimidation tactics won't—" Rosevier was saying, and Quinton interjected.

"Your partner is cheating you," he said.

Rosevier frowned and cocked his head to the side, as if he hadn't heard.

"Gervais is cheating you. You're partners, right? Split everything down the line fifty-fifty?"

Rosevier nodded. "Yes, that's right."

"Well, he makes, on average, 20 percent more on everything than you do."

"That's impossible. I check every transaction myself."

Quinton stepped back and pulled his blade away from the shop owner's throat. "Look for yourself. There are two sets of ledgers. It's right there on the console. Go ahead. Have a look."

Rosevier looked at the console screen, peering at the data on it. He scrolled through a few pages, and then Quinton blanked out the screen. Rosevier frowned and looked at him.

"Do we have a deal?" Quinton asked. "You give me the power

core, and I give you that report. There's fifteen years' worth of data there. Do we have a deal?"

Rosevier looked away and seemed to be considering it. He rubbed his eyes and shook his head, muttering Gervais's name. Then he looked at Quinton. "I'm afraid not. Um, don't get me wrong. This is huge and worth more than an old power core I'd have trouble offloading anyway, but I can't make a deal with you given this," he said, gesturing toward the console. "I'm truly sorry about that."

"You're sorry? What more do you want? I just . . ."

Alerts appeared on Quinton's HUD.

*Power regulator . . . disabled.*

*Power core levels falling.*

*Twenty percent.*

*Eighteen percent.*

*Fifteen percent.*

*Twelve percent.*

Quinton tried to move but couldn't. He looked at Rosevier, who gave him a knowing look. "What have you done to me?"

"I'm afraid you're worth more in trade than doing business with you directly," Rosevier said and inclined his head a little while pressing his lips together. "You can't move. Just a little suppression field that interferes with motor control."

*Nine percent.*

Quinton stopped trying to move in the hopes that he'd consume less power.

*Seven percent.*

Quinton began to panic. He knew he should try to conserve his energy, but he was about to go into standby. Rosevier must have guessed what Quinton was. He'd pull out his ESS and sell it to the highest bidder. Then Quinton would be enslaved.

He felt a mental shudder.

Enslaved.

*Five percent.*

A large panel next to the console opened, and a small storage container was deposited onto the ground.

"Oh, it looks like that power core you need just arrived," Rosevier said. He leaned down and opened the container. Inside was a cube that glowed in a faint yellow. He picked it up in one hand and regarded Quinton for a moment. Then he walked over, casually tossing the precious power core up in the air and catching it, and pushed back the hood covering Quinton's head.

"The suppression field drains that power core you have in your chest."

*Three percent.*

"There's something else I haven't told you," Quinton said.

Rosevier looked amused. "What's that?"

"Gervais has also been lying to the Mozeyian Outpost finance officer. You haven't been paying the proper fees based on your actual income."

Rosevier's expression faltered. "Then they'll take it up with Gervais."

Quinton laughed. "He's not here, so they'll come after the next best thing—you."

Rosevier's eyes darted from side to side while he considered the implications.

"I don't know as much as you do about this outpost, but my guess is that they take being cheated very seriously, and when they learn about you—"

"Stop."

"Turn off the suppression field."

Rosevier did, and Quinton's power core was holding at only 2 percent. There was no way he could make it back to the ship.

"Now replace the power core in my chest."

"You'd trust me to do that?"

"No, you idiot. I don't trust you at all, but you're all I've got. To keep you honest, I have a timed message waiting to be sent with all the incriminating evidence. And if you get any other ideas, I also tasked your automated delivery system to offload your entire stockpile as a generous donation," Quinton said.

Rosevier narrowed his gaze and sneered.

"You have less than two minutes. Now get over here and replace this thing," Quinton said, opening his chest piece.

Radek went on standby—not that he could actually do anything while the power core was being replaced, but he'd be the first to come back online.

Rosevier regarded Quinton for a few long moments and then nodded. He'd been beaten. All that was left was damage control. "You'll stop everything if I replace the power core, right?"

"I said I would. Now quit stalling."

Rosevier reached inside the agricultural unit's chest piece and initiated the shutdown-and-replace procedure.

Quinton's perception of everything around him went dark.

# CHAPTER NINETEEN

QUINTON SNAPPED BACK INTO CONSCIOUSNESS.

*System diagnostic running.*

*All systems operational.*

*Upgraded power core operating at 100 percent.*

*Veris initiation complete.*

*System startup complete.*

*Autonomous mode has been activated.*

He remembered the last time he'd woken up. The agricultural unit had gone through a startup sequence that exposed a number of broken systems. Some were even critical, but somehow there were enough working that Quinton was able to keep going. This time, not only was the startup sequence quick, but systems were green across the board. He was still in danger, but at least he didn't have mechs hunting him. He couldn't expect to have everything go his way, but it was gratifying not to see a warning about the power core on his HUD.

Quinton raised his gaze and saw Rosevier standing a few feet away.

"I did as you asked. Now do your part," Rosevier said.

Quinton didn't respond right away. The agricultural unit's

internal systems were all available to him, which hadn't happened when he'd first awakened. This improvement must have been due to a combination of having a functioning power core and the repairs Simon had done. Even some of the precision rodent-mitigation systems, which had the focused sonic generator, were now available for his use.

"We had an agreement," Rosevier said.

Quinton brought up the subroutine that was set to deliver the incriminating evidence to the Mozeyian Outpost's financial officer. He also accessed the command sequence that would offload all of Rosevier's current inventory. The timer was running out, but he hesitated.

"You were going to sell me," he said.

"I was," Rosevier replied. "Can you really blame me?"

Quinton stormed closer to him. "Yeah, I really can."

"We made a deal."

"We had a deal before, and you double-crossed me," Quinton said and put the countdown timer on the nearby console.

Rosevier's façade began to crack. "Don't do this. You'll ruin me. They'll kick me off the station, and I have nowhere to go. I did as you asked. I don't know who you are, but I think you're a man of honor."

Quinton laughed. "Trying to appeal to my good nature, huh? I think you're getting desperate. I think the moment I stop that timer is when you'll do something foolish."

He brought the sonic wave generator online, and a small cylinder raised from a hidden compartment on his forearm.

"Take your revenge then, but don't ruin everything I've built."

Quinton was taken aback by his reply. Somehow, Rosevier's logic had prioritized his life's work over his own life.

Rosevier's gaze darted to the timer and then back to Quinton. "You're right. You hear me?" he said, his voice rising. "You're right. I was going to—"

Quinton extended his hand and a focused wave of sonic

power shoved Rosevier into the wall, hard. The shop keeper crumpled to the ground, unconscious.

Quinton glanced at the console and watched the timer run almost all the way down. Then he stopped the message and the inventory offload command.

*A deal's a deal.*

He glared at the man on the ground. Rosevier possessed logic to the point of being almost completely dispassionate, but not completely. Did that make him only partially human?

Quinton looked around at the things in the storage room. He needed to prevent Rosevier from interfering with his escape. He'd probably regain consciousness soon, and while slamming him into the wall again would give Quinton a certain amount of satisfaction, he didn't intend to stay there that long. He looked at the console and then walked over to it, accessing the inventory system. The console was unlocked, and it took him little time to find what he needed. When he stepped away from the console, he had the location of a bio-containment system. Rosevier didn't deal only with spare parts but anything from exotic plants to certain types of animals.

On the floor underneath a dark metallic shelf was a long capsule that looked to be large enough to accommodate Rosevier. It would be a tight fit, and Rosevier probably wouldn't be comfortable, but Quinton didn't really care about that. He retrieved the storage container and brought it back over to the console, opened it up, and forced Rosevier's body inside. It was more than a little cramped, but the double-crossing shop owner would live, which was much more than he deserved. Quinton activated the bio-containment protocols, which did a quick analysis of the container's contents, and then engaged the appropriate life-support option to ensure that Rosevier would survive through a short stasis period. He set the wake-up time for seventy-two hours. He should be long gone by the time Rosevier was released. The process was extremely quick.

Quinton opened the wall panel for the automated inventory system. He then lifted the storage container and pushed it into the cargo elevator that was used to transport containers to the warehouse. He selected the coordinates for a shelving unit in the warehouse far away from the exit. When Rosevier regained consciousness, it would take him even more time to find his way out of the building. Then Quinton closed the doors and watched as the cargo elevator disappeared from view.

He felt more than a little bit of satisfaction at extracting a small token of revenge for what Rosevier had tried to do to him. He needed to be more careful. The trouble was that he'd thought he *was* being careful. Now he needed to get out of there.

Quinton walked through the storage room and back into the storefront. He searched for another way out, but the only exit was through the front door. He glanced up at the vent above him, but it was much too small for him to squeeze into.

He pulled his hood over his head and accessed the storefront's video feeds. The enforcers had just walked over to the shop's door. Quinton hastened to the side and hid behind a stack of . . . He had no idea what the stack was. It looked like a pile of haphazard parts, but it gave him more than adequate cover.

The front door opened, and several Mozeyian enforcers walked inside. They called out for Rosevier.

"Activate his personal locator," an enforcer said.

"He's not here. It looks like he's on the warehouse level," replied the other.

"What the hell is he doing down there? Actually, never mind. Send a detachment down there immediately. He might be trying to hide contraband. Let's get out of here."

The enforcers left without checking the storefront at all. Quinton waited for them to move onto the next location and saw that, despite the enforcers' presence, activity in the open area had returned to normal.

Quinton came out from behind the stacks and went to the

front door, peering outside for a few moments before opening it. The door split down the middle and pulled to either side, allowing him through. With a determined stride, he headed out into the most crowded area he could find. Then he went to where Maelyn and the others had been, but they were no longer there.

He shook his head. Things had just started going his way. He scanned the crowded area, looking for the others, but couldn't find them. He wasn't supposed to access the outpost's systems, but what choice did he have?

He brought up a list of the public systems that were on hand for anyone to use. He then opened a comlink back to the ship.

"This is the *Nebulon*," Simon said.

"It's me, Quinton."

"Quinton!" Simon exclaimed. "What are you doing?" he asked quickly.

"I don't know where Maelyn and the others are. We got separated."

There was a brief pause.

"We haven't heard from Maelyn either," Simon said.

"I think they're in trouble. The last time I saw them, they were surrounded by . . . Actually, I have no idea who they were. They weren't Mozeyian enforcers—I know that much—but they didn't look friendly either," Quinton said.

"All right, stand by. I'm going to try to reach her," Simon said. "And don't . . . just wait for me, okay?" he said and then added after a few seconds, "Wait a minute, did you find a power core?"

"Focus, Simon. I have a great story about that, and I'm fine for now," Quinton replied.

"Okay, stand by," Simon said.

Quinton glanced around, feeling out of place and that, at any moment, he would draw unwanted attention.

"She's not responding," Simon said.

"I can track her through the comlink."

"No, don't do that."

"Why not?" Quinton asked. "If this is because you're worried about it being detected, then don't be. I haven't been detected yet. I've been careful."

"No, it's not that," Simon said quickly. "You said she was surrounded by some people. If that's the case, then if we try to track her and they detect the signal, it might make things harder for her."

"So what do you suggest I do?"

"I'm trying to think of something," Simon replied. "No, I haven't heard anything yet. I know. I'll let you know as soon as I do."

Quinton assumed someone else had just come to the bridge and Simon was speaking to them. "Who was that?"

"Guttmann," Simon replied. "He's been checking in every fifteen minutes."

Quinton considered finding another biological storage container for Guttmann. Would anyone really miss him if he were gone?

"I think you should head back to the ship. It's what Maelyn would want," Simon said.

Quinton had no idea what Maelyn wanted. She made an outward show of keeping her motivations transparent, but he didn't trust her. He didn't trust any of them. Even if he returned to the ship, what would he do then? Now that his power core had been replaced, he could focus on finding the source of the activation signal or maybe even a better host for his PMC.

What if he just left? He could go back to Rosevier's store and see if there was a ship he could appropriate for his use. He could steal a ship and then he could do what he wanted, but how far would he really get if he did that? The galaxy had changed, and he was still finding his way. He couldn't do what he needed to alone, which meant he couldn't leave the others behind. He had a much better chance of succeeding with them than on his own.

"Quinton, did you hear me?" Simon asked.

"I heard you."

"Good. You should be able to find your way back to the *Nebulon*. Hopefully, by then we'll have heard from Maelyn," Simon said.

"That's not going to work," Quinton said.

He heard Simon sigh through the comlink. "What are you going to do?"

Quinton used the agricultural bot's power sensor to find the camera feeds in the area.

"Quinton?"

"Need a minute," he replied and then muted the comlink. He needed to concentrate. If there were enhanced detection systems capable of noticing what he was about to do, he'd need to get out quickly.

He followed the data connection to the video surveillance system, which cached recent footage before it was uploaded to the main system. He checked the feed from fifteen minutes earlier and saw Maelyn and the others being escorted out of the area.

Quinton began to follow the corridor they'd taken and reactivated the comlink. "I'm going to follow them."

"How?" Simon asked.

"I don't have much time, but the outpost's video surveillance system stores the video feed even after it's been uploaded to the main system. If I wait too long, it'll be overwritten," Quinton replied.

Simon was quiet for a few seconds. "That's . . . That's pretty smart."

"Thanks. I'll let you know when I find them. Oh, and we might need to make a quick exit."

"I'm already on top of that."

"Good," Quinton said and closed the comlink.

He walked through the corridors that connected the large

open decks of the outpost. Whoever had taken Maelyn and the others seemed to be making their way toward another docking bay. Quinton quickened his pace, hoping to catch up with them. The last video feed he checked was only seven minutes old, so he wasn't far behind. Each time he checked, he didn't get the impression that Maelyn and the others were actually prisoners. Becker glanced back the way they'd come a few times, but that was it.

Quinton brought up the most recent video feed on his HUD. Becker kept watching their surroundings but didn't look as if he was going to make an escape from their captors anytime soon.

He increased his speed, weaving his way through the crowded corridors to the next open area. He must have reached the central part of the outpost because he'd emerged onto another massive plaza. There were eight crosswalks that connected to the other side. High above, he saw the edges of the semi-translucent shield, along with a wide expanse of the stars beyond. Aircars flew overhead, providing quick transport to the far side of the outpost.

He checked the nearby video feeds and saw Maelyn and the others enter the nearest crosswalk. Checking the timestamp, he saw that he was only thirty seconds behind them now. He hastened over to the crosswalk. Small booths were interspersed along the way, making a direct path across all but impossible. It would slow the others down as well. Most of the peddlers glanced in his direction with a practiced eye capable of determining whether he was an easy mark, but they soon averted their gaze. Quinton supposed that Becker's Yezierian disguise was good for something.

He crossed the middle of the crosswalk, and it was a straight-open shot to the other side. Spotting the back of Maelyn's head, he closed the distance as much as he dared without drawing any notice.

He opened a comlink to Maelyn. "Miss me?" he asked. "I'm a short distance behind you."

The men surrounding her came to a stop, and the rearmost

turned toward him. A moment later, Maelyn and Becker turned as well, followed by Vonya.

Quinton froze, unsure what to do.

"Wallace," Maelyn said, speaking to the man nearest her, "I neglected to tell you that we left someone behind."

Wallace looked at Quinton and narrowed his gaze. "You're traveling with a Yezierian now?" he asked while trying to peer under Quinton's hood.

"Not exactly," Maelyn said. "I'm sure you can understand the need for discretion."

Becker cleared his throat. "I already told you that I spotted some of Lennix Crowe's people on the outpost. They're searching for us."

Quinton walked toward them without saying a word.

"That's close enough," Wallace said.

"Low profile, Wallace. Remember?" Maelyn said.

"I told you not to contact anyone, and instead, you called someone from your ship."

Maelyn rolled her eyes. "They sent him to look for me."

Wallace frowned and regarded Quinton for a moment. "How'd you find us?"

Quinton glanced at Maelyn, who gave him a small nod. "It wasn't that hard," he said and turned to address her. "Captain, Simon and the others became concerned when you didn't check in."

Maelyn nodded, and her gaze flicked to Wallace. "I was already on my way back. There's no need for you to provide an escort."

Wallace shook his head. "I have orders from Brandt himself."

Becker shook his head. "We don't have time for this. What difference does it make whether you bring us in or we meet you there? I already told you that Crowe isn't going to just let us go."

Wallace looked unconvinced. "We're on the outpost. There isn't much he can do to us here."

Becker's face deadpanned. "You don't know what he's capable of or what resources he has at his disposal."

"You should listen to him, Wallace. Becker was high up in Crowe's Union," Maelyn said.

Wallace shook his head. "You'll forgive me if I don't take the word of a turncoat salvager. And besides, what could you have done to Crowe that would make him hunt for you here?"

Maelyn regarded him for a few moments and frowned. Then, a klaxon alarmed sounded overheard.

"Emergency jump will initiate in thirty minutes. Return to your ships immediately. This is not a drill," a monotone, dispassionate voice sounded after the alarm. The automated message repeated itself several more times.

General activity seemed to increase all at once as people began to leave the area.

"We have to get out of here," Becker said. "An emergency jump means there's an attack force on its way here now."

Maelyn stopped. Wallace's men watched them, looking ready to reach for their weapons if they thought it was necessary.

"From one ship captain to another, you can't ask me to abandon my ship," Maelyn said.

"I won't," Wallace replied. "I'll take you to your ship, and then we'll both get out of here."

They continued. Quinton walked next to Maelyn while Wallace led the way.

"Where did you go?" she asked.

"I was in one of the shops when the enforcers came."

"We got sidetracked by Wallace. We need to get you back to the ship. What's the power core reading at now?" Maelyn asked.

"It's fine. I found a new one."

Her eyes widened, and her gaze slid down to his chest. "But someone would have had to swap it out. You would've gone offline."

"I did, and don't worry about it. The shop owner won't be

coming out of stasis for three days," Quinton said and explained what happened.

Maelyn shook her head slowly, and Quinton couldn't decide whether she was more concerned for him or the fact that she'd lose her big payday if something happened to him.

"Great," Becker said. "We got what we came for. Now let's get the hell out of here."

Maelyn opened a comlink to the ship. "Simon, I want you to move the ship to this docking platform. I need it done quickly," she said and was quiet for a moment, listening. "He's here."

Fifteen minutes later, they entered the docking area where Wallace's ship was located, and Wallace received a comlink from his own ship. He glanced at Maelyn for a moment and then closed the comlink.

"The *Nebulon* has taken up position nearby, I assume under your orders," Wallace said.

"That's right. We'll execute a jump once we're away and then transfer back to my ship. Is that acceptable?" Maelyn said.

Quinton admired her instincts. Moving her ship nearby meant that Wallace couldn't simply execute a jump without being followed. Maelyn seemed to be quite adept at neutralizing risks.

"Very well," Wallace said and led them to his ship.

Quinton walked with the others. He expected the patrons on the outpost to question why they needed to leave, but they didn't. They hardly took a moment to acknowledge the change, and business ceased. He was still connected into the outpost's computer systems. Reading the flow of data that traveled at the speed of light was becoming increasingly easy for him, and he could scarcely explain how he was doing it. It was as if he'd gained an awareness of which data streams to follow, and he wondered if Radek had had something to do with it. His VI assistant had been unusually quiet since the new power core.

The Mozeyian Outpost's power systems were being rerouted to the jump drive network and also the outpost's defenses.

Quinton didn't know what the outpost had for defense, but whoever was in charge of them must've determined that there was a significant threat. Was Becker right? Did Crowe have warships with enough firepower to threaten the massive outpost?

Quinton glanced at Becker. The salvager wore the concentrated look of one determined to keep moving forward with each dogged step he took.

Wallace turned toward one of the access ramps that led to his ship. Every ship Quinton had seen so far looked to be designed for transporting cargo and defense, and Wallace's ship was no different. There were mag cannon turrets on top, as well as a few below. Their worn-looking barrels indicated many years of service, but there were a few empty turrets where the mag cannons should have been. It looked as if they hadn't been part of the ship's original construction but were an add-on, which meant their armament was less than that of an actual warship. Despite all that, the ship was much like everything else Quinton had seen in the galaxy—battle-worn but determined to survive. The ship might not be as pristine as the day it had launched from the shipyards, but it still had teeth and wouldn't go down without a fight.

They walked up the loading ramp and headed inside.

# CHAPTER TWENTY

THE INTERIOR of the ship matched the exterior. As he walked the corridors, he noted dingy yellow metallic walls, and yet Quinton couldn't see a speck of dirt. He sampled the air with his sensors and noted that the atmospheric scrubbers kept the air fresh and free of contaminants. The ship was simply old and probably beyond its intended life cycle, but someone had kept it serviceable long past when it should have been scrapped for parts. Given the patchwork he'd seen on the hull, he thought someone must have cobbled together enough working parts to keep the ship serviceable, but he wondered if anyone was building ships anymore.

The loading ramp closed, and Wallace led them toward the center of the ship where the bridge was located. Their armed escorts stayed with them, but Maelyn didn't seem to mind. Becker strode behind her as if their armed escorts didn't matter to him in the slightest. Quinton wondered if it was for show, but perhaps Becker really didn't perceive them as a threat. He glanced at Vonya, and the lavender-skinned beauty smiled at him reassuringly.

The command deck had the standard workstation layout that

was at once vaguely familiar to Quinton, though he couldn't remember why. The command chair was occupied by an older woman, who stood up.

"Sitrep, Elsa," Wallace said.

"We just got clearance to decouple from the docking platform, and we can be underway in a few minutes, Captain," Elsa said.

Wallace nodded and peered at the main holoscreen. There was a mass exodus of ships as they fled the outpost as quickly as possible. Quinton spotted the *Nebulon*, which had positioned itself on an intercept course.

"I see the *Nebulon*," Quinton said.

Wallace looked at him and frowned.

"Yes," Maelyn said. "We need to get back to our ship immediately."

Wallace shook his head. "You know I can't do that. Admiral Brandt's orders are that we bring you back to the fleet. Cantos signed off on the orders as well."

"Wallace," Maelyn said.

"I know what you're going to say, but I can't. Not this time. Brandt's orders are clear."

"I understand, but Brandt doesn't know everything," she replied, and Wallace pressed his lips together. "I claim captain's privilege."

Quinton glanced at the others. He had no idea what "captain's privilege" meant, but the others seemed to know.

Wallace regarded her for a few moments and stood up. "Very well, Captain Wayborn. Let's take this to my ready room. Elsa, you have the conn."

"Yes, Captain, I have the conn," Elsa replied and returned to the command chair. "Captain, what about them?" she asked, tilting her head toward Quinton and the others.

"Rosser, take them to the meeting room and keep two men posted outside," Wallace said.

"Understood, sir," Rosser said.

Quinton and the others were escorted off the bridge and taken to a meeting room a short distance away. They were left alone, and Quinton looked at Becker and Vonya. He couldn't help but think they were the extremes of who he could have been stuck with. By all outward appearances, Vonya was calm. She sat down in one of the chairs and closed her eyes as if she was meditating. Becker rolled his eyes and walked to the other side of the room.

"What's captain's privilege?" Quinton asked.

Becker looked at him for a few moments, his thick eyebrows pulled together, and then he shook his head.

Vonya sighed. "Captain's privilege is a courtesy between starship captains whereby they are granted a private meeting to discuss options for peaceful recourse."

"That's new, I guess," Quinton said.

"It's a waste of time," Becker said.

"Why?"

"Because it's just people pretending to be civilized. There's nothing to compel Wallace to let us go," Becker replied.

"Ordinarily, that might be true," Vonya said, "but they're both from the DUC."

"DUC?" Quinton asked.

"Dholeren United Coalition," Vonya replied.

Becker rolled his eyes. "They're a migrant fleet of refugees who dream of a galaxy that no longer exists."

"They work toward peaceful coexistence by welcoming anyone from the old federations to become part of the coalition," Vonya said.

"They're welcome to the galaxy's rejects," Becker said. He checked his weapon and returned it to its holster.

Quinton turned toward Becker. "What the hell happened to you that made you so bitter?"

Becker glared at him and Quinton watched him closely,

expecting him to go for his weapon, but he didn't. "None of your goddamn business. Look, we're not friends and we'll never be friends. You're just a means to an end."

Quinton grinned. "I wasn't offering to be your friend, but you look like you have all this pent-up emotion about the galaxy. I figured you wanted to share your feelings. Get some of it off your chest."

Becker's mouth was partially opened. "My feelings," he rasped and narrowed his gaze.

Vonya stood up and walked between them. She moved with a feline grace that encompassed her entire body in such a way that was just pleasing to look at. Even Becker's gaze softened.

"Fine, I'll stop," Quinton said and looked at Becker. "How do you know Crowe tracked us here?"

"I know how he operates. He won't let this go. Not if he knows what you are," Becker said.

"Yeah, but how would he know that?"

Becker sighed. "Crowe has been around for a long time. You don't get to his position by employing incompetent people. Nate Carradine would be able to figure it out."

Quinton remembered the older man who'd been with Crowe on the hangar deck. He barely remembered that the man had been there but had no real impression as to what his capabilities were, so he'd have to rely on Becker's opinion. Despite his own opinions of Becker, the one thing the salvager was not was a bad judge of a situation. He had keen instincts for detecting a potential threat.

"Why go through the trouble?" Quinton asked.

"You don't even understand what you're worth," Becker said and held up a hand. "Now, before you say something stupid, let me finish. You know you can be controlled."

"So you've said. I don't know how, though."

"Neither do I, but Carradine would be able to find out how,

and he's loyal to Crowe. I think they've been partners for a long time," Becker said.

"What does controlling me get him?"

Becker glanced at the door, and Quinton wondered if he was looking for a way to avoid answering the question.

"I can start guessing, if you want," Quinton said.

"You'd give him an unrivaled advantage, which is something he needs."

"What do you mean? Why would he need an advantage?"

Becker glanced at Vonya for a moment and then looked at Quinton. "Crowe isn't the most powerful salvager. There are others who are a lot more powerful, and none of them are willing to give up their relative positions and territories."

"Territories," Quinton said.

"Stepping on each other's toes goes with the business, but let's just say that Crowe might have overstepped and brought unwanted attention. That's why he won't let this go. He'll come at you any way he can."

Quinton considered this for a few moments, and Vonya returned to her seat. "Let him try."

Becker looked at the door. "I wish I knew what they were saying."

"Captain Wayborn is quite capable. I'm sure we'll be on our way soon," Vonya said.

Quinton figuratively frowned in thought and checked for open system access, immediately finding several that were available. Wallace didn't know what Quinton could do, so he should be able to listen to their conversation without raising any alarms.

He accessed the ship's systems and brought up the video feed for the captain's ready room.

"I already told you that it's dangerous to bring Quinton to any of the fleets," Maelyn said.

"Because you believe he's an actual Personality Matrix Construct from one of the older federations."

"Yes, either Jordani or Acheron."

Wallace exhaled forcefully. "Where did he come from? Has he been lurking around for a few hundred years?"

"No, he was recently activated, but it's complicated."

"Your propensity for finding trouble never ceases to amaze me. What am I dealing with here?" Wallace asked.

"You're not dealing with anything."

"He's on my ship."

"I told you we needed to get back to my ship."

Wallace rubbed his forehead and dragged his hand over his face and down to his beard. "Geez, Maelyn, stop mincing words with me. He could be in our systems right now."

She smiled a little. "He probably is by now. He's inquisitive by nature, I think. Like I said, it's complicated. None of which I need to delve into right now."

Wallace looked up at the ceiling for a few moments. "Do you really think he's listening to our conversation?"

Maelyn shrugged. "It's not important. No, seriously. Quinton is dealing with certain limitations, which might actually be helping him to retain his sanity."

Quinton's thoughts began to race. He supposed that if he'd been in his actual body, his pulse would have increased, along with a healthy release of adrenaline, none of which applied to his current . . . situation, but his mind was still human, equipped with years of conditioning, along with billions of years of evolution.

Wallace leaned forward. "This is supposed to reassure me."

"You asked for honesty. I'm leveling with you. We don't have a lot of time."

"You intend to bring an unstable PMC that inhabits an agricultural bot back to the migrant fleet. Are you insane? That's beyond reckless."

"Give me some credit, Wallace. That wasn't the plan."

"Oh, so you have a plan. This should be interesting."

"I'm thinking that you could actually help me," Maelyn said. Wallace raised his eyebrows. "I need you to contact Brandt and brief him. Then he can meet us away from the fleet. It'll be safer for everyone."

"I don't even know how Brandt will react to this. He might not want anything to do with it."

Maelyn pursed her lips in thought. "In that case, you'll need to bring Cantos into it. She'll at least listen to reason."

"Reason," Wallace said, and shook his head. "There's nothing reasonable about this. I have half a mind to toss that thing off the ship."

Quinton tried not to take it personally, but every person's reaction to the fact that he was a PMC was to immediately put as much distance as possible between them and him, and it was wearing thin.

"Don't do that," Maelyn warned.

"Do what?"

"Threaten him," she said. Wallace looked up at the ceiling again, which amused Quinton because he was listening and watching them through the comms system, which was located at the console on Wallace's desk. "He'll listen to me, but if you threaten him, there's no telling what he'll do. He's capable of much more than he knows."

He didn't know if Maelyn was building up his capabilities to get Wallace to cooperate or if those were her own opinions of him. She knew he was listening in and still said those things anyway.

"You're playing a very dangerous game, Maelyn," Wallace said.

She smiled and waggled her eyebrows once. "Those are the only ones worth playing. Now, before you say anything else, I have a deal with Quinton. It's mutually beneficial for both of us."

"What kind of deal?" Wallace asked.

"He helps us gain access to technology and resources we

wouldn't otherwise be able to access, and we help him get a more suitable body. Ideally, we retrieve his DNA so his physical body can be regrown."

Wallace regarded her for a few moments. "You promised," he began and stopped with a slow shake of his head.

Maelyn held up her hand in a placating gesture. "Some chance is better than no chance at all. Someone activated Quinton. We have no idea who or why. Like I said, we don't even know for sure which federation he comes from."

"Jordani or Acheron." Wallace sighed. "There isn't a good choice either way. What are you going to do when he regains his memories and has full access to his ESS? Have you thought about that?"

"That depends on him."

A comlink opened from the bridge.

"Captain," Elsa said, "the Mozeyian Outpost has decreased their countdown to jump by more than half. They're going to jump much earlier than expected."

Wallace stood up. "Understood," he said and looked at Maelyn. "We're finished here. I'm on my way back."

Quinton was accessing the ship's communication systems, which covered a wide variety and was interlinked to every single system on the ship. He'd had knowledge of the outpost's broadcast moments before Elsa contacted Wallace.

"Why are you so quiet all of a sudden?" Becker asked.

It took Quinton a few moments to register that Becker was speaking to him.

Meanwhile, Maelyn said to Wallace, "Are we agreed then? Will you help me out?"

"Let's go see what we're dealing with first. Something must have happened for the outpost to move up its jump window. I don't like this at all," Wallace said.

They left Wallace's ready room, and Quinton returned his

attention back to his immediate surroundings where he found Becker staring at him, his head tilted to the side.

"Didn't anyone tell you that it's not polite to stare?" Quinton asked.

Becker's lips lifted a little. He'd almost cracked a smile. Then he shook his head. "I wasn't sure if you were still there anymore. You might have just broken down. You know, you don't look so good."

"You're not getting rid of me that easily. Come on, Vonya, they're coming for us."

Vonya stood up and interlaced her long fingers in front of her.

Becker frowned and then his eyes widened a little. "You were listening to them? You were listening to them in the ready room."

If Quinton could smile, he would have. As it were, it was just a strange feedback from the agricultural bot systems of an expression that had no meaning for it. The bot's systems couldn't interpret the emotional data—in this case, a fair amount of satisfaction at the note of alarm in Becker's voice—packed into the response, or in this case, a smile. "How does that saying go? If you're not cheating, then you're not doing it right."

Becker chuckled and seemed a little surprised that he'd done so. The door opened.

Rosser stood outside. "They want you back on the bridge. Follow me."

They left the room and returned to the bridge. Wallace narrowed his gaze as if he preferred that Quinton wasn't there at the moment, but it was something he had to deal with. Maelyn gave him a confident nod.

Quinton turned his attention to Wallace. "I'm still here, Captain. Sanity still in check."

The others around them looked bewildered at his statement. Wallace winced. Now there could be no doubt that he'd listened in on their conversation.

Quinton looked at the main holoscreen. He had access to the ship's scanner array and noticed that the plot was crowded with ships fleeing the outpost.

"Elsa," Wallace said, "put us on an intercept course with the *Nebulon*. We'll be doing a high-speed pass," he said and looked at Maelyn. "The outpost is charging their jump drives. We need to make minimum safe distance and won't be able to slow down. You can make it to your ship by using one of our escape pods."

Maelyn smiled, looking as if she'd gotten exactly what she expected. "Thank you, Captain. I owe you one."

"You have no idea," Wallace said and glanced at Quinton. "But if your arrangement works out, then it could be good for us all. Safe travels, Captain Wayborn."

"To you as well, Captain, and your crew," she said.

She led them off the bridge, and Rosser escorted them to an escape pod. Maelyn went in first and the rest of them followed.

"It took you long enough," Becker said to Maelyn.

"Wallace took some convincing," Quinton said.

Maelyn arched a dark eyebrow. "I knew you were listening to us."

"I was, and I don't see how it changes anything." Even after he said it, he still didn't feel right about it. The constant suspicion of the people he surrounded himself with was wearing on him.

Maelyn regarded him as if trying to guess what his thoughts were. Quinton supposed that was one advantage to having a metallic, expressionless face—it didn't give anything away. A few moments later, she turned her attention to the escape pod systems. After a short wait, the pod was jettisoned from Wallace's ship, and they were on a direct path to the *Nebulon*. Maelyn opened a comlink to the ship. Simon, sounding very much relieved to hear from them, was only too happy to retrieve the escape pod.

Once they were back aboard the *Nebulon*, they headed to the bridge.

Simon smiled a greeting. "I'm glad you all made it back safely."

They were flying on a trajectory away from the outpost at best speed possible amid the other fleeing ships.

"Any trouble while we were away?" Maelyn asked.

Simon shook his head. "No problems here."

Quinton glanced at the main holoscreen, which showed a multitude of ships. At a casual glance, it looked almost chaotic, but then he spotted something peculiar. "That's odd. There's a group of ships on an intercept course with us."

The others turned their attention to the main holoscreen. It was difficult for the others to see because of the mass exodus from the outpost. Ships were jumping away as soon as they reached the minimal safe distance, so the plot on the main holoscreen was a bit confusing. Quinton highlighted the ships for them.

Simon hastened to the nearest workstation. "That isn't right. Scanners indicate that they're JFS warship design."

Becker cleared his throat. "It's Crowe. He's here."

Maelyn sat in the captain's chair. "We're not far enough away for a jump."

"You might not have much of a choice," Becker said.

The calculations appeared on Quinton's HUD. Maelyn was right—not much of a surprise there. The other ships were heading directly toward them, but they should be able to jump away before they reached them.

"It will be close," Quinton said.

"I suggest you all strap yourselves in. This is where it gets interesting," Maelyn said.

# CHAPTER TWENTY-ONE

"WITH ALL DUE RESPECT, Captain, I think it would be best if I wasn't on the bridge," Vonya said.

Maelyn looked at her for a moment and then nodded.

"You two," Becker said to Guttman and Oscar, "we can't be here either. Go ahead and I'll be right behind you."

Guttman and Oscar left the bridge.

Quinton watched them go, and then looked at Becker. "Running away?"

Becker ignored him and looked at Maelyn. "I'll keep my comlink open, and if I can think of something that will help, I'll let you know."

"How very upstanding of you. You're with us in solidarity, but not on the bridge where someone can see you," Quinton said.

Becker gritted his teeth and inhaled, nostrils flaring.

"Quinton," Maelyn said, "it's for the best. No need for us to confirm anything for Lennix Crowe."

Since Crowe had managed to track them all the way here, they weren't going to hide the fact that they had escaped his space station with some help. Quinton thought Crowe was the type of person who didn't let small details slip past his notice, especially when those "details" were high-ranking salvagers in his organization. Becker turned around and left the bridge.

Quinton looked at Maelyn and shrugged. "I'm not going anywhere."

"I didn't expect you would, even if I wanted you to," she said, sounding mildly annoyed.

"It's because we're all so trustworthy," Quinton replied just as frostily.

Maelyn gritted her teeth a little and then exhaled softly. "Do you have to be so . . ." she said and paused, pressing her lips together.

Quinton waited a few moments for her to continue, but she didn't. "Everyone here is looking out for themselves, so why should you expect anything different from me?"

Maelyn regarded him for a few moments, making him feel a little exposed. What did she see when she looked at him? Was it just an old service bot? Or did she see *him*, a Personality Matrix Construct that was the very essence of who he'd been when he'd resided in his human body? Quinton tried to recall his own face, and it was like trying to peer at a star map through a dense billowing cloud. He had enough to give him an impression but none of the details. Why was that fundamental knowledge kept from him? Was this part of the lockdown protocol? Did the others treat him like some kind of ghost in the machine because they wouldn't allow themselves to acknowledge that he was alive? They must know. They had to know. Quinton's artificial robotic eyes glowed a pale green. Maelyn had to know. He felt a sudden surge of longing for not just Maelyn but also the others to believe that he was more than a ghost from the past. He was more than what he could give them.

"Captain," Simon said, "we're being hailed. It's Crowe."

Maelyn held Quinton's gaze for another moment. "This isn't over," she said and then looked at Simon. "Understood. Patch the others in so Becker can observe."

"Yes, Captain," Simon said.

Quinton went to stand to the right of the captain's chair, and the vidcom came to prominence on the main holoscreen.

Lennix Crowe, wearing a black uniform, sat on the command bridge of a Jordani Federation destroyer. The crew was focused on their workstations, and their holoscreens glowed a pale green. Crowe lifted his dark-eyed gaze, and the video feed closed in so only his head and shoulders appeared.

"Captain Crowe. I didn't expect to see you here," Maelyn said.

On the upper-right side of the main holoscreen was a countdown timer for their jump drive to engage.

Crowe looked at her and arched one eyebrow. "Captain Wayborn, you've stolen something from me."

Quinton watched as Maelyn's eyes widened in mock surprise. "I don't think so. I'm sure it's just a simple misunderstanding."

"Is it though? I thought you were smarter than this. Did you think I wouldn't figure out what you've got there?" Crowe said, inclining his head toward Quinton.

Maelyn glanced at Quinton and laughed. "Imagine my surprise when we learned that the agricultural bot had something extra, but no, we didn't steal it from you. As you might recall, this agricultural unit was claimed by my sysops expert, Simon Webb, who accompanied your salvagers."

Crowe's gaze hardened, and he leaned forward. All pretenses of cordiality were gone. "I like you, Maelyn. You have a firm understanding of how things work. That's why I'm going to give you a chance to just hand it over."

"Excuse me," Quinton said. "Since you know what I am, then you'll also know that I'm not an 'it.' Furthermore, no one is handing any part of me anywhere without my say-so."

Crowe looked at Quinton for a moment and shook his head a little. "A PMC who believes they're still alive."

"A fool who believes they're in charge," Quinton said. Crowe glowered at him, his mouth forming a silent snarl. "I thought we were just stating the obvious here."

Crowe leaned back in his chair. "I'm really looking forward to meeting you in person."

"I can guarantee that this feeling won't last for long, but I'm afraid I'm also going to have to decline your offer to meet," Quinton said.

"It wasn't an offer, and besides," Crowe said, looking at Maelyn, "I think a suitable arrangement can be reached."

"But our business has already concluded. You're just trying to take what's rightfully mine," Maelyn responded innocently.

"Trust me when I say that you won't like it if you make me take him forcefully."

Quinton laughed. The countdown timer was almost finished. "Look who has a big bad warship. I bet you can't wait to use those weapons of yours. Are you really sure you want someone like me on there? You can ask the captain here for confirmation. I'm afraid I can't help getting into places I shouldn't be."

"Captain," Simon said, his voice going high, "they're targeting us."

Maelyn nodded once and looked at Crowe. "You'd risk losing access to the Mozeyian Outpost by firing weapons here in such close proximity to the outpost and all these other ships?"

Crowe shook his head. "Maybe I was wrong and you don't realize what you have, but if I can't take him from you, then no one will have him."

"Oh, I know exactly what I have, and you can be sure that you're never going to take him from me," Maelyn said, her tone becoming the hardest battle steel. Then she looked at Simon. "Execute jump."

Crowe leaned forward and smirked.

The *Nebulon*'s jump drives didn't activate, and Maelyn frowned. "Simon?"

"I'm trying, but we can't get a field lock. The calibration won't align. The nav computer has the coordinates, but it's like something is preventing an alignment," Simon said.

"I can override—" Quinton began to say.

"No!" Maelyn said with such command authority that he instantly stopped speaking.

Crowe laughed, drawing their attention back to the main holoscreen. "It seems that you're not going to get as far away as you originally thought."

"Simon," Maelyn said.

"I know. I'm looking, Captain."

"Don't bother. I'll just tell you," Crowe said and looked away for a moment, considering. "Never mind. I'll tell you in person when I get there." He closed the comlink.

Maelyn brought up her personal holoscreen. "The jump drive is online. So that's not it. What about the nav computer? Simon, run a diagnostic."

"Ship disablers," Quinton said.

"What?" Maelyn asked.

"Ship disablers. They're outside the ship. The JFS used them to prevent ships from making FTL jumps. Any kind of long-range drone could deploy them. Crowe hasn't been here long, so he didn't fire anything from his ship, but what if he had help? Someone on the outpost maybe?"

Maelyn looked at Simon.

"I hate to say it, but he's right," Becker said, his voice sounding over the comlink speakers on the bridge.

"It won't hurt nearly so much the more you say it," Quinton replied.

"Enough," Maelyn said. "Scanners aren't showing anything."

"They wouldn't," Becker said. "They're small, but they link up to form a field that you can't bypass. We'll have to go out there and destroy them."

"Are they attached to the hull?" she asked.

"I'm not sure. They could be, but they could also be maintaining position close by. We'll need our weapons for this," Becker said.

"Hold on a second," Quinton said. "Doesn't this ship have some kind of point-defense system?"

Simon nodded. "We do, but since the scanners didn't detect anything, we have no way to tell them what to fire on."

Quinton could just access the point-defense systems, along with any of the ship's other systems, but he didn't. Instead, he looked at Maelyn. "With your permission, Captain, I'd like to use the point-defense system on the ship."

"To do what exactly?" Maelyn asked.

"It's better if I just show you."

Maelyn considered it for a few seconds. "Go ahead," she said.

Quinton cranked up his frame rate, tentatively at first, expecting some kind of an alert to appear on his HUD, but none came. His new power core was in pristine condition and barely registered the additional draw as he raised his frame rate to the max. His thought processes sped up so much that time slowed down for everyone else. He was in the *Nebulon*'s computer systems, connected to multiple data streams that his army of VIs acknowledged. They awaited his commands. The strength of a PMC was the ability to simultaneously access multiple systems at once while being partnered with VI assistants that enabled the PMC to outperform any combat VI system alone. He unpacked a suite of VIs that took the aged scanner arrays and delved deeper into their detection capabilities, dialing them in to sense the tiny robotic swarm that surrounded the array. Without Quinton's augmentation, the ship's VI had rightfully classified the swarm as benign, given the fact that the ship was flying through crowded space. But the system didn't have the protocols required to make that determination. It wasn't designed for it. The protocols were for civilian use, and what he had access to was something much more capable.

There were two sets of point-defense cannons, each having

kinetic and energy-based weaponry. They were lightweight, which wouldn't save them if they came within firing range of Crowe's JFS destroyers. He had to assume that Crowe had long-range missiles, which could reach them easily despite the other fleeing ships and the outpost, but Crowe wanted to take him intact. Quinton needed him to believe he could still do that.

He sent a new data feed to the main holoscreen, along with updated targeting parameters for the point-defense system. Then he slowed his frame rate back to normal time.

Maelyn glanced at the main holoscreen and did a double take.

Simon stood up, his mouth hanging open. "This," he said and looked at Quinton. "You did this?"

"Yes, now say goodbye to our pesky swarm," Quinton said and engaged the *Nebulon*'s newly enhanced point-defense cannons.

Both the kinetic and energy armament fired, sweeping their range of fire. Quinton engaged the maneuvering thrusters, and the ship rotated on its axis. The robotic swarm was beaten back. He was careful not to hit any of the other ships nearby. After a few seconds, the swarm was reduced to almost nothing.

Simon went back to his workstation. "I still can't get the jump drive to engage."

Quinton had the ship's sensors make another active scanner sweep, but nothing was detected. "There has to be something on the hull. I'm sorry, I can't do anything about that from here."

He withdrew from the ship's systems and felt a sense of emptiness from the loss of connection. For a few moments, he'd felt closer to "whole" than he'd felt since he'd woken up. Accessing the ship's systems had felt familiar and touched upon the very things those same VIs that had helped him also had to keep him ignorant of, locked away inside the ESS. He wanted to fully access the ship's systems again just so he could feel the complete immersion, chasing that feeling of wholeness. It was such a powerful urge that Quinton opened several data connections—not to do anything but just to feel whole again.

"Well then, we'll just have to go outside and take a look for ourselves," Maelyn said.

Quinton looked at her and nodded.

"Becker, Guttman, and Oscar, meet us at the rear airlock," Maelyn said. Simon stood up, intending to go with them. "Not you," she said to him. "You stay here and monitor Crowe's ships. As soon as we clear out the remaining disablers, I want you to execute a jump when we're back inside the ship."

Simon looked as if he was about to protest but didn't. Then he said, "Aye, Captain."

Maelyn turned toward Quinton.

"Lead the way," he said.

She nodded, and together they left the bridge. They headed toward the airlock near the middle of the *Nebulon*, which put them as close to the scanner array as possible. Quinton waited for the others to put on their EVA suits.

Maelyn grabbed a pair of boots with thick bottoms and tossed them toward Quinton. "Put them on. You need to wear them," she said.

Quinton glanced at the boots for a moment.

She gestured toward his feet. "You can't magnetize those footpads, yes?"

He checked the agricultural unit's feature list. "You're right, but the artificial gravity kept me attached to the ship before."

"Yeah, but we didn't have warships bearing down on us then."

Becker walked with the others inside the outer airlock, giving him a "get on with it" look.

Quinton quickly slipped on the boots, and the straps automatically adjusted to his metallic frame. He took a few steps, allowing the boots to self-adjust for maximum effectiveness, and they molded themselves to his peculiar foot shape. For the first few moments, it was like wearing two sets of shoes at the same time, but soon, the bot's motor control helped him compensate so he could walk normally, and he joined the others inside the airlock.

"About time," Becker muttered.

Oscar looked at Quinton, regarding him for a moment, and then said,

"Nice trick with the sensors and point-defense systems."

"Thanks," Quinton said.

"How did you do that?" Oscar asked.

The exterior airlock doors opened, revealing the Mozeyian Outpost's massive structure off to the side. Even though they'd put some distance from it, the outpost was still the largest thing in the area.

"Save it," Becker said.

"We've got work to do," Maelyn said.

"What are we looking for?" Guttman asked. He kept glancing around, and Quinton realized he was searching for the swarm.

"The swarm is gone," Quinton said.

"What's to stop it from coming back?"

"The swarm was part of the disablers attached to the ship," Becker said. The others looked at him. "I've never used them myself, but I've seen them before. Someone could have deployed them right from the maintenance airlock on the docking platform."

"That might have been useful to know earlier," Quinton said.

"Knock it off," Maelyn said. "We thought we'd outrun Crowe's agents. That's all there is to it. So, let's get the disablers off the ship and get out of here."

Quinton watched as the others nodded. Maelyn had a command authority that others had come to respect, even if this was only a temporary partnership.

She led them toward the sensor array, and they all engaged their mag boots. The artificial gravity field was weaker at this part of the ship, and Quinton realized that this was where the fields overlapped. Inside, the ship was fine, but here the weakness in gravity was enough that, with enough force, they could be jettisoned into space.

The scanner array was a series of sensors that were networked and located in different areas of the ship. The *Nebulon*'s navigation computer depended on the array to send the jump coordinates to the jump drive system. Quinton suspected that he could have found a way to override the safety systems and gotten the ship to jump anyway, but the risk was high that they wouldn't end up where they needed to be. It was no use getting somewhere quickly if they died in the process.

They reached the first in a series of sensors, which looked like tiny gray towers, a little bit taller than they were. Quinton scanned the sensor array for additional power signatures that didn't stem from the ship's power core. He filtered out everything else, and an object highlighted in red appeared on his HUD.

"I found one," he said and sent the targeting data to the others' suit computers.

The disablers were dark gray cylindrical-shaped devices that attached themselves to parts of the ship. A minimally charged plasma shot from a hand cannon or rifle was enough to destroy them, and they made quick work of removing the disablers on the nearby arrays.

Maelyn opened a comlink to the bridge. "Is the nav computer able to lock in the coordinates?"

"Negative, Captain, although it does take a few moments to cycle before it fails to lock on," Simon replied.

Quinton looked at the Mozeyian Outpost, and a series of massive maneuvering thrusters came online. The outpost was now moving away from them with increasing speed. He saw bright flashes from the other ships as they jumped away.

"Captain," Simon said, "I've detected a massive energy spike from the outpost. They're charging their jump drives. You need to get back inside."

"We can't. We have to clear out the last sensor array," Maelyn said.

"Now wait just a minute," Guttman said. "He's right. We can't be out here when that outpost jumps away. The gamma burst alone will kill us."

"Go back inside then," she said and started heading in the direction of the last sensor array.

Quinton caught up to her. "He's right. You need to get back inside the ship. I can take care of this."

Maelyn didn't slow down. "You're not shielded from gamma rays any more than we are."

"I know, but it won't affect me like it will you if you're caught out here. Let me take care of this for you," Quinton said.

Becker walked over to them. "The captain of the ship belongs on the bridge," he said. Maelyn shook her head and rolled her eyes. "Simon is as good as they come, but he's not the captain. We'll get this done."

She glanced at the others, who were already heading back to the airlock. Then she looked at Quinton. "All right," she said and handed him her rifle. "There's a maintenance hatch near that last array. I'll make sure it's unlocked for both of you."

Quinton took the rifle and gave her a quick salute by touching two metallic fingers to the side of his forehead. Then he ran toward the last sensor array.

Running with mag boots wasn't like running anywhere else. It took a lot of coordination, and even then, people couldn't do it well without the assistance of an EVA suit computer VI. He heard Becker following, and he wasn't that far behind. Becker knew what he was doing.

They made their way along the hull, approaching the last sensor array. It had a long shaft that extended ten meters from the hull. It was small in comparison to the ship, but they'd have to climb it. Quinton spotted a few of the ship disablers that had attached themselves to the shaft.

He glanced at Becker.

"I'm just protecting my investment," Becker said.

"I didn't think you'd taken a liking to me," Quinton said.

Becker looked at the shaft and walked over, preparing to climb.

"Wait. I can get up there faster. Why don't you go secure the hatch?"

Becker regarded him, then shook his head and smiled. "She *is* a beauty. I can see why you'd want to impress her," he said and raised his rifle. He shot the lowest disabler, leaving a slight scorch mark on the hull.

Quinton thought he hadn't heard correctly and checked his short-term memory.

Becker leaned toward him. "The thing is that I don't think she's into robots."

Quinton jumped up and grabbed the sensor. He swung around to the other side and shot the dark gray disabler. "I don't think she's into idiots either, so that rules us both out," he said, climbing higher.

Becker grinned and headed for the hatch. Quinton watched him go for a few moments, then continued his climb. The disablers seemed to have congregated on this particular array. The sensor wasn't just a solitary shaft but also had offshoots like the branches of a tree. At the top was a small dome about two meters in diameter. That's where he'd find the last disabler.

Quinton accessed the ship's systems and brought up the sensor systems. The readout nearly made him miss the handhold he was reaching for. He opened a comlink to the bridge. "Are you seeing this?"

There was a cluster of long-range missiles heading toward them, weaving their way through the fleeing ships.

"Yes," Maelyn answered. "Did you clear that last array?"

Quinton scrambled up to the shaft. "I'm working on it. It might be a good idea to bring the weapons systems online."

The point-defense systems were online, but he didn't know what kind of missiles Crowe had on those destroyers. Quinton reached the bottom of the dome and climbed toward the edge. The outpost's thruster went dark, and he saw the massive system of networked jump drives on the outpost reach the apex of their capacitor's capabilities. He glanced downward and saw that Becker had made it to the hatch and had just gone inside.

Quinton climbed over the edge and reached the top side of the dome. In the center was a ship disabler. He reached down and tore it from the hull, then threw it away from the ship. He scanned the area, looking for additional disablers, and none appeared.

"We're clear," Quinton said.

"Good work," Maelyn replied. "Now get back inside. We're charging our own jump drive now."

Quinton didn't respond. He hastened toward the edge and pulled himself down toward the hull, where he disabled the mag boots and pulled himself toward the ship. He then pulled his feet to his torso and pushed away from the sensor array. He'd pushed off at an angle that took him toward the hull.

The agricultural unit didn't have anything like the maneuvering thrusters that an EVA suit had, but he hadn't thought anything of it and had been in the middle of congratulating himself when he realized that he was "flying" headfirst toward the hull. The distance to the hull appeared on his HUD, and he quickly calculated his velocity.

A comlink opened from Becker. "Nice work. How do you plan on not bouncing off the hull?"

Quinton bit back a retort, and the bot's internal systems struggled to find a way to deliver his intentions but couldn't because it wasn't capable of conveying freaking facial expressions. He didn't know which made him more irritated—the fact that he couldn't make facial expressions or that Becker was right.

He increased his frame rate, and time slowed down. He

secured the rifle to his back and did a few quick simulations for the best way not to bounce off into space. He extended his metallic arms in front of him, and if he'd been standing upright, his hands would have been over his head. The agricultural unit's hands were a composite alloy that was incredibly strong. He needed to redistribute the impact while propelling himself forward.

Even with his frame rate just above normal, Quinton was increasingly aware that he was rapidly approaching the hull of the ship. He'd done the calculations and tested them in a simulation. Now all he had to do was execute the maneuver and hope nothing broke on the agricultural bot's body that had been out of service for over a hundred years.

*Why did I do this to myself?*

Quinton executed his semi-controlled crash into the hull and skipped across its surface like a rock across a calm lake. He tried to reach for something to grab onto but couldn't. His feet dragged across the hull, and then he remembered the mag boots. He activated the boots and boosted them to maximum, which began to slow him down. Windmilling his arms, he tried in vain to push himself back toward the hull. It didn't work, and he imagined Becker was laughing at him. As he moved over a part of the ship where the artificial gravity field was stronger, he began to angle back toward the hull. That, in combination with the drag from his mag boots, allowed Quinton to come to an awkward stop. He regained his footing and looked around. He'd overshot the hatch by a good distance in the direction of the ship's engines.

"Get back inside!" Maelyn said, and there was no mistaking the urgency in her voice. She must have been monitoring him from the bridge.

"I'm on my way."

"Move it. You've got to run. Now!"

# CHAPTER TWENTY-TWO

QUINTON SPUN AROUND AND RAN. He'd overshot the hatch by more than seventy meters. Even with mag boots and the aid of his VI assistants, he could only move so fast in near-zero gravity, which was nothing like an all-out run at the speeds he could maintain in a one-g environment.

The *Nebulon* lurched to the side, pulling Quinton off balance before he could push himself off. Only one of his mag boots kept him attached to the hull, and he scrambled to get his footing under control while grabbing onto a nearby handrail. His view of the Mozeyian Outpost twisted away. A bright flash illuminated the backdrop of the ship and momentarily overwhelmed his vision. Maelyn had angled the ship away from the outpost so that when it performed its colossal FTL jump, the *Nebulon* shielded him from the brief but intense wave of gamma radiation. She'd saved his life. An intense gamma wave could easily damage the internal components of the agricultural bot. He had no idea if his ESS was sufficiently shielded against the intensity he'd just observed and wasn't curious enough to push the limits, but he wasn't out of the woods just yet. He had to get inside the ship before they could execute their own FTL jump, and there were still long-range missiles on an intercept course with the ship.

Quinton ran, quickly closing the distance to the maintenance hatch. He rounded the corner, expecting the hatch to be open, but it wasn't. He peered through the rectangular window and saw Becker standing there. He had two fingers pressed to the side of his helmet near his ear, and his head was turned away as if he was having a separate conversation.

Quinton accessed the comms systems nearby and heard Becker speaking.

"Say that again, Guttman," Becker said.

They must have been using a private channel of their own because Quinton couldn't hear the reply. Becker's mouth hung open a little, and he looked at Quinton with his brow furrowed.

Quinton banged his fist on the hatch. "What are you doing? Unlock the door. Let me inside."

Becker inhaled deeply and glanced away from him for a few silent moments. Then he shook his head. "I can't," he said, his voice sounding thick.

Quinton glared at Becker with smoldering emerald eyes. "You can't?" he growled and jerked on the hatch.

He couldn't believe it. Becker wasn't going to let him in. He tried to access the hatch control systems, but they were offline.

Quinton opened a comlink to the bridge. "Becker won't let me in. He's locked out the controls. They're offline."

"Maelyn," Becker said, his tone calm and even. "You have to listen to me. We can't let him inside."

"I don't know what game you think you're playing, but you open that hatch right now," Maelyn said with a steely edge to her voice.

Quinton looked at Becker, who shook his head. Quinton studied him for a few moments. His shoulders were tight, and he stared off to the side without seeing. His heart rate was elevated. Becker was afraid—not of him or Maelyn but something else.

"You know I can't do that. They'll destroy the ship. We can't let him back inside," Becker said.

"Dammit, Becker," Quinton said and slammed his metallic fist against the hatch again. He wished he had the strength to tear it off the ship and force his way inside.

"Override his controls," Maelyn said. She must have been speaking to Simon.

Becker regarded him, his jaw set and his gaze hard.

"Why not?" she said.

"He can't override the controls," Becker said. "I've disabled all systems access. They're on manual. The only way they're getting open is if you come down here yourself, but there isn't time for that. You have to trust me."

Quinton wanted to punch the hatch again but didn't. Instead, he said, "Becker, look at me."

The salvager raised his gaze.

"Crowe is not going to get us. There's still time. Let me inside."

Becker sneered and rolled his eyes, shaking his head again. "You think I'm afraid of Crowe? He's here, but so are the Sentinels. They're here, and they're hunting for *you*."

Quinton glanced over his shoulder and then chided himself inwardly. The Sentinels weren't right behind him, waiting to pounce on him unsuspectingly.

"You don't know that," Maelyn said, speaking to them now. "If you don't open that hatch right now, our deal is off, and nothing will stop me from throwing you and the rest of your crew off my ship."

"I don't believe you. You know I'm right. I have to do this." Becker paused for a second. "You'll never get here in time, and he can't make it to another airlock." Becker scowled at him and gritted his teeth. "He's in the ship systems. They're going to scan us and detect a PMC presence. What do you think is going to happen then?

You know how this is going to play out. They'll take out the ship without any hesitation or remorse, using weapons that will outclass anything available in this sector. Sentinels can't be reasoned with."

"I'll get out of the ship systems. They won't be able to detect me," Quinton said while trying to think of a way to get back onto the ship. Becker was right. This was the closest access hatch in the area.

"No, you won't. You can't help yourself," Becker said and then added, "You're in the ship systems. Look at the sensor feed. Look at Crowe's ships."

Quinton accessed the active sensor scan and saw that the JFS destroyers were now heading away from them. They'd altered course. He looked at Becker.

"You see it too. Even Crowe is running away from the Sentinels. This isn't personal, Quinton. But I'm not giving my life for you."

Quinton spun around and scanned the area. He couldn't see the Sentinels. He didn't even know what those ships looked like, but they were on the ship's sensors, and they were broadcasting their position. The sensors detected six ships, but they were too far away to determine what kind of ships they were. The Sentinels increased their speed, heading toward them. Quinton tried to think of why they would do that but couldn't come up with anything. He didn't know what scan they could do that would reveal his presence to them.

"Simon, are you there?" Quinton asked.

"I'm here."

"Have they scanned us? Have they already detected me?"

Simon didn't reply right away. "It's not that simple, but I don't think so."

Quinton looked through the hatch window and saw Becker watching him.

"You see?" Becker said. "He doesn't know."

"There has to be another reason they're heading toward the ship then," Quinton said.

He heard Maelyn begin to say something else, but he interfaced with the ship systems once again. Immediately, all the data streams were at his disposal, and his VI assistants waited for him to direct them. He felt an urge to turn them loose and take over the entire ship's systems, but he hesitated. Controlling the ship wouldn't help him.

"Radek, can you give me anything here? Any ideas?" Quinton asked inwardly.

An image of the plot appeared on his HUD, and it highlighted the long-range missiles that were still heading toward them at an unhurried pace. They'd likely increase speed once they got closer. They weren't close enough for the *Nebulon*'s point-defense systems to be effective, and the other ships would likely treat it as an attack. Crowe had been trying to intimidate them, but he'd also destroy the *Nebulon* to keep anyone else from using Quinton. Bargaining chip aside, Quinton didn't care for being treated like some kind of commodity.

He brought his attention back to the sensor plot. There were ten ships between the missiles and the *Nebulon*. The missiles had to be part of this. He just needed to figure out a way to use them or take them out of the equation.

Quinton accessed the *Nebulon*'s comms system and opened a broadcast subspace link to one of the other ships. The automatic comms systems that registered a ship-to-ship broadcast acknowledged it, and he was in. He bypassed their almost non-existent security measures, feeling as if what he'd just done was something he'd done many times before. He then opened separate comms channels to the remaining ships in the area.

". . . I don't know. He's broadcasting a signal," Simon said.

"Can't you lock him out?" Becker asked.

"No, I'm not going to lock him out," Maelyn said. "Quinton, tell us what you're doing. I want to help you."

Quinton cranked up his frame rate, allowing him to work with the world of data streams and subspace communications much faster than if he'd stayed in normal time. He was risking breaking the internal components of the agricultural bot that wasn't designed for such use, but he didn't have a choice. Becker wasn't going to let him back inside the ship, and he needed to convince him.

The other ships hadn't even detected the missiles in range. Their captains were too focused on jumping away from the system. He quickly calculated the highest probability of the trajectory the missiles would take to the *Nebulon*. Two of the ten ships on the path jumped away. Now he only had eight to work with. A quick query into their systems revealed that only five of the ships had some type of point-defense systems. He severed his connection to the other ships. They wouldn't be able to help. He offloaded copies of several VIs onto target ship systems because it would make what he was trying to do much easier by spreading the workload. Their access was tied directly into Quinton's ESS, which contained a data library for ship systems. The point-defense systems were rudimentary, with a solitary kinetic mag cannon that wasn't well maintained. A single small mag cannon couldn't provide adequate coverage, but these weren't warships. They were freighters meant for salvage and carrying cargo.

Quinton turned his attention to the maintenance records and winced inwardly. He'd be willing to wager that the captains of those ships mainly focused on maintaining the engines, trusting that running was a better option than relying on a nearly out-of-service point-defense system. Those systems had Cerberus protocols in their foundation, but given the state of the actual weapons, he could probably count on them being only 20 percent effective, and that estimate was generous.

He had five ships to work with that were in relatively close enough proximity to be effective. He put up their jump drive countdown timers while coming up with a firing solution that accounted for all the variables. He wouldn't test fire the mag cannons because that would alert the missiles' own sensors, and they would take evasive action. He needed to take them by surprise by having the mag cannons fire all at once.

Quinton uploaded his firing solution to the VIs he had on the other ships' computing systems, along with instructions for the VIs to delete themselves when the systems reset, which was the standard operating procedure for faulty systems. The captains would run a diagnostic on the faulty system, detect Quinton's VIs as anomalies, and then reset those systems.

The cluster of long-range missiles flew along their trajectory toward the *Nebulon*, increasing their speed. The mag cannons began firing a salvo at the missiles. Some of the mag cannons stopped firing after only a few seconds, while others increased their rate of fire, as if the cannons needed a bit of warm-up as they cleared their throats. The missiles' smart defense systems were taken by surprise and couldn't evade the sudden onslaught. They were destroyed without so much as a self-destruct protocol being engaged. Quinton ordered his VI assistants on the other ships to utilize the ships' sensors and search for any other missiles. He set the task to expire after fifteen minutes and withdrew from the other ships' systems, including the *Nebulon*'s.

Quinton returned his frame rate back to normal time. "It's the missiles," he said. "The Sentinels must have detected the trajectory of the missiles and were coming to investigate the ship. They haven't detected me at all."

Becker raised his eyebrows. "It's good in theory, I'll give you that, but I'm not letting you back on board."

As if to emphasize his determination, Becker sent a command to turn off Quinton's mag boots, and Quinton grabbed onto a handrail by the hatch. He could have taken control, but he waited. He could hold on for as long as he needed to.

"He's not in the ship systems anymore," Simon said.

Quinton put the comlink session on hold so he could think.

"Radek, you've got to give me something here. How can the Sentinels detect that I'm a PMC?" he asked.

"They must have protocols to detect the unique system access used by PMCs. Withdrawing all access, including latent subroutines, should erase all evidence of your manipulation of the system. Beyond that, they might be able to detect the leuridium power signature of your ESS, but sufficient shielding should prevent them from detecting that," Radek replied.

"Well, what would give me sufficient shielding?"

"It's hard to estimate because we don't know the scanning capabilities of the Sentinels' ships."

"For the love of—Take a damn guess," Quinton snapped.

"The highest probability for adequate shielding would be near the ship's reactor core. It's an area that must be shielded from the rest of the ship. Sensors in that area are designed for detecting containment breaches, not minuscule power core signatures," Radek said.

Quinton reconnected to the ship's systems and executed the cleanup protocol, which would theoretically erase all evidence of his activities in the ship's systems. Then he reactivated the external comlink that was connected to his shoulder and heard the others arguing. "I have a way to keep the Sentinels blind to me, but you need to let me back on the ship," he said and waited a few moments. "Becker, they're coming toward us right now, and if we jump away, they'll just follow us. We need to let them scan the ship."

"You're a damn fool," Becker replied and adjusted a setting on his assault rifle. "Maelyn, turn off the artificial gravity in this part of the ship, and I'll make sure the Sentinels won't detect us anywhere near Quinton."

Becker wasn't bluffing. A sufficiently charged plasma cannon would do the trick, and Quinton had nowhere to run. He didn't have time to fight Becker right then.

"I'm not in the system, and I removed all traces of being

there. If I can get to the ship's reactor core, there's enough shielding there to prevent the Sentinels from detecting my ESS. Since I'm not in the systems, that's their only other way of detecting what I am," Quinton said and paused for a few moments. "Come on, Becker, think about it. You know I'm right. I thought you wanted to get your big payday. This is how you do it. This is your only chance."

Becker looked away from him, his dark-eyed gaze intense.

Quinton silently urged him to open the hatch. "It's the only way. The Sentinels aren't stupid. They're going to realize where I came from, and then they're going to come after the ship anyway. Your only chance is to help hide me from them."

Becker glared at him. Then he sighed and collapsed his assault rifle, deactivating it. The hatch opened.

Quinton stepped inside and closed the hatch. Becker had removed the control panel, which was why the hatch had to be manually opened. A few seconds later, the gray interior airlock door opened, granting them access to the ship. He brushed past Becker without saying anything. He knew the layout of the ship and began to run toward main engineering.

"Don't worry about the doors," Maelyn said. "I'll take care of them as you head to the reactor. Now run!"

That was all the confirmation Quinton needed, and he sprinted down the corridor to a maintenance shaft. He slid down the ladder to the lower levels, plunging down several decks, and only slowing his descent at the last possible moment. He emerged from the shaft and ran down a dimly lit, narrow corridor on the most direct path to the reactor room. Bulkhead doors shut behind him as he made his way to the rear of the ship. Since he'd withdrawn his access from the ship's computer system, he felt like he'd been submerged in a sea of darkness. He'd ignored it at first, but the longer he went without access, the more he felt like he was stumbling around in the shadows, cut off from everything.

Quinton knew the layout of the *Nebulon*, having committed

it to memory when he'd first come aboard, but he checked the posted signs above the bulkhead doors and the faded remnants on the walls just the same. It was easy to get turned around in these maintenance corridors. All he needed was to get lost on a ship that wasn't overly monstrous by any stretch of the imagination.

He emerged from the maintenance path into the main corridor. Amber lights flashed outside the main reactor chamber as the doors began to open. Quinton bolted toward them. As soon as he was inside, the outer doors closed.

Quinton had a strange feeling that he should be breathing heavily. It had been a while since he'd felt the need to breathe. Stress and habits of the mind fueled well-established behaviors that he hadn't entirely put aside, and that was a good thing. Those habits reminded him that he was still human.

A nearby wallscreen flickered to life, and he saw Maelyn's face.

"All right, sit tight. I'll let you know when the Sentinels have done their scan."

Quinton nodded. "I guess if they've already detected something, none of us . . ." he couldn't finish what he'd been about to say. Maelyn had saved his life. He knew she'd had her own reasons for doing so, but he couldn't ignore what she'd done. She could easily have agreed with Becker, and then he would have been space dust.

Maelyn's lips lifted a little. It wasn't a smile or even the hint of one, but more of an acknowledgment. Regardless of what it meant, it reassured him.

"Thanks," Quinton said.

Maelyn looked away from the video feed toward what must have been the main holoscreen on the bridge. The image on the wallscreen Quinton watched split to show the bridge and the data feed on the main holoscreen.

A group of eight ships was highlighted. They were on an

intercept trajectory that would bring them close to the *Nebulon*. A scout group. That must've been what they were—a Sentinel scout group—but who controlled them? They couldn't be autonomous, but Maelyn and the others had said they hadn't communicated when hailed.

"Jump drive is ready, Captain," Simon said.

"Understood," Maelyn replied.

If they jumped now, the Sentinel scout ships were close enough to determine where they'd gone. They had to wait, and Quinton hated it. Waiting to be scanned by the Sentinels went against every instinct he had. He glanced at the others on the bridge, seeing that Simon and Kieva were sitting at a pair of workstations. The doors to the bridge opened, and Becker walked in.

Maelyn ignored him, keeping her attention on the main holoscreen.

Quinton questioned the logic of just lying down and exposing their throats to the Sentinels. They were putting themselves at the mercy of something they didn't completely understand. He frowned inwardly. That wasn't entirely correct. Everyone else had more of an understanding about the Sentinels than he did. He needed to rectify that, but what could he do if he couldn't access the ship's systems or give away his presence in any way?

There was nothing he could do now. They'd taken their chances based on his plan—Maelyn most of all. She was the captain.

*Radek, I hope you're right.*

An idea came to mind, and Quinton spoke. "Can you record them? The data feeds from this encounter."

"We are," Maelyn replied in a hushed tone.

Quinton was glad she'd kept the comlink session open and a live data feed to the bridge. It was his only connection. Did she suspect that if she kept him in the dark, he would access the ship's systems even though he'd promised not to? He was tempted. He wanted to know what was going on, and he'd become accustomed to having information readily accessible. Perhaps it made up for having such limited access to his own ESS.

A data overlay came to prominence on the main holoscreen. SN-DISCOVERY PROTOCOL INITIATED.

"They're scanning us now," Simon said.

Quinton was already still, but he wanted to hold his breath and be very still, or else he'd be detected. It was preposterous, but that was what fear was. For him, it was a fear of the unknown, but he'd also noticed anxiety in the others. Whatever the Sentinels were, they'd generated a universal dread among the ship personnel, along with a certainty of death if the Sentinels decided it was necessary. Becker had been willing to kill Quinton to save himself, which he understood. He didn't like the man, but Becker wasn't a coward. He'd thought they were all going to die if Quinton stayed. That was all there was to it. Quinton supposed he couldn't fault Becker for that.

He watched the wallscreen, feeling oddly exposed, as if something dark and sinister was lurking around the nearest corner. He resisted the urge to turn away.

"Oh my God! Did you see that?" Simon said.

Quinton saw that one of the Sentinels had accelerated past them with a sudden burst of speed, quickly followed by the others.

"They're attacking those ships," Simon said.

Quinton watched the data feeds on the main holoscreen and saw that Simon had highlighted the ships being attacked. If he had a mouth, it would have been hanging open in shock. The Sentinels' targets were the ships he'd used to destroy the long-range missiles.

"Why are they attacking them? It doesn't make sense," Simon said.

*I did this*, Quinton thought to himself. Those spacers were being murdered by the Sentinels, and it was all his fault. He sank to the floor, leaning heavily against the wall. He wished he could sink through the floor or become invisible. He was the reason those people were dying, all because he'd thought he was being clever. He'd left a few temporary VIs on those ships to provide protection should any other missiles be fired at them, thinking he'd protected them. The ships hadn't jumped away.

"Do you see the energy beam's power signature? I've never seen a magnitude that high. It melted through the hull in milliseconds," Simon said.

Becker came closer to Maelyn and then looked pointedly at the camera. "You're not so clever now, are you?"

Simon looked at Becker in surprise. "What are you talking about?"

"Those spacers are being slaughtered because of him," Becker said, jutting his chin toward the camera feed showing Quinton slumped against the wall in shame.

Kieva frowned. "I don't understand."

"Becker's right," Quinton said, and the others all looked at him. "I accessed those ship's systems and used their point-defense systems to take out the missiles. Then I left a temporary VI in place to scan for other incoming missiles. I didn't think . . . Those ships were moments away from jumping. They should've been gone."

"It's not your fault," Maelyn said.

Becker turned toward her. "You've gotta be kidding me! He's the reason the Sentinels destroyed those ships. Those spacers are dead because of him."

The last ship Quinton accessed had managed to execute a space jump, but a few moments later, several ships from the Sentinel scout force jumped also, no doubt in pursuit of them.

"You must see that," Becker continued.

Maelyn stepped toward him and thrust out her hand. A burst

of energy came from her palm stunner, shoving him back. He tumbled several feet away.

"You," she hissed, striding toward him. She swung again, and another burst of energy threw Becker back toward the doors to the bridge.

He slowly stood and raised his hands.

"Get off my bridge before I throw you off this ship," Maelyn said and pulled out her sidearm. "Changed my mind. Throwing you off is too good for you," she growled and pointed her weapon at him.

Becker hastened backward, stumbling a little.

"Captain!" Simon said.

Becker held up his hands.

Maelyn sneered, her nostrils flaring. Then, through gritted teeth, she said, "Get out!"

He scrambled to his feet and fled. Maelyn headed back to the captain's chair. "Execute jump."

"Aye, ma'am, executing jump," Simon replied.

Maelyn sat in her chair and activated her personal holoscreen. Quinton glanced up to see her face still red with anger, but she tried to soften her features when she looked at him. "This wasn't your fault. You didn't know."

"Yes, it was. I should have listened. Becker was right," Quinton replied.

"He's an asshole. Unforgiving and rigid."

Quinton looked at her. "That doesn't make him wrong."

She started to speak again, and he shook his head. "I'd like to be alone."

Maelyn regarded him for a moment and then nodded. The comlink to the bridge disconnected, and Quinton saw the monitoring system for the reactor register a power spike as the *Nebulon* jumped away.

# CHAPTER TWENTY-THREE

THE *NEBULON* HAD EMERGED from its jump some time earlier. Quinton made a conscious effort not to know how much time had passed. It actually required mental effort and assertion on his part to blank out his HUD, which was designed for ease of access. His HUD wasn't the agricultural bot's default interface. It had been altered when Radek adapted the bot's systems for PMC use. Quinton had his own HUD that was combined with that of the agricultural bot. All the data feeds normally within view were now invisible, and he didn't want to think about any of them. At some point, the heavily shielded doors to the reactor core opened, and he guessed that was Maelyn's way of urging him to leave the core.

Quinton stood up and walked out, leaving the reactor core behind. He tried to keep his mind blank, which was impossible. He wasn't even required to physically rest, so his mind was always active. There should have been something in his training to accommodate this, but those memories were unavailable—big surprise.

*Those spacers had been slaughtered because of him . . .*

Snippets of the events that had taken place a few hours before, along with Becker's condemnation, kept coming to the forefront of his mind—

*Three hours and fourteen minutes.*

Quinton stopped walking. He clenched one of his robotic hands into a fist, hoping the simple act of squeezing really hard would provide an outlet for his rage. He'd settle for feeling a strain or an explosion of breath, or even being able to grit his teeth, but he couldn't do any of those things. There was no buildup of corporeal pressure, but pressure was building in other ways. He hadn't wanted to know how much time had passed since he'd aided in the murder of spacers who were fleeing for their lives.

He glanced at dark gray walls of the corridor and focused on a blemish the maintenance bots hadn't been able to scrub clean. It wasn't the only imperfection evident on the old ship. He imagined striking the wall and feeling the force from his hands and shoulders dispersing throughout the rest of his body. He knew that if he struck the wall with enough force, he'd leave a mark . . . *his* mark. A few moments of heavy silence passed, and then Quinton resumed walking. The corridor walls had gotten off easy because a small part of him had cautioned against it. The agricultural bot was old. What if he broke something important? And for what?

He wanted to walk aimlessly and allow his feet to guide him, but that was impossible. Movement required a destination, so either he could spend his time picking obscure destinations on the ship, or he could go to the one place that made the most sense to him. It wasn't a logical kind of sense, but it was the only place he could think to go and not see anyone else.

Quinton walked into Simon's workshop and closed the door. The workshop was empty, with only the ambient glow of the amber lighting overhead. They were watching him. Maelyn would definitely be monitoring his location, and Quinton felt less inclined to try to hide it. He just wanted to be left alone.

He crossed the workshop toward a shelving unit on the other side and crouched. He was close to the shelves without making any contact. He could see the door to the workshop and stared at it for a few moments.

*. . . slaughtered . . .*

*You're not so clever now . . .*

Quinton was able to recall Becker's voice with stunning clarity. He didn't know what the Sentinels were capable of, and he hadn't listened to the others. They'd tried to warn him in their own subtle ways, while at the same time trying not to overwhelm him with information about a galaxy he scarcely understood.

The pitter-patter of small footsteps drew his attention, and Stumpy leaped down to the floor from some shelf he'd claimed as his own. The creature's sizable ears perked up, and his large round eyes regarded him with the vertical irises of a nocturnal predator. Then Stumpy walked toward Quinton, crouching on all fours. The creature vocalized at a high pitch that wouldn't have been heard by any of the others unless they'd augmented their hearing.

Quinton repeated the cadence of Stumpy's vocalizations, and the creature paused to peer up at him warily.

"Aren't we a pair," he said softly. Then he sighed inwardly. Here he was, sitting in a dark room, identifying with an animal slightly bigger than a rodent.

Stumpy leaped toward him, and he easily caught the creature in his hands, raising him toward his face. Stumpy cocked his head to the side and peered at him.

Quinton cocked his head in imitation. "Well, I'm not homesick for *your* planet. That's for sure."

Simon must have been feeding him because he didn't look as scrawny as Quinton remembered. The bare patches of fur were starting to show new growth. A few good meals and some rest in a safe place had done wonders for the little guy, but he had to be lonely. Quinton remembered the group of them that had climbed into the vehicle while he was fleeing from the hunter mechs. None of the others could have survived. The atmosphere was becoming toxic, at least in that region of the continent.

He lowered his hands to the ground, and Stumpy stepped off. He went a few feet away and sat on the floor, grooming himself. Quinton supposed that conveyed a certain level of trust. Stumpy was probably the only one on the ship who trusted him.

He spent the next few minutes watching the creature clean himself, doing a rather thorough job of it. Grooming must have been impossible on the planet because of the toxic nature of the fallout. He wanted to believe that not having access to the bulk of his memories was worse than being cut off from your species on a dying planet, but that would push the boundaries of his self-pity too far. He wasn't that far gone, and he decided not to dwell on it.

Quinton glanced at the wallscreen nearby and stood up. He wouldn't stay huddled in some dark corner. He didn't have to be inside the system in order to use it. He lamented the almost painfully slow access to information, but direct access seemed foolish to him right then. He increased the luminosity of the lighting in the workshop. He could see just fine in the dark, but he had the feeling that staying in the dark was the same as hiding, and he didn't want to hide anymore.

The wallscreen workstation was equipped with a holographic projector, and Quinton enabled several holoscreens. They were blank screens with a standard interface, waiting for him to initiate an action. He paused for a few moments, considering what he needed to do first, and then brought up the data recordings of their encounter with the Sentinels.

"Radek," Quinton said.

A holographic, semi-translucent sphere appeared.

"I need you to help me analyze this encounter."

"Analysis would be much quicker if you accessed the ship's computer system more directly than using this interface," Radek replied.

Had the VI expressed a note of disdain? Quinton dismissed it. VIs didn't have a preference for how they worked. Radek was merely pointing out the fact that working this way was suboptimal.

"Understood, Radek. Let's just work this way," Quinton replied.

He began querying the *Nebulon*'s computer system and realized that Simon had already pulled all data related to the Sentinel encounter into one place for him to review.

On one holoscreen, Quinton pulled up the communication logs that began with the initial broadcast from the Sentinel scout force. He compared that with the active scan data and tried to see whether the *Nebulon*'s systems had even detected the scout force jumping into the area.

"Radek, see if you can pinpoint the jump insertion of the Sentinels from this log data."

The shimmering orb turned his attention to the data on the holoscreen and seemed to study for only a second or two. "Impossible to predict to any degree of accuracy."

"That's what I was afraid of," Quinton said.

Thousands of ships had been fleeing the Mozeyian Outpost, and the *Nebulon*'s sensors hadn't been able to cope with all that information. All he had to work with was the initial broadcast detected by the ship's communication systems.

He studied the data on the screen. "The Sentinels arrived in-system and started broadcasting their presence. Why would they do that?"

"Are you asking me?" Radek asked.

Quinton glanced at him. "Well, no. I'm thinking out loud. It helps me organize my thoughts."

Radek was silent.

"Is there something you'd like to share about the Sentinels?" Quinton asked.

"I don't have enough data to establish a pattern, but in this instance, based upon the data, I believe the Sentinels were following their own established protocols."

"Destroying ships because their scans and systems access revealed a PMC presence?"

"That, too, but your question had to do with their initial broadcast. They announced their presence. Perhaps they expected compliance from whoever received the broadcast," Radek replied.

Quinton considered this and tried to think of what kind of compliance the Sentinels expected. A ship broadcasting its location was the best way to establish intent and avoid collisions. This was more of a concern when in close proximity. Compliance also meant that the Sentinels had a task to perform, and any ship within range of the broadcast was expected to just let them do it. Scanning ships and remote systems access to search for PMC activity seemed extreme, but according to the others, this activity was considered normal. The fact that successful detection of PMC presence resulted in an attack meant that the protocols were being followed irrespective of the lives aboard the ship.

"So much for rules of engagement."

Quinton looked at another holoscreen that was displaying the Sentinel attack data. These were warships, and they'd fired on civilian freighters. After destroying those ships, the Sentinels had moved on to scan the other ships. Even after two of the Sentinel scout ships had FTL-jumped out of the system to pursue a fleeing ship, the others continued. There was a certain level of detachment reminiscent of a VI control system. It had been almost a hundred years since the Federation Wars. Why were the Sentinels still around?

Quinton searched for other log data with previous encounters but couldn't find any.

"Your search for previous encounters with Sentinels in the ship's logs didn't yield any results, but this isn't your first encounter with them," Radek said.

"What do you mean? I think I'd know it if I had."

Radek opened another holoscreen. "These are the ship designations from the broadcast that came from the scout group," he said and brought up another screen. "This is the ship designation from the hostile ship encountered in the Zeda-Six Star System. The base designations are the same."

Quinton looked at the screens.

*SN-Seeker-901 – Broadcast hail. Zeda-Six Star System.*

The ship had changed course to pursue him while he was leaving the system. It had been a lone Sentinel scout ship.

Quinton looked at the designation for the scout group.

*SN-Seeker-SF-301 – Broadcast hail. Mozeyian Outpost.*

*Seeker-SF . . . Seeker Scout Force.*

It was a military designation. He recognized the hierarchical references, but which federation military had created the Sentinels?

If he'd allowed that ship to scan him when he was fleeing the Zeda-Six Star System, it would have destroyed him for sure. But why had the Sentinels been there in the first place? Had they tracked the activation signal to Zeda-Six and come to investigate? Had the hunter mechs on the planet been following some latent protocol that originated from the Sentinels, and was that the reason they wouldn't communicate with him in the first place?

Quinton stared at the two holoscreens, allowing his thoughts to explore the questions on his mind. If the Sentinels were hunting for him, then maybe he *should* leave the *Nebulon* and get a ship of his own to track the activation signal. How much could he trust the other people on this ship? Becker had been ready to hand him over to the Sentinels and flee the system. Guttman and Oscar would be sure to follow Becker's lead. But what about Maelyn, Simon, and Kieva? Maelyn had supported him, but could that change, and was it really fair for her to do so? Quinton thought Simon and Kieva would follow Maelyn's lead, but perhaps not as doggedly as Guttman and Oscar followed Becker's. Then there was Vonya. The door to the workshop opened, and he stopped in mid-thought.

Vonya entered. The Servitor had changed her clothing, which now covered significantly more of her smooth lavender skin but still didn't leave anything to the imagination. Her long platinum hair was tied back into a simple ponytail, accentuating her high cheekbones. Her gaze warmed at the sight of him, and she smiled a little as she closed the distance between them.

Vonya glanced at the holoscreens. "Am I interrupting you?"

Quinton wondered whether she had just happened to find him here or had been sent here by someone else. "I was just thinking about the Sentinels."

She came to stand by his side, looking completely at ease. He'd expected that the others would want to remain distant from him, except he hadn't realized it until just that moment.

"Time for quiet reflection is often time well spent," Vonya replied. She looked at the data on the holoscreens. "What's so special about Sentinel ship designations?"

Quinton wasn't sure how the others would react if they learned that the Sentinels were more aware of him than they'd originally thought. It wasn't that he intended to hide it from them, but he hadn't decided whether he wanted to share it with them yet.

"That's what I was looking at. I don't have any memories of Sentinels."

Vonya regarded him for a few moments. "It must be frustrating for you."

He knew she was trying to soothe him, perhaps lull him into a sense of confidence, false or otherwise. "It is," he said, and was glad to have someone acknowledge it. "Radek was just pointing out to me that we'd encountered a Sentinel when we left the planet I was activated on."

Vonya's eyes darted back to the holoscreen. "Really!" She pursed her full lips, which drew his attention. "That can't be a coincidence."

"Only if my luck changes," Quinton replied, and she chuckled.

"You'll need that. Constant vigilance is exhausting. Being able to regard the situation you find yourself in with a bit of dry humor allows for relief."

"It doesn't change anything. Are you going to keep trying to counsel me?"

Vonya looked at him. "Not if you do not wish me to."

Quinton didn't reply. He didn't know what he wanted.

"It's what a Servitor does."

"What's that exactly?"

"We attend to people's needs and provide advice when desired."

Quinton wondered just how many things could be grouped under "attending to people's needs."

"And what do you get out of it?" he asked.

Vonya arched a platinum eyebrow toward him. "The satisfaction of knowing I've touched the lives of others in a meaningful and positive way."

Quinton made an unintelligible sound.

Vonya frowned a little and then smiled. "Do you find it amusing?"

"Would it offend you if I did?"

"No. There are many people who don't fully appreciate our ways."

"I bet there are a lot of people who try to take advantage of you."

"Many *think* they do," Vonya replied.

There was something in her gaze that Quinton hadn't seen before. It was like a comfortable knowledge of one's place in the galaxy, but there was also a certainty that she was playing a game at a higher level than most people comprehended. He had dismissed the Servitor out of hand, but perhaps she was much more dangerous than he'd initially thought. He just didn't understand in what form Vonya's particular brand of danger would manifest. Did she even know?

"Interesting," Quinton said. "So did Maelyn ask you to check on me?"

Vonya quirked an eyebrow at him, and her eyes twinkled. "Would it bother you if Captain Wayborn sent me to you?"

"You didn't answer the question."

She exhaled softly, managing to make even that look graceful and alluring at the same time. He might be stuck in a robot body, but he wasn't dead. Vonya was a beautiful woman if one preferred the utter perfection of female symmetry—from the deliciously feminine features of her face, to her long slender arms, and down to the tips of her fingers.

"Yes, she did," Vonya said finally. "She believed it might make you feel better if I spoke to you."

"Did she send you to Becker too?" he asked and almost immediately wished he hadn't. Almost, but not quite.

Vonya drew herself up, looking neither annoyed nor offended. "I prefer to get to know the entire crew. It helps the captain if I contribute in this way."

"That's just it. We're not a crew. We're passengers on Maelyn's ship, along with a whole lot of promises."

Her eyebrows pulled together in concern, and a small part of him liked the attention, the comfort in the illusion that he wasn't alone. But it *was* an illusion. This was just another of Vonya's tricks.

"We share a common goal that will benefit all involved," she said.

Quinton glanced at the holoscreens. "I don't know if it's going to work out the way you think it will."

As she regarded him for a few moments, the door to the workshop opened and Maelyn walked in.

Quinton glanced at her as she strode into the workshop, coming toward him. She was a formidable woman, the bearer of a fierce beauty that was at once at odds with Vonya's stunning perfection. But her beauty was real. She had thick dark brown hair, tanned skin, and subtle blue eyes that blazed when one was lucky enough to be caught in their crosshairs. He'd seen her raw anger as she handily removed Becker from the bridge. She was a woman who was used to command. He hadn't seen it when they'd first met, and he wondered how he could have missed it. He'd seen her as strong and kind, and very much a product of the harsh realities of this galaxy, but Quinton didn't really know who she was. She was tenacious and seemed to keep to herself and a trusted few. But what did she really want?

Maelyn looked at him with a coolness that was reflected in her blue eyes. Quinton studied her and then cranked up his frame rate, slowing down his perception of time and elongating the moment. On second thought, he'd been sure her eyes were pale green. He checked his memory and found that the color of her eyes had changed. On the deck of Lennix Crowe's hangar bay, Maelyn had had eyes of celestial blue. Then, sometime after they'd escaped from Crowe and were on the Mozeyian Outpost, they'd been a pale green with hints of brown in them. Now they were a blue that was as intense as the largest star burning the hottest.

Quinton lowered his frame rate back to normal. She blinked, and there was a calm set to her mouth. Her jawline was on the square side but not in any way masculine. Where Vonya was tall and slender, Maelyn had an athletic body that was properly proportioned and no less perfect than Vonya's engineered physique. Quinton had never taken the time to admire it. He'd only sneaked a few glances during their time together. He was a man, after all, and if he wasn't looking, then there had to be something wrong with him. Becker had detected something in the way Quinton regarded Maelyn.

She looked at Vonya for a moment. "Thank you, Vonya," Maelyn said and turned toward Quinton. "I asked her to check on you."

Quinton nodded. "Well, it would have been her or Simon."

Maelyn tilted her chin down and sighed.

"I know what you're doing. You send in a friendly face and then we can gloss over the fact that this situation—me being on this ship— is spiraling out of control."

She smiled widely, her eyes gleaming with amusement. "You really don't think much of us, do you?"

"Would you? Since I met you, it's been all about what I can do for you. I'm so valuable that Crowe is willing to commit vast resources to capture me. Are you saying you would do any less?" Quinton asked and then added, "No, you're always much more subtle than that. Why use a blaster when you can use empty promises?"

"Quinton, that's not fair," Vonya said.

Maelyn raised one of her hands in a placating gesture. "On the contrary, Quinton is being very fair."

He felt the annoying urge to frown, which came with the added bonus of an error about not having a mouth to hang open.

Maelyn pressed her lips together for a moment, but there were still hints of a smile around the edges. "However," she said, "the promises I made to you aren't empty."

Quinton looked away from her toward the holoscreens—not because he needed to see the information on them but to buy himself a few moments to think. He turned back to her. "I don't think this arrangement is going to work out between us."

"Are you breaking up with me?"

He felt the urge to frown yet again, along with the irritating feedback on non-capability. He leaned away from her. "What?"

Maelyn laughed, and despite himself, it was a sound he found soothing to his artificial ears. "Will you at least hear me out and then make a decision?"

Quinton's guard went up immediately. *Are you breaking up with me? What did that even mean*, he thought. Aloud, he said, "What? That's it? You'd just let me go? I wouldn't have to bargain for it or take more direct action to secure my freedom?"

Maelyn's eyebrows rose for a quick second. "Are any of us really free?" she asked and held up her hand. "Never mind, don't answer that. But to answer *your* question, yes, I'd let you go. You're not my prisoner, Quinton."

"What about Wallace?"

Maelyn inhaled deeply and arched a dark eyebrow. Vonya watched them both with keen interest. "That's not something you need to concern yourself with. I can take care of myself."

"I know you can take care of yourself, but I thought—"

"I know what you thought, but look, I'm going to level with you. That's what you want, isn't it?" Maelyn asked.

Quinton nodded.

"First, you're right. I'd considered sending Simon to check on you. You two have a rapport. You obviously wanted to be alone, but when I saw that you were working in here, I thought it would be best for you to see a friendly face. Vonya was nearby and said she thought she could help you," Maelyn said.

Quinton glanced at Vonya, who nodded once.

"It was highly manipulative, and I offer my heartfelt apologies for being concerned for your well-being."

He grinned and shook his head. "All right, fine. There wasn't some nefarious motivation on your part, and I appreciate your concern. Thank you."

Maelyn inclined her head in a small nod. "I said I was going to level with you, and I am. You want to track the activation signal and get out of that body."

"Preferably into my own body based on my biological scan data."

"I don't understand," Vonya said.

"As part of the upload process for becoming a PMC, biological scan data was always retained as a backup," Quinton replied.

Vonya frowned. "But it's been so long. Are any of those records still around?"

"I don't know for sure, but I do have access to resources that might help," Maelyn said.

Quinton didn't respond. He waited for her to continue.

"You always have the option to wander the galaxy on your own, but I'm not sure how successful you'd be."

"I don't know. I'm pretty determined," he said.

"Of that I have no doubt. Let me tell you why coming with me is your best option. I'm from the Dholeren United Coalition. There are several large nomadic fleets that form the coalition, and it's made up of people from multiple federations. They were displaced during the Federation Wars, as well as in the aftermath. There were many roaming groups just looking for safety."

"Nomadic fleets? Why didn't they resettle on a habitable world?"

"Some did. Actually, a lot of them did, at least initially. Then various salvager groups and pirates raided those areas. Why work to build a permanent settlement when someone else was just going to come and take everything you own?" Maelyn said.

"Couldn't they defend themselves?" he asked.

"It's not an all or nothing, Quinton. People did try to defend themselves, and some succeeded for a little while. But eventually, defending a habitable world wasn't a viable long-term option. You see, not only were they the victims of remnant militaries, but the worlds were also visited by Sentinel scout fleets. You've seen what they're capable of. There are records of them visiting the same devastation on newly minted colonial worlds. So, what would you do?" she asked with raised eyebrows. Quinton was silent. "Moving around was their best option. And the DUC is more accepting of people from all federations than other groups."

"Okay, I'm with you. Keep talking," Quinton said.

"Since the DUC accepts refugees from all over, we have access to a pretty robust knowledge base. There might be someone with knowledge about PMCs and that signal used to activate you," Maelyn said.

"Is that before or after they try to enslave me? I don't know if I can go along with this without full access to my own memories. I mean, there seems to be a common hatred of the Acheron Confederacy. What if you learned that they were the ones who activated me or somehow there's a connection there? What would you do then?" Quinton asked.

"I don't know how people would react to that," Maelyn said. "I don't even know how the DUC leadership would react, but I don't think it would matter because you're the key to unlocking technology and access to data that we simply don't have right now. It's been locked away from us. So regardless of people's prejudices, they will *need* you, just like you need us. Whether you want to admit it or not, your best chance at surviving is with me."

Quinton regarded her for a few moments. No matter how he tried to dissect it, Maelyn made some very good points. He wanted to find a flaw in her argument, but he couldn't. She'd already acknowledged the risks associated with going with her.

"I'll do everything I can to help you," she said.

"Why? Why would you make a promise like that? I don't know if I can trust you, and you don't know if you can trust *me*."

"Eventually, you'll have to trust someone. That is, unless you plan to remain alone."

He didn't need Radek to tell him what the probability for

success was if he decided to go off on his own. Whether he liked it or not, he needed to stay on the *Nebulon* and see this through.

Quinton gestured toward the holoscreens. "Since we're being honest, I think you should know that I've encountered the Sentinels before, but I didn't know what they were," he said and told her what had happened during his escape from the Zeda-Six Star System. "What do you think?"

Maelyn peered at the data on the holoscreens and then looked at him. "You're right. They might be hunting for you. I think we should assume that they are."

"So, you still think bringing me to the DUC nomadic fleets is a good idea?" Quinton asked.

"Our options are limited, but I'm not bringing you to the civilian fleets. We're going to meet at a neutral location to protect the fleet," Maelyn said.

"I just don't know how the Sentinels could have tracked me here."

"It could just be coincidence. It's certainly not the same scout ship, but they must have a central command that they report in to."

"Central command—COMCENT," Quinton said. "Maybe we can find out what they know?"

Maelyn shook her head. "No way. It's too well protected, and you saw what they can do. That was only a scout force."

"Okay, but when the scout force reports to COMCENT, that means there will be more Sentinels looking for me," Quinton said.

"Not just you. I wasn't—There've been other reports of PMC activity."

"What kind of reports?" he asked.

Maelyn shook her head. "I don't know, other than the fact that there have been rumors, and it's something that would be quite concerning if it was true."

Quinton considered this for a few moments—more than a

few moments to be exact, thanks to his internal clock. "You're worried that another war will happen. The Sentinels will increase their activities and maybe become more aggressive. That's what you're afraid of."

"That's what *you* should be afraid of," she replied.

There was something in the certainty of her reply that made him think he would be foolish not to listen to her. Yet, he wasn't sure how he could go on avoiding the Sentinels, and he said so.

"Everyone avoids the Sentinels. You wouldn't be alone in that," Maelyn said.

"I can't promise that I won't access computer systems when I come across them. I can try and limit my footprint, so to speak, but I can't stumble around any more than I already am," Quinton said.

Maelyn looked at him for a few long moments and then nodded slowly. She didn't like it, but what choice did he have? He thought about the salvager ships that had been destroyed by the Sentinels. There had to be a way for him to mask his presence.

"So, are we still on to meet with the leadership of the DUC?" Maelyn asked.

She wasn't going to take anything at face value or she wouldn't have asked. She didn't demand or expect his cooperation.

"Yes, let's see what we can find out," Quinton replied.

She smiled a little. "Good. I'll make the arrangements."

"Do those arrangements still require the presence of Becker, Guttman, and Oscar?" he asked.

He really didn't have any problems with Oscar, but he doubted Oscar would leave Becker.

Maelyn's gaze hardened. "We have a deal," she said, as if that explained everything.

"I'll never trust Becker."

She inhaled and sighed. "You don't have to trust him, and he doesn't have to trust you."

Quinton couldn't help but detect the warning note in her voice. Becker had challenged her authority and come up short. She could use the blaster, but Quinton thought she preferred mutual cooperation. He decided he'd play along for now. He'd much rather work with Maelyn than against her. But regardless of what anyone said, he would keep a close watch on Becker and his men.

# CHAPTER TWENTY-FOUR

THEIR MEETING with the Dholeren United Coalition leadership was delayed. There were concerns that the meeting would draw attention from the Sentinels or even Lennix Crowe, so extra precautions needed to be taken. Maelyn explained that the additional security measures were because of her report that had been delivered by Captain Wallace. A DUC admiral by the name of Severin Brandt had sent Maelyn a recorded message. The DUC admiralty didn't want to chance an open connection with Quinton on the *Nebulon*. From a security standpoint, Quinton approved of the precautionary steps being taken, but he was still impatient to get on with it. Vonya had commented about a saying that referred to "idle hands opening the way to mischief."

Quinton had some free time on his hands, so he stayed busy by analyzing the current data from the Sentinel attack. The standard protocols they followed were extreme, as if the entire galaxy were in one big interstellar war and the Sentinels retained some kind of emergency powers that allowed them to violate just about every pre-Federation War law to protect people.

Spacers had always scanned each other. It was the only way to determine what kind of ship or other installation they'd encounter in a given star system. But the Sentinels accessed ship systems and then determined whether they were going to obliterate those ships, colonies, space stations, or just about any settlement found across the galaxy. It was a gross abuse of power, and it had led the survivors of the Federation Wars to take extreme measures of their own in order to avoid combat with the Sentinels and each other. Genetic augmentation had always been practiced, but Quinton's limited memory of it indicated that it had been highly refined to fit unique circumstances, such as adapting to a habitable world. But post-Federation War, people had taken genetic manipulation to a whole new extreme where they could almost scarcely be called human anymore.

Quinton looked at Simon expectantly. They were alone on the bridge.

"What you're asking is impossible for me to duplicate," Simon said.

"It's not impossible."

He'd been directly interfacing with the *Nebulon*'s computer systems while conversing with Simon at the same time. Multitasking was actually getting easier for him, but it did require increasing his frame rate, so sometimes his conversation with Simon was a little off-kilter.

"Do you know how to do it then?" Simon asked.

"That's the point. Radek has helped create cleanup routines that effectively mask my presence in the system and will remove all traces that I can think of, but that's the problem. What if we missed something? We need a way to test it," Quinton said.

Removing traces of his presence on the ship's computer system was simple in theory but had proven to be frustratingly difficult to implement. In all instances, Quinton had to disconnect from the computer system to avoid detection. That was the easiest thing to do, but it severely limited what he could do.

"You can't go around making changes to the system, even if it's less efficient. You also access information quicker, which leaves a trace, and no, telling the *Nebulon* to stop logging activity won't work either because there are limits to how many processes the ship's computing system is able to monitor," Simon said.

"That's the part I don't understand. What if you'd made the improvements or found another way to do what I can do, but without being a PMC?"

"Then any Sentinel we encountered would become hostile."

"That would mean that there haven't been any improvements to computing systems since the Federation Wars."

"I wouldn't go that far," Simon replied. "That's an oversimplification. There have been changes and improvements, but innovation has slowed down, and anything we do requires that we consider how the Sentinels would react."

"I know you told me that there have been multiple war efforts to stop the Sentinels, and they were all put down hard, but I just don't believe that all the options have been explored," Quinton said.

Simon shrugged one shoulder. "Regardless, I can't guarantee that even with Radek's improvements for hiding your presence you wouldn't be detected by the Sentinels. Think about it. They're not dumb machines that keep doing the same thing over and over again. They adapt too. Based on the reports of every encounter we know about, the Sentinels aren't stagnant in the methodology they use."

Quinton was quiet for a few moments while he considered. "I just want to be thorough. There has to be a way to fool them, but we can't wait to encounter a Sentinel to test out our ideas."

Simon pressed his lips together while he peered at the data on the holoscreen in front of him. "Much of our detection capabilities for PMC activity stem from what the Sentinels use."

"They shared it with you?"

Simon snorted and shook his head, grinning. "We had the capability beforehand. It came out during the Federation Wars when multiple federations were producing their own PMCs, so the ability to detect PMC activity was born of necessity."

"I see," Quinton said. "How long do you think they'll delay the meeting?"

"Not that long. They'll want to keep it a secret, but they also can't sit on this for any great period of time," Simon replied.

The door to the bridge opened and Maelyn entered, along with Becker.

"Any word from Brandt?" she asked.

"Not yet," Simon said.

Maelyn nodded and looked at Quinton. "It shouldn't be too much longer."

"Let's hope not," Becker added.

The salvager had gone back to treating Quinton as he'd done before—slightly indifferent with the occasional proverbial jab.

"What I'd like to know is how Lennix Crowe was able to track us to the outpost," Quinton said.

"He has an effective network of informants," Becker replied.

"We were only there for a few hours. Can they normally track someone that fast?" Quinton asked.

Becker leveled a look at him. "You think it's me. That I somehow informed Crowe of our location."

"You did work for him. Maybe you decided that changing sides . . ." Quinton paused, choosing his words, ". . . ending your employment was a hasty decision, and how else could you rectify such a decision but by offering me up to Crowe?"

Becker chuckled and then nodded. "It's tempting, and I can see why you'd think that, but you'd be wrong."

"Am I?"

"You don't get it. Crowe doesn't offer second chances."

"Is that so," Quinton replied. "Apparently, I'm pretty valuable. He must want what I can do in the worst way. I can see him making an exception in this case."

Becker glanced at Maelyn and rolled his eyes. "There are

rumors that Crowe is in trouble with the Collective. That's why he'd like to get his hands on a PMC."

"The Collective?" Maelyn said. "Draven is after him?"

Becker arched an eyebrow, then nodded once. "These are just rumors."

"What kind of rumors?" Quinton asked.

Becker scratched the stubble of his beard. "Crowe tried to claim something that didn't belong to him, or he failed to deliver on a big promise, and Draven plans to absorb Crowe's Union."

"That's it? One bad deal and Crowe's entire operation is at risk?" Quinton asked.

"There's also a rumor that Crowe tried to steal something important from the Collective. It doesn't really matter," Becker said and glanced at the main holoscreen for a moment. "All I know is that demands were increased across the board. They wanted us to bring in as much salvage as we could. Crowe became obsessed with resource allocation."

Maelyn pursed her lips. "If he had the Collective breathing down his neck, that would explain a few things."

Quinton looked at her.

"I'd thought Crowe wanted you in order to sell dumbed-down versions of you, or he'd use you to help his operation run more efficiently, but I might have been wrong. He needs you to survive, or . . ." She stopped speaking and looked at Becker, and then they both looked at Quinton.

"Why do I get the feeling I'm not going to like where this is going," Quinton said, dryly.

"Crowe needs you in order to take on the Collective," Maelyn said.

"Wait, what?" Quinton began and stopped. "I'm assuming he has a way to enslave me, but how does that mean he can suddenly take on the Collective?"

Maelyn and Becker didn't look at each other, but there was some kind of deference evident between the two of them.

"I thought we were done hiding things from each other," Quinton said.

Maelyn tapped her fingertips on the nearest workstation and then turned toward him. "You could give him a tactical advantage in space combat. It would be enough of an advantage that Crowe could start nibbling away at the Collective."

Becker exhaled explosively and shook his head. "That would be a huge power play," he said and frowned. "That would really shake things up."

Maelyn nodded.

Becker regarded her for a few moments. "One day, I'd like to find out what you were really doing trying to infiltrate Crowe's organization."

"Who said I was trying?" Maelyn said dryly.

Becker snorted.

"I understand this is important, but how much of an impact would this have?" Quinton asked. He was getting tired of being in the dark about . . . everything.

"The Collective is a known entity," Maelyn said. "We avoid them whenever possible, but sooner or later you have to deal with them. They're one of the largest purveyors of just about anything you can think of, but at a cost." She pressed her lips together. "The dominant faction of the Collective came from the remnants of the Tilion Empire Fleet. They had one of the most intact military fleets at the end of the Federation Wars. The Tilions had already been quite militaristic. They sought to fill the void the Jordani Federation left after both they and the Acheron Confederacy destroyed themselves. I'm afraid there's a lot of history here that you'll need to learn about in order to understand."

"What a surprise," Becker said. "Quinton needs another history lesson."

Quinton looked at Becker with what he hoped was a menacing glare. The agricultural bot's facial features weren't meant to convey much in the way of emotion, but he thought he could change the eye color to something more menacing.

"There are a few lessons I'd like to teach you, Becker," Quinton said.

Becker's smile didn't reach his eyes. "Anytime."

"Not now," Quinton replied. "I think I'll take a page out of your book and wait for . . ." He glanced at Maelyn and didn't finish.

"Now that we have that out of the way, I think we can move on," she said.

"We still don't know how Crowe was able to find us," Quinton said while making a quick change to Becker's wrist computer configuration. "We checked the ship for trackers and didn't find any, so that was a dead end. I checked the subspace communication logs and didn't see anything out of the ordinary."

Becker frowned and looked down at his wrist for a moment.

Maelyn nodded. "I think we'll be safe for the time being. Crowe's not going to know where the DUC leadership wants to meet us, and even if he did, he might get more than he bargained for. Admiral Brandt isn't going to take any chances where that's concerned."

"Crowe's too smart for that," Becker said.

"How so?" Simon asked.

"He won't attack unless he thinks he has a tactical advantage. He's not above sacrificing some of his ships, but he won't commit to an all-out assault against anything the DUC has in their arsenal," Becker replied. He looked down at his wrist computer and then let out a startled yelp, tearing it off his wrist and rubbing the area where it had been.

"What's wrong?" Simon asked.

Becker looked at his arm and then at his wrist computer, which was now on the floor. "I don't know. It just started burning," he said and bent down to retrieve it. Then he glared at Quinton.

"You gotta watch those configuration settings. Sometimes you can overclock them, and who knows what can happen?" Quinton said.

Simon looked at Maelyn, his eyebrows raised and mouth partially open. Becker turned away, grumbling while he accessed his wrist computer's configuration settings.

Quinton thought it would be too much for Becker to handle if he actually laughed, but inside he felt a wave of satisfaction at Becker's frustration. Sometimes a little bit of payback could go a long way.

Maelyn looked as if she was about to speak, but a comlink registered on the main holoscreen. Simon looked at Maelyn, who gestured for him to acknowledge it. A brief message appeared on-screen that contained a meeting time and a set of coordinates for them to follow.

"It looks like we've gotten our invitation, gentlemen," Maelyn said.

Since Quinton was already in the *Nebulon*'s computer system, he had access to the navigation computer, and the destination appeared on his HUD.

"That's not right," he said.

Simon frowned. "What do you mean? The message is definitely from the DUC."

Quinton saw Maelyn's lips curve slightly.

"Oh, the message looks authentic, but the coordinates take us to the center of a star system. And I mean inside the actual star. That's not right," Quinton said. He looked at Maelyn and waited.

Becker followed his gaze. "What is this? What's going on?" he asked.

"It's just a security measure," Maelyn replied. "Trust me when I say that we're not going to jump into the center of a star."

Quinton thought she sounded confident, but he didn't like not knowing where they were going. "What are the real coordinates then?"

The edges of Maelyn's lips lifted a little. "Captain's privilege," she said. Then she walked over to the captain's chair and opened a ship-wide broadcast. "We'll be jumping to a neutral location for our meeting with the DUC leadership. Kieva, I need you to report to the bridge."

Maelyn closed the comlink.

Quinton looked at Becker, who didn't seem bothered by not knowing their coordinates, but Quinton didn't believe that for a second. He studied the coordinates, hoping Radek might see something he couldn't.

"It irritates you not knowing where we're going," Becker said.

"And you're not?" Quinton said. "At least *I'm* not pretending to be fine with being kept in the dark."

Becker smirked. "Shouldn't you be able to figure it out? I mean, I thought PMCs were supposed to be highly capable of this sort of thing."

Quinton knew Becker was goading him, but that didn't mean it wasn't working. It was. He hated not knowing where they were heading. There were millions of possibilities based on the coordinates alone, but he could reduce those if he kept their potential destinations within jump range. However, that still left them with too much data to predict the meeting's location with any degree of accuracy. So, no, he couldn't figure it out.

"You do have limits. That's good to know," Becker said smugly.

Quinton made a mental note to come up with creative ways to frustrate Becker. The man had a temper. He could make that work for him, but he had more important things to consider at the moment.

He didn't think Maelyn would tell him, even if he asked. If Admiral Brandt was really concerned about security, then this could be just the first in a set of coordinates until they arrived at the actual meeting place.

In thirty minutes, Quinton would find out. He couldn't help

but think that if Crowe was willing to do everything in his power to control Quinton, then what would stop the DUC from doing the same? Any fleet admiral worth their stripes would see the tactical advantage of what Quinton offered. Wouldn't he want that for himself? He needed to be prepared in case this meeting went sideways. He chuckled at the thought, which drew a few inquiring glances in his direction.

"It's nothing. I just thought of something funny," he said.

Becker looked away from him, and Maelyn arched an eyebrow.

"It's not worth repeating," he said. He then added, "Quinton's privilege."

Maelyn leaned back in her chair and smiled. "Very well. Enjoy it."

He wouldn't go so far as to believe his little play on words had been clever, but he did like her smile. He walked over to Simon's workstation on the bridge.

"How capable is the DUC fleet?" Quinton asked.

Simon's expression faltered.

"I'm not looking for specifics," he added quickly. "But if Crowe somehow found this meeting place, how safe would we actually be?"

Quinton's biometric sensors showed that Simon's heart rate had increased. The young engineer looked away from him for a few moments.

"I . . ." Simon said, drawing out the word. "The DUC does have defensive capabilities, but there's a higher priority for threat detection and avoidance."

Quinton considered this for a few moments, hoping he'd misheard what Simon had said. "Threat detection and avoidance . . . Are you saying that running away is standard fleet doctrine for the DUC?"

He heard Becker chuckle.

Simon swallowed hard, his expression serious. "Sometimes it's the best option. You keep moving around and you live. Stay and fight, or even attack, and a lot of people will die."

Quinton turned toward the main holoscreen. It was clear that Simon wasn't comfortable with that answer, and he'd accidentally touched on a sensitive subject.

"I wasn't judging."

"Yes, you were," Simon said.

He waited a few seconds before responding. "You're right. I, um . . ." Quinton didn't know what to say. He didn't want to offend one of the few people on the ship that he actually liked and respected. Simon had helped him, both with repairs to the agricultural unit and as a companion.

"It's okay, you're from a different place and a different time. A place I wish I could have seen," Simon said.

Now Quinton really didn't know what to say. "I'm going to go stand over here," he said, gesturing behind him.

Simon nodded and focused his attention on the workstation holoscreens in front of him.

He'd been standing off to the side for a few minutes when he heard Maelyn clear her throat. When he turned, she gestured for him to come over.

"Is asking what you're thinking about part of 'Quinton's privilege'?" she asked.

"It might be."

"I'm sorry, but I can't disclose the actual meeting location. You don't have to worry about it though."

There was a flurry of sensation errors as the agricultural bot's internal systems failed to interpret the spike of Quinton's emotions. He really hated that.

"I want you to trust me," Maelyn said.

Quinton let out an audible sigh. "I'd like to, but it's not just . . ." He paused for a second, reconsidering. "Don't worry about it. Let's just get through this part in one piece."

Maelyn nodded. "Fair enough," she said.

It took several jumps for the *Nebulon* to reach the star system for the meeting with the DUC. Admiral Brandt had put them on a tight schedule, but Maelyn was familiar with standard DUC protocols, even for a secret meeting. Once they entered the star system, there was a subspace communications beacon that gave them the coordinates for the next star system. Once the beacon transmitted its message, it engaged the self-destruct protocol. Quinton suspected that it also contacted the DUC to keep them apprised of the *Nebulon*'s progress. However, he didn't try to access the communications beacon to confirm this.

"We're here," Maelyn said.

The confirmation showed on the main holoscreen, along with the star map of a binary star system that was about the most unfriendly place Quinton had seen yet. When they formed, a binary star system gradually stabilized after billions of years. The binary star system they were in now was the result of when two individual solar systems collided. The two stars were in a celestial tug-of-war until, eventually, one absorbed the other. This process could also take billions of years. But what Quinton was seeing was that the individual star systems had once had a system of planets with them, and all that was left of the rocky planets were massive asteroid fields. One day, a long time from now, they might re-form into new planets, but Quinton would never be around to see that. The larger Jovian planets hadn't even settled into a stable orbit yet.

A video comlink registered with the *Nebulon*, and Maelyn acknowledged it.

On the main holoscreen, the head and shoulders of an older man appeared.

"Captain Wayborn, I'm glad you made it."

"Thank you, Admiral Brandt. I've come as you requested."

Brandt shifted his gaze toward Quinton. "I'm looking forward to speaking with you when you come aboard the *Astra*."

He looked at Maelyn. "Captain, your shuttle is cleared to board, and be advised that security measures are in place."

"Understood, Admiral," Maelyn said.

The comlink severed, and the main holoscreen went blank. They set a course for the waypoint.

Quinton looked at Maelyn. "What security measures do they have in place?"

Becker looked at him. "It means don't go poking around."

Quinton glanced at him and then turned back toward Maelyn, waiting.

"Becker's right. They'll have additional security measures in place that are specifically designed to detect and prevent PMC access. So please, show some restraint," Maelyn said.

Quinton had suspected that the DUC would take precautions against him, but he couldn't help but be a little curious as to what they had in place and whether he could bypass it. The temptation began to build up—

"Quinton," Maelyn said.

"I'll play nice as long as they do," he replied.

Maelyn nodded and had Simon set a course for the waypoint.

Quinton had already hardened the communication capabilities of the agricultural bot. Communications could work in a number of different ways. Data communications between computer systems required that one party send information while the other received it. However, even the most hardened security systems had to account for the vulnerability of the initial communication. Neither sender nor receiver was totally secure. This was why he had effectively sealed off every conceivable way for a comlink to register with him unless he approved it. Furthermore, he had routed all comlinks to a virtual sandbox that was controlled by Radek. It was an additional layer of security that gave Quinton some comfort. He couldn't get around the fact that he was vulnerable, and the odds were stacked in everyone else's favor because of his ignorance of the galaxy. He'd have to improvise if the situation called for it.

A short while later, they boarded the shuttle and Maelyn flew them to the *Astra*. The DUC *Astra* was a Tilion Empire cruiser that had been heavily modified during its lifetime. Quinton could still see the original design elements, which pointed to a heavy cruiser design. He supposed he should be thankful that it was an actual warship and not some kind of converted freighter. According to the shuttle scanners, there were two more cruisers and a civilian transport ship.

No one was left behind on the *Nebulon*. Becker kept looking in Quinton's direction, as if there was something he wanted to say. Quinton was sure it was nothing he wanted to hear, so he ignored him.

The shuttle flew through the hangar bay shields, and Maelyn landed the shuttle. After opening the side doors, the loading ramp extended to the ground. Quinton was closest to the door, but he waited for Maelyn to lead the way. She was the captain, after all, and as he was almost constantly reminded, this was her ship.

She looked at him for a moment and then exited the shuttle. Without a backward glance, Quinton followed her.

He hadn't known what to expect when he got out of the shuttle. He thought there would be an escort of some sort, and definitely armed soldiers. There was a large group of them, but the hangar deck was essentially empty. They were the only ship in attendance. He glanced around and thought this would've been a good ambush site.

Rows of black-armored soldiers held their assault rifles in front of them. Power signatures appeared on his HUD, showing that the armor and rifles were fully charged. A DUC delegation walked through a break in the rows of soldiers. Quinton recognized Admiral Brandt as he strode over to them. Walking next to him was a woman with blonde hair and a mixture of mature and youthful features. Quinton found that he couldn't estimate her age, but if her eyes were any indication, she looked to be of an age of experience and intelligence. There were other people who followed them, but he assumed the most important people were the two in front.

Maelyn came to a stop and said, "Director Cantos, Admiral Brandt, I'd like to introduce you to Quinton."

"Severin Brandt," the admiral said. He paused for a moment, taking in Quinton's appearance. "I have to admit I didn't expect . . ." his voice trailed off.

"I didn't expect it either," Quinton replied, breaking the awkward silence.

Director Cantos laughed. "Well met, Quinton. Sherilyn Cantos, one of the elected leaders of the Dholeren United Coalition."

Quinton felt an urge to stand up straighter. Maelyn introduced the rest of the crew.

Brandt looked at Quinton after the introductions were concluded. "My understanding is that some kind of activation signal was sent to the Zeda-Six Star System and that's how you came to be here."

"That's the long and short of it," Quinton replied. Then he added, "The reports you've no doubt read are accurate. I have limited access to my Energy Storage System. This body was the best of the extremely limited choices available."

Brandt chuckled without humor. "I can identify with that—the limited choices, I mean."

Brandt looked at Cantos, his eyebrows raised. She gave him a small nod and then looked at Quinton. "We also heard about the Sentinel attack near the Mozeyian Outpost."

"Crowe's Union ships were there as well," Maelyn said. "He opened hostilities against my ship. Quinton was helping to defend the ship, but he didn't fully understand the capabilities of the Sentinels."

The rest of the delegation looked at Quinton, as if trying to somehow peer past the rough exterior of the agricultural unit. Maybe they were trying to find his ESS.

"Captain Wayborn said we might be able to help each other," Quinton said. He figured that if they were being formal, he should address Maelyn by her title.

Sherilyn Cantos interlaced her fingers in front of her and regarded Quinton calmly. "Yes, we'll get to that, but I'm interested in your intentions."

"My intentions," Quinton repeated, "are that I'd like to get out of this body. I'd like to be put back in my own body so I can have access to my own memories. You have no idea what it's like to be so close to who you once were and have it kept from you."

"That's just the thing. We don't know who you are," Sherilyn said.

"I'm happy to get to know you, if that's what it will take to get your help, but I don't have a lot of time," Quinton said.

The barest hints of a smile lifted Sherilyn Cantos's lips. "You misunderstand me. We cannot find any record of a Quinton Aldren at all in our records." She looked at Maelyn. "We've checked all of our data repositories."

"Surely there must be some kind of mistake," Maelyn said.

"I'm afraid not," Cantos replied.

"So what if you can't find a record of me. Aren't your records incomplete?" Quinton said.

"They might be," Brandt said. "But it could also be that your records were erased. We've compiled documentation over the years from all the old federations. They came from all the refugees that joined the DUC and have been pieced together for a century. So you must understand that our records are probably the most intact you'll find."

Quinton was quiet for a few moments. "Does that mean you're not going to help me?"

"That's what we're trying to decide," Cantos said.

He didn't like where this was heading.

"We think Quinton is from either the Acheron Confederacy or the Jordani Federation. He predates the Federation Wars," Maelyn said.

"If he's from the Acheron Confederacy, that may complicate things. This could be some kind of latent ploy from Grand Admiral Browning. If that's the case, no good can come of this," Brandt said.

"Hold on a minute," Quinton said. "I don't even know who that is, so I'm not anybody's ploy. I came here because I needed help. Maelyn said you were my best option and that we could help each other. You need access to technology and resources that only I can give you. Do all those wants go away because you suspect some kind of connection to this Admiral Browning from the Acheron Confederacy?"

The others around him went into a stunned silence, which wasn't the response he'd been hoping for. The environmental detection systems in the agricultural unit showed him the nearest data access points, and he wanted to access the *Astra*'s systems to find out who Browning was.

Brandt stepped closer to him, and Quinton noticed that the nearby soldiers watched them intently. "Browning was a monster. He's the reason the Federation Wars lasted as long as they did. He's responsible for trillions of deaths. The Acheron Confederacy is gone. We've taken in refugees from there, but they've cut all ties to their former federation. And it's a good thing too. Their contributions are the reason this galaxy is in the state it's in. Entire worlds have been destroyed. Entire civilizations are gone. And all of this has given rise to anarchists in the form of warlords wielding old federation military might. I realize that your memories are an issue for you, but trust me when I tell you that I would love to forget the things I've seen. And I'm not the only one. So please don't act high and mighty, flippantly challenging our concerns."

Brandt had spoken evenly and coldly, which was much more effective than if he'd been yelling. Quinton looked at Director Cantos and saw the same battle-steel resolve in her gaze. In addition, there was general agreement from everyone who was standing nearby. He saw the same haunted bitterness in their gazes, although some didn't shine quite so brightly.

Quinton looked back at the crew of the *Nebulon*. Simon gave him a small nod and a look of encouragement. Becker merely looked at him impassively. Kieva and Vonya watched with keen interest, as did Guttman and Oscar.

He turned and started to walk back toward the shuttle. Every soldier in the area readied their weapons, pointing them at him in a seemingly single fluid motion. He halted. The soldiers carried kinetic-style rifles that had computing systems he could access. "So you don't intend to help me, but you're not going to let me leave. Is that right?" he asked.

Brandt looked at Cantos.

"Who's in charge here? Because I'm not sure if it's you, Admiral Brandt, or if it's you, Director Cantos. Who should I be speaking with?" Quinton asked.

Brandt looked over at his soldiers. "Stand down."

The soldiers lowered their weapons but didn't look any less dangerous because of it.

"Leadership is shared in the DUC," Cantos said.

"Are you authorized to help me? Maybe I should have started off with that, because right now, I feel like I'm wasting my time. And as you can clearly see, my time is limited," Quinton said, putting as much edge in his voice as he could.

"We are authorized to negotiate," Cantos said.

"Okay, what do you want?"

"We have other ways to confirm your identity, but it will require your cooperation," she replied.

"I can be reasonable," Quinton said. He thought he heard Becker mutter and clear his throat. "What do you have in mind?"

"We have in our possession a data relay console that was frequently used by PMCs during the Federation Wars. They were part of the subspace communications network relays," Cantos said.

"And you want me to access them as a way of confirming my identity," Quinton replied.

Cantos nodded.

"Before I do anything, I'm going to need some assurances from you."

Brandt exhaled explosively. "I don't see how you're in any position to request assurances."

"Don't you even want to hear what they are before you make your decision?"

Brandt regarded him coolly.

"I'll take whatever test you have for me, but regardless of the results, I want your assurance that you won't try to stop me from leaving here," Quinton said.

"That is a reasonable request," Cantos said. He looked at her and waited for her to continue. "You mentioned before that you would like to get back into your own body. That means Maelyn told you about the DNA vaults."

"That's right. The DNA vaults have the genome of all PMCs ever uploaded," Quinton said.

Admiral Brandt shook his head. "That was the practice before the end of the Federation Wars."

"The vaults were often attached to military outposts, but most are no longer around. The ones that remain are guarded by Sentinels. I'm telling you this so you'll understand that what you want might not be possible for us to deliver," Cantos said.

"I understand there's a risk. Let's get on with it," Quinton said.

Cantos brought up her wrist computer and accessed her personal holoscreen. "I'm authorizing you to use this data access module to access the console."

A data connection comlink initialized, and he accessed it. A challenge protocol presented itself, and something in Quinton's ESS responded with the proper authentication codes. This back and forth went on for almost a full minute before he was granted access.

*Confirm PMC identity.*
*Quinton Aldren, G class.*
*Acheron Confederacy Navy – SP.*

Quinton cranked up his frame rate to the max. The act of authenticating with the PMC communication console had activated more parts of his ESS than ever before. Data windows appeared on his HUD.

*Data update available. Commence download.*

The PMC console was following a standard set of protocols that were included in the update file. Quinton brought up a secondary interface and queried for the activation code used to initialize his PMC.

*ACN – PMC recovery protocol.*
*Activation code trace running.*

A long list of coordinates appeared in front of him, and Quinton copied it for future reference.

There was very little doubt that he had been part of the Acheron Confederacy Navy, but the information available didn't indicate a rank or anything like that. His classification was *G class*. He didn't know what that meant either.

Quinton then queried for DNA vaults that contained his unique genome. As the list appeared on his internal HUD, he wondered how many of those installations would still be intact.

His session with the PMC console closed before he was ready. They must have set some kind of time limit for access in anticipation that he could increase his frame rate to quickly access data.

He returned his frame rate to normal and looked at Director Cantos. "It worked, although I would've preferred a little more time."

"A precaution on our part. What did you discover?"

"There is a record of my genome, and I saw my identity. I'll transfer the data to you. I'm from the Acheron Confederacy Navy, although there was no record of anything more than that. There's no rank or ACN identification for me other than a PMC classification," Quinton said.

Cantos looked at Brandt. His eyes narrowed. "It could be some kind of special project. I'll have it investigated."

"Here are the lists of the coordinates for the DNA vaults. I assume you can compare these locations to your own star charts," Quinton said.

Director Cantos regarded him for a few moments. "Thank you for sharing the information with us. I also want you to know that we don't hold the fact that you are from the Acheron Confederacy against you, but for our own protection, we do need to confer with the rest of the DUC leadership before we agree on a way forward."

Quinton looked at Maelyn, who gave him a small nod. "All right."

Director Cantos smiled. "Thank you for understanding. I invite the rest of you to take your ease. We have a place for you to wait, and refreshments will be served."

Quinton didn't have any need for refreshment, but he certainly had plenty to think about. He'd been able to decipher the activation code, but there was a strange reference in it. He needed time to do his own analysis of the DNA vault locations. It wasn't just a simple list of the coordinates. It looked like there was other information in the data upload he'd received.

They were escorted out of the hangar bay. Simon glanced at him a few times. Maelyn walked behind Brandt.

Director Cantos turned toward Maelyn. "Captain Wayborn, there are several things we'd like to discuss with you away from your crew."

"I'm at your disposal," she replied.

The group split and Quinton wanted to go with Maelyn, or at least listen to their discussion. No doubt they were going to be discussing him.

Maelyn looked at him before she joined the others. "It's fine. I'll regroup with you in a little while. At that point, I'll tell you everything I'm authorized to tell you."

He leaned toward her and said quietly, "I don't think they're going to help me."

"They're concerned, Quinton, and with good reason, but I'll convince them that this is our best option."

Maelyn rejoined Director Cantos and Admiral Brandt, and Quinton went with the others.

# CHAPTER TWENTY-FIVE

REFRESHMENTS WERE INDEED SERVED. Becker, Guttman, Oscar, Kieva, and even Simon immediately went over to the food and drink that had been set out on a table for them. Quinton supposed they were getting tired of the food available on the *Nebulon*, but he couldn't be sure about it. Any table of delicious food in a room full of hungry people was sure to make them swoop down for a meal. Quinton's gaze slid to an assortment of fruits in a wide variety of colors.

Vonya looked at him with a pinched expression.

"You better join them before there's nothing left for you," Quinton said.

She glanced at the others before turning back to him. "Do you miss it?" she asked and gestured toward the others.

Becker noticed them and looked pointedly at Quinton before he took a hearty bite of his food, chewed it, and then swallowed, looking content.

Quinton hadn't thought about eating. Somehow, he'd managed to avoid it. Simon sometimes snacked while they were working, but it was nothing like the spread here. The agricultural unit had highly sensitive receptors equipped for scent, but he'd disabled them. He was tempted to turn them back on so he could smell the food. The others kept commenting about it.

He looked at Vonya. "Sometimes," he said and meant it.

She nodded with a sympathetic expression and then joined the others.

Quinton couldn't remember why he'd volunteered to upload himself into a Personality Matrix Construct. He must have been part of an Acheron Confederacy Navy project, but none of the records he'd found indicated what. At least he'd found the coordinates to DNA vaults that had his identification. He could become human again, as long as the vault was intact. The vaults had been established to offload PMCs who had decided to end their artificial existence.

His thoughts turned to the activation signal. He was able to decipher it, which meant he could trace it back to its origins, but what if Brandt was right and the activation signal was just some kind of latent protocol? He'd forgotten to ask them about the rumors of PMCs getting activated and whether there was increased Sentinel activity concentrated in a particular sector of the galaxy.

Both of Quinton's choices were dangerous. Tracing the activation signal to its origins ran the risk of the agricultural bot breaking down permanently, and trying to find a DNA vault established for the Acheron Confederacy Navy was risky for everyone.

"Quinton," Radek said inwardly, "you asked that I check Becker's activities according to the *Nebulon*'s computer systems."

Quinton was pulled from his thoughts. "Oh yeah, that's right. What did you find?"

"I believe Becker was conducting an investigation of his own."

"So he was watching me while I was watching him?"

"Not entirely," Radek replied. "He was checking ship maintenance logs."

A report appeared on his HUD, and Quinton looked at the log data. Becker had spent a lot of time reviewing the ship's automated maintenance routines, particularly trash and waste removal, which struck Quinton as odd because those systems were automated. The only time people actually checked those activities was when they stopped working or when those systems were due for manual inspection, which, according to the logs, Simon had done several months prior.

Quinton glanced at Becker. "What were you looking for?" he asked sub-vocally and then returned his attention to Radek. "Was there anything else he was doing?"

"Nothing out of the ordinary. He'd been trying to see what you were doing, but with the cleanup VIs you have running on the *Nebulon*'s systems, that effort has halted."

"Thanks, Radek. Good work," Quinton said.

His comms session with Radek ended. He thought about Maelyn and wondered what she was discussing with the DUC leadership. The *Astra* had security measures in place to detect whether Quinton tried to access their systems. He didn't want to risk it, but he wanted to know what was going on.

He had turned his attention to Simon when a tauntingly logical idea pushed to the forefront of his mind.

*I shouldn't do this. I told her I'd play nice*, Quinton thought.

Simon's comlink was active and ready to receive a connection to Maelyn. He was her second-in-command, and it was probably their standard protocol that contact was maintained, if possible. Now that Quinton had noticed the comlink, he couldn't stop thinking about it.

*Simon, Simon, why are you doing this to me?*

There must've been other comlinks in whatever meeting room Maelyn was in, but would it have something that could prevent subspace comms? Something that worked from ship to ship, but with personal comms? It could be done, but there was only one way to find out.

Quinton used Simon's comlink to open a data connection to Maelyn's comlink and set the priority to the lowest level so it wouldn't generate an alert. He nearly grinned when Maelyn's comlink accepted the connection. When it was this easy to gain access, how could he *not* do it?

He brought up Maelyn's comlink interface and engaged the microphone so he could listen. He thought about activating the vidcom capabilities, but that might be noticed by the others. The only way he was going to see what was going on in that room was if he accessed the *Astra*'s systems, which would surely be detected, unless they were bluffing about their ability to detect PMC activity.

*No, no! Focus*, he chided himself.

Maelyn's comlink microphone became active, and he immediately heard someone speaking.

"You asked for options. I'm giving you options," Brandt said.

"The options aren't even plausible," Maelyn replied.

"We don't need this kind of trouble. We have enough to deal with considering the heightened Sentinel activity. We need to manage the migration of the entire fleet, and we need to do it by reducing our risk exposure," Brandt replied.

"You just don't like the fact that he's from the Acheron Confederacy. You're letting it cloud your judgment," Maelyn responded.

Quinton wasn't sure if Maelyn was answerable to Brandt. He wasn't even sure if she was in the DUC Navy despite being a ship captain. She seemed to hold a post that was answerable to multiple groups or leadership types.

"I do have a bias, and rightfully so. Any time we've conducted operations that had something to do with the Acheron Confederacy, it cost us in lives and loss of ships. Sherilyn, we don't need this," Brandt said.

"Yes, we do. What about the recolonization effort? The Acheron Confederacy had a detailed record of habitable systems that they kept secret from the rest of the galaxy. They used automated terraforming systems," Maelyn said.

"She has a point, Severin," Cantos said.

"I'll give you that," Brandt replied. "It's not like I wouldn't want to get my hands on the alleged resources kept at an Acheron military facility, but I've chased these leads before, many times—not just for the Acheron Confederacy but for any other federation that had a military. Many times, they'd been picked clean or destroyed, or there was a Sentinel monitoring station in the area."

"You've seen the reports of overcrowding on migrant fleet ships. The answer to our problems is not to simply acquire more ships. People need a home. We'll never have a second chance if we don't have a safe place for people to go," Maelyn said.

"Your heart is in the right place, Maelyn," Cantos said. "But whenever we've tried to colonize, even in secret, eventually the raiders come. It's a never-ending cycle."

"I understand that, and eventually, the secret would get out. But we would have a head start. No one else has this knowledge. No one else is working with a PMC. Quinton could help us do this if we helped him in return. It's the only way this is going to work," Maelyn said.

"I think we should wait and see if we can find somebody who has expertise with PMCs. They could probably help Quinton. He's stuck with limited access to his ESS. We don't know what will happen if he gets access to all his memories," Cantos said.

"Agreed. We should wait," Brandt said.

"Quinton doesn't have a lot of time," Maelyn said. "Simon has done the best he can with maintaining the agricultural unit, but we don't have any place to move his ESS to."

"That's hardly a reason for us to move faster than we choose to. My understanding is that if the agricultural unit were to cease operating, then Quinton would be forced to withdraw completely into his ESS. He'd be less dangerous that way," Brandt said.

"That's not fair to him," Maelyn replied.

"This isn't about being fair. This is about ensuring our survival. You'd put our fate into the hands of a PMC?" Cantos said, then added, "I know you want to help him, but there are bigger things at work here. The DUC needs our protection."

"Then don't give us any resources. I can take the *Nebulon* and scout a few of these locations. I could report back, and you could make a decision after that," Maelyn said.

"And we just overlook the fact that Quinton could take control of the *Nebulon* any time he chooses?" Cantos said.

"He could. And he could have done it way before now, but he didn't."

"Does he trust you?" Brandt asked.

"A little. Maybe more than a little, but he's become increasingly aware of the precariousness of his position. How would you be?"

"I've been backed into a corner before," Brandt said.

"I'm surprised you've allowed yourself to get caught up in something like this," Cantos said.

"Should I have just ignored the situation? No, I don't think so," Maelyn replied.

"Do you trust him?" Brandt asked. "When it comes right down to it, do you think Quinton will act like any other PMC ever encountered?"

"He hasn't exhibited any signs of losing his sanity. He's remarkably strong-willed and stubborn. I think those were traits the ACN looked for in its PMC candidates," Maelyn said.

"That's because he was recruited to help fight a war. I've never heard of the G class PMC," Cantos said.

"I can do some checking into that to figure out if we even know what the designation means," Brandt said.

"I think if we treat Quinton fairly, he'll reciprocate," Maelyn said.

"Thank you for your assessment. We're going to leverage our

extensive resources to see what our next step should be. Please inform your crew," Cantos said.

There were a few moments of silence before Maelyn replied, "Understood, Director Cantos. I'll see to the maintenance of the *Nebulon*."

Quinton severed the connection to Maelyn's comlink. They were going to make him wait because they wanted to consult with PMC experts. They might be looking for the best way to control him. He kept reviewing what he'd heard. Maelyn continued to defend him. It was both gratifying and reassuring, and it made him not want to disappoint her.

A few minutes later, Maelyn joined them in the conference room. She walked over to Quinton and told the others that they needed to talk. They moved to the other side of the room.

Quinton looked at her. "I was listening," he said.

Maelyn frowned and then looked down at her at wrist computer. Then she glanced at Simon, figuring out how Quinton had overheard her conversation.

"What are you going to do?" he asked her.

"I'm going to help you. There's too much at stake if I don't," Maelyn said.

"Was the Acheron Confederacy really terraforming worlds in secret?"

"That's one of the oldest rumors in the galaxy. Some people say it's just a foolish dream that gives spacers hope. It makes them continue to explore, but no one's ever found one."

"Well then, we might be the first," Quinton said.

Maelyn smiled.

"Why are they so hesitant about this?"

"Brandt and Cantos have been alive for a very long time. They were young when the Federation Wars began. I guess you could say they've witnessed the great collapse and the dark times that came after. They might appear harsh to you, but it's not without reason," Maelyn replied.

Quinton considered this for a few moments. "And you're going to disobey them to help me?"

Maelyn frowned. "No, I'd disobey them to find the DUC refugees a homeworld. Someplace safe from the Collective and people like Lennix Crowe. Some spacers thrive without setting foot on solid ground, but most people don't. We need our terrestrial roots planted on a homeworld that can be defended."

She wanted to find a home for the migrant fleet, and judging from Director Cantos's response, it wouldn't be the first time. Quinton wondered how many times they'd tried to colonize a new homeworld before giving up on it. Still, he'd thought there might have been other reasons for what Maelyn had in mind.

"Oh," Maelyn said with a playful glint in her eyes, "and there's you, of course. Can't forget about that."

Quinton chuckled a little, feeling relieved. "I grow on you after a while. It's part of my charm."

# CHAPTER TWENTY-SIX

MAELYN WENT over to the table and began selecting food to eat. Quinton noticed that she seemed quite deliberate with her selection and only took small amounts. He glanced at the others and saw that they'd exhibited the same behavior. He'd expected Guttman and Oscar to pile on the food with exuberant proportions of debauchery, but they hadn't. Quinton supposed they were on their best behavior.

Maelyn sat and began eating while Becker joined her. The two spoke quietly. He didn't want to stand there staring at them, so he decided to shift his attention elsewhere. The rest of the crew was farther down the table. Guttman and Oscar were speaking with Vonya and Kieva. Simon waved him over.

"I never got a chance to ask you about how it went accessing that PMC console."

"Authentication took longer than expected, but after that, things went much more smoothly. The session didn't last very long," Quinton said.

Simon nodded. "They're just taking precautions, but they might let you access it for longer next time."

"If you say so," Quinton replied, unconvinced.

He glanced toward Maelyn, and a HUD overlay appeared on his internal heads-up display. The thermal analysis suite showed that the skin temperature on her cheekbones had increased. She was still speaking with Becker, and the two of them seemed completely at ease with one another. He didn't need a wide array of sophisticated sensors to inform him that there was some level of attraction shared between them, and he wondered when that had happened. *Had* it happened, or was he simply seeing something that wasn't there? Why did he care anyway? It was as if Becker didn't remember Maelyn throwing him off the bridge using a palm stunner and then threatening him with her sidearm.

"I *do* say so," Simon said, interrupting Quinton's thoughts.

He looked at Simon. "What?" he asked.

Simon finished chewing his food and swallowed. "I said that I do think they'll let you have another crack at the console. Did you learn anything else from it?"

Quinton looked down at the table and saw a few large nuts. "Do you mind?" he asked.

Simon glanced down at the table. "No, go ahead," he said, gesturing to the nuts.

Quinton picked up a couple and peered at them. "The authentication process accessed parts of my ESS that I hadn't known were there."

"What do you think it means?"

Quinton tossed a nut up in the air and deftly caught it. He tossed it up again. Then snatched it out of the air again and allowed it to glide across the back of his metallic fingers. He switched hands and did the same with both of them. "There was also an update."

Simon watched Quinton's finger dexterity with open appreciation. "Impressive," he said, inclining his head once. "Did the update affect the lockdown?"

"That's a good question," Quinton said. He hadn't thought to check that. "No, at least not as far as I can tell. I don't have any more access to my ESS than I did before. However, I'm able to retain the knowledge gained from the PMC console."

He saw Becker lean back, grinning. Quinton flicked the nut, and it darted across the room and clipped Becker on the back of the neck. Becker's hand came to his neck, and he turned toward them.

"Sorry about that. It must have slipped," Quinton said, gesturing with his hand.

Simon frowned. He'd seen what Quinton was doing and knew that he hadn't slipped. Becker shook his head, and Maelyn stood up.

Quinton looked at Simon, but before he could say anything, the door to the room opened and Admiral Brandt walked in. He headed straight toward Quinton.

Maelyn joined them, and Becker followed her.

"We've checked the vault locations against our current star charts," Brandt said. "It looks like there were indeed facilities at these locations, but many have been destroyed. Here, look for yourself."

The DUC fleet admiral activated his personal holoscreen and made it bigger, showing a galactic representation of the nearby sectors. "It looks like Sentinel fleets have discovered the vaults and cleaned house."

Quinton looked at the galaxy map. Radek ran a quick comparison of the list of vaults from the PMC console and compared it with the locations on the map. Brandt was right.

"Are you sure they've all been destroyed? Maybe some of them have been left intact or at least partially operational," Quinton said and looked at Maelyn. "Could we go look at a few of them? Maybe the data here is wrong."

Maelyn shook her head, and several of the others did the same. "The data is accurate. Salvagers would have picked those locations clean a long time ago. They have exploration drones that scout the old federation star systems. Also, the Sentinels wouldn't have left any of the infrastructure they found operational if it was designed for PMC use."

Brandt nodded. "Those systems would have been the first ones targeted."

Quinton looked at the galaxy map and tried to think of a solution. How destructive were the Sentinels? How well hidden were the vaults? Despite what the others had said, he still believed there must be something the Sentinels had overlooked. Star systems weren't inconsequential. There were lots of places to hide things. Usually, the best place to hide something was in plain sight, but the others were unwilling to even scout out some of these systems.

"It was a long shot at best, but we'll keep searching," Brandt said and shut down his personal holoscreen.

Quinton had committed it to memory, so he didn't need it on display.

"He's right," Maelyn said. "We'll keep searching. We can also find a more suitable body for you to use. There are several groups that specialize in androids, which will give you more access to your ESS."

She was just trying to help, and Quinton appreciated it, but he didn't want to find another cobbled-together android body to stick his ESS in. That was no way to live. He wanted to feel what it was like to be human again and not some shadowy reflection or memory. He'd gotten his hopes up when they'd shown him the list of vaults.

Maelyn looked concerned and glanced at Simon.

Quinton focused his attention on accessing the ESS. He didn't try to access his memories, but there were parts that had been activated when he'd authenticated with the PMC console. He brought up the deciphered activation signal used to bring him online. He then used the key to authenticate to his own ESS.

*Access granted.*

*Mission parameters updated.*

Quinton studied the message that appeared on his HUD.

"There's another vault," Quinton said finally.

The others became quiet.

"Where?" Maelyn asked.

He projected an image of the galaxy map, along with the coordinates of a star system that had been locked away in his ESS.

Brandt peered at the coordinates. "It's not in our data repositories."

"That's good. That means no one has been there," Quinton replied.

"There's no way you can know that," Becker said.

Quinton ignored him and looked at Brandt. "If I was in the ACN, then this could be a military installation. There could be things there that you could use. Didn't you say that ship upkeep is a huge issue, with more things needing repairs and not enough parts being fabricated?"

"That's true," Brandt said. Lips pursed, he looked at Maelyn.

"I think it's worth looking into," she said.

"Will you send ships to help scout the area?" Becker asked.

Brandt peered at the galaxy map and then looked at Quinton. "How do you know there's a vault there?"

Quinton had hoped this detail would've escaped the fleet admiral's notice. "I don't. When I authenticated with the PMC console, I received an update, and the lockdown protocols lessened. These coordinates have to do with the activation signal that brought me online."

Becker exhaled explosively. "The truth is you have no idea what could be at those coordinates."

Quinton was quiet for a moment while he squelched his irritation. "No, I don't," he said finally. "But there has to be something there. My ESS was in a hidden storage facility on Zeda-Six. I don't understand why there was a lockdown protocol used in the first place, and this unit is insufficient to find that out. But the fact that there are Acheron Confederacy military installations hidden out there and that I happen to have a set of coordinates associated with the activation signal is too much of a coincidence. None of you have to go with me. Lend me a ship and I'll go scout it myself."

Brandt shook his head. "Ships are among the most valuable commodities in the galaxy. We're not going to just give one to you."

"I'll take him," Maelyn said, and Brandt looked at her. "We need this, Admiral. We both know it, even if Cantos doesn't want to admit it."

Quinton thought Brandt had the look of a man who didn't approve of the current situation, and nothing was going to change that.

The DUC admiral inhaled deeply and sighed.

"I'll need your authorization to leave the ship," Maelyn said.

"This is ridiculous," Becker said, rounding on Maelyn. "There could be anything at those coordinates. Send a recon drone, and if none of those are available, then wait. The Sentinels targeted all Acheron Confederacy star systems for a reason. Browning was the most cunning officer before he turned against them. The man was a butcher. None of you have questioned whether Quinton is part of something Browning set in motion all those years ago."

Maelyn glanced at the star map. "Those coordinates are nowhere near the Acheron Confederacy. They're not in any claimed territory. It's just another red giant star system with minimal resources."

Becker shook his head. "This is more dangerous than you're letting on. I've led countless salvage missions in the verse, and there's a reason my team survives. We may not get the biggest bounties, but we more than make up for it by living to salvage another day. There's a right way to do this, and going recklessly to these coordinates is the surest way to die quickly."

"You don't have to come, Becker," Quinton said.

Becker scowled and turned back to Maelyn.

"Quinton's right," she said. "You've helped us get this far. Admiral Brandt can see that you're suitably compensated."

Brandt nodded. "That won't be a problem, and based on Captain Wayborn's recommendation, I'd even offer you a position in the DUC fleet."

Becker looked down at the floor for a few moments and then looked at Maelyn. "That's not what I want."

"I've led more than a few missions myself. I promised Quinton I would help him, and I intend to do that. I see no reason for you to remain aboard my ship," she said.

Quinton wanted to cheer or pump his fists in triumph, and he couldn't decide which, but the expression on Becker's face almost made him feel sorry for that reaction.

"I'll need some time to coordinate things on our end," Brandt said to Maelyn. "But I can give you clearance to leave."

She regarded Brandt, and something unspoken passed between them.

Brandt left the room.

"What just happened?" Quinton asked.

"The DUC leadership could relieve him of duty. He's sticking his neck out for this," Maelyn said. "But the potential gains outweigh the risks. Having said that, Quinton, I want you to know that if the situation is too dangerous to proceed, we'll regroup with the DUC and decide our next move."

"That sounds more than fair," Quinton said.

She looked at the others. "None of you are compelled to go. Service on the *Nebulon* is voluntary."

"I wouldn't miss this," Simon said.

Kieva nodded. "I'm with you, Captain."

"I'd like to go with you, if that's all right," Vonya said.

Maelyn nodded once and looked at Becker and the others.

Becker glanced at Guttman and Oscar. Guttman was shaking his head, muttering something about dying.

Becker sighed and looked at Quinton. "This better not be a waste of time."

Maelyn looked at Guttman and Oscar.

"We'll go," Guttman said.

She smiled. "All right, then. We leave at once. We'll need to do some planning on the way."

Becker arched an eyebrow. "You're not sure how long Brandt will give us clearance."

"Something like that," Maelyn said and headed for the door.

Quinton followed her. "Thanks," he said.

She gave him a small nod. "Don't thank me yet."

"You and Radek have a lot in common."

Maelyn looked at him and frowned. "Your VI?"

"Yeah, he doesn't know what to make of someone conveying appreciation either," he said.

She smiled a little. "In that case, you're welcome."

Quinton snorted, and they headed back to the main hangar bay where the *Nebulon* waited for them. He glanced back at Becker, thinking about what the man had said. He was right. They didn't know who had sent the activation signal or why, and it could be true that he was merely being used as a pawn in someone else's game, but Quinton was determined to control his own destiny. And that included finding his DNA so his body could be regrown and he could finally get out of this damn agricultural bot.

# CHAPTER TWENTY-SEVEN

THEY REACHED the main hangar bay, and a deck officer spoke with Maelyn for a few minutes. The rest of them headed to the *Nebulon*. Quinton walked behind Becker.

The loading ramp extended from the *Nebulon's* shuttle, and he heard Vonya speaking with Simon, asking him about preflight checks. The others climbed aboard, and Becker turned toward Quinton.

"I didn't think you'd decide to come with us," Quinton said.

Becker was cradling something in his hand that Quinton couldn't see. He shrugged one shoulder and tilted his head to the side in a so-so kind of gesture. "You were right about one thing—we don't know what we'll find."

"Don't tell me I've made a believer out of you."

Becker regarded him. "No, I still think you're an idiot."

"The feeling is mutual, but I have to know. Why are you coming?"

"Do you want to know if I'm coming for her?" Becker said and jutted his chin toward where Maelyn stood talking to the deck officer.

"That doesn't matter to me," Quinton said.

Becker laughed a little. Then he flicked whatever he was holding in his hand straight toward Quinton's face. Quinton caught it easily. It was a thick oval-shaped nut that looked exactly like the one he had thrown at Becker earlier.

"Quick reflexes," Becker said and walked up the loading ramp.

Quinton followed him, and Maelyn soon came on board.

They prepped the shuttle for launch and flew away from the *Astra*.

Everyone aboard was quiet, and Quinton felt an urge to break the silence, but he couldn't think of anything to say.

"Radek," Quinton said inwardly, "do you know anything else about those coordinates?"

"I have the same level of access that you do. Again, if I knew more or thought I could offer some insight that would assist you, I would notify you," Radek said.

Something in the VI's response pulled at his curiosity. "Why do I get the feeling you're not telling me something."

"I am not deliberately omitting information that you need."

"Or perhaps I'm not asking the right question," Quinton said and considered it for a few moments. "Do you have any further information about the coordinates based on your analysis? Something out of the ordinary, perhaps?"

Radek didn't respond right away, and the seconds seemed to accumulate. Then he said, "You've mentioned several times that the coordinates became available from your ESS after you authenticated with the PMC. This is inaccurate."

"How?" Quinton said, ignoring the agricultural unit's error message about not being able to frown. "How is it inaccurate? It's perfectly accurate. I was able to get the coordinates after I authenticated with the PMC console and received the update from it."

"Neural patterns indicate that the coordinates became available while you were focused on the activation signal and the locations of the DNA vaults the DUC representative had. It could also be that these thought patterns in your construct might have influenced the lockdown to change behavior."

If Quinton had a mouth, it would have been hanging open like a fish out of water. "Are you saying that my thought process can influence the lockdown protocol?"

"Unknown, but as part of my analysis capabilities, I have to note all the variables in order to reach an accurate theory on what changed. As a VI, to ignore your thought processes at the time would be negligent on my part. However, I don't feel comfortable estimating the probability that all variables influenced the result. The process would need to be repeated several times in order for a pattern to be established."

Sometimes Quinton felt like the two of them spent a lot of time going around in circles when they spoke, but he thought about Radek's response for a few moments. He had asked the VI for it, and it was clear that Radek hadn't volunteered his idea because he didn't think it would help. Radek might've been right, but Quinton wasn't so sure. VIs handled the PMC interface with . . . well, with everything. They could probably monitor things that he wasn't even aware of, so why not his thought process. The way the brain worked in the matrix construct was intricate and stretched the limits of any intelligence, be it virtual or otherwise. People were always trying to figure out how the mind works, such as why some ideas seemed to spread like beams of light bursting from a pulsar, and others just didn't seem to generate any momentum.

"It's interesting, I'll give you that. I don't know what to think about it. Either way, we'll both understand more about this lockdown once I get out of this body and have full access to the ESS," Quinton said.

The shuttle docked with the *Nebulon*, and they returned to the ship.

Maelyn looked at Becker. "Are you familiar with the munitions systems on the ship?"

Becker nodded.

"We were resupplied by the *Astra*. Can you check them? I'd like a visual inspection," she said.

"Will do, Captain," Becker said, smiling. "Oscar, Guttman, you're with me."

Quinton went to the bridge with Maelyn and Simon. Kieva and Vonya headed to the main engineering section to check on an automated maintenance hatch that was putting errors in the logs.

Simon sat at his workstation. "Updates from the *Astra* are complete. Navigation computers processed the updates, and we're ready to go on your orders, Captain."

"Thank you, Simon. Set a course for the closest jump point. I'll have coordinates for you momentarily," Maelyn said and went to the main holoscreen.

Quinton joined her.

The screen showed a star map of the current system, and she inputted their destination coordinates.

"It looks like we'll need a minimum of six jumps to get there," Quinton said.

"That's right, and the closer we get, the more updated our information will be on our destination," Maelyn said.

Calibrating the jump capacitors for the jump drive systems was required as part of routine maintenance. The fastest they could reach the coordinates was forty-eight hours, and that just brought them within the vicinity.

"We need to talk about something," Quinton said.

Maelyn arched an eyebrow, intrigued. "All right, what do you want to talk about?"

"I need to . . ." he began and stopped. "I'm going to need to be in the *Nebulon*'s systems, fully integrated. I know you're all worried about this."

"If there are Sentinels there, then . . ."

"Then we should execute emergency jump procedures and leave. The reason I need to be integrated is because we might get a challenge protocol from the Acheron military facility that's likely at our destination. We might have only one opportunity to communicate," Quinton said.

Maelyn inhaled and sighed, then glanced at the star map.

"I'm expecting that there'll be some kind of challenge protocol, and I'm hoping there's something in here"—he tapped on his chest piece where his ESS was housed—"that I'll be able to respond with like I did with the PMC console."

Maelyn crossed her arms in front of her and tapped two fingers on her full lips, considering. "If we're wrong, whatever is there might just decide that we're hostile and attack us. I don't want you integrated with the system when we jump in. We don't know what's on the other side, but if we do receive a challenge protocol, I'll give you permission to interface with our comms systems. Not before. We need to scout the system, which means we'll be doing passive scans until we're confident of what's there. Then we'll go for a closer look."

Quinton would rather have been integrated with the system before they jumped to their destination. It was just more efficient, and he could react much quicker to the information that would be available. He tried to think of a scenario where delaying his integration with the *Nebulon* would increase the risk, but the fact of the matter was that he just wasn't sure.

"All right, we'll do it your way. You are the captain, after all," Quinton said.

Maelyn smiled. "There's only one captain." She paused for a moment. "I know it's a struggle for you when you integrate with ship systems."

"The struggle comes when I need to pull out of them. Working within them makes me feel whole, like it's what I was meant to do."

She nodded. "There's a reason for that."

"What do you mean?"

"Helping PMCs cope with their new environment required a certain manipulation. VIs help bridge the connection, but they also engage brain patterns for reward centers of the brain. This helps condition PMCs to function more efficiently," Maelyn said.

"We're conditioned to enjoy it," Quinton said while considering the implications.

"It's what I read. It was one of the reasons PMCs became disassociated with who they were and became more machine-like."

"So, are you saying that Radek is manipulating me?"

Maelyn nodded. "To a certain extent, but not with malicious intent."

"I don't understand what you're trying to tell me, so why don't you just come right out and say it."

"Think of it like an addiction. Have you noticed that you continue to look for excuses to interface with ship systems or any computer system, for that matter?"

Quinton shook his head. "It's what I'm supposed to do. It's what I was trained to do."

"It's one of the reasons the Federation Wars consumed the old federations. You need to be aware of the danger. I'm not trying to tell you not to utilize your capabilities. I'm trying to warn you that there are consequences of which you might not be aware."

Quinton regarded her for a few moments. "You know, this isn't who I am," he said, gesturing toward his body.

Maelyn's eyebrows pulled together. "I know, Quinton," she said.

"And I know it's easy to forget. This is all anyone sees."

"If there *is* a DNA vault at those coordinates, we'll be able to regrow your body, and you can offload out of your ESS. Everything will work out," Maelyn said.

He looked at the star map, unsure what to say to her.

"I *am* curious to see what you really look like. I've tried to imagine it, but I really have no idea."

Quinton looked at her. "You've tried to imagine it? Were you dreaming about me?" he asked and chuckled.

She looked at him with an almost deadpan expression. "Wouldn't you like to know," she said, her eyes gleaming as she walked away from him, heading toward the captain's chair.

Quinton laughed. "You're right. I *would* like to know."

She didn't answer him.

He studied the star map on the main holoscreen, thinking about what Maelyn had said. He was aware of his PMC training, much like he was aware that he could walk. He couldn't remember learning how. He could just do it. Sometimes when he thought about what he could do, those skills felt like being able to walk. He couldn't remember being conditioned or predisposed to want or need to integrate with computer systems, but he couldn't rule out Maelyn's warning either. The knowledge was likely within his ESS. Maybe Becker was right and they should wait—try to find a better android that was more capable of housing his ESS, but he'd gotten the impression from Admiral Brandt that these weren't readily available. He supposed that made sense. Why keep highly sophisticated androids around if the Sentinels would just determine them to be PMC technology and destroy them, despite the collateral damage. A century of such behavior would severely limit Quinton's options for finding a more suitable replacement body. Pursuing the DNA vaults was his best option. Traveling the galaxy in an old agricultural bot wasn't a long-term solution.

A lot of what Becker had said now had Quinton thinking. He had perfect recall of all their encounters, and he was able to simultaneously review everything Becker had said since they'd first met.

Quinton stayed on the bridge until after the *Nebulon* executed its FTL jump from the star system. Now, they were on a recharge cycle. The ship was capable of making continuous jumps, and the length of time required to recharge the capacitors was dependent upon the distance they traveled. They didn't need to push past the red line because it wasn't safe. The farther they jumped, the greater the risk for computational errors for their destination. Even with their best sensors, when dealing with interstellar distances, they were still looking back in time. That was why after each FTL jump, they did a sensor sweep, which updated the navigation systems. There were also navigation stations deployed throughout the galaxy that were connected through a subspace communication net. These were the most reliable way of getting a nearly up-to-date picture of their target destination, although this only got them part of the way. Navigation stations were only in sectors that spacers traveled to. Before the Federation Wars, they'd been maintained by the governing federation, and the sensor data was shared throughout the galaxy.

Quinton left the bridge. He needed to talk to Becker, which wouldn't be easy because the man became irritable whenever they were in close proximity. The feeling was mutual, but Quinton wouldn't let that stop him. Becker was a seasoned salvager who'd spent years delving into the skeletons of a bygone age to retrieve anything useful.

Becker and his crew were inspecting one of the *Nebulon's* smaller kinetic point-defense turrets that was in a storage bay. Hiding turrets in this way gave them a small advantage in dicey situations. Point-defense turrets weren't meant to dissuade an aggressor, so there was no need to advertise a ship's defensive capabilities. The *Nebulon* also had point-defense masers, which resided on the outer hull of the ship. The *Nebulon* was a small freighter meant for speed, maneuverability, and combat avoidance, with limited long-range combat engagement capabilities.

"I'm telling you, Vonya's massages are the best thing I've ever felt," Guttman said.

Quinton slowed down as he came near the storage bay doors

and saw Guttman standing near the base of the mag cannon. He was accessing the console and running a diagnostic.

"Is that only because she won't sleep with you?" Oscar asked.

Quinton glanced up and saw that Oscar was standing on a counter-grav maintenance platform hovering near one of the ammunition loaders that fed the cannon.

"I'll get there, don't you worry," Guttman replied. "It's still showing a degradation for the actuators at anything above half speed."

"I'll take another look," Oscar said. He lowered the counter-grav platform and moved to the other side of the loader.

"She's been training me on giving massages too. Her skin is amazing. I don't know if it's all Servitors or just hers, but it's the perfect combination of smooth and firm," Guttman said.

Oscar grinned and stepped back from the loader, leaning on the handrail to peer down at Guttman. "Let me get this straight. Our resident Servitor is rewarding you by letting *you* massage *her*?"

"Well, it's give and take," Guttman said quickly.

"Riiight," Oscar said, drawing out the word as long as possible. "It's never gonna happen, my friend."

"Keep telling yourself that. What is it *you* do with her? Calibrations?"

"I just enjoy talking to her. She's interested in piloting, so I've been running her through simulations," Oscar replied.

Becker exhaled explosively from the other side of the turret where Quinton couldn't see him. "Enough! I'm tired of hearing about it. You're both stuck in the friend zone. Move on."

Guttman laughed. "Is that why you keep trying to sweet-talk the captain?"

Quinton had heard enough. He walked into the room. "Is this what you guys talk about while you work?" He looked up at Oscar and studied the loader. "The angle of the loader is a little off. That's why it keeps underperforming."

Oscar turned back toward the munitions loader and studied it. "It's not showing up for me."

Quinton quickly climbed up the turret. "Looks like something hit it pretty good and knocked it out of alignment."

Oscar frowned. "I get that, but I can't see it with the scanner."

"Oh. The sensors I have are highly accurate for this fine-tuning kind of work, although the designers probably didn't have this in mind," Quinton said, gesturing toward the turret.

He told Oscar the adjustments he needed to make, and Becker circled over to their side, riding his own counter-grav maintenance platform.

"All right, Guttman, run another test," Oscar said.

Guttman initiated another test that fed ammunition through the loader on one side of the turret and into the loader on the other side. He increased the speed. "That's good. We're able to get to 70 percent now."

Quinton studied the loader, looking for anything else out of alignment, but couldn't find anything. He wanted to get it to 100 percent.

Becker chuckled. "If you're looking for perfection, it's not going to happen. Guttman's right, 70 percent is really good for these old turrets."

Quinton looked at him and then glanced at Oscar, who nodded.

"That does it for this one," Becker said. "Guttman, let the bridge know that they'll be able to run a live fire test in a few minutes."

Becker and Oscar lowered to the ground, and the counter-grav platforms sank seamlessly into two depressions on the floor.

Quinton leaped down and landed nearby.

"Thanks," Oscar said.

"No problem," Quinton replied.

Becker looked at him for a moment. "What do you want?"

"I wanted to talk to you."

Becker rolled his eyes. "I'm a little busy."

They cleared the turret platform, and the airlock doors closed. The turret began to rise, moving out of view.

Guttman and Oscar walked ahead of them.

Quinton suppressed a flash of irritation, thinking that this was going to be even harder than he'd initially thought.

"I need your help," he said.

The three men stopped in the middle of the corridor and turned around to look at him.

"I know. It's shocking," he said.

Becker recovered first. He turned to Guttman and Oscar. "You guys go on ahead."

The two men shrugged and continued onward. Becker raised his eyebrows and waited for Quinton to speak.

"Look, I understand why—you know what, never mind that. I don't care about what happened. All I know is that we need to work together so that we can both get what we want," Quinton said.

"What is it that you think I want?"

"Come on. Do I need to spell it out for you?"

"I'm genuinely curious."

"You want to set yourself up with a star union of your own, running different salvage operations with ships and all that," Quinton replied and paused for a moment.

"You've got me all figured out."

"I know that you're above and beyond your comfort zone for a man who takes risks regularly."

Becker turned around and walked away.

Quinton hastened to catch up to him. "You asked."

Becker shook his head. "You said you need my help."

Quinton nodded. "I do. Did you know I have perfect recall? Believe me, it's not all it's cracked up to be. There are some things I'd like to forget, but lately I've been thinking about some of the things you've said, and I'm beginning to think that your issue with me is a lot more personal than you let on."

Becker stopped, and steel entered his gaze.

"I'm not here to talk about your past. I'm just telling you what I think. I need you to keep an eye on me."

Becker snorted. "I never intended not to."

"You don't get it," Quinton said and told Becker about what Maelyn had explained to him about the behavior modification that came with PMC interfacing with computer systems. "I'm not going to be anyone's pawn, but I realize now that I might not be the best judge."

Becker frowned. "What do you want me to do?"

"Just what you wanted to do before. I want you to terminate me if I . . . you know," Quinton said and stopped.

"Does Maelyn know about this?" Becker asked.

"No, and while I think if push comes to shove she'd do what's needed, I do think she'd hesitate. You wouldn't, and that's what I need."

Becker crossed his arms and leaned back against the corridor wall. "This is something," he said and chuckled without any humor. "How do you know I won't just do it, you know, for fun?"

"I don't."

"Uh-huh."

"I don't know what we're going to find. I know what I want to have happen, and I'm going to do everything I can to make sure that it does, but I need . . . There are things I don't understand."

Becker unfolded his arms and stood up straight. "Even if I agreed to this, how would it even work?"

"You mean you haven't already thought up a way for me to meet an early demise?"

"Oh, I have. It usually involves explosives."

While Quinton didn't like the thought of being blown up, he couldn't fault the logic.

"It would never work. You'd be able to stop a remote detonation in any case."

"Then you'll have to stay close." Quinton watched as Becker thought about it. "To be honest, I didn't think you'd hesitate."

"I'm just trying to figure out how I'll know if it needs to be done. I'm thinking about the aftermath. I don't want to do this and have the DUC try to hunt me down for taking you away from them," Becker said.

Quinton considered it for a few moments and then transferred a file to Becker's wrist computer. "This is a recording of our conversation. It's unalterable, and they can verify it. That should get you out of any trouble with the DUC."

Becker opened his personal holoscreen and examined the file. Then he closed the session. "You're serious about this."

"I am," Quinton replied. "Why would you think I'm not serious?"

Becker pursed his lips and then shook his head. "It doesn't matter," he said quietly.

"The next thing I need is for you to tell me more about the Federation Wars," Quinton said.

"We already told you about them," Becker replied and began walking down the corridor.

"You gave me an extremely high-level version of events, but I need to know more. I need any advantage I can get, so don't hold anything back."

Becker sighed. "This could take a while."

"We have two days until we get to that system. I'll help you with whatever Maelyn has you guys doing."

Becker considered this for a few moments. "All right, I'll tell you. But if you do anything to irritate me, like overclock my wrist computer so it burns me, flick something at my neck, change the shower settings to suddenly become ice cold, or make stupid comments, then that's it. I'm serious. The nonsense stops now."

Never before had Quinton wanted so badly to take a proverbial jab at Becker. It was a good thing the agricultural bot couldn't show facial expressions. "I'll be the absolute vision of cooperation."

Becker glared at him and kept walking.

*Yeah, this is going to be tougher than I thought.*

# CHAPTER TWENTY-EIGHT

OVER THE NEXT TWO DAYS, Quinton learned a few things about Toros Becker. The man had a tireless work ethic. He simply stayed on task until the job was done. They had to use stimulants to stave off weariness while they went through the *Nebulon*'s systems. Even with the stimulants, Maelyn tried to make them rotate for a few hours' rest. Not everyone complied.

Quinton had spent much of his time with Becker, the most time the two had spent together since coming aboard the *Nebulon*. He thought that if Becker could ever get over his hatred of machines and all things related to PMCs, they could actually work well together. Well, he hadn't actually thought that. It had been more or less suggested by Maelyn, but the notion was wishful thinking on her part. Quinton was satisfied that Becker wasn't trying to kill him, which meant that he had to do the same. He didn't want to kill the man . . . at least, not anymore, but if Becker pulled another airlock stunt, then all bets were off.

"What is it, Quinton? I can hear you thinking," Becker said.

They were in the galley, and Becker was wolfing down his breakfast. He swallowed his food and stifled a yawn.

"Take a second to chew your food. I don't need you choking

here in the galley," Quinton said.

Becker continued to take enormous bites. His dimpled chin bobbed up and down quickly while he chewed.

Quinton had received a crash-course in the recent history of the galaxy. They'd had to do their best to estimate when he'd been uploaded into an ESS.

"I just don't get it," he said. "The Acheron Confederacy goes from breaking the Jordani Federation's tyrannical control to an all-out conquest of every other star nation and federation alike? It doesn't make sense, and I'm not saying that because I'm from there."

Simon sat across from Becker. He leaned forward. "What's so hard to understand? We've seen many star nations rise up to become the dominant force in the galaxy. That's how the Jordani came to prominence. The Acheron Confederacy was just next in line."

"Maybe," Quinton said.

"Browning was the first," Becker said.

Grand Admiral Elias Browning, along with several galactic fleets under his command, had begun waging war against star systems almost seemingly at random. The Acheron Confederacy disavowed Grand Admiral Browning, but there was a general agreement that the Federation Wars started with Browning's betrayal of the ACN. Many atrocities were attributed to him.

"From war hero to war criminal. I don't understand how that happens," Quinton said.

"Maybe you'll understand better once you get your memories back," Simon said.

Becker gulped down his water. "It's not that far of a stretch. Lennix Crowe increased the Union's influence and reach, which brought him in direct opposition with the Collective. Draven wasn't just going to sit by and let Crowe keep challenging the Collective. He needs to put them in their place, or else other unions will rise up and challenge them."

"Browning was truly awful," Simon said. "He butchered space stations and colonies. And that was *before* the problems with PMCs started happening."

"I've heard you say that before, and I guess you're right. I just think there's more to it. Who controlled the Sentinels?" Quinton asked.

"Sentinels were created from remnants of federation militaries banded together to combat PMC-controlled systems and fleets," Simon said.

They'd talked about this before, and Quinton didn't see any advantage to circling back to discuss it again. Galactic history had been cobbled together through reports of fleeing survivors as they sought to avoid being pulled into the desolation. Quinton also noticed that there seemed to be discrepancies in what the crew members recalled as the "history" of the galaxy, but they were unanimous in the fact that Admiral Browning's exploits had plunged the galaxy into all-out war the likes of which had never been seen.

Simon checked his comlink and then looked at the others. "We're nearly to the jump point. We should get to the bridge."

Becker nodded while taking one last mouthful of food and then stood. They left the galley. Quinton had believed that learning more about galactic history would help him with what they were going to find, but he wasn't so sure anymore. The more he learned, the more questions he had.

They did a long-range sensor sweep as they headed to the target star system, hoping that they could learn more about it as opposed to jumping in blindly.

The red giant was an old star, but they'd recently discovered that there was a singularity in orbit around it. In galactic terms, it slightly outmassed the star that was still slowly consuming it. Because of the singularity, they had to jump farther out in the star system.

Simon went to his workstation. Maelyn sat in the captain's

chair, and Quinton and Becker stood nearby. Kieva sat at her workstation next to Simon. The others were in a common area midship, but they were comlinked to the bridge.

"Execute jump," Maelyn ordered.

The *Nebulon* jumped to the outer edges of the target star system. Passive scanning systems came online, and they set a course to the interior of the star system, believing that this was the most likely place for an ACN facility to be located.

"Not the most peaceful star system we've ever been to," Simon said.

Quinton looked at the data on the main holoscreen. He wasn't integrated with the ship systems yet, so he was reliant on the *Nebulon*'s computers to make the data being gathered available. The singularity in this system must have been a recent event —in galactic terms. The other planets in-system had an orbit that hadn't completely stabilized yet.

The star system was lifeless. No planets here could support anything remotely livable. Perhaps with hundreds of years of terraforming it could be different, but there were much better systems available for supporting life.

Quinton looked at Maelyn. "Passive scans are only going to get us so far."

He was impatient to be integrated with the *Nebulon*'s systems, but he'd promised Maelyn he would wait for her permission.

"No other ships detected in the system," Simon said. "In fact, I don't see anything that indicates anyone has ever been here."

But it was too soon for them to conclude that there was nothing there. Quinton needed to broadcast a specially crafted comlink.

"You're up, Quinton," Maelyn said finally. "Interface with the *Nebulon*'s systems and broadcast your signal. Let's see if anything's waiting for us out there. Simon, I want the emergency jump coordinates ready to execute."

Quinton accessed the *Nebulon's* computer systems and saw that the emergency jump coordinates were already loaded into the navigation computer. He cranked up his frame rate and then took control of the communications array, uploading a modified protocol for a broadcast signal that included the activation signal used to bring him online. He then initiated an active scan of the system. If they were going to broadcast a communication signal, there was no reason not to initiate an active scan.

"Broadcasting now," Quinton said, then added, "I'm adjusting to juggling multiple frame rates." His voice sounded even more monotone, with less emotional inflection. It felt strange, as if he were in two places at once. His perception of time was at once normal, like everyone else's, and as fast as the agricultural bot's internal systems would allow. It was a risk because, despite their best efforts, the agricultural bot's internal systems weren't designed for this kind of computational capacity. They were being pushed beyond their limits, but he had to push them. If this was some kind of Sentinel trap, he'd need to react quickly.

A response came via a subspace comlink, which contained a challenge protocol similar to what he'd encountered with the PMC console, but it was more complex, comprised of multiple layers of protocols requiring a response. Since he was directly interfacing with the ship systems, the response protocol authentication came from his ESS. He provided a vast array of authentication codes that he hadn't even known were inside his ESS, as if it were responding autonomously.

Quinton pinpointed the location of the subspace comlink to a large moon that orbited a Jovian planet. He focused an active scan pulse at those coordinates and could detect only a comlink array there. There was no other facility detected. The array probably had another subspace comlink to a facility that managed the challenge protocols. They could still execute an emergency jump, but he suspected it would be close. If they ended up in a dampening field, they couldn't simply jump away.

He'd sent the last authentication code and was waiting for a response.

"I received a reply and am working through the authentication protocol. So far, it's just like the PMC console," Quinton said.

"Where did the reply come from?" Maelyn asked.

He updated the main holoscreen with a flashing icon to indicate the location.

"Simon, set a course for those coordinates," Maelyn said.

"Are you sure you want to do that?" Becker said and then held up his hands in a placating gesture. "I mean, he hasn't received a response yet. There hasn't been an all-clear invite."

"Whatever's over there could just be coming online, and that's taking some time," she replied.

Becker turned his attention to the main holoscreen and didn't say anything else.

Quinton was tempted to send another transmission but decided to wait. A few minutes passed before a reply finally came. "We're authorized to approach. They sent us a secondary set of coordinates. I'll put it on the main holoscreen."

The coordinates were located on the other side of the star system.

"We can get there quicker with a micro-jump," Maelyn said.

"Initiating micro-jump," Simon said.

Becker looked at Quinton and appeared as if he wanted to say something.

"That was the only reply I got. It's an invitation," Quinton said.

Becker inhaled deeply and sighed. Then he nodded.

The *Nebulon* jumped to the other side of the star system where a small asteroid field was located.

Several warnings appeared on Quinton's HUD. The agricultural bot's internal systems were wearing out. Power levels from his core were fluctuating, and he returned his frame rate back to normal time.

"System resources aren't meant for the excess load. Recommend avoiding overtaxing the system," Radek said sub-vocally.

Quinton quickly acknowledged the list of warnings. "Understood," he replied.

"Quinton," Simon said with concern in his voice. He had the agricultural bot's status report on one of his holoscreens.

"What's wrong?" Maelyn asked.

The power fluctuations returned to normal. "It's fine. I just overdid it," Quinton replied.

Maelyn looked at Simon. He refreshed the report, then nodded at Maelyn.

"Erratic orbital patterns are being reported for our destination," Quinton said. A few moments later, the warning appeared on the main holoscreen.

"No weapons systems detected," Simon said.

Quinton looked as if he was peering at the main holoscreen, but he was interfaced with the *Nebulon's* sensor array and accessing the data in real time before the *Nebulon* put the data through its own analysis. He could have deployed his VI assistants into the *Nebulon's* systems, but they might be detected by a Sentinel scan. Even though he was in the system, he was simply using it by inserting himself into key areas that didn't require actual manipulation. It was one of the protective measures he and Simon had come up with to limit their risk exposure should the Sentinels suddenly show up.

"The trajectory suggests a pattern of ships docking with one another," Quinton said.

A high-res image appeared on the main holoscreen.

"Would you look at that," Becker said.

"It's a station, all right. They've just kept it hidden," Maelyn said.

"Quinton's signal must have caused it to activate," Simon said.

"I thought the activation signal had come from here, but how can that be if the station is only coming online now?" Quinton asked.

He glanced at the others.

Maelyn shook her head. "I don't know. Maybe the signal was relayed through here."

It was possible. The coordinates were unlocked from within his ESS, which meant that someone had put them there. They had wanted him to come here.

Another window appeared on the main holoscreen, which had a series of images on them. "These are archival images of the stations that contained the DNA vaults for the Acheron Confederacy," Maelyn said.

They were cylindrical in appearance, with only a few docking ports. When compared with the live video feed from this star system, the station was much larger. Multiple sections of the station had docked together, and its overall length was over three thousand meters.

Simon leaned back in his chair. "Look at the size of it."

"Captain," Kieva said, "I've received a remote autopilot request from ACN starbase Endurance."

Maelyn looked at Quinton.

"I've had no other contact from them," he said.

"There can't be anyone there. Not if it's been hidden all this time," Becker said.

Maelyn nodded. "Authorization granted."

The *Nebulon* flew toward the middle of the massive station. Quinton peered at the high-res image, and his own analysis appeared on his HUD. Entire sections of the station's walls had a rocky outer layer that made it appear as if it were just another asteroid. He easily picked out point-defense turrets that, upon first pass, looked to be in pristine condition. The surrounding asteroid field shifted, and rays of starshine gleamed off the battle-steel plating.

The *Nebulon* was guided into a central hangar bay. Thick armored doors opened as they made their final approach.

"Is this like anything you've seen before?" Quinton asked.

Becker studied the live video feed on the main holoscreen. "It looks like a standard station design, but they've usually been destroyed by the time we find them. This one looks operational."

Quinton looked at the others as they watched the holoscreen. Simon kept shifting in his seat as he tried to keep track of the data streams on his workstation, but he couldn't stop himself from gazing at the main holoscreen. There had to be a DNA vault there.

The *Nebulon* landed in a vast but empty hangar bay.

Quinton glanced at the others and then opened a comlink to the station. He connected immediately, feeling as if he'd been pulled inside a massive computer system that had been specifically designed for PMC access. He wasn't sure if he was more relieved to be accessing the station or if *it* was just enthusiastic to have someone who'd finally answered its call.

"Systems are still coming online. There is an atmosphere. Life support is functioning normally," Quinton said and paused for a few moments. He chuckled a little. "There's a lot of information."

"Can you throttle it down so you don't get overwhelmed?" Maelyn asked.

"It's being throttled down. The VIs are working on it. I don't know where to begin. There's so much here," Quinton said.

"Focus on what we came here for first. You need to find out if there's a DNA vault, and can you authorize data access so Simon can access the station?" Maelyn said.

The station was managed by its own VI that was less sophisticated than Radek. Quinton requested station access for Simon, and it was immediately granted. Then he began a search for a map of the interior layout.

"I'm in," Simon said.

"Good. Begin searching for a world database. We need to find out where their secret colonization projects were located," Maelyn said.

"And ships. Don't forget to look for ships. There are more hangars than this one. They can't all be empty," Becker said.

"I have the schematics for the interior. Making them available to everyone now," Quinton said.

Maelyn nodded and stood up. "Let's get the away team ready. Kieva, I want you to monitor our progress from the ship. Send a comlink to Admiral Brandt giving the all clear, and include our current coordinates."

Becker looked at Maelyn. "Brandt was following us?"

"Of course. I kept them apprised of our progress," she replied.

"I guess I expected him to be a little bit more cautious."

"Ordinarily yes, but . . ." Maelyn said and gestured toward the main holoscreen.

Becker nodded in agreement.

The others were leaving the bridge, and Quinton hastened to catch up. They met up at the main airlock where Guttman and Oscar distributed weapons to everyone.

"I don't think we'll need those," Quinton said.

"That's why you're not in charge," Becker said. Guttman and Oscar grinned.

"It's just a precaution," Maelyn said. "Sometimes, these places have automated defenses."

Vonya glanced at the sidearm that Guttman was trying to hand to her and shook her head.

"Take it just in case," Maelyn said, and then Vonya slowly reached out for it.

Quinton looked down at the gauss rifle he'd been handed and slung it onto his back. An analysis of the station's atmosphere didn't reveal any foreign contaminants. The station was as pristine as the day it had been fabricated.

He opened the airlock and walked down the loading ramp. The nearest wall displayed a massive black and gold emblem of the Acheron Confederacy Navy—two golden triangular halves that angled away from a sphere on a black background. Beneath were the words "Perseverance. Endurance. Fortitude. Readiness."

The others joined Quinton, and he watched them take in their surroundings in silence. Every ship and space station he'd been on since he'd been reactivated had had a long service record. They'd been patched up and were well beyond their design specifications. He glanced at the others again. Becker and Guttman had the beginnings of a scowling expression. Vonya calmly took in the sight of the ACN emblem as if she was studying something she hadn't seen before. Maelyn had a tightness in her eyes that bordered on resentment, as if she'd been betrayed. Simon and Oscar looked at the emblem with a thoughtful frown but nothing more. Quinton wondered if this was how the members of the DUC would react once they got here.

Quinton made a clearing-his-throat sound. "I wouldn't go around commenting on how much you hate the Acheron Confederacy here. Just a little advice."

Becker shook his head and then strode toward the hangar bay doors that led to the station's interior. Quinton and the others quickly caught up with him. The sensors detected their presence, and the automatic doors opened.

"Has anyone or anything tried to contact you?" Maelyn asked.

"No, there are a lot of systems still coming online. There's a tram system a short distance ahead of us. Maybe we should split up to explore this place," Quinton said.

"He's right," Guttman said. "We'll cover more ground that way. There are a few other hangar bays, smaller than this one, but I want to check them out to see what's inside."

They reached the end of the corridor, which emptied into a small plaza where a tram system was online. There were several trams waiting to be boarded.

Guttman and Oscar headed toward a tram on the left. Guttman turned around. "Becker, are you coming?"

Becker shook his head. "Negative, you guys go ahead and report back in. I'll catch up with you."

Guttman's lips formed a thin line. Then he shrugged and nodded. They walked onto one of the trams and left the station with just a slight hum as the counter-grav plating sped the tram away.

Maelyn frowned. "I'm surprised you didn't go with them."

Becker almost glanced at Quinton but covered it up with a slight shake of his head. "I thought I'd stick with you and see what else the station has for us."

"We need to look for a bio lab. That's where we'd find a DNA storage vault, along with a medical capsule and material to grow Quinton's new body," Simon said.

"I like the sound of that. We should always do what Simon says," Quinton said.

Simon smiled, and they climbed aboard a tram. "I think that used to be a game a long time ago."

"What game?" Becker asked.

"Never mind that now," Maelyn said. "We need to take this tram . . . Oh, it's a combination elevator system as well. We just input the bio lab destination."

Quinton had already selected the destination before anybody could use the interface. "You sound surprised by the elevator system."

"I am, only because . . . I just hadn't expected it to be here, that's all," she said.

She looked around the gleaming interior of the tram as if she expected to see something that wasn't actually there. Quinton noticed the others doing the same.

The tram slowed down and then stopped, and then they began to rise. They ascended forty decks before the tram came to a stop again, and the rear doors opened.

The corridor beyond began to light up as they walked off the tram. The interior lighting had a tinge of yellow to it, reminding Quinton of the light of a yellow main sequence star. The agricultural bot's sensors detected trace amounts of ultraviolet radiation, which people needed in order to stimulate production of essential vitamins, but it also had a positive psychological effect on spacers who spent long periods of time away from a planet.

As they walked the corridor, Becker looked at Quinton. "Do you even know how you transfer back into a body?" he said and frowned. "And don't give me any flack because I don't know the technical terms. You know what I mean."

Quinton searched the data available on his ESS for the procedures and couldn't find anything. "I don't know, but why would I need to know? They'll have the procedure here. They'd be prepared for it since these DNA vaults were so widespread. Or I just need full access to my ESS."

Becker nodded and didn't say anything else.

The bio lab revealed bright white walls and amber-colored holoscreens that flickered to life as they walked inside. There were several medical capsules farther inside.

Simon whistled. "Look at how many of them there are," he said and looked at Quinton. "As long as we have the right stock of materials, these are capable of regrowing a body for you."

Internally, Quinton laughed with anticipation. He was so close.

Maelyn received a comlink from Kieva. "Go ahead, *Nebulon*."

"Captain, I received a response from Admiral Brandt, and they'll be at the station within two hours. He'd like you to have an update ready for him when he arrives," Kieva said.

"Understood," Maelyn said.

"Ask her if she's detected any broadcast signals from the station," Becker said.

Maelyn asked.

"None detected," Kieva replied.

"Very well. I'll be in contact," Maelyn said and closed the comlink.

Quinton accessed the bio lab systems and began a search for his DNA profile.

Simon sat down at one of the workstations. Quinton looked at the others. "I've given you all access to the station's computer systems, including Guttman and Oscar."

Vonya sat next to Simon and watched him work while Becker opened a comlink to Guttman and let him know.

Quinton put the status of his search on one of the nearby holoscreens.

"I didn't realize there were so many of them," Maelyn said as she looked at the screen, her face etched with sorrow.

"Neither did I," Quinton said quietly. There was a long list of DNA profiles, and each one of them had been a person like him. All at once, he felt a profound sense of emptiness. Most, if not all, of the people on this list were dead. They had died during the Federation Wars. Even though their DNA profiles were here, they couldn't regrow their bodies because they lacked the minds to go with them. A PMC was required—otherwise the body that was regrown would be lifeless.

"We should take a copy of this back to the DUC in case they find any other PMCs," Quinton said.

Maelyn nodded soberly. "We will," she promised and looked at Simon.

"I have a data uplink to the *Nebulon* already online, and I'm moving information across."

Quinton tried to focus on something else, but he kept watching his search window, unable to do anything else. Then the search stopped.

*DNA profile match.*

Quinton read the status window a few times before he believed what he saw. "That's it! That's me! I'm in there. Do you see it? I'm in there!"

Maelyn smiled and nodded enthusiastically. Even Becker tilted his head in an acknowledging nod.

"Oh boy," Simon said. "I just found the procedure to get Quinton back into a body. It's complex, and there are risks involved."

"What kinds of risks?" Maelyn asked.

"Based on this," Simon said, pointing to the data on the screen, "it's almost like they'll be scanning his consciousness again before it will be allowed to be transferred back into his body. There's a risk of rejection."

"What?" Quinton asked. "My body isn't going to reject my mind. The two go together."

"No, I understand that, but I'm just telling you what's here. There *is* a risk. Also, there's some kind of integrity scan to confirm that the PMC is stable," Simon said.

Becker chuckled. "And here I almost regret making all those instability jokes."

"Ha, ha, very funny," Quinton replied. Then he looked at Maelyn. "I don't care what the risks are. I can't stay in here," he said, gesturing toward the agricultural unit's chest cavity.

"I know," Maelyn said. "Are there any other androids on the station that would be a suitable match for him?"

Quinton balled his mechanical hands into fists. "No!" He backed up a few steps. "I'm not going into another android. We're going to bring one of those medical capsules online, engage the restoration protocol, and follow the procedure. Enough is enough."

Maelyn gave him a long look, and Quinton knew that her concerns were justified, but he had to get out of this body. Maybe it wouldn't have been so bad if he had full access to his ESS, but he didn't, and he'd had enough. He finally had everything he needed to make this happen, and he wasn't going to lose this opportunity.

Maelyn looked at Simon. "What do you need?"

"We need to transfer his ESS into one of those chambers. There's a cradle inside that's designed for it. We just need to place it there," Simon said.

Maelyn looked at Quinton. "We need to access your ESS."

Before she finished speaking, he had ripped the chest plate from the agricultural unit's body, exposing the ESS. The decagonal shape of the ESS glowed pale blue, and its surface pulsed from the leuridium core.

Maelyn looked at it, and her eyes widened a little. She leaned forward to get a better look.

"Wait! You can't touch it," Quinton said.

"Why can't we touch it?" Becker asked.

"I was going for some heightened drama," Quinton said.

Becker frowned at him.

"I was just joking. It has defense capabilities that will neutralize anyone who tries to tamper with it. Either it will knock you out or your heart will stop beating. Either way, it's not worth the risk." He looked at Maelyn. "I need to have Radek initiate the release, and the ESS will disconnect from the agricultural unit. Then you can use an anti-gravity field to transfer it into the cradle. Will you do that for me?"

Maelyn nodded and smiled. "Yes, of course I will."

"I don't know," Becker said. "It would make for a nice decorative piece on the *Nebulon's* bridge."

Quinton was so excited that he wasn't even annoyed. "Once I'm done with it, you can do whatever you want."

Becker received a comlink from Guttman. "Looks like they found a couple of ships that they want me to see. Everything seems under control here," he said and looked at Quinton. "I'm going to go meet up with the others."

Quinton looked at him for a few moments. "Thanks," he said.

Becker gave him a nod and left the room.

"What was that about?" Maelyn asked.

"Just a contingency plan."

She glanced at the door Becker had used and then back at Quinton. "For what?"

"It's really not important. We didn't end up needing it," Quinton said and gestured toward his ESS. He felt oddly vulnerable. Maelyn arched an eyebrow. "He was going to do something for me in case things got out of control."

She tilted her head to the side a little, waiting for him to continue.

"It's not important," Quinton said and looked at Simon. "Are we ready? Can I give Radek the go-ahead?"

Simon nodded. "Yes, we can start the upload process now. That will give us time to get the other things in place."

Quinton thought Maelyn looked annoyed, but he didn't want to get into it right then. She grabbed the small handheld gravity field emitter used for transferring dangerous substances and powered it on. Two prongs ejected from the end and began to glow.

"Here goes nothing," Quinton said. Then he had Radek initiate the release protocols that would detach him from the agricultural unit.

Quinton had to withdraw from the station's systems, as well as those of the *Nebulon's*. Being cut off from everything made him feel diminished, less alive than he'd been mere moments before, but it would only be temporary. He probably wouldn't even notice the missing time. Just as Radek was initiating the release protocols, he remembered that he'd forgotten to ask how long the process was going to take. He probably should've asked that, but it was too late to . . .

# CHAPTER TWENTY-NINE

QUINTON DIDN'T WAKE up like he expected to. He'd thought that when he woke up, the others would be looking down at him as he regained consciousness in the medical capsule. He'd be inside a newly grown body that was his own, taking his first breath, and he'd have full access to his memories. Instead, he just sort of became aware, but even that wasn't the right way to say it. He wanted to frown and tried to organize his thoughts. He felt an increasing sense of awareness, as if he'd been floating in an empty void, and now he was being pushed toward an invisible barrier.

An image of a video feed appeared in front of him showing the bio lab, which was empty. The agricultural unit he'd been housed in stood to his left. Its chest panel had been torn open. The bot's metallic alloy had splotches of a white filmy substance that, at first glance, one would think could be scrubbed off, but Quinton knew better. The bot had been exposed to a harsh atmosphere for a very long time. He hadn't taken time to look at the agricultural bot's appearance because it was more upsetting than comforting. Now that he was no longer trapped inside, he wanted to destroy it because if he didn't, there was a chance that his ESS would somehow end up inside it again. Quinton knew it was foolish, but that didn't change how he felt.

Turning his attention to the medical capsule, he tried to peer inside, and the video feed zoomed in closer. His body was inside. He could see his legs—*his* legs—and his body up to his chest. His head and shoulders were blocked from view because they were inside some kind of chamber. The capsule was filled with a liquid that had a yellowish tinge to it.

A silver sphere appeared in the video feed. The sphere looked like liquid mercury—silvery and highly reflective.

"Quinton?" Radek asked. The sphere flashed along its edges.

"I'm here," Quinton replied. "What's going on? How come I'm not in my body?"

"Regrowth is only 65 percent complete and requires a full reanimation check for adequate muscle stimulation and response," Radek replied.

He glanced at the agricultural unit again. "Where am I?"

"Your ESS is still active and is undergoing an integrity check as part of the revival protocols."

He felt an urge to shake his head, except he didn't have one, which made having the urge highly distracting. "Something's wrong. You wouldn't have awakened me otherwise. I was supposed to wake up inside my own body. Where is everyone? How much time has passed? What's going on?" He tried to access the station's systems and couldn't, which increased his anxiety about the situation to whole new levels.

"Wait," Radek said. "I have you restricted for your own protection. Please don't override it until I've explained a few things to you."

Since Radek was asking him not to override his restriction, it meant that Quinton *could* exert some level of control over his situation. He calmed down a little. Radek was afraid of what Quinton would do and was trying to protect him.

"Endurance Starbase system utilization is extremely high

because of a massive data dump to a DUC ship called the *Neseverous*."

"The DUC is already here? How long have I been out?"

"It's been five hours since you were taken offline. I've been monitoring the process the entire time."

"Why would the DUC try to do a massive data dump? It would be quicker to just query the system for the data they wanted. Simon knows this. He would have told Maelyn if she didn't already know it," Quinton said.

"I'm unaware of the communication between Maelyn and the DUC fleet."

"What do you mean 'unaware'? You're in the station's computer systems. It's just a matter of monitoring comlink activities. Maelyn wouldn't have blocked access," he said.

"I'm not actively inside the station's computer system. I reside within your ESS, which is inside the cradle awaiting transfer into your biological form."

"Then how could you know that the station's computer system is being highly utilized?" Quinton asked.

"Because the computer system told me."

Quinton couldn't fault the logic. The extremely limited VI that managed Endurance Starbase had probably reprioritized, or more likely was given a high priority for the data transfer, which was making his own analysis and download take even longer.

"Then why did you wake me up?"

"Too much time had passed, and no one from the *Nebulon*'s crew has returned to check on your progress," Radek said.

Quinton considered this for a few moments. The only way to find out what was happening on the station was for Radek to wake him up. "I understand. Remove the restriction. Let's see if I can figure out what's happening here."

"Done," Radek said.

Quinton's awareness shifted to a phalanx of holoscreens that represented his interface with Endurance Starbase's computer system. Radek helped to organize the data feeds Quinton could now access so he wouldn't be overwhelmed by the sheer volume of information available. Instead, he was overwhelmed by the fact that the station's sensors detected two opposing fleets locked in an engagement. He saw that the *Astra* was among the DUC ships engaging the other fleet. He opened a tactical workstation holoscreen and designated the second fleet as hostile. He didn't know who they were.

Quinton opened a comlink to Maelyn.

"Wayborn here."

"Maelyn, it's me, Quinton."

"Quinton!"

He located her position near a residential section on the other side of the station. Simon and Vonya were with her.

"Who's attacking us?" Quinton asked.

"Wait a second, I'm going to patch Becker in," Maelyn said.

Becker joined them. "The transport shuttles in this hangar aren't space worthy. I have no idea why. They look like they've been cannibalized for parts."

"Becker, Quinton is awake," Maelyn said.

Quinton heard something loud from Becker's comlink connection, and then an impact alert came to prominence.

"Who's firing on us?" Quinton asked.

"Becker, are you all right?" Maelyn asked.

Becker exhaled explosively. "Yeah, we're fine. That was close."

"The DUC fleet is fighting Union ships," Maelyn said.

"Crowe is here?"

"Are you in a body yet?" Becker asked.

"No, it's not ready."

"How are you awake?" Maelyn asked.

"Radek woke me up. He was monitoring the integrity check for my ESS and received an alert from the system because of the data dump to the *Neseverous*. It's degrading the entire system."

"I told you that you shouldn't have given Brandt your access codes for the station," Becker said.

"Never mind that," Maelyn said. "Quinton, how much time is left for the transfer?"

"The body regrowth is now at 72 percent. How did Crowe find us so fast?"

Another impact alert came from a different part of the station. Someone was using kinetic artillery and was taking shots at the station.

"Hey, since you're just wasting time, can you make yourself useful?" Becker said.

"He's right, Quinton. Are you able to help us?"

"How?"

Becker cursed. "How about engaging the station's point-defense systems for starters. Does this place have anything that can shoot back? The DUC isn't going to last long against Union ships. I bet Crowe brought everything he had here."

Quinton winced inwardly. He accessed the station's point-defense systems and brought them online, assigning targeting priority to Union ships.

"How did Crowe find us?" he asked.

The tactical holoscreen showed the two fleets pounding on each other with mag cannons and maser beams. It appeared that both sides had ships fleeing the battle, and several were now going offline. Becker was right—Crowe's Union ships were outmaneuvering the DUC fleet ships.

"You guys need to get back to the *Nebulon*," Quinton said.

"Tell us something we don't know," Becker said.

"The tram system is down," Maelyn said.

Quinton accessed the station's transport systems. After the station had been hit, it must have initiated safety protocols that precluded the use of the tram system.

"I think I can override it," Quinton said. "Maelyn, follow the maintenance corridor to your left. It will take you to an emergency transport station that should get you most of the way."

He heard Maelyn speaking to Simon and Vonya. "Why won't the bulkhead door open?"

"I don't know, but she said she meet us farther..." Simon said, and Quinton ignored him while he tried to find a way to help Becker. Then he paused.

"Becker, it's time to come clean. Did you tell Crowe our location?" Quinton asked.

"What? Not this again. No, dammit! Telling Crowe where we are is a death sentence."

Quinton still had his perfect recall from their time on the *Nebulon*.

"Why were you so interested in the *Nebulon*'s maintenance logs? You kept reviewing their activity."

"Look, we can talk about this or you can help us get out of here. We're stuck in a small hangar bay with ships that can't take us anywhere," Becker said, scowling.

"What was so interesting about the automated maintenance systems?" Quinton asked.

"Maelyn, he'll listen to you. Can you tell him to help us?" Becker asked.

"No, I don't think so, Becker. Answer the question," Maelyn replied frostily.

Becker cursed and lowered his voice. "I was trying to find out if someone on the ship was giving away our location to Crowe."

"What does that have to do with the maintenance systems?" Quinton asked.

"What did you find out?" Maelyn asked.

"Nothing. I couldn't find anything firm, and I knew that if I made an accusation, I'd be on the top of everyone's list of betrayers. Maelyn, I'm telling you that I did not do this," Becker said.

"I'm not convinced," Quinton said. "In fact, I think I'm going to vent the atmosphere in that hangar bay."

"Wait!" Becker cried out. "Guttman and Oscar are with me."

"It could be any one of you," Quinton replied and accessed the life-support systems for Becker's location. He heard Guttman shout in the background about the ventilation system flushing out the atmosphere.

"Stop it! I was checking the maintenance systems because sometimes you can schedule a subspace comlink to coincide with the ship's automated systems used to manage repair drones. That's what I was checking for. You can look for yourself," Becker said.

Quinton opened a comlink to the *Nebulon's* systems and checked the logs. Becker was right. Someone could have done what he'd suspected, but they hadn't.

"Quinton, I know you're in the *Nebulon's* systems. What did you find?" Maelyn asked.

"He's right. Becker is right. Someone could have done it, but they didn't try to mask a subspace comlink. However, unless jump drones are part of routine maintenance, I think whoever was feeding Crowe information was using them," Quinton said.

He heard Becker gasp and then begin to cough. Either Becker was caught in an elaborate lie and had become the leader of all deceivers, which Quinton didn't believe he would do, or he wasn't the traitor. He restored life support to the hangar bay.

Becker inhaled several lungsful of breath before he could speak. "I told you it wasn't me."

"Then who the hell was it?" Maelyn asked.

"I don't know," Quinton replied. "Since the drones were operating under an automated maintenance system, there isn't a clear identification of who added them. Whoever did this is subtle, capable, and able to . . ." he paused for a moment, his mind racing. "Maelyn, is Vonya with you?"

"No, we were separated. Do you think it was Vonya?" Maelyn asked and then scowled. "It has to be her. Neither Kieva nor Simon would do this. Vonya has spent time with everyone, 'finding her place and getting to know the ship.' She fed me a Servitor's sad story, and I ate it up like a fool," she said bitterly.

"Not for long," Quinton said and began searching for Vonya.

Maelyn wasn't the only one who'd been fooled by Vonya. She'd fooled them all. His perfect recall brought up every interaction with the beautiful Servitor, looking for some kind of sign that she had been lying to them. Why had she done it? Was she just loyal to Crowe, or was he somehow coercing her to work for him? He'd find out soon enough. There was nowhere on this station that she could hide from him.

Quinton accessed the station's life-sign tracking system and was able to locate everyone on the station except Vonya.

"I can't locate her. She doesn't appear to be anywhere on the station," he said.

Maelyn opened a comlink to the *Nebulon*. "Kieva, did Vonya return to the ship?"

"Negative, Captain," Kieva replied.

"Understood. If she returns to the ship, don't let her come aboard," Maelyn said.

"Captain, what's going on? Vonya has been such a great addition to the crew—"

"Kieva, she's been using jump drones to inform Lennix Crowe of our location and who knows what else. I don't have time to go into it. We're on our way to you. Prep the ship for launch," Maelyn said.

"Aye, Captain," Kieva replied and closed the comlink.

Since the bio-detection systems on the station couldn't locate Vonya, Quinton started checking for door-access control systems, which included the airlocks. "How did you get cut off from each other?"

"Can we focus on getting off this station?" Becker said. "Can you use your illustrious access and find us a ship to escape on? I don't know that we could make it back to the *Nebulon* if we had to run."

The tram systems were offline due to damage from a mag cannon blast that had penetrated the station's armor. Emergency bulkhead doors sealed off the damaged sections, and Becker and the others were stranded. He accessed the stations logs for any ship that had been left there.

"There might be something, but you'll have to head away from the central station. There's a dark hangar bay that was sealed for storage. You'll need to restore power and then see if the ship inside is space worthy," Quinton said.

"Can't you restore the power?" Becker asked.

"No, it's entirely cut off from the station, but it might be your best bet. It's closer than trekking all the way back to the central hangar," Quinton said.

Becker growled in disgust and disconnected the comlink.

"What's the status of the regrowth?" Maelyn asked.

Quinton checked it. "Ninety-seven percent complete," he replied and felt a surge of anticipation. "I think Vonya is off the station. An exterior airlock was accessed shortly after you were cut off, and a repair shuttle's been taken."

"Can you contact the shuttle?"

"I can't. There's no response. She could have taken the comms systems offline in order to prevent me from accessing it. I can't track her," Quinton replied.

Maelyn sighed heavily. "Okay, we'll deal with her later. Will the station's point-defense systems stay online after you begin the transference protocol?"

Quinton glanced at the holographic sphere that hovered nearby. It bobbed once. "Radek says it will."

"Good—" Maelyn said as an alpha priority alert appeared on all of the holoscreens around him.

The alert was for unauthorized access to the station's computer systems.

"What the hell," Quinton said as more alerts appeared.

"What's wrong?"

"There's been unauthorized access to the station's systems. Someone has bypassed the security systems," he said.

"Can you block their access?"

He was trying that, but the first thing the infiltrator had done was to create alternative access points, and as Quinton blocked them, they appeared somewhere else from an entirely different subsystem. "I'm trying, but they keep coming back."

"Quinton, I think you're in danger. You need to get out of the station's computer systems."

He raced to block the unauthorized access and tried to think of a way to stop whoever it was. If he took the entire system down, then the point-defense systems would be taken offline, as well as internal systems. Maelyn was right. They were all in trouble.

"Crowe wouldn't come here unprepared. He wants to capture you, and there are infiltration protocols that can be integrated into a system to do just that. They already have access. You need to pull back and begin the transference protocol. It's the only way to avoid being taken over," Maelyn said.

Quinton had multiple holoscreens up, and he was furiously trying to eradicate the rogue VI that was infiltrating the station's computer system. It was a race, but he thought it was one he could win.

"Quinton, you need to listen to me," she said.

The rogue VI began spawning even more copies of itself at a rate he hadn't thought was possible.

Maelyn called out to him again.

"What about you and Simon? You haven't made it back to the ship yet."

"Don't worry about us. We can take care of ourselves. I've redirected the tram to take us to the bio lab. We'll leave the station together."

Quinton looked at the status for his new body.

*Regrowth complete.*

He hesitated.

It was all right there for him. All he had to do was to order Radek to begin the transference protocol, and his PMC would be merged with the brain of his new body. He'd be whole again. This was what he wanted. This was why he'd come here. He looked at the bio lab through the video feed and saw the medical capsule. His body was in there. He could have a new life. This was it.

"Quinton," Radek said, "shall I engage the transfer protocols?"

He wanted to tell Radek to do just that, but the words wouldn't come. He glanced at the tactical workstation holoscreen that showed Union ships pushing back the DUC fleet. Inside the station's computer systems, a vicious infiltrator VI was attempting to assert control. What would it do if it couldn't get to him? Would it simply stop what it was doing, or would it turn its attention toward taking control of the station's computer system? He didn't know. Maelyn and Simon were on their way to the bio lab, and Becker and the others were trying to find a ship to escape in.

But what was he doing? The enemy was closing in all around him, and what was he going to do?

He could engage the transference protocol, and if it worked, wake up in a new body of flesh and blood. He'd have access to all his memories. All the answers he'd sought would be his, but what good would that do if they all died? What good would it do for him to survive here while everyone else died around him?

Quinton looked at the two fleets battling for control of an Acheron Confederacy Navy space station. Who'd hidden it here? Why had the coordinates been in his ESS, and why was he here?

The holoscreens rearranged themselves in front of him—the tactical holoscreen, a video feed of the tram that Maelyn and Simon rode, the central hangar bay where the *Nebulon* waited, and a holoscreen where he saw Becker, Guttman, and Oscar running down a corridor, racing for a safe way off the station.

Rising above the other holoscreens was a video feed of the interior of the bio lab. He still couldn't see his own face that was hidden inside the capsule. And here Quinton was, at the cusp of ending this ordeal. He'd fought for this, risked his life for this. He glanced at the other video feeds. Theirs was a harsh galaxy, but in rare moments he glimpsed the older ideals when things hadn't been so dire.

He dismissed the video feed of the bio lab, and it disappeared.

"No, Radek, there's been a change of plans," Quinton said.

# CHAPTER THIRTY

"I MUST ADVISE AGAINST THAT," Radek said.

"I'll take it under advisement."

He needed time. He was in a virtual holding area where he could use the station's computer systems but not directly interface with it the way a PMC was meant to. Quinton pulled up the central computing core location and opened a direct connection to it. He needed to interface with the computing core if they were going to have a fighting chance.

"The body can wait," he said.

He uploaded his own VI suite into the computing core, and his assistants began a quick assessment of the new environment. Then they facilitated additional connections to his ESS.

*G Class PMC Access Level.*

Quinton became aware of the access level seemingly before the curious thought had formed in his mind. He was a Galactic class Personality Matrix Construct, which carried the highest level of access and interface with ACN computing systems. Radek raced to unload the concepts that hadn't been available to him while he'd resided in the agricultural bot. Quinton hadn't fully understood just how feeble a connection to living the bot had provided. It was like using the flimsiest material to hold the weight of a Titan-class battleship. He brought up the specs of the ship of the wall that formed the foundation of the Jordani Federation Navy. He knew its armament, as well as the kind of fleet deployments that made the best use of the interstellar fortress.

Quinton cranked up his frame rate, and his perception of time sped up while virtually no time at all passed for the others. He was no longer bound to the pitiful hardware of a decaying old robot, and it was glorious. He didn't need to worry about hardware that was about to fall apart. He was in an ACN Starbase Alpha meant for picket duty, protecting strategic star systems on the fringes of federation territories. The starbase had the armament equal to that of a small fleet. There were weapons systems that had never been brought online. He'd only engaged the point-defense systems, but the starbase was designed to deal out significant punishment to any who sought to destroy it. It was technology meant for fighting a war, and Quinton was the only one who could command it.

He tasked a VI with the sole purpose of blocking the infiltrator VI that had been unleashed by Lennix Crowe. Quinton's VIs were capable of learning and adapting through the use of Sapient Combat Simulations. They essentially took action while running countless simulations to help sway the outcome to achieve his objective. As they engaged the advanced rogue VI, they tried to adapt to tactics that were taking place on a virtual battleground of the station's computing system. They'd slow the rogue VI down, but it would eventually adapt.

Quinton shifted his focus to the space battle occurring dangerously close to the starbase. The DUC fleet ships were being pushed back by the Union ships. Because his frame rate was so high, he was looking at a snapshot of the situation that was in the midst of progressing. The DUC fleet hadn't been defeated, but his own analysis indicated that it couldn't fight the Union ships for much longer. He knew what Admiral Brandt was fighting for —habitable worlds that they could keep hidden from Crowe's Union and the Collective. The DUC migrant fleet was made up of galactic refugees and comprised the migrant's most capable warships. They were enough to make any aggressor think twice before engaging in hostilities, but Crowe would never relent until he either had what he wanted or destroyed it.

Quinton checked the status of the station's weapons systems. Several missile silos were coming online, but it was going to take time for the autoloaders to bring actual missiles to the silos. Safety protocols required that the missile tubes go through an integrity check before being cleared for duty. The starbase wasn't combat ready. He needed a faster response. Then he found it. The station had twin particle cannons that wouldn't take long to charge. They were designed for a quick response, unloading a devastating attack that could tear through kinetic shields and the reinforced multi-alloyed hull of a Jordani warship.

Quinton instructed the starbase's combat VI to divert power to the two particle cannons.

The starbase also had heavy mag cannons along its underside. They'd immediately passed the startup protocols, and Quinton received a green status for them before he moved on.

While interfacing with an advanced computing core like the ACN station, he wasn't limited to the physics of normal time as observed by humans. He found that he could multitask and partition his focus, but there was a cost. The more he partitioned his attention, the less focus he was able to apply to a complex problem. That's where his VI assistants helped because they handled the technical aspects of his orders.

There were physical limitations. The particle beam cannons needed time to prime before they were able to fire. The more powerful the beam, the more they needed to prime, but he was impatient. In normal time, it would take mere seconds to prime, but for Quinton, it seemed to take significantly longer.

He created a virtual Sapient Combat Simulation, leveraging the combat VI to come up with a firing solution that would be sure to get Lennix Crowe's attention. Once he had his firing solution, he authorized the combat VI to execute.

Twin particle beam cannons came online, fully primed, and fired a devastating beam at the Union ships. His targets were along the edge of the Union ship deployment. He hit one destroyer-class vessel directly in the main engines, and the other one was hit midship, where the bridge would be located. The main engines of one destroyer went offline, and it began spinning out of control. The closest ships in the area evaded it, thanks to the quick thinking of their captains.

The particle cannons fired again, this time focusing on one ship. The particle beam shredded through its shields and hull, devastating its defenses. Then Quinton fired his mag cannons at the target. The particle beam exposed the ship's interior, and kinetic artillery tore through the rest. The ship broke apart as its main reactor failed.

Union ships shifted their targeting priority to focus on the starbase's weapons, and a bombardment from kinetic weaponry slammed into the starbase defenses. Point-defense turrets unleashed the fury of their armament, barely holding back the bombardment.

Quinton opened a comlink to the DUC ship *Astra*.

"This is *Astra* actual," Brandt said.

"Admiral Brandt, I've taken the pressure off your ships. If you regroup, you'll have a chance to make another attack run while I have their attention," Quinton said.

There was a long pause.

"Admiral, I have control of the starbase," Quinton said.

"Quinton, where is Maelyn? The last I heard, you were getting a new body," Brandt said.

"I still am. I'm just delaying it. Can you regroup?"

"Understood. Give us some time to regroup, and we'll hit them with everything we've got," Brandt said.

Quinton closed the comlink. The point-defense systems were belching out artillery, trying to hold off the Union fleet's bombardment, but some were penetrating through his defenses. He analyzed the Union fleet. They had two JFS heavy cruisers that were protected by smaller destroyer-class ships, along with several squadrons of light attack craft. He needed to give the DUC fleet time to regroup, but that didn't mean he had to take a beating from the Union ships.

Quinton opened a broadcast comlink to the two cruisers. Two of the five missile tubes in the station had failed their integrity check. He diverted missiles to the other three tubes. Autoloaders rushed to deliver missiles to their silos.

Union ship *Devastator* acknowledged his comlink. "Who is this?" a man asked.

"Well, who's this?" Quinton asked in turn.

"This is Lieutenant Henderson of the Union ship *Devastator*."

"That sounds very impressive, Lieutenant Henderson. I'll make sure I target your ship first. Now put me on with the commanding officer."

"You haven't told me who you are."

Quinton sent a data packet through the comlink. "Henderson, do you recognize the coordinates I just sent you? They are for the precise location of the command bridge that you're actually sitting in on that ship. In essence, I know exactly where you are. I know just where to point my weapons. If you don't put me on with Lennix Crowe right now, I'm gonna unleash the full armament of this ACN Starbase Alpha."

Quinton was bluffing. Oh, he knew exactly where the bridge was located on that ship. That wasn't a ruse, but particle beams wouldn't be enough to destroy the bridge. They were too far away, and it would take a sustained blast for a bit longer than it had taken to destroy the smaller ships.

A video comlink came online and showed Lennix Crowe's face. "Captain Wayborn, are you going to beg for your life?"

"Close, but you got the wrong person. I'm Quinton. I'm the PMC you're trying to capture. That infiltrator VI was a nice touch. I have to admit I didn't see that coming. Courtesy of your lavender-skinned spy, I presume."

"Are you going to stick with a voice-only comlink? Don't want to show me your face?"

"That's a bit difficult right now because I don't have a face," Quinton said. Instead, he opened a video channel but used Crowe's face, tweaking his appearance by giving him a man bun, horns sticking out of his forehead, and painted lips. "There. How do you like that? I think it's some of my best work yet."

If he'd been in Crowe's position, he probably would've just kept firing on the starbase. However, the bombardment from the Union ships slowed down.

"I'd rather take that starbase intact. The armament stores alone are worth a fortune. Can we come to an arrangement?" Crowe asked.

"You could retreat to minimum jump distance and then get the hell out of here. Would that work for you?"

Crowe smiled a non-smile with a smoldering gaze. "I'm sure you've analyzed the tactical data. The DUC can't win and neither can you. I'm going to take that starbase. You see, I think you have minimal weapons available to you, and you're just trying to buy yourself some time."

Sometimes Quinton got tired of people not doing what he wanted them to do. "Believe what you want."

Crowe nodded. "I will. I know the DUC is regrouping. We've got something special planned for them. As for you, well, that's a problem that will resolve itself."

If Quinton had teeth, they would be clenching right now. His mind raced. He'd underestimated Crowe's determination. The man could not be bluffed. He had all the cards, and he definitely had the upper hand.

"We'll see about that," Quinton said, his own voice sounding raspy. "You might take the starbase, but I'll see to it that it costs you everything."

Crowe laughed, and Quinton was about to sever the comlink when Crowe spoke again. "My infiltrator VI is based on Sentinel technology. It's the technology that was designed to destroy you. There's no way you can beat it. All I have to do is outlast your attack. Then, I'll come aboard, retrieve your ESS, and you'll be mine."

Quinton severed the comlink. He wished there was a panel in front of him for his hand to smash, but at the same time, he felt a tugging sensation at the edge of his thoughts. It was as if there were something he should be remembering, but he couldn't quite get it. Without warning, it blazed like a beacon to the forefront of his mind. He froze, unable to do anything. Radek and his army of VIs demanded direction, but he couldn't give it.

*Please be wrong.*

He turned his attention to the communication systems of the space station and felt as if the ground was falling away from his feet. The infiltrator VI had taken control of a communications array and was broadcasting a subspace comlink. There was only one intended recipient, and Crowe didn't even realize what he'd done.

Quinton opened a comlink back to the *Astra*. "Admiral Brandt, you have to break off the attack. You need to get out of here. Leave the system immediately!"

"Impossible. We're about to regroup for our attack run."

"Break off the attack, or all your ships will be destroyed. You'll lose everything."

Active sensor readings from the station detected new FTL

jump emergent points into the star system not far from their location.

"Now isn't the time to give up," Brandt said.

"You don't understand. The Sentinels are here. Check your active scans. They're still jumping into the system. It's a fleet. It's too much for you. Get out of here," Quinton said.

# CHAPTER THIRTY-ONE

A FEW SECONDS DRAGGED BY, and while Quinton waited for Admiral Brandt to acknowledge the inevitable, he ordered his VI henchmen to bring up every weapons system operational on the ACN starbase. Sentinel ships continued to jump into the star system, swelling the number of ships beyond those of Crowe's Union ships. But that was just it. Space fleet engagement wasn't just a numbers game. Classes of ships and their capabilities in combat greatly influenced the outcome of any fleet engagement. The starbase scanner array included the ability to run active scans through subspace. Quinton's curiosity spiked for nanoseconds, and Radek quickly provided him with the knowledge framework that surrounded FTL scanning. He didn't know if either the DUC ships or the Union ships could run active scans through subspace, but the Sentinels could. They were already adjusting their trajectories to put them on an intercept course with the starbase.

"They're coming up on our sensors now," Brandt said. "How'd they find us?"

"It was Crowe. He's trying to use an infiltrator VI to take control of the starbase, and it's based on Sentinel technology. My guess is that it has a few extra capabilities that he wasn't aware of and couldn't account for. They sent out a broadcast that brought the Sentinels here."

Quinton heard Brandt order his astrogator to plot a new course for the DUC fleet.

"It's not too late for you to get away," Quinton said. "You can micro-jump to the edge of this star system and then retreat. I'll hold them off as long as possible."

Admiral Brandt was quiet for a few moments. "I don't know what to say."

"Save it for later," Quinton said.

The comlink to the *Astra* closed, and he saw that more and more ships of the DUC fleet had altered course.

Union ships were still on an intercept course for the starbase, and he wondered if they hadn't detected the Sentinels yet. Quinton focused his attention on the Union ships. Their fleet was comprised of older Jordani Federation ships that had probably been repurposed or abandoned in a shipyard. The JFS fleet used to coordinate their fleet engagements with what the Jordanis thought was secure communications, but the starbase was able to detect the subspace signals used by the Union ships. Quinton sent out a broadcast of his own, disguising his signal as an acknowledgment from the two Union cruisers, except his signal uploaded a very precise and very deliberate data signature unique to when a PMC was prevalent on a ship's computer systems. The effect was almost immediate. A portion of the Sentinel fleet altered course, heading for the Union fleet.

Quinton felt a moment's satisfaction imagining Crowe scrambling to figure out what had happened. But he didn't have a lot of time to relish the thought and turned his attention to the starbase.

Becker, Guttman, and Oscar had found a ship inside the hangar bay that had been offline, and they'd restored power to it.

Quinton didn't recognize the kind of ship it was, but the designation indicated it was some kind of prototype.

Quinton opened a comlink to Becker. "You need to leave."

"I know that, but we're still trying to access the ship here. It looks like it has a jump drive, but it's been on emergency standby for a really long time," Becker said.

"You know all this, but you can't access the ship yet?"

"It's not like we're standing around here doing nothing. I got the data from the console here in the hangar. Can you access the ship?" Becker asked.

Quinton opened a comlink to the ship and received a PMC challenge protocol. Authentication was done quickly, but he detected that it had required access to his ESS. He really needed to figure out what else was stored there beyond his unique PMC.

ACN *Wayfarer*.

A loading ramp opened from the sleek outer hull, and Quinton heard Becker call out to the others. Quinton initiated the ship's startup protocols.

"Thanks," Becker said. "It sounds like the bombardment stopped."

"Not for long. As soon as the engines are ready, get out of here and meet up at the emergency jump coordinates," Quinton said.

"Where's Maelyn? Last I heard, she and Simon were heading to you."

"They're next on my list. Look, the Sentinels are on their way here right now, and they're going to attack. You don't want to be here when that happens."

Becker began shouting orders to the others and then said, "Quinton, thanks. I'll see you at the rendezvous."

He severed the comlink. Becker had almost sounded like he'd meant it. Maybe the salvager wasn't so bad . . . Who was he kidding? Becker was still a pain in the ass, but that didn't mean Quinton was going to abandon him.

He opened a comlink to Maelyn.

"The tram just stopped," she was saying when she acknowledged the comlink.

"I stopped it," Quinton said. "And now I'm sending you back to the *Nebulon*. I'm overriding the safeties because there isn't a lot of time."

The tram began heading away from the bio lab, but it slowed down after a short distance and came to a stop. He sent another override to force the tram to return to the central hangar bay where the *Nebulon* would be, but the tram wouldn't respond.

"What did you do?" Quinton asked.

"You think you're the only one who knows how to override a system?" Maelyn replied.

The tram began heading back toward the bio lab, and there was nothing he could do to stop it. The only thing he might be able to do was to shut down the tram system altogether, but that would leave Maelyn and Simon stranded, which wasn't what he wanted.

"Dammit, Maelyn, stop it. The Sentinels are here, and they're coming to destroy the starbase. Brandt and the DUC fleet are in full retreat. They're getting out of here, and that's what you need to do."

"I'm not going to leave you here."

"You have to."

"No, I don't. You don't get to tell me what to do," Maelyn said.

The tram's velocity increased. She must've been guiding it on manual control.

"Maelyn, you have to listen to me. I have a plan for getting out of here."

"You're just saying that. You don't have a plan."

"Yes, I do. My body is waiting for me. I'm going to download my PMC into it. There's an escape pod not far from the bio lab that's capable of micro-jumps. I can get out of here, and then you can pick me up in the *Nebulon*. Look, I'll show you," Quinton said and sent her the location of the escape pod.

"It could work," Simon said.

Maelyn sighed. "You better be there," she said.

Quinton saw the tram come to a halt, then begin speeding back the way it had come. "I will be. I promise."

His awareness was surrounded by all the systems that were connected to the computing core. With the starbase's resources at his disposal, he was able to slow down the infiltrator VI significantly but not completely.

He received an alert that the hangar bay doors where Becker and the others were had opened. A quick view of the video feed showed the ship flying out of the hangar. Becker, Guttman, and Oscar had escaped.

The tram had just arrived at the plaza near the main central hangar. Quinton urged Maelyn and Simon to run. The starbase's combat VI showed that Union ships were now engaging the Sentinels while retreating. A large group of Sentinel ships had broken off from the main group and were now heading toward the starbase.

Hyper-capable missiles were loaded into tubes. Those were new. At some point, Radek had made the knowledge of them available. He executed a firing solution, and missiles with high-yield antimatter warheads flew from the tubes. Once clear of the starbase, they went into hyperspace, shifting from normal space for less than a second before returning almost on top of the Sentinel fleet ships. Antimatter explosions tore through even the Sentinel warships, causing massive destruction. At the same time, twin particle beam cannons fired on the Sentinels ships, and he devoted all mag cannons to targeting them as well. Quinton had unleashed the full combat capability of the Acheron Confederacy Navy starbase. The Confederacy might've been gone, but Quinton was still here. He wasn't sure what that meant, but he knew the Sentinels used lethal force at the slightest detection of a PMC, and he wanted to make them suffer.

"Quinton," Maelyn said, "we've reached the *Nebulon*."

"Good. Launch immediately," he said and heard the monotone intonation of his voice because he was stretching himself entirely too thin.

The starbase's main central hangar had two hangar bay doors on each end of the starbase, and he opened the doors away from the battle.

"Execute a micro-jump as soon as you're clear of the hangar bay doors," Quinton said.

He was ready to take over the *Nebulon*'s systems if Maelyn didn't cooperate, but the *Nebulon*'s engines engaged, and the ship sped toward the exit.

"We're on our way. What's the status of the transference protocol?" Maelyn asked.

"Transfer has begun," Quinton lied.

The *Nebulon* flew through the hangar bay doors and executed a micro-jump. A second later, it appeared on the fringe of the star system.

"We'll maintain our position here in case something goes wrong with the escape pod," Maelyn said.

There was something in her voice that clued him in that she had caught on to what he was doing.

"Quinton," she said.

The first wave of powerful spinal-mount particle weapons that were fired from the Sentinel battleships slammed into the starbase. It quickly burned through the shields and began melting through the armor, destroying a missile tube. One of the missiles exploded, but it hadn't been armed, so the damage was minimal.

A barrage of alerts appeared in front of him. Sentinel ship weapons were powerful, and he adjusted his analysis of their capabilities. The tactical plot still showed Union ships fleeing the area. One of the Union cruisers had been destroyed, but it wasn't

Crowe's. His ship was still making best speed away from the battlefield.

*Run, you bastard. Run away.*

Maelyn called out to him.

The recent battle developments wouldn't reach the *Nebulon* scanners for another fifteen minutes, so she couldn't know what was happening.

"No need to wait around," Quinton said.

The last of the Union ships jumped from the system, but they weren't followed by the Sentinel ships. Those ships changed course, heading for the starbase. He didn't know if they had somehow figured out what he'd done to trick them or if they'd decided he was the bigger threat.

"What do you mean? The transference shouldn't take that long. You need to pull back into your ESS," Maelyn said.

Quinton felt all kinds of urges for muscle movements he wasn't even capable of, but they were ingrained into the human psyche. He was a physical being and needed to release the tension from his emotions. They rooted him into his own humanity.

He pulled back from ordering his VIs. They were frantically trying to come up with a superior firing solution against the approaching Sentinel fleets. His combat VI focused the starbase's firepower on the support craft and then began shooting their heavy hitters. The Sentinel ships looked like they were an amalgamation of multiple federation militaries. The information he had on hand was for specific federation militaries, which helped but wasn't exactly conclusive.

"I'm sorry," Quinton said.

"What did you do? Just get to the escape pod. It's all you have to do. Complete the transfer. Then get to the escape pod. Just do it!" Maelyn said.

Quinton looked at the video feed from the comlink to the *Nebulon*. He saw Maelyn sitting in the captain's chair. Her shoulders were drawn up tight, and her face was almost rigid.

"I can't do that. I have to stay here and take care of this."

"Yes, you can. You can do this," Maelyn said almost pleadingly.

Quinton added a video feed to the comlink and showed her his face—the face of his human form inside the medical capsule. His eyes were closed, and the body floated in amber liquid.

"I figured you'd want to see this at least once," he said and created an avatar that resembled his face for the comlink.

Maelyn swallowed hard and leaned back into her chair for a moment. Then she slammed her fist down. "Just get to the escape pod!"

Quinton shook his head, and his makeshift avatar mimicked the movement. "There isn't an escape pod. I lied."

Maelyn's eyebrows pulled together, and her face became a tight frown. "I thought you weren't a hero."

He chuckled. "I'm not. I just don't like to lose."

Her full lips lifted in a sad smile. "Neither do I," she said, her voice sounding thick, almost strangled with emotion.

"I know," Quinton replied. "Tell Brandt that at least this part of the Acheron Confederacy didn't fail."

"Is that why you're doing this? Because everyone blames the Acheron Confederacy for the Federation Wars? Do you think this will make everything better? It's not your fault," she said.

Quinton looked at her and felt a stubborn gleam in his eyes. Then the comlink severed.

The Sentinels had destroyed the comms array he'd been using and overwhelmed the starbase's point-defense systems. They weren't trying to preserve their numbers. They were playing a logistics game, and their objective was clear. Quinton threw himself into the fight by using every weapon that was still operational and overriding any and all safeties for critical systems. Wreckage from the Sentinel ships formed a small debris field. He kept at it, trying to take as many of them out as he could. At least he could make the bastards pay.

The general condemnation of the Acheron Confederacy bothered him. At first, he'd been indifferent to it largely because he hadn't had access to his memories. But when he'd learned that he was from the Acheron Confederacy, coupled with his perfect recall of recent events, he found that he wanted to learn more about it. The more he learned, the more he questioned the general consensus, at least in part. There was sufficient historical evidence to support that, for some reason, the ACN had begun fighting with the other federations, but it wasn't clear why. There'd been no formal declaration of war. At the center of it all was a rogue grand admiral by the name of Elias Browning. Quinton couldn't put all the pieces together because he didn't have enough information, and now he wouldn't get the chance. Maybe Becker was right and he was someone else's pawn in a war that was no longer being fought.

He looked at the tactical plot and heard his avatar sigh. He turned his attention toward it and wanted to glare at it, but he couldn't because glaring required . . . Despite having access to every type of sensor throughout the starbase, he felt detached. A body grown using his DNA was in the bio lab, and it was going to die, just like he was about to. The Sentinels pushed forward, firing their superior weaponry at the ACN starbase. He'd destroyed many of their ships, and the Sentinels' rate of fire had diminished. There were limits to even their technology.

Quinton pulled back from the weapons systems, trusting his VIs to do the best they could against an unwinnable battle. The Sentinels had been created to hunt down and destroy PMCs, but what if there was a way he could convince them that he wasn't a threat. Would they even listen?

He found a backup comms system that was still operating and sent out a broadcast, which included the challenge protocol he'd encountered on the PMC console.

A response was sent.

*Authenticate.*

Quinton had expected that the stored information in his ESS would offer up his clearance codes as part of the authentication process, but it didn't.

"Quinton Everett Aldren, Acheron Confederacy Navy."

*Unknown Personality Matrix Construct.*

*ACN Rank.*

He didn't know his rank, but the knowledge became available from his ESS. "Commander," he said.

His ACN commander's identification transferred from his ESS to the comlink and then to the Sentinels.

*Confirmed.*

"I'm not a threat. You can stop trying to kill me," Quinton said.

*Threat anomaly confirmed.*

*Prevention of spread is required.*

He didn't understand, and he wondered if the Sentinels were nothing but a malfunctioning, overpowered virtual intelligence that needed to be turned off. He sent a series of commands through the commlink, ordering the Sentinels to cease all hostilities.

*Security override has failed.*

*Hostile PMC host detected.*

*Probability of spread 100 percent.*

*Targets confirmed.*

Several Sentinel destroyer-class ships began to maneuver away from the rest in the direction that the DUC and Union ships had gone. Quinton detected a surge of energy to their jump drives and targeted those ships. His remaining particle beam cannon fired first, and he spiked the energy levels past critical. The Sentinels were attempting to hunt down the others. He wasn't going to let them.

The particle beam burned through the Sentinel destroyers, piercing one ship's hull and tearing into the next ship in the formation. The remaining Sentinel ships refocused their fire on the starbase. They were closing in on his position, but they weren't moving fast enough. The starbase had limited maneuvering that any ship could outrun, but he engaged the engines, heading *toward* the Sentinel fleet.

Pieces of the starbase began to break away under the heavy fire from the Sentinel ships. Mag cannons went offline. Point-defense systems became inoperable. He'd expended most of his stockpile of missiles, with the exception of those that he'd lost from enemy fire. Then his remaining particle beam cannon stopped firing.

Those were all the weapons available. He'd given everything he had, and now he was going to die—alone.

"Quinton, I've done as you've asked. The body has been destroyed," Radek said.

"Was it painless?" he asked.

"The body remained in a comatose state and never achieved awareness."

"Collapsing stars, Radek! Your bedside manner still sucks."

Radek didn't reply for a few moments. "No pain was felt."

Quinton chuckled. "That's good. I'm going to join him in a few minutes," he said while giving his authentication for the self-destruct sequence, which would also destroy a large number of Sentinel ships.

"Look at them, Radek. They're trying to run," he said.

Radek didn't reply.

The good thing was that when the starbase blew up, he wouldn't feel a thing. The bad thing was that he'd never get a chance to feel anything again. Why was he so afraid? He felt it there, deep inside—irrational and primal. In the short time he'd been reactivated, hadn't he done something? Had it been worthwhile? He didn't know, but at least it was something. He would have liked to have seen more of the galaxy, but the Sentinels . . . The blast radius of the starbase was enough to get most of them. He wasn't sure how many would escape. Perhaps some of the damaged ones would, but they wouldn't recover enough to follow Maelyn and the others. He used the time he had left trying to find his records in the ACN starbase's computer system. He'd found his DNA record, but what about his service record.

There wasn't one. There wasn't anything listed. He didn't need to check more than once. Why didn't he have a service record? He had an ACN rank. Why wouldn't his service record be here? Someone had activated him. But maybe it had only been some latent protocol from an automated system. If that was the case, perhaps it was better that he never regained his memories.

Quinton's thoughts halted. The starbase's self-destruct timer was reaching critical mass, but he could still access his ESS and access the knowledge of who he was. With his frame rate cranked as high as it was, he'd have time to take in all the memories that were locked away. He just wasn't sure if he wanted to. He'd pulled back from the starbase's computer core. There was no need for him to be aware of all the systems going offline and the damage reports anymore. He knew what was about to happen.

He wondered what he would find in his ESS, but at the same time, he was afraid of what he'd find. Maybe he was fortunate not to have to remember a lifetime of experiences and people who were all gone. Why go through so much pain and loss when he was about to die?

Quinton thought about the people he'd encountered, the friends he'd made. They were enough for him. He didn't want to spend his remaining time remembering a world that no longer existed and instead chose to think about the people he'd met. The variants of humans he'd encountered perplexed him because of the lengths the people had gone to survive in this galaxy. He thought about Simon and how he'd been the first person to figure out what Quinton was. Simon was the only person who had tried to help him without demanding something in return—some last vestige of decency, or perhaps Simon hadn't aged enough to be as pragmatic as someone like Becker. Then he thought about

Maelyn. She was something else. At least he'd been able to show her his face. It had been important to him that they all saw him for what he was and not that damn agricultural bot body he'd been trapped in. He was relieved that he wasn't in there anymore.

Quinton brought up the video feed of the bio lab and looked at the agricultural bot, standing stone-still like a lifeless husk. Then he closed all the data feeds, even the timer for the self-destruct. He'd had enough of being connected to everything.

# CHAPTER THIRTY-TWO

THE *NEBULON* WAS on the fringe of some nameless star system. The one thing that Maelyn actually liked about being captain of her own ship was that there was very little opportunity for idleness. There was always something that required attention, but now the ship felt empty.

She headed to the bridge to meet with Simon and Kieva. They'd been in this star system for ten hours, and passive scans had shown that there was no one else there.

Kieva entered the bridge and walked over to Maelyn and Simon. "Have we heard from the others?"

Simon shook his head. "Nothing."

"Becker got what he wanted, and that's all," Maelyn said.

Kieva frowned a little. "I really thought he meant to join us. They all said they couldn't rejoin the Union."

Maelyn wasn't surprised, at least not much. She shrugged.

"I keep thinking we're going to hear from Quinton," Simon said and held up his hands in a placating gesture. "I know. I just thought he would've found a way to— I thought he would've found a way off that starbase."

"So did I," Kieva said.

Maelyn's throat became thick, and she swallowed. Quinton had been struggling to find his place and make sense of the galaxy. She thought about their last conversation, trying to glean some kind of insight, but it was a waste of time. "He's gone," she said.

Simon nodded, and his shoulders slumped a little. He looked away from her. "I know. I just don't want him to be," he said and smiled a little. "I liked having him around."

"Me too," Kieva said. "He was quite charming. It must've been hard for him being trapped in that agricultural bot."

"Can we just move on? No sense wasting time kicking a broken jump drive," Maelyn said a bit more harshly than she meant to.

Simon and Kieva shared a glance.

"Vonya covered her tracks too well. I've been over the system, trying to figure out how she did it. Quinton and Becker were right. She used the automated maintenance schedules and just added a jump drone to the routine maintenance and waste-disposal system. We probably would've figured it out eventually," Simon said.

Maelyn felt a spike of irritation. Vonya had fooled her as well, and she hated that. "You mean we would've eventually noticed that our stock of jump drones had dwindled? She must've known she was on some kind of time constraint. I'd love to get my hands on her again."

"I spent the most time with her," Kieva said. "She seemed so convincing. I've never heard of a Servitor being a spy."

Maelyn scowled. "Because she wasn't a Servitor. She was just in disguise."

"Well, it was a pretty convincing disguise," Simon said. The two women looked at him, and his eyebrows raised as he shrugged.

"We'll need to be more careful in the future—more secure with who we allow to access our systems, and . . ." Maelyn said and paused, clenching her teeth. "I'm the one that usually does the misdirection. I really want to find Vonya."

"If that's her real name," Simon said. "Probably not, and we don't even know if that's what she really looks like."

"She could have gone anywhere," Kieva said.

"Not anywhere," Maelyn said. "She'll need to report back to Lennix Crowe."

"Captain," Simon said, "it's not that I wouldn't want to go on another hunt with you, but we should probably report to Admiral Brandt. He might have different plans for us, especially once they've reviewed all the data they got from the starbase."

Maelyn felt the muscles in her shoulders loosen. Simon was right. Hopefully, there'd be some clue to where the Acheron Confederacy had hidden the colony worlds. "We will, and we'll do it now. There's no point waiting here any longer," she said.

Kieva went to her workstation and brought up the astrogation interface.

Simon looked at Maelyn. "Are you all right?"

"I'm fine," she said probably a little too quickly. She sighed. "I'm annoyed. I thought things would've gone differently."

He nodded and touched her shoulder, then went to his own workstation. Maelyn sat in the captain's chair. She was eager to be away from the star system. She wanted to believe they'd gotten actionable data from the starbase, but there were no guarantees. If they hadn't, she still had a mission. Crowe's Union wasn't going to stop. One thing she knew about Lennix Crowe was that he wouldn't quietly disappear. The Collective wouldn't let him.

"Coordinates are in the nav computer, Captain," Kieva said.

"Let's go," Maelyn said.

Lennix Crowe sat in his ready room near the bridge of the Union ship *Devastator*. He leaned back heavily and rubbed the tension from his forehead.

The door chimed, and he glared at it. He just wanted five minutes alone.

The door chimed again and opened. Lennix scowled.

"We need to talk," Nate Carradine said.

"If you were anyone else, I would . . ." He let the thought go unfinished. "What couldn't wait? The Sentinels haven't found us."

Carradine shook his head. "No, I don't think they were as interested in us as they were in that starbase."

"The infiltrator VI needs a lot of work. Who cleared it for use?" Lennix asked. He wanted to know who he was going to severely punish.

"Let's not be too hasty with the consequences. The infiltrator VI did its job. We needed something that could help us capture a PMC. I believe if we'd had more time, it would have succeeded," Carradine said. He sat down on a couch and leaned forward, resting his elbows on his knees.

"It also broadcast a signal to the Sentinels and brought them there. I wouldn't necessarily call that a success. Quite the opposite," Lennix said.

"It needs refinement. That doesn't mean we should execute the person most capable of fixing it. Wouldn't you agree?"

Lennix inhaled deeply and stood up. He didn't reply. He didn't need to.

"Have we heard from our asset?" Carradine asked.

"She hasn't reported in yet."

Carradine nodded. "I'm sure she will when she's able. None of us are where we expected to be right now."

"My friend, you have a serious knack for making an understatement, but I agree. I didn't think she was up to the task."

"Does this mean you've reconsidered her capabilities?"

Lennix tilted his head to the side once. "We'll see. She hasn't shown up yet. Anyway, the PMC is gone, so we'll have to move forward with our contingency plans."

Carradine stood up. "You sure about this? Trenton Draven can be negotiated with."

Lennix shook his head. "Not this time. And I'm not gonna watch everything I've built be absorbed by the Collective. We'll simply need to move our operations."

"Understood. I think we should look for more PMCs. It stands to reason that there might be others being activated."

Lennix regarded him for a few moments. "That's a big 'if.' Hoping for something to fall into our collective laps isn't a good strategy."

"Given the losses we've sustained, it might be our only strategy," Carradine said.

Lennix clenched his teeth. If that damn infiltrator VI had done its job properly, he would have been on that ACN starbase and in control of a powerful PMC. It wouldn't have mattered that he'd lost so many ships. He could replace ships. He'd have to anyway.

Lennix stood up, and Nate joined him. No more sitting around.

# CHAPTER THIRTY-THREE

QUINTON WOKE UP, which was at once perplexing and unexpected. He should've been dead. The self-destruct had destroyed the starbase and all the attacking ships in its vicinity. That was his last memory, and yet here he was.

*System diagnostic running.*

The words appeared amid the darkness of his thoughts. Where was he?

*Veris initiation complete.*

*System startup complete.*

*Autonomous mode has been activated.*

"Hello, Quinton," a familiar voice said.

His eyes opened, but he narrowed them as he saw the curve of a nearly transparent ceraphome ceiling in front of him. There was a circular room beyond that was dimly lit with the azure glow of ambient lighting. He'd never seen this room before in his life, and he took in the smooth white walls bathed in a bluish light with the clarity of enhanced optics.

"Radek," Quinton said and was startled to hear his own voice with such clarity. "What happened? How'd did I get here?"

A status window appeared on his HUD.

*Energy Storage System integration with cybernetic avatar complete.*

*Personality Matrix Construct integration optimal.*

"I'm just as surprised as you are. I went to active status at the same time you did," Radek said.

Quinton looked down. He was in some kind of storage container, which he'd think about in a minute. He raised his hands. They looked like his own hands but for the chrome-colored "skin" of the advanced composites that comprised his musculature. He had a full-sensory interface. He could see, smell, and feel. He glided the tips of his fingers along the smooth walls of the cool storage container. As he did so, he noticed the muscles in his arms move in a perfect copy of true flesh and blood.

He wanted to see his face but was only able to see an obscure reflection in the ceraphome window.

"I have a partial log from the starbase," Radek said. "In its final moments, a subspace comlink request opened to this place. A data transfer occurred, and your PMC was integrated with the ESS in this cybernetic avatar."

Quinton frowned and actually felt the artificial muscles of his face contract. "That shouldn't have been possible. There wasn't enough time to transfer that amount of data."

"Correct," Radek said, "but the data was compressed. Are you sure you didn't initiate the transfer?"

"Me? How would I even do that? The last thing I remember thinking was how much I didn't want to die," Quinton said.

"Perhaps if you initiate a connection to the ship, there'd be more information available to help us figure out what happened."

He connected to the ship's computer system. The ship was called the *Wayfarer* and was a star-class jumper. There was a brief PMC challenge protocol that ended quickly. He could crank up his frame rate to review the particulars, but something else caught his attention.

"We're not alone," Quinton said.

"The biosensors indicate three people are aboard this ship."

He opened the storage container and stepped out. This body was so easy to use. It felt just as natural as an artificial body could feel. He looked at the ship's identifier and chuckled. He knew who was on the ship.

"We'd better get to the bridge before they break something," Quinton said.

He thought about opening a ship-wide broadcast but decided not to. He wanted to see the looks on their faces, so he walked toward the door and left the room.

The lighting in the corridor dimmed for a few moments before returning to normal. Quinton's first thought was that they'd already broken something. He headed to the bridge and found Becker, Guttman, and Oscar arguing.

"What did you do?" Becker asked.

"Nothing," Guttman replied. "Ever since we got that crazy data burst, nothing's been right."

"Well, just reset the system then," Becker said.

"We can't," Oscar said. "We don't know where we are. The jump drive isn't like anything I've ever seen, and the navigation system contains star charts that are seriously outdated. We're lucky to even be here."

Becker growled. "The ship's computer system keeps bumping me off."

"Same here," Guttman said. "Wait a minute, you don't think this is happening on purpose."

"On purpose?" Oscar asked.

"Yeah, like Quinton sent us here as a joke to get revenge," Guttman said.

Becker sighed and shook his head. "Doesn't matter," he said. "What? It doesn't. I'm the captain, so we'll just need to figure out what's wrong with the ship and then be on our way."

Quinton smiled, and it felt so good that there were no

annoying errors thrown up in response. He walked onto the bridge, and the others went silent.

"I loan you a perfectly good ship, and you're out here stranded in the middle of nowhere. You're lucky I happened to be around," he said.

Becker narrowed his gaze.

Guttman's mouth hung open, and then he shook his head. "You see, I told you he wasn't helping us."

"Quinton, is that you?" Becker asked.

"In the flesh," Quinton said and frowned a little. "Sort of anyway." He laughed. Becker and Guttman didn't. Oscar laughed but looked uncomfortable. "Hey, I didn't expect to be here. And no, I didn't do this on purpose."

Becker inhaled and sighed. "How did you get off the starbase?"

Quinton held up his hands. "I'm not sure, really. I'm still piecing things together."

He strode to the captain's chair and sat down.

"What are you doing?" Becker asked.

Quinton arched an eyebrow toward him. "This is my seat."

Guttman and Oscar looked at Becker, who continued to watch Quinton. His brow furrowed, and his gaze went cold.

"You're welcome to try to take command," Quinton said and stood up, but that didn't convey what actually happened. He had moved so fast that he was in front of Becker well before a second had ticked away on the ship's clock.

Becker's eyes widened, and he tried to step back. Quinton didn't let him. "I have a few enhancements, but look, I don't want any trouble," he said and let Becker go.

"All right," Becker said.

Quinton regarded him for a few moments. "I need to hear you say it."

Becker looked away and shook his head. "All right, Captain."

Quinton glanced at Guttman and Oscar, who immediately

called him captain. Then he looked at Becker. "Now that we've gotten that out of the way, I'm hoping we can help each other. This ship wasn't meant for you. It was designed for someone like me."

"Why?" Becker asked.

Quinton returned to the captain's chair and sat. "I'm not sure, but I'll figure it out—with your help, that is."

"What are you going to do with us?" Guttman asked.

"Well, that depends on you. I'm hoping we can come to some kind of agreement—you know, like a temporary alliance. I could actually use your help," Quinton said.

Becker pursed his lips in thought. "What do you need?"

Quinton rubbed his hands together and glanced at the outdated star charts that Oscar had on the main holoscreen. "There's a whole galaxy out there. Help me fix the ship, and we'll take it from there."

Becker looked at Guttman and Oscar. The two men nodded, and Becker turned back to Quinton. "You've got a deal."

"Excellent. I've got a good feeling about this," Quinton said.

"What about our rendezvous with Maelyn?" Becker asked.

"We're not going to make it, but I'm sure we'll catch up with her sooner or later."

He considered sending Maelyn a message but decided not to—at least not yet. There were still too many unknowns, and he needed some time with his new ship. He was better off if people thought he was gone. He glanced at Becker.

"You're probably right."

"I'm glad you agree," Quinton replied. "All right, we've got some things that need immediate attention, one of which is the food replicator." He looked at Guttman. "I thought you'd find that one important if you'd like to eat anytime soon."

At the mention of food, Guttman's glower vanished in the face of more mundane needs.

"We'll also need to check the life-support systems as well. The ship's been offline for a very long time," Quinton said.

Becker nodded. "And the nav system."

"He's right. The data hasn't been updated in forever," Oscar said.

Quinton nodded and smiled inwardly. He'd learned a few things since being brought back online, such as the importance of keeping people on task so they didn't get into trouble. He needed their help to explore the galaxy, and they needed time to get used to him being the captain.

Guttman left the bridge, and Becker walked over to Quinton.

"This new body. Does it give you full access to your ESS?"

"It does."

"And?" Becker said with raised eyebrows.

Quinton smiled. He'd been expecting this. "Captain's privilege."

# AUTHOR NOTE

Thank you for reading Acheron Inheritance, Federation Chronicles Book 1. I hope you enjoyed it. One of the questions I often get has to do with the amount of research I do when writing a book. While some things I do have to research, there are other subjects that I'm just interested in. One of my go-to resources for this book was Superintelligence by Nick Bostrom, particularly the chapters on speed intelligence. It's an interesting book with lots of concepts that fascinate me, so while crafting the story for the Federation Chronicles, I wanted to explore technology that I hadn't used before in my stories (Along with some familiar ones). Man-in-a-machine or Man-Computer Symbiosis isn't a new concept, but this is my own version of playing "What if..." in a galactic society. It's fun and sometimes a little bit scary to think that no matter how far we advance, we're still vulnerable to technological leaps and how we use them.

Another question I often get—after when will the next book be released—is how many books will be in this series. I figured I'd just tell you that I plan to write three books in the Federation Chronicles series.

Only three?

Yes, but plans can change, and if readers really enjoy this universe, then there are always more stories that can be told in it. The galaxy is a very big place with lots to explore. This brings me to my request from your dear reader. Please consider leaving a review for Acheron Inheritance. Reviews are essential to help spread the word about the book to other readers. Your reviews also help Amazon decide whether to show my books to other readers. If you don't want to leave a review, then don't worry about it. I get it. Telling a friend who might like the book also helps a lot.

Again, thank you for reading one of my books. I'm so grateful that I get to write these stories.

**If you're looking for another series to read consider reading the Ascension series or the First Colony series. Learn more by visiting:**

### https://kenlozito.com/my-books/

I do have a Facebook group called **Ken Lozito's SF readers**. Answer two easy questions and you're in. If you're on Facebook and you'd like to stop by, please search for it on Facebook.

Not everyone is on Facebook. I get it, but I also have a blog if you'd like to stop by there. My blog is more of a monthly check-in as to the status of what I'm working on. Please stop by and say hello, I'd love to hear from you.

**Visit www.kenlozito.com**

THANK YOU FOR READING ACHERON INHERITANCE - FEDERATION CHRONICLES BOOK 1.

If you loved this book, please consider leaving a review. Comments and reviews allow readers to discover authors, so if you want others to enjoy *Acheron Inheritance* as you have, please leave a short note.

**The Federation Chronicles will continue with - Acheron Salvation - Federation Chronicles Book 2**
**Visit KenLozito.com to learn more.**

If you're looking for something else to read consider the following series I've written.

**First Colony - A story about humanity's first interstellar colony.**

**Ascension - A story about humanity's first alien contact.**

# ABOUT THE AUTHOR

I've written multiple science fiction and fantasy series. Books have been my way to escape everyday life since I was a teenager to my current ripe old(?) age. What started out as a love of stories has turned into a full-blown passion for writing them.

Overall, I'm just a fan of really good stories regardless of genre. I love the heroic tales, redemption stories, the last stand, or just a good old fashion adventure. Those are the types of stories I like to write. Stories with rich and interesting characters and then I put them into dangerous and sometimes morally gray situations.

My ultimate intent for writing stories is to provide fun escapism for readers. I write stories that I would like to read, and I hope you enjoy them as well.

If you have questions or comments about any of my works I would love to hear from you, even if it's only to drop by to say hello at KenLozito.com

Thanks again for reading *Acheron Inheritance - Federation Chronicles Book 1*

Don't be shy about emails, I love getting them, and try to respond to everyone.

# ALSO BY KEN LOZITO

Road to Shandara

Echoes of a Gloried Past

Amidst the Rising Shadows

Heir of Shandara

**Broken Crown Series**

Haven of Shadows

Made in the USA
Monee, IL
11 November 2020

47271120R00218